SLEEPING WARRIOR

THIS AIN'T A GAME

PATRICK F. SULLIVAN

outskirts
press

DISCLAIMER

Sleeping Warrior is a work of fiction. Names, characters, businesses, places, events, locales, and incidents are either the products of the author's imagination or used in a fictitious manner. Any resemblance to actual persons, living or dead, or actual events is purely coincidental.

The cover, back cover and binder were designed by cal5086 who produced the items through fiverr.com (2019).

The book title and front cover illustration is derived from a dawn viewing of a series of stacked rock formations of the same name in the Haleakala Crater. The photograph on which the cover is based was taken near the 10,023-foot summit in the moments following the sun's emergence above Haleakala, "The House of the Sun". The Hawaiian People are descended from great mariners. The mariner's world lasts in the moment of observation, change lurks just out of view. Nothing lasts, Volcanos in essence are pending. Perhaps the Warrior sleeps pending the need for him to waken.

This view of the Sleeping Warrior occurred from inside Haleakala Crater, Maui, Hawaii in 2008 by MaryLynn Sullivan, MD. After ascending some 10,023 on a mid-summer's night through falling snow one needs to be in position just as that summer snow evaporates into a wispy predawn cloud cover. Out of darkness the Sleeping Warrior appears. A trick of perspective, gone in seconds. Like life it was worth the trip.

Irish Diplomacy

The ability to tell a man to go to hell
so that he'll look forward to making the trip.

Author Unknown

CONTENTS

1

LOOKING FOR A HOME-COOKED MEAL

The hard work was good. For a long time, work was just frustrating. No, that's wrong. Being unable to do work I took in stride before was frustrating. When did I start feeling good being tired after hard labor?

Fatigued, not overwhelmed. Where did that come from? Am I going Puritan? Would I look good in the starchy black outfit and funny hat? I know Puritans don't drink the devil's brew. Do they eat French food? I'll have to wait until tomorrow to join up. Tonight, I'm for Gabrielle's and French cuisine.

Abruptly I'm staggering forward. That's something new. My hike toward normal has been long and winding. The step-up to her bar requires a large step up from the sidewalk. A few weeks ago, I'd leaned against on the left side of the frame with my shoulder, thrusting my body into the barroom—like the rising step into a western saddle stirrup.

If I followed the leaning step with a dragging lift of my right leg I'd be in the barroom. Talk about Mt. Everest. At least on Everest one doesn't fear the slam of the solid core door pinning one's head. Don't ask, it was embarrassing. I was on the aluminum walker at that point. The door fetched me a stiff clout.

That struggle with sudden death wrapped the bar in a pall of silence. Patrons' reaction differed. There was pity, sympathy, a few snickers. More averted their gaze hoping I'd refrain from sitting near them.

Some seemed to fear I'd fall on them, giving them my disease. I was blown up. It wasn't Bubonic Plague--no rats in my pocket with Bubonic.

Tonight is better. No one notices my entry. Outcast by mankind though I may be, at least I'm ignored. Small progress it is, but progress. Not being noticed will suffice.

Being among people feels good. Hungry and physically tired is nice. Not long ago, my efforts to enter Gaby's often resulted in my tumbling through the doorway and struggling to grab the back of the nearest booth in an effort to avoid a face plant on the floor.

Tonight, feigning nonchalance, I stroll to the bar. I even manage to find an open barstool to sit on. Surprise, surprise. I don't fall off.

I'm early for dinner. The staff is changing shifts.

From the barstool, I people-watch. Chicago was once the world's capitol for gawking at fellow diners. Now, we dine in isolation. The afternoon's professional drinkers are packing up, giving way to an urbane dinner crowd. The afternoon's uncut gems depart for wherever uncut gems go at dinner time. Upwardly mobile diners are arriving, choosing their spots. Some stop to chat with familiar gems sharing a parting drink with an acquaintance. The day bartender ignores me. The old fart usually ignores me. I appreciate the anonymity, but a drink while spectating might be nice. I live in Bridgeport, but I remain in Bridgeport on sufferance. I am not of Bridgeport, if one lived here a hundred years they might not be of Bridgeport. Am I suggesting the place is clannish? Just a little. Money talks, bull-shit walks with the creatures of the evening. In a city of neighborhoods, Bridgeport stands out.

Carl Sandburg in his (1916) poem, "**Chicago,**" called it the "City of big Shoulders." Bridgeport knows to a man that Sandburg was speaking of them.

Outside the bar window, the evening is going all misty. City code mandates a sidewalk pedestrian view into liquor premises. The art of the Shanghai not limited to San Francisco.

Out of the evening mist march M.D.s, masters of the Mercantile Exchange, board traders, and lawyers seeking to dine. Male and female apex predators on the hunt for dinner and what not. In their wake follow the remora seeking love, marital self-interest, and entertainment.

The neighborhood has a whiff of the Levee district. Danger scents the air.

Here it's mostly safe. The food is good. The drink is excellent. I came to Gaby's tonight in search of a home-cooked meal. My grandmother was French-Canadian. As a child, on cold wet nights my friends went home to mac-and-cheese. Gram cooked me crab Lorraine when my parents worked late. One's own comfort food is a personal thing.

After I came back from Afghanistan in my own personal basket, I developed a distaste for wet dreary nights. I hope fog over the river doesn't bring rain. In Afghanistan, even with the green of night-vision, it was hard to see on wet and cold nights. Why my distaste for wet cold weather? It wasn't wet the night I fell from grace. It may have been cool, not wet. We were in the mountains at about 8,000 feet above sea level at night. It was cold. The air was dusty, not wet.

The mind plays tricks. Getting wacked is a serious thing. Then again, the taste of wet, cool air reminds me of air gurgling through a tracheal-tube. For a moment I listen in fear for that wet snorkel gurgle to announce my new life is a dream into which I've retreated to save my sanity.

It may be better to just live the life before me, playing the cards I've been dealt.

Since Afghanistan, cold, damp nights seem filled with menace. Maybe it is just vague foreboding. Dark with potential. Like disaster, life is lurking just around the corner.

Scars acquired on one's soul in the Shah-I-Kot at the seat of the kings, seem to fade slowly. In time I'll fit in. I have a few Frankenstein scars where they sewed my head on. The bolts are hidden, not protruding below my ears. If I need to hide the scars, I can always wear a turtleneck.

I am fairly certain there will come a point when I stop scaring off women and children. It is good to have goals.

I hate premonitions. Something is gonna happen. People will come, people will go. Shit will happen. Will I have to decide? Could I actually do something?

Change is inevitable. Feels like the change bus will be stopping outside Gaby's tonight.

Today, the Greek insisted we be at work when the sun came up. We've been splicing keel sections on our skipjack. Wooden sailboats are a niche market. We are working our niche. This ain't art, we need to sell a boat. Never push craftsmanship, but we're reaching the breaking point in terms of finances.

Enough sailboat talk. Time to ponder imponderables.

Joe left the boatyard while I washed up. Strange, what's up there, Sherlock?

The Greek seems in a hurry of late. Joe does not like to hustle. Unless money or love is involved. The Greek always has a scheme. This has the texture of love to it. Twice last week I smelled a woman's scent in the hallway outside my door. I might have heard the click of stiletto heels out there on concrete stairs.

Joe has a life to live. He definitely wants me out of his hair. Partnership has limitations.

When I came back to Chicago, my bodily motion was shambling and my walk a stuttering stupid display. Mornings, I could see Frankenstein's monster staring back at me in the mirror. I was clumsy and doddering when shaving, but my fear of opening the neck scars and bleeding to death have yet to be realized.

With my doddering walk, I move with the monster's stiff gait. I know I'm not a monster, but I've experienced mothers grabbing their child's hand and crossing the street after seeing me coming. Maybe, they were afraid I would fall on them. Maybe I just feel I appear a monster as a result of my dark deeds.

So, in my head, I'm scary to look at. Being this scary to look at, am I ready to go out ass grabbing?

I suppose that once having grabbed, I really am afraid I might get grabbed back. Then what will I do? Will I be able to do much of anything? A bridge to cross when I come to it.

I return to my room surveillance. My scan stops on Gaby's bartender. No. Not crabby old Karl--the day man. Karl's off shift. He left ignoring me and my parched throat. Surprise there. The evening bartender is Jill. Jill Ryan. Watching Jill is personal, different from peeping out at the lives of others from inside Frankenstein's head. Jill is tall, slender, a born runner. One morning I saw her running the river walk at sunrise. Been an early riser since. At dawn, she runs northeast along the river walk toward the Loop.

Like Pavlov's dog, I've been trained to stand facing the northeast, waiting to salivate should she return.

Being the average Frankenstein-looking male, I find it a pleasure to watch a woman I care for coming into view.

Jill has the long gliding stride of a long-distance runner. Lacking intestinal fortitude and a backbone, I've been satisfied to just watch Jill striding into view, flying past, gliding southward toward home. If I had any guts, I'd talk to her. She always waves, says hello. Not me, I'm a macho man safe behind a face of stone. Maybe I'll nod today as she passes; I'm feeling very conversational. Or, I could just pretend I don't see her. I could look like I'm doing something, not standing with bated breath waiting on her return.

She's so damned sweet. I'm not. Watching Jill run by makes my ears burn. Burning ears? What am I, twelve? She makes my head spin. I fear at any moment I'll go all Labrador retriever on her. Who knows, I might start humping her leg. Wouldn't that be nice. Woof, woof. I bet I'm cute when I slobber.Having a very hard time staying away from that one. She's just a kid, she doesn't need some old fart trying to jump her bones. Not yet thirty and sounding old fartish. Stay away from me, girl. I'm losing my ability to stay away from you.

I start running again. My runs are also before dawn in that grey light. Fancy that. I tell myself. I picked the grey light of dawn, because no one will see me, except maybe Jill. As my balance returns, running has to be re-learned. I use the Apache dog trot run ten paces, walk ten, repeat. Got to start somewhere.

Friday, we are stacking cedar planks on our curing rack. Joe shoves me, then drapes an arm over my shoulder. He points toward the river walk, "There she is, Galvan. Wave. It's OK to look. She knows. I know. The whole neighborhood knows. She's an eyeful. If you don't look, you'll sulk.

"She's gonna be in class all day, stupid. She won't run by again to-day, however much you watch for her."

Jill spots us. She stops short. Almost walks over. I could offer her water, a coffee. Could make her breakfast. She waves. Joe does a little flutter wave. He shoves me forward. I stumble. I freeze, lost for a thing to say. Jill does an odd two palms up shrug, spins on her heel. She pivots south, striking out at a steady pace toward home. Home is in the apart-ments above Gaby's. Gaby likes to rent her small apartments to women in school. Must be a mother-hen thing, no kids.

With her hair and make-up always perfect, she's probably studying cosmetology. I could read up on that stuff. It'd give me something to talk about with her. I'll search it on the net.

Jill's voice speaks from nearby, "Yes?"

I provide my usual snappy answer, "Huh?"

Where did she come from? She's standing directly in front of me. She speaks, "What? You've been sitting there staring at me for five minutes. Say something, Galvan."

Think, Galvan, got it. I'll just relate to what she's studyin. "Love your hair and make-up, tonight. Really lovely. Did you do it this way before school, or is it a kind of in-house learned thing?"

Jill glances down, her face contorted in a confused smirk," Thank you, I think, Mr. Galvan. We try to practice hairstyles during the dissection class. I named my cadaver Irma. If you need any pointers, honey, just ask. Did I ever tell you that you're beginning to drive me nuts, Galvan?"

She relents. "Would you care for something more?" With raised brow for punctuation, Jill adds, "I didn't think you would. Such a waste, hon'."

Not wanting her to leave, a bit thirsty, I abruptly blurt, "Jameson, Black Barrel on ice. When things slow down."

Jill cuts me off with a hand swipe, "I'll deal with you in a minute. A paying customer awaits. Duty calls, Galvan."

Jill walks up to a pair of bikers. Haven't seen bikers in here before. They must have settled in while I was daydreaming. We've had some in the hood lately. Caucasian, 40s, living well enough to be overweight. The colors are the same I saw around the bike row on Halsted south of 31st street, down from the pantry.

The shorter one speaks to Jill. She appears skeptical. The biker holds up two fingers, gesturing to himself and his partner. He then indicates a woman seated on a barstool between us.

Jill speaks to the woman, who has her back to me.

Where did the woman come from? If Gaby is having a best dressed competition tonight, this one already won.

Jill points to her glass. The woman shakes her head negatively, motioning for a larger glass. Her existing glass contains the remains of a colorful mixed drink.

The woman regards her biker benefactor. Apparently, she raised him. He flinches but extracts one then two bills from his shirt pocket. Cheap-skate frowns, then sees me watching and glares my way. Jill takes the bills, displaying neither liking nor trust of the dude. The well-dressed woman turns at the biker's hard-eye toward me. Not only well dressed, pretty, eastern European. Poised, elegant.

Focusing on me, she startles. She snaps her gaze away, then swings back swiftly. In an instant I get stabbed by an icy glare, before receiving a dazzling saccharine smile. Jill spots the by-play between the woman and me. I turn away. I am a mere spectator. I don't have a dog in this fight. It is not worth a fight. Jill has already told me off.

The seated brunette has very short hair, lovely fine features, and my interest upsets her. The woman must be slumming. Whatever silly game she's at with that matched pair of rough-cut gems is her business. Time to mind my own business. There is no accounting for bad taste. A glance as I turn away, tells me the brunette is getting nervous. Her posture and body language are wrong.

Jill carries their drinks to the trio on a small tray. She sets a rock glass of Jim Beam in front of each biker. As Jill pivots to set the large mixed drink before the brunette, the host-biker hovers his hand over the glass, snatching the remaining drink from the tray. His maneuver felt strange to me as he did it.

Odd. The little fat guy places his palm over the mouth of her goblet. When he lifts the drink it sloshes about as he sets it before the brunette.

The guy swipes his palm over his jeans. What? That all looked wrong. Why? The biker once more angrily glares at me. The brunette swings back to me. She has an angry defiant hint to her glare. With obvious effort she forces a second pleasant smile. The biker takes his change, tosses a dime tip on Jill's tray. Jill pinch lifts the dime as one might a dead mouse by its tail. Walking to the register she drops the dime in a jar marked, 'Poor Box'. Something is off. Did the guy palm powder into the woman's drink? Maybe lint fell from his sleeve into her glass? I look. No lint floating, bottom residue? Not certain. Must be me. Dude is shabby and gross.

Who am I to judge? I'm sitting by myself. He's sitting with some upper-class model. I usually don't find women with short hair attractive. This one would be a stunner with her head shaved into a mohawk. The boy-cut, dark hair is actually cute. The crisp silk jacket and emerald green blouse over black skinny-jeans and 100mm heels work. The heels make her my height. Good taste in clothes, if not in men. Glancing at Jill and the brunette, I realize I am not dead. The brunette casts another indifferent eye on me from beneath her long, swept back bang. She doesn't care for my watching her. The woman seeks out my gaze then rejects me. It must be love. This woman acts more the hunter than fearful prey.

Damn, Lady. I was star-gazing. Forget I looked.

I offer a defensive, sheepish smile. Then, as I turn away, she gives me the 'copper-stare'. Is she after them and waving me off? Or, might she be working me? Then, she could be short-handed and tailing the pair. Giving me the bum's rush is probably an effort at economy of motion.

Or, I could just be nuts. Too many what ifs, best to let it go. Who might she be? Local? Feds.? Which Feds? She appraises me with the slow police stare. OK, lady, you told me. Don't yell 'hands up', I'll faint.

She shifts into a victorious sultry smile. A perfect smile. She has more gleaming white teeth than a great white shark. The woman is every inch a Princess. Careful, Princess, if you grab those tigers by their tails, they might eat you. Not my business.

Jill steps back in front of me. Her mind is whirring behind that steady gaze. Our eyes lock. Jill mimics the saccharine smile Princess gave me earlier. Jill's attitude toward me just changed.

I ask, "What?"

Teasing smile, "You want to do her hair, too?"

"I don't want to do anything connected with that scary wench. I make boats. I was trying to make conversation with you. I figured because of the many lovely ways you wear your hair, that you worked at it. Joe told me you were in class all day. I meant to chat with you this morning. I missed the opportunity."

I continue, "I don't know women very well lately. Then I probably never did. Since life changed for me, I seem unable to come up with much to say. I was trying to compliment you on how nice you looked. I thought it had something to do with your studies. I have no idea how you learn your trade."

She's confused. Why? Because I'm clumsy? I definitely have to improve my boy-girl talking skills.

The corners of her mouth twitch upward, uncertainly. Jill nods, then saunters toward the shelved bottles arrayed before the bar mirror.

Searching, she finds a bottle of Jameson Black Barrel.

Jill walks up, squaring off to me, "So. You talking to me again, Galvan? If you have no interest, why do you spend your day staring? Say hello, don't stare. We'll work it out, hon'. Black Barrel?"

Ever the conversationalist, I nod.

"I don't understand your case of the roving eyeballs. You're not the first guy I've had stare at me. What do you see? What is it? Are you rethinking things? Why were you undressing that high fashion bitch with your eyes? Honey, that bitch in her five-thousand-dollar outfit is too scary for you. She won't understand. Don't worry, I'll protect you, Little Mister."

"My mother used to call me Little Mister when I refused to do what I was told."

"I'm not your mother, Galvan. If I think there's something you should do, I'll speak up. I'm not shy. "

Jill positions the bottle of Black Barrel on the bar in front of me. From below the bar, she produces a whiskey rock-glass, setting it before me. Taking up shiny tongs, she extracts a single ice cube from below the bar.

Jill drops the cube into the glass. There's an audible crack. I am receiving her bartender show. I wasn't watching the cube fall. I haven't ever been this close to Jill before. Helplessly enthralled, I watch Jill intently. I try not to stare, but my eyes sweep over her.

Naturally, I get caught watching.

Her brow furrows. She catches my eye. Her eyes betray a sense of confusion once more.

Shrugging, Jill pours a splash of black barrel into my glass, sets the bottle on the bar, corks it. No spout, one must avoid evaporation with the good stuff.

Out of the blue Jill slaps my cheek. Well, more a tap than a solid blow. Jill's hand lingers a moment, almost a caress, "You're staring at my boobs like you've never seen a girl, Hon'. In this line of work that happens. Now. Why is a guy like you always tossing me long, hot stares?"

I redden. I struggle to find an answer. Everyone looks, why can't I look? I answer, in expectation of another whack, "Your inherent beauty?"

Jill snatches my head between her palms, tilts it down to kiss my forehead. "If only. You, my dear, are an enigma."

I reach for her to bring those gorgeous lips to mine. Jill is thoroughly surprised, pulling back as our lips brush. We study each other a long moment. Jill's smile turns down into an accepting frown. Up go the hands into that palms up shrug. Why does she do that?

Jill takes my twenty from the bar, walking away. She makes change at the register.

Jill places my change before me. Then saunters away, shaking her head. She saunters away from me a lot.

Long ago, Grandpa Silky noted that I had to be his grandson, because we were both leg-men. The conversations one has with one's grandpa. Studying the flex of Jill's departing stride I decide Grandpa was right.

In the silence of her wake, I mutter something on the order of, "Thanks for the drink, young lady."

Jill spins on me, annoyed, "Really. How old are you, Pops?"

With chagrin, I answer.

Jill responds, "Moron, look at me. Don't call me young lady. I know your self-image got blown up along with your ass. Jeez, let the grandpa Moses wall between us drop, hon'. Life-choices aren't the only thing that has me wondering about you."

She returns, arms crossed over her chest. Leans on the bar with her elbows.

Our mutual stare levels. Brown eyes challenge my green. Are they brown or something else, intriguing...

We are quite close. Jill's warm breath brushes my skin. I have an overwhelming urge to taste her lips. I move toward her—she smoothly slips back a step.

Jill says, "You are home. You're jumpy. I get that. Where you are coming from, is what is confusing me. I'm looking at you. Now, you're finally looking back? When you figure out if I have what you're looking for let me know, huh?"

Jill steps away, asking, "Should I walk into the restaurant to let Gabby know you're here for your weekly crab casserole?"

"Funny girl. Do you have time to join me? "

Jill halts mid-stride, surprised, "Will wonders never cease? Are you asking me to dinner? You and Joe confuse me, Galvan. OK, I get it. Yes. I'd love to have a platonic dinner with my buddy. We could discuss hairstyling and make-up. Won't that be fun. Not tonight, Galvan, my feet are already killing me from roaming rounds at school. I have a bar to tend. Another time?"

"If I throw in a foot-rub?"

"Don't be annoying, honey. I'll let you take me to dinner. Unless I get a real offer from some guy in the meantime. Friends is fine, but I'm like everyone else, I'm looking for something."

Her smile flickers. "Jealousy in those cold green eyes? Not dead after all, are you, friend?"

Friends? That has got to be the worst place a guy can find himself. I've been told. Oh well, not her type. That's life in the big city.

I leave her for the restaurant and enjoy the crab lorraine.

Gaby stops by during dinner, "Are your intentions toward my bartender honorable, Galvan?"

"Karl? I have no interest in Karl. Can't stand him. Oh, Jill? I have been in lust for Jill since the instant I saw her. I've tried to be nice, but I'm too old to be in phase with her. Chit-chat is about all she'll let me do."

Gaby smiles. "So, that wasn't you kissing the woman at the bar just now? You two have more going on than either will admit. Don't wait too long. If she escapes your clutches, poppa, you'll be sad. Tonight, she is off at ten."

Forewarned is forearmed. I pay my check and return to the bar, planning for the future. We are all subject to the weaving of the Fates. More colloquially, shit happens. Think fast, here it comes.

My exuberant mood disappears as I re-enter the bar. The air is charged. I'm rusty, but I've been there. I can still pick up bad vibrations. I thought those skills gone. I guess they didn't go very far.

Having seen the elephant, one is easy to recognize when it walks up. After a year flat on my back, I thought the ability to see elephants gone. Obviously, the elephant doesn't go away, it just tiptoes in the background.

Studying the scene before me I think of Shakespeare's, 'Double, double toil and trouble. Fire burn, and cauldron bubble. The shit is gonna hit the fan.' I paraphrased the last part.

The bar has become fricative. Little sparks are bridging the air molecules around me. Jill is frowning at Princess. Princess is scared. Her pet biker has arisen, to stand dominant over her. I'll call him, Tweedle Dee. He is sharing a companionable leer with the larger Tweedle Dumb sitting north of him.

Play with fire, get burnt fingers.

Dee and Dumb appear ready to feed. They seem to be in lust with Princess. Whatever plan they have for her this evening is one she does not view favorably. Her face reflects her poorly concealed anxiety. The shorter, fatter Tweedle Dee calls Princess,' Baby Cakes.' Did Dee is suggesting they step outside. For what? A romp in the park, or maybe an alley? Her eyes are filming over. She's in some kind of trouble. She looks off-balance. Her expression brings to mind victim interviews Those women suffered unhappiness and a sense of loss on their part. Dignity and self-worth are hard earned possessions, difficult to recover when stolen.

At the heart of weaponized Rohypnol lurks sexual degradation of the victim. Rohypnol nullifies a woman's capacity to resist, while making the victim extremely susceptible to suggestion of sexual conduct.

Princess is fighting to hold on, but she's losing her battle. The Princess appears to be under the influence of the big R.

It has been a while since I observed the drug take hold, but Princess has that dopey, suggestable look flickering over her features. Not good. She got dosed. I'm out of practice, but I did see a little white powder in the bottom of her glass. The glass sits on the bar half empty before her. Trouble is in the offing. Onset whacks a person in under 30 minutes. Drowsiness, maybe sleep, depending upon dosage level, followed by excitation. The up and down roller coaster ride has begun. Abruptly, Tweedle Dee, grabs Princess by her left sleeve. The other, Twiddle Dumb, rises in unison with his ugly partner.

If they try to frog-march Princess out to the parking lot, I'll have to do something, maybe stop them until the police arrive, assuming someone calls. Either way I get my ass kicked. It's not the time for would've, could've, should've. On occasion, one has to do something. People have been telling me all day to do something. Fish or cut bait. As I step in, I notice the Northside-Johns around me are feigning blindness, and showing spectator indifference. One who sticks out seems absorbed in carefully polishing his spoon. The taste of fear is exhilarating for those who like to watch. Some are leaving already though.

Their taste for fear appears to be ebbing in favor of personal survival. I should mind my own business. I'm a broke-down stumble bum. I care about Princess even if the girl dislikes me. This pair enjoys the way their intimidating costume and body mass conveys power.

The body-mechanics of Tweedle Dumb's moves predict the application of an imminent pimp slap to the face of Princess. His left palm spreads, streaking forward. Princess cowers away. Dumb's going to blind-side her. Princess is already wobbly. The roofy is gonna put Polly-Pure-Heart down hard. If I don't do something, I become part of the audience. Fuck it. Tweedle Dee distracts her attention by hauling Princess sharply to him by her sleeve. Princess lifts off her stool, surging forward. She arches her back, seeking space. Her shoulder cap and sleeve part. Her butt slaps onto the leather-covered stool. Tweedle Dee smirks. He's done a funny. Dee laughs, enjoying his little joke. Tweedle Dumb half-steps quickly inward extending his reach. Princess, jaw agape, glances at severed sleeve. Her eyes flash. She has more grit than I expected.

Hook up, step into the door. Jump-time, Galvan. No more time for navel gazing. Time to see if I can fight. I'll probably get my ass stomped. They can kill me but they can't eat me. I glide forward, cutting an angle to block his shot. In front of me, Princess shifts. She moves fluidly.

Dum doesn't. Princess rebounds off her stool, lunging forward. Her hand snatches Dee's rock glass as her torso slips past. Princess cocks her arm in the shadow of her breast. The glass is couched, hidden from Dee's view. Damn, we got a bar fight. Tweedle Dee is going to catch it. Nice.

If you're afraid don't lose your head. Fear will slow the world around you. Some call it Chi. Others insist it is just adrenaline gushing from the adrenal gland. It is a friend in need. The surge allows one to fight or take flight.

Adrenaline operates in the tiny linkage space between nerve endings in synaptic gaps where it acts as a neurotransmitter. It facilitates receipt of incoming observation and outgoing action.

Adrenaline locks neural passageways in the full-on position. Riding the adrenaline wave, will wear one down quickly. Arriving fast, it is quickly exhausted. Do something before you go tap-city, you old fart. About me, everyone slows to a crawl. I'm less disabled than I thought. Adrenaline has arrived. A friend in need is a friend indeed. Tweedle Dee turns toward Tweedle Dumb for a moment's chuckle. Dumb shrugs, smiling in bad natured approbation. They are really going to go for broke with Princess. If stupid effervesced, bubbles would come out the dumb brothers' ears. Princess has it timed just right, sweeping her glass up into view. Wham. Her large, half-glass of deep-red wine plunges into Dee's eyes. Ohhh. Nice shot.

Princess holds the glass like she would brass knuckles Shelunges, and corkscrews a tight, hard overhand-right to the center of Dee's face. The blow snaps Dee's head back. Good girl--she put her whole body into the punch.

Dee plummets to the wet floor. Lands solidly on his ass among glass shards. Ouchhhhh! Tweedle Dumb steps in, swiping a hard left for the woman's skull. Princess ducks beneath Dumb's swipe. Her left hooks around Dumb's arm, smacking him hard to the cauliflower ear. His eyes bulge a second.

Dumb recovers in time to snatch the nape of her neck. He's quick for a big man. He now controls her head. The body follows the head. Dumb hauls Princess to him, bringing her face forward, seeking to maximize impact with his incoming fist.With his marriage-of-gravity, Dumb will flatten her face. Dumb is saying, "Time for the consequences, bitch."

Bitch? If you have nothing good to say, say nothing. Maybe I get a few of my own, before I catch my ass. Popping the clutch, I step inward smacking Dumb's inner forearm, driving my knuckles to rake his nerves toward the wrist. His hand snaps opens, releasing Princess. Tweedle-Dumb's face reflects shock. Good to be alive won't last long. Princess keeps moving. Freed of Dumb's hold on her, Princess reaches behind her to snatch her barstool, spinning it and hurling her barstool against Dumb's shins. Somebody's not ready to take her beating. I could appreciate this one.

Fighting for balance, Tweedle Dumb shifts his weight onto his back leg. He overcorrects rearward, stumbles for balance. Remember, Galvan, do something. I continue to slide between Princess and Tweedle Dumb. With my left knee, I pop Dumb's back knee outward. His knee buckles, he staggers back. Tweedle Dumb skims the top of my head with his fist, a glancing blow. I lurch back, the bar whirling a little.

Princess sweeps her body around and behind mine, settling to my left rear. Oh good. To get Princess he'll have to walk through me. From the size of the lad he probably will likely do it--and soon.

I expect her to stumble on her six-inch heels, she doesn't. Princess comes to rest, torso pressing my back. In the doing, she regains her balance without disturbing mine. Tweedle Dumb rocks forward, charging me. The boy is quick, but the weight of his large gut impedes his effort to overcome the backward stagger. No, Dumb's edges are too sharp. My adrenalin is roaring. Dumb's left hand grasps my right shoulder. He's radaring me as he did to punch Princess. The move will guide his incoming right fist to my head.

The boy must need glasses, or he's a one trick pony. I disrupt his plan, rising as I time his move. I step rearward with my left foot, and I pin his hand to my shoulder, dragging him with me. The edge of my right flicks hard across his Adam's Apple. Dumb gags. My hand swings up and over his pinned arm. My throat chop circles over, then beneath his locked right arm, twisting it.

Tweedle Dumb arches back, then plunges face forward with a screaming gurgle. Dumb's groin smacks Tweedle-Dee into Dee's rising face, sprawling Dee back flat on the wet floor and its glass shards. Dee must fall down a lot. Family reunion time, I dump the gasping Dumb on Dee.

I observe the Greek leaning in the doorway to Gaby's office. He stands with his arm wrapped tightly around Gaby's shoulder. In his free hand Joe holds a baseball bat.

The Greek says, "Looks like you're getting better, Kid, but the girl seems to have done most of the fighting. She looks bad; get her out of here. I'll handle these two."

Joe the Greek and Gaby? How about those apples?

Princess molds to me from shoulder to hip. Silky was right, girls are softer than boys. I loved his kind grandfatherly sayings. Princess brushes her right hand down my right side. She stops at my right hip, over my pistol. Princess just frisked me. I think she's the cops.

Peace seems to be restored. Joe's dress shirt is open over a black t-shirt. He's packing heat.

Joe has a gun, a bat, and Gaby. Gaby has a motherly smile as she studies Jill. Jill is glaring at Princess and has a most annoyed expression. Dee and Dumb have each other.

What have I got? I got Princess. My next move: "Come, Princess, let's us escape."

Jill appears more dismayed. Should I give Princess back? No, I can't give Princess back.

Princess came close to having her face mashed. Princess shamed the Wit Brothers. Until the Rohypnol wears off, I'll need to keep her upright and fleeing. I snatch Princess by the hand. She hesitates. I nod to the Tweedles trying to rise from the floor and draw Princess to me. Her expression relaxes. Her earlier look of distaste warms a bit. It must be the Ruffies. Princess presses her torso to my side. We exit, fleeing on foot. I had left my chariot at home. Her keys are in the purse Jill just picked up during the fight. Jill still holds Princess's purse as we depart.

Up and down gangways we run. We stop at a gas station. I buy Gatorade and seltzer water to flush her system. Princess gets the restroom key from the attendant. The fog is heavier now. There are echoes of revving motorcycles in the mist as she returns.

I march us north by stages. When we reach the river-walk we are just south of the Pere Marquette memorial.

The memorial is a seventy-foot-tall, two-foot-thick, dark wooden cross. The cross marked where Father Marquette and Louis Joliet landed as voyageurs in the Age of Discovery. Well, where the fifty-foot wooden cross used to be--crosses are sort of out of favor these days.

Princess is winded from our run. I hand her the Gatorade, telling her to drink to get the Rohypnol out of her system.

She shrugs, wraps an arm around mine. Princess kisses my ear, bites the lobe. I push her back. I guess that Ruffies do that to a girl.

We share seltzer water and Gatorade. Princess plunges at me out of the blue with a kiss. She tastes like Gatorade and warm friendly woman. I push her back, again. She giggles.

Looking at her, I note half-lidding eyes. She's may be leaving the excitation phase. The drug effect may be dissipating. I must be tired from all the running, and the adrenaline rush in the bar.

Ruffies are a roller coaster ride. The drug induces periods of excitation, suggestibility, drowsiness. The length of the effect span depends on dose size and activity.

The motorcycle thrum shifts closer in the fog. Princess leans into me, trembling in the cold mist. Cold or scared? I walk Princess east toward our boatyard. We walk in silence. I get an occasional sloppy neck kiss. Princess and I continue to pass the Gatorade from hand to hand.

She's getting a red mustache from the Punch Gatorade. I swipe the red stain from her lips with my thumb. She looks at me with extreme earnestness.

She swipes her thumb over my lips doing the same to me. Princess thrusts herself against me, grabbing my head and we are locked in a deep kiss. She is all tongue and soft lips. Lost, I succumb. Princess is hard to resist. It's been a long time between kisses. She kisses well.

We walk in the fog. I realize we've been holding hands. My head hurts. Long day into night.

When Princess is not full of Rohypnol, the flirting will be kaput. Now she's swiping hips with me and giggling. When her head clears, she's done with me. Too pretty, too well built. I wouldn't know what to do with her. Apparently, I'm willing to try.

Excuses, excuses. I love to lie to me. Lying keeps me from having to come out and see if I can still function after my fall from grace.

Princess grabs me by the ass. We stare at each other. Princess has large dreamy eyes. She smiles seductively. She's wobbly. I wrap an arm about her shoulders, just to help her walk. In an instant, my hand slides to her hip. I kiss her again. My hand slips to grasp her bottom. She pulls her face away to study my expression. She smiles wickedly, and we are back at it.

I force myself to stop. Things are getting out of hand. I'll just end up doing what I tried to stop.

I hate this Sir Galahad shit. Princess smiles knowingly, snuggles in. We walk.

Sorry, Princess, we won't be singing in the rain tonight, you'll have to settle for stumbling in the fog.

2

RAINY DAY BLUES

Where am I? Who am I? How did I get here?
I awake in damp cold clothes. My face is wet. My left sock is soaked and sagging off my foot.

A misty rain hugs the turgid surface of the Chicago River below me. Lovely.

Question one answered. I am lying on my chaise lounge on my concrete balcony exposed to the weather.

Who am I? Me? Am I the me I was before Afghanistan? Having been a bit dead was I reborn as a new me? More likely, I'm a mélange of before and after. Being dead droops, a lead weight fixed onto the line running between segments of time.

Now for the most significant question. How, when faced with a variety of options, did I put me out here in the rain on a chaise lounge. Must've wanted to chill out.

I was successful in the chilling. I am frozen.

I have a smallish triangular jib sail over me, thus the wet sock.

At least I chilled on my own balcony. I'm not nestled at the curb on a busy wet street. I'm not drunk on a bar floor. I didn't wake in a strange bed. Things could be worse.

I live on the second floor of an old warehouse. We fitted out the land and building to serve as a boatyard. Our first floor is devoted to the shop. The second floor is mine. Well, the loft in the back is mine. I share the floor with our sail loft. The Greek has a penthouse on the roof.

The balcony of my floor supports a stationary crane for use in lifting boats or other cargo from the river. Its employment as a balcony is secondary. The deck surface on which I stand is cold and wet. Misty, rainy, muffled in fog, a Chicago morning has broken on this fine spring day.

Feet and face wet. Mouth as dry as the Gobi Desert. My head pounds. I turn my head too quickly, luckily it doesn't fall off. Perched on the patio table before me sits a half empty bottle of Black Barrel. I've developed such a healthy lifestyle.

I poisoned myself--didn't succeed in killing me yet. At the moment I can sit down and roll in search of sleep. I'll get up, after the poison kills me. No, I need very much to quit the drinking.

I'm done sleeping. I am somewhat short of dead. I gather and spread the jib to dry in the loft area.

Water, water everywhere; I need something to drink. A glance tells me the grey-brown pudding of a river down there is still flowing south-westward toward the Gulf of Mexico. So I'm not in a different plane of existence

We'll be lucky if the South Branch of the Chicago River hasn't dissolved our concrete launch ramp. I'm afraid to look. If I look my head will fall off. If it lands in the river, I'm not going in the pudding to retrieve it.

I stiffly stagger to the kitchen area seeking a few gallons of water to slake my thirst.

During my death march, I snatch my wet socks, roll them together and fling them onto the loft balcony. There's a washing machine up there, I think.

Head clearing is of the essence this bright spring morning. I pour ice cubes into the stoppered kitchen sink as it fills with cold water. I plunge my head into the sink's icy depths. Damn, that's cold. I remain submerged long enough to freeze my hair. Enough. I'm as awake as I'm likely to get. Didn't eliminate my hangover, at least I'm conscious. I dry my face with a dish towel, contemplating my sins.

I'll have to repent, redeem my salvation, get my shit together and quit drinking like that. With so much to do, I pull on cross-trainers.

This is a very funny-looking living room. We bought the building from an old Romanian. When we rehabbed the building, the Romani taught me how to sew with his industrial sized sewing machines.

Joe appointed me vice president in charge of sewing, by saying, "Do I look like a seamstress, asshole?"

Sail lofts require space to lay out bolts of fabric. We built wheeled cutting-tables which physically interlock the sewing machine tables onto lay-out tables. When not in use the tables sit along outer walls.

I left room for a workout area when we re-purposed the space. I don't have a girl. I do have a gym. There's yet hope. The Greek's 100-pound heavy bag hangs from a fixed derrick along the wall. Mi casa, the Greek's other casa. My speed-bag platform has an adjustable crank mechanism to raise the bag platform in case I get taller. Hasn't happened yet.

The platform is so the peanut bag's base is positioned at my chin level. The small peanut-bag has the quickest rebound. I have a need for speed. I test air pressure by squeezing. It is good to go. Like the third bear's bed, not too hard, not too soft. Just right.

I beat different rhythms at varying speeds to clear my mind. My head clears. My neck loosens. Regular bag use quickens the eye.

As in meditation, a cleared mind tends to drift. Maybe, like grandma says, an idle mind is the devil's workshop.

Unbidden, Shah-I-Kot comes to mind. It is a place name that means, 'the seat of the king'. The last redoubt for the kings of Afghanistan since Alexander the Great upset their apple-cart. A place of retreat from which to sally forth to attack the invader rear guard. The Shah-I-Kot Valley looks like a bull-frog run over by a truck. The frog's head rests high up in the king's lap. There are few ways out; the frog's head, hands and feet mark exit trails. The frog's head rests in a basin at the foot of a 12,000-foot peak sitting southwest of Gardez. The city is the capital of Paktia Province. Gardez is positioned at 7,000-feet above sea-level. Shah-I-Kot is positioned in the suburbs of the Hindu Kush Mountain range of Victorian fame. Isolated is a fair description of the Shah-I-Kot Valley. There are few roads in, few out. Thin air at altitude hinders helicopter transport. Runways are even more rare. The trails of the Shah-I-Kot have been prime routes for smuggling for centuries. Routes run through the Hindu Kush into Pakistan in the south and Iran in the west. Our team operated out of the suburbs of Gardez. I wasn't there for Operation Anaconda. I was once in Gardez, and am now in Chicago, a confirmed civilian.

In Gardez, I was under contract to Department of the Treasury working with the secret service relative to infringements of the United States currency. The secrets do that, have done so since the American Civil War. I don't think old Allan Pinkerton who served during the American Civil War still runs the Washington office, but he might.

Infringements of the currency is subject to interpretation. The powers that be were determined that the jurisdiction extended to the secret service over the currency manipulations of the Columbian drug cartels was not dissimilar to jurisdiction over Taliban manipulation of the currency in support of terrorism.

Everyone in government wanted in on the War on Terror. We went in. The Drug Enforcement Administration and Alcohol Tobacco and Firearms (ATF) leadership was like-minded.

We were a U.S Joint Terrorism Task Force (JTTF). Abbreviation means you are in. We were in. The Feds talk like that. In the early days the FBI was not always represented in JTTF. It was something about all those planes someone left behind the Chinese wall. Why they forgot to mention the planes, I don't know.

Wondering why the bureau wasn't present on our detail, I asked the Navy Chief Petty Officer who ran things for us. He told me a parable.

Not long after 911, during the very early days of Afghanistan, our chief was a young SEAL sniper seated at near the rear load door of a helicopter, loading for a twilight trip inbound for Afghanistan.

The Seals boarded. The Green Berets boarded. Recon Marines boarded. An Army Ranger Dog handler boarded. The copter was pretty much at load weight.

A pair of guys in fatigues bearing the FBI Logo sought to board. The crew chief told them, 'No room.' The Bureau contingent was upset when told to stand down.

A gray-beard walked up in non-descript battle rattle. He spoke to the crew-chief. The load-master nodded. Gray-beard took a seat between the Marines and the Army, who made space.

The bureau contingent registered a heated complaint.

The crew chief's response, "New York Police Detective. He's OK. "

The bureau representative demanded, "Why not us?"

His response, "No room."

My chief sternly studied me, "Your question, Detective?"

I repeated my, "Why no FBI?"

Our chief answered, "No room."

Fancy that. I thought we were the only ones who didn't like the bureau.

Our original deployment was supposed to involve issues in the Afghan banking industry. There was no genuine Afghan banking industry. Money business is handled through the medieval Hawala system. Hawala, the original no paper banking system.

Thus, we went off-reservation. We purchased loyalty. Later, we audited the accounts of the disloyal. My contracted sojourn in the Hindu Kush was set for two years. My visit was cut short of two years. Never stay at the party too late.

In the field, my final excursion was northeast of the seat of the king's pants. We were in a village whose name I can't recall. Maybe I don't want to recall the name, I can be a real wuss.

Big Bob tripped an improvised explosive device (IED)–a terrorist's weapon of mass destruction in the millennial war. My potato got mashed. My neck got broken. When taken out by medivac I was soaked in blood. For clerical purposes I was listed as a civilian clerk, deceased by mischance.

I was indeed dead for a time, before modern medicine interceded. At present, I'm fairly certain that I'm not dead. Fairly certain, not sure, awaiting developments.

I have intermittent episodes of Post-Traumatic Stress Disorder (PTSD) during my idle-mind-is-the-devil's-workshop moments. Wandering down that memory lane is not necessarily for the best. The psychiatrists suggested that I arc the experience toward a positive mental outcome. If I failed to provide a happy ending, the devil tended to provide his own less happy version.

Thus, as I wander, I force myself to recall an old TV commercial. In the commercial Ken and Barbie are going out to play tennis. Ken has a pastel sweater knotted over his shoulders. Barbie wears the kind of tennis skirt that shows her ruffled underpants. G.I. Joe fights off T-Rex, steals a red Corvette, pulls up at Barbie's in the nick-of-time.

Barbie jumps in the 'Vette with G.I. Joe. The 'Vette' crashes into a sleeping cat before disappearing into the distance.

Ken has a good cry.

I'm just a guy, it always works for me.

I glance at the wall clock, 7:30 AM. I mentally probe the screws, nuts, and cages holding my head on. Still attached, I guess. I'll know for sure if my head falls off. The impact tempo on my speed bag increases at the speed of creeping annoyance.

I force down my inclination toward self-pity. Battling PTSD requires a proactive stance. Glancing down at my big feet, I conclude my stance is good. No sense wandering off to la-la land when there's a chance you won't come back.

I glance to the wall clock. How did it become 8:15 AM so fast? Looking down, I view a pattern of sweat droplets circling my stance. Bag rhythm hovers at third level. That third level resonates as a ripping sound.

Something distracts me. What?

I feel watched. I scan around me. Nobody on the balcony. No one behind me. Is he planning a long shot? The watcher could be at river level. I sweep left to right, reading the terrain. My eyes sweep upstream on the river walk.

Jill is standing on the river-walk, looking up. At what?

She's staring at me. Why? What did I do? Hasn't she ever seen a drunk working off a hangover?

Jill stares at me, hands on hips. Her hair is draw back into a pony tail. Mist droplets sparkle delightfully on her pony-tail.

Jill's wearing a soft, misted powder-blue hoody over an orange top. She looks to have been running. Her hood is down, splayed over her shoulders. Black leggings, orange and powder-blue running shoes complete her outfit.

Jill looks nice in most settings. She's easy on the eye on even a rainy day. I return her bemused stare.

As is our habit, Jill speaks first," I think you killed him, Big Man. "

Confused, I answer, "I'm fine. Sorry about last night. I literally had to run. Can I make you breakfast."

Jill nods, "How do I get in?"

"Walk over to the gray metal door in the lot. I'll buzz you up."

Jill walks toward the lot. Momentarily, the doorbell sounds.

I hit the buzzer. I hear the lot door open. There is a metallic thud as it closes. Footfalls, she bounds up the stairs. A knock. Who might that be?

I snatch a towel from the stack on the couch that I forgot to put away yesterday. I open my steel, commercial door admitting Jill.

Jill crosses my threshold, taking the offered towel. "Thanks. I'm soaked. The mist turned to drizzle on my way back from the old post office."

Pointing to my speed bag, she says. "I heard the thrum of the bag in the fog a quarter mile upriver. It was eerie at first. I couldn't figure out what it was. The noise echoed off the mist walls. Haunting. I was searching for a source of the noise. Then I spotted you. You were beating the thing to death."

"So, this is where you and Joe live. Roomy. What do you call your decorating, industrial? Factory modern?"

Confused I say," Joe doesn't live with me. He lives in the penthouse upstairs. We spent more than enough time in close proximity overseas."

"Gaby said you two were friends. She told me you lived over here in the boatyard. Is this loft apartments or a factory?"

"We build sailboats downstairs. This is the sail loft, those are layout tables and under the dust covers are industrial sewing machines. We won't need them until the next boat is ready."

"How many boats are you guys making?"

"We have the one in progress. We bought and repaired a couple more. One sold, the other is in Burnham Harbor."

"No wonder."

"No wonder what?"

"No wonder I couldn't find this place. Karl, the day bartender, told me you love-birds lived in a boatyard. I couldn't find any boats."

"When I mentioned that I saw you two downstairs on the dock. Karl said I might be surprised if I asked to see your love nest. He suggested if I was that curious, I should knock."

"This morning. I saw you banging away on that bag. I didn't want to bother you, but I thought it wouldn't hurt to ask. I've been living in dorms and apartments for years because of school. I must be nesting. It's spring, I'm desperate to decorate something. I had time this morning. I went for a run. Obviously, you're up. Mind if I look around?"

"Jill, the Greek and I are not a couple. We've been partners in a lot of things. We're not life-partners. Your bartending colleague is playing you. On the police department, we were partners as detectives. We paired up as press imbeds with a Navy unit in Afghanistan. We're partners in this boatyard. We're not life partners.

"The absence of boats out in the lot stems from the fact we're working with wood. It reacts to humidity and temperature change. The boats we've worked on to date have been small boat repairs. We kept them in the shop to acclimate the new and existing wood. Our baby in the making sits downstairs in its cradle, if you want to see it."

Jill says, "That explains a lot. What a surprise, I never thought I'd hear you put our baby and cradle in the same sentence."

My face reddens, "Explains what? Our business model? Why there are no boats in our lot? I have nothing against babies or cradles, Slim. If you're in a mood to discuss the potential for some preliminary work, we can talk about it over breakfast."

"What it explains is all the time you've spent staring. Karl was right, I got surprised."

"I thought my interest in you was obvious."

"Come on in, I'll rustle up some Eggs Benedict. Make yourself at home. "

"Got coffee?"

"I'll get water going for the French Press. If you need more towels, some are on the couch."

While I cook, I explain, "Joe lives upstairs. I've got an apartment in the rear loft on this floor. My loft has the bedroom, bathroom, and the laundry stuff. The kitchen and living room are down here, obviously. "

I add water to simmer in the lower pan of the double boiler. I separate yokes, slide them into a bowl. Lemon juice, white pepper and Worcestershire Sauce are whipped in. The Bearnaise sauce simmers in the upper pan.

Jill wanders, looks around, dries her hair. As she saunters by, I burn my thumb. Time to watch breakfast, not Jill.

Distracted, Jill is stretching, hands over her head, loosening kinks after her run. She seems preoccupied with framed photographs on the wall. Jill's orange top clings wetly to her in the cool air. She gazes my way quizzically.

In my role as village-idiot, I stand sucking my burnt thumb. That, and ogling Jill's form.

Jill startles, looks down, frowns. To distract I nod to the open balcony doors, "Sorry, the open door is making it nipply in here." A great line, that, genius at work.

She says, "We just met, Galvan. It's about three minutes since I discovered you like girls. You had your look. Toss me your hoody. Mine's wet."

"I've been talking with you since the snowstorm, Jill."

"Yeah. Talking, not hawking. I thought you and Joe were a cute butch couple. When you were given the opportunity, you showed no interest. Let me adjust."

Flummoxed, I pop more sour dough English muffins from the toaster. I butter them, placing the muffins over the warm toaster as I whisk butter into the warming hollandaise sauce.

Slow down, Galvan, you'll get a more harmonious outcome.

Adding apple vinegar to simmering water. I break eggs sliding them in.

Jill continues her survey.

Meanwhile, I decide Jill's form is made for Lululemon leggings. Feeling my gaze, Jill zips my hoody, bunching it to her waist for warmth. That definitely hides neither leggings, nor more importantly, form.

Jill doesn't mind the attention. She's moderating my intensity. We just met. Looks allowed. Not time yet for soulful gazes. Jill walks over to my bow rack under the balcony. She selects a longbow and holds it out. "Nice bow, show me?"

I answer, "Let's eat, I'll show you after breakfast."

Jill looks up, becoming distracted. Timing is everything. I turn back the heat on my sizzling Canadian bacon. I slide slices onto muffins, ladle a poached egg onto muffin-halves. Then top each with a dollop of sauce.

Lifting the plates, I turn to the breakfast island asking, "Ready?"

Timing is everything. Mine's gone awry.

Jill's stalking toward the door. "I see you already have company, Galvan. You should have said something. The purse is in Gaby's office. Karl opens at ten."

The door slams behind Jill. Footsteps echo on the stairs. The lower door slams.

What did I do?

A noise above me. I look up.

Princess stands on the landing, looking down at me. She's wearing my dress-shirt mostly buttoned. Through the white material I catch a glimpse of black lace. Princess has long, toned legs.

I forgot she was up there. I must've really drowned my sorrows last night.

I forgot I put Princess to bed up there after her Rohypnol poisoning. I sprint to the dock balcony, trying to come up with an excuse. None comes to mind.

Noise in the lot. Joe is entering spewing gravel from his Stinkin-Lincoln.

Wearing my hoody, Jill strides to Joe. He listens, shakes his head in dismay, glances up at me.

Too late, now. Jill's convinced of my perfidy.

Princess strutting around half-dressed on the balcony overhead didn't help. Whether or not I did the dirty deed, Jill thinks I did.

With that dose of Rohypnol, Princess won't remember whether I did or didn't. From her garb and stance, she thinks I might have.

Even at this distance there is something funny in her eyes. Doubt? Fear? Confusion? I guess she has a right to all of the above. I'll work an explanation into the breakfast conversation.

Below me, Joe wraps an arm around Jill's shoulders ushering her into his Lincoln.

Movement on the point across our inlet catches my eye. A man is standing in the bushes. The man is watching Jill get in Joe's car.

Haven't seen this guy before.

He is downstream of our spring. The water is still clear running in the inlet at that point. He looks in my direction. People seem to feel you looking at them. Seeing me surprises the guy. He drops his chin, turns and walks inland toward the city playlot south of the point. Strange dude, I wish I had a better look at him. He seems familiar; it was almost as if he knew me when he looked up.

Princess comes up behind me. She snakes an arm through mine. Barefoot, Princess is still tall. I turn toward her.

We are standing eye to eye.

Her gaze is probing. She asks, "What are you looking at?"

I gesture toward the point across the inlet, "There was a strange man standing near the water, watching our lot. He's gone now. Probably nothing."

Studying her I ask, "How are you feeling? Are you groggy still?"

Her gaze is stern. "What happened last night?"

My answer, "You were sitting in the bar at Gaby's last night with a pair of bikers I hadn't seen in there before. I'm pretty sure the short fat one palmed Rohypnol into a mixed drink he bought for you. The sugary flavoring in the drink covered the taste."

"I saw him do the palm move, but I didn't pay attention to it. I was talking with the bartender."

"The pretty young girl who just left in a huff?"

"Yes."

"Why did she bring us breakfast? Is she a friend?"

I look at the pots on the counter. Princess is observant, but not always. She's younger than I thought. She appears to be a kid. She must have washed her face when she got up. Without the smoky eyes she might be Jill's age.

Tense again, "Where's my purse?"

Jill just told me it's locked in Gaby's office. I'll take you to get it after breakfast. They won't be open for a couple of hours. You look like you need breakfast."

"What happened? Did they do anything to me?"

"I don't know about before you got to the bar. After you were in the bar you threw a drink in one guy's face and punched the daylights out of him. They tried to hustle you out. You fought them. I helped you a little."

"Why is my purse in the bar, and how did my jacket get ripped?"

Tweedle Dumb ripped it trying to drag you to the parking lot."

"You said earlier you didn't know them. You know his name, now. How did you know he was dragging me outside?"

"The big guy said it was time for the consequences, the lot was kind of mentioned. Something about a walk in the park or maybe it was a party in the parking lot."

"I named the short fat guy, Tweedle Dee. That would make the bigger one Tweedle Dumb in my memoirs."

Princess raises her chin, tilts back her head to eye me, "Are you being funny, Officer Galvan?"

"Trying my best, Officer Sugar."

"I'm not in municipal law enforcement."

"Should I call you Agent Sugar, Princess?"

"My name is Dimitrieva, Nadia Dimitrieva. I'm not any kind of princess. Why did you think I was a police officer?"

"You frisked me in the bar as you slithered over my back, you fist fight like it wasn't your first rodeo, you've been interrogating me almost since you got out of my bed. The only ones who use that bullshit municipal law enforcement jargon are the miscreants from the bureau."

"I'm not the police, dear."

"Not by a long-shot, Agent Sugar.

"By the conceited tone and the air of superiority, you be the 'G. Why you lookin at me?"

The woman's eyes misted "What happened to me last night. You have a dab of lipstick smeared on your ear and down your neck. What did you do to me, god damn it?"

Got me. Princess Nadia slumps on the couch, looking desolate. She appears to have lost self-respect, her sense of worth gone. Victimization is a horrible thing to realize in the light of day.

Apparently, I am the type capable of doing things worse than death to innocent women everywhere. So, I try for the truth. "The bikers slipped what I think were ground up Roofies in your drink. You drank enough of it to get wrecked. Never drink from something the bad guys give you, Nadia. Ask for bottled beer, it's harder to dope."

"You pretty much fought them off. I helped, then hustled you out. They chased us around the neighborhood in the fog. You were fading fast. I got some Gatorade and seltzer water. Forcing fluids can water down the Rohypnol, the drug passes from your system with the fluids."

"What about my lipstick on your neck, Galvan? What did you do to me? Did you enjoy throwing a quick one to the drugged slut."

I lift the almost empty Gatorade punch bottle, "Ease up on yourself, lady. Whatever you want to pin to my tail, you won't prove rape. We ran out of Gaby's. You were wrecked. The drug made you susceptible to suggestion and relaxed your inhibitions. I brought you here. You got a little uninhibited. The red stuff is not from when you felt amorous. It's not lipstick. Its girl-flavored Gatorade slobber."

I continue, "I put you to bed, then I slept out there on the balcony. Your virtue remains intact as far as I know. I just put you to bed."

"Where are my clothes?'

"You'll find your jacket up in the bedroom, I tossed it on a chair. It got ripped when you were tussling with the 'Wit Brothers' in the bar. I tossed it on a chair while we undressed you. Your shoes are under the chair."

"Who said you could undress me?"

"You kept taking things off and flinging them at me. I kept putting things back on. You were having a great time. We eventually compromised on the underwear."

"You stripped me down to my underwear?" Princess asks incredulously

Amused I say, "No. You completely disrobed on your own, Princess. The drug they fed you was probably Rohypnol. They call it the date rape drug. Inhibitions drop followed by amnesia. When I came down here last night you were as dressed as I could get you and sleeping under a throw."

I conclude, "Go up and find the clothes. Put them on while I finish breakfast. There's a washer and dryer up there if you need them. The shower and tub are down the hall upstairs. Don't worry, the door has a lock. Lock it. There's an iron in the closet, if you need it."

"Holler when you're ready and I'll nuke your breakfast."

Princess Nadia stands glaring at me, fists on hips.

Annoyed, I say, "GO. I did nothing to you. I tried to help you fight off a pair of would be rapists. If you were pure as the driven snow before you sat down in Gaby's last night, you remain so. Go put some clothes on."

"We'll pick up your purse when I take you home. You drink coffee?"

Nadia nods stonily and retreats to the loft.

While the shower is running, I call Gaby to verify Princess Nadia's purse is in Gaby's safe. Gaby says it will be there waiting for us.

On returning, wearing clothes, Nadia is nervous. Perhaps with time alone, she took time to review her notes. She seems to again be convinced of my perfidy. I have to get this one out of here. Grandpa Silky was right, never invite the 'G' into the house. Like annoying relatives, they never leave.

I don't care if she's nervous. My landline was in-use while I cooked, the light on the phone down here was red part of the time she was upstairs. I should have listened in. Didn't, should have.

Nadia carefully descends the staircase from the loft wearing the four-inch heels from last night. She joins me carefully positioning herself with her back to the door, across the table from me before allowing her eyes to meet mine.

Cool and steady is a good description of her gaze. Ms. Dimitrieva says in a saccharine, snide tone," Good morning, Galahad. I may owe you an apology. I suppose you deserve a thank you. For your assistance, last night."

I'm gifted with a 100,000-Watt smile. She delicately sips her coffee. Surprised, princess stares at her cup, "That is good coffee."

I walk to the warmer extracting our Eggs Benedict. I pour Hollandaise over the eggs and Canadian bacon. The muffins are sourdough. I say, "Pick your poison. Sorry about the nuke, you were on the phone for a long time. "

Nadia looks confused, then annoyed. Trying for innocence she asks, "Phone?"

I point to the message machine attached to the landline alongside the lounge chair.

Worried, she thinks a moment, then points at the plate in my left hand. I set it before her. She sips her coffee, then glances at it skeptically.

I say, "ENOUGH."

I pick up her cup and take a sip. With a new fork I take a small slice from her Eggs Benedict and eat it. "I didn't poison you. I didn't sexually assault you. I put you to bed. I'm beginning to think I should have drowned you. Eat your breakfast so we can get your stuff and you can go home."

"Damn it, Francis, I had to call work."

How does this wench know my first name? I'm targeted for something.

Mad, Princess cuts a tiny piece, takes a bite, chews.

Her face changes into a smile. She savors the eggs, dabs her lip with the napkin. Sips her coffee. Says, "This IS good."

Princess wolfs her breakfast in contentment.

"What were the spices you used in that sauce? It was perfect."

"The usual, maybe a little brucine."

"I don't know that one."

"Brucine is a member of the Strychnine family."

"You gave me Strychnine? You poisoned me?"

"I didn't say that. I'm yanking your chain because you're tailing my ass. What do you think I did, Princess?"

I continue, "Don't worry. A single dose of brucine doesn't kill. It's a cumulative dose weapon which causes renal failure--hair loss."

Princess snatches her hair, to see if it falls out.

"Don't worry, Kid. I am just fucking with you."

"You said you didn't."

"I didn't have sex of any kind with you last night. You'd know if I did."

"Yeah? Why?"

"We'd both probably be smiling more when looking at each other, and sneering less."

"Why do you know about the poison?"

"Jan Michael Vincent used it on Arthur Bishop in '**The Mechanic**'. I looked up brucine after I saw the movie on Turner Broadcasting."

"I must have missed that part. You're talking about the Jason Statham Movie, right?"

"No. The original was with Charles Bronson. Jan Michael Vincent coated Bronson's glass to kill him. Bronson died instantly from what looked like a heart attack. To kill like that you'd have to dose the victim starting with a milligram the first day, two the second, etc. it would take a month or so. In the end you could coat both glasses, let the victim choose one, then drink with him from the other without hurting yourself. It would kill him not you."

"How do you know that? Why do you know it?"

"It was in 'The Count of Monte Cristo'."

"The movie with that hunk, Jim Caviezel?"

"No, the book by Alexander Dumas. If you're worried, you could have your lab run a test using liquid chromatography-mass spectrometry on a blood sample. I didn't poison you.

Seeking to continue her interrogation, over calling herself an ambulance, Princess says, "It was nice of your little bartender to bring us breakfast. Did you pay her? I'll buy. I'm sorry if I scared the girl off. She seems a simple soul."

She adds, "Be careful, I think that poor girl has a crush on you."

I shrug. "If Jill was interested, she ain't now. You saw to that, Princess, with your black lace La Perla floor-show."

"My what sharp eyes you have, Mr. Wolf. Did I look that bad?"

"Ms. Dimitrieva, you are stunning to behold. I'll probably wake many nights dreaming of you naked, descending from my loft."

"I WASN'T NAKED, FRANCIS GALVAN."

I respond, "Today. You were walking around naked, up there, during the night."

Princess called me by first and last names this time. Barely knows me, but knows a great deal about me. Nadia seems to have made a study, or at least an investigation of me.

Nadia plays with her coffee cup, rolling it between her palms, asking coyly, "Have you been back long?"

"From where?" I ask.

"Let me rephrase my question. Where on earth did you go for so long?" Nadia says.

I answer, "You got me. I'm dead. I got kicked out of hell; I tried to take over. Just got back. Sniff my wrist, you can smell the sulfur. Come, I'll drive you to Gaby's to get your stuff."

Her facial expression flickers uncertainly. Annoyed I say, "Pick one, honey: girl or hunter?

I rise. Princess follows languidly, but reluctant. We take my SRX back to Gaby's. A Fed sits in his 'G' car across the street, next to the Greek's Lincoln.

Is the Greek up early, or did he stay late? Gaby's door is locked. Nice, I knock. The curtain moves. The Greek says," We're closed, go away asshole.

Finding it nice to be loved. I respond, "It is I, dearest. We're here for Princess's purse and flame-thrower. She left her things on the bar last night before the festivities."

Joe opens the door. He looks me up and down. "Sorry, kid, I thought it was some other asshole; you all look alike." Feeling overcome by the rapturous welcome, Princess and I enter.

Walking behind the bar, the Greek flips a bar towel over his shoulder, turns to face us with his arms folded across his chest. He glances from me to Princess looking her up and down, before turning back to me with a raised eyebrow. He smirks.s "You'd be hard to resist."

Princess and the Greek exchange hard stares. She says to me, "My name isn't Princess, asshole."

Joe smiles in recognition, saying, "Oh, you know him."

Nadia gives the Greek an icy glare, inquiring of him, "My purse, big-and-dumb?"

Joe calls back to Gaby's office, saying, "The asshole is here with the giant 'G' broad."

Gaby appears, followed by Jill. Both appear angry. Let me guess at whom. Jill carries a large rectangular sterling silver tray, with matching warming cover.

Nadia asks Jill, "My purse, honey?"

Jill dramatically places the tray on the bar. Jill looks at Gaby. Gaby glances at Princess. Then gestures to Jill, who lifts the sterling-silver cover from the tray.

Arranged neatly are Nadia's purse, handcuffs, an FBI badge-case, emblazoned 'FBI' on its leather flap, car keys, and a neat stack of cash on which rests various credit-cards weighted in place with a Glock Model 26 Gen-4, 9 mm 10 shot automatic with a round in the chamber.

Gaby says, "Please check the purse and its contents."

Nadia's face reddens, she mumbles something about being sure it's all there. She checks anyway. When the contents go back in the purse, Nadia thanks Jill.

Jill stares, coldly.

The two women glare a long moment. At first, nothing passes between them.

Then, BOOM, Nadia says sweetly, "I'm so sorry I slept with your boyfriend last night, dear. If he had mentioned you I would have declined. Sorry, didn't know."

"Didn't know, or didn't care?" says Jill.

"There you have it. We just popped out of bed, and you brought breakfast. Embarrassing."

"Funny. When I passed the building earlier, Galvan was wrapped in a boat-sail sleeping on a chaise lounge, snoring in the rain. After he showed me the loft, you wandered out of the loft half-dressed, looking chubby and confused. It appears you weren't very memorable, he forgot you were up there."

Oblivious, Nadia asks, confused, "He snores?"

"Does he ever. Sounds like a foghorn, dear. I heard his snoring down the block."

"You apparently didn't sleep with Galvan, dear. The fleet is in town, maybe you banged some sailor. What with the bar-fight you probably had a very busy evening. If Galvan had put himself any further away from you, he'd have been in the river."

"Regardless, he is your boyfriend?"

"No, Galvan is not my boyfriend. Friends like him I can do without. He spends way too much time with biker sluts. Yuck."

Nadia's blue eyes harden to a blue crystal before regaining composure. She says, "That's good, I'd have felt bad about our evening if I thought you two were, what? I don't know? Together?"

Nadia spins on me. She folds herself about my torso, thrusting her tongue down my throat. We are bound together for a moment eye to eye, then she quickly breaks contact. She slips past, slapping my ass in passing.

At the door Nadia pauses, turns to Jill as she speaks to me, "Thank you for being my hero last night, Galahad. It was wonderful. I owe you a wake-up. See you soon?"

Nadia draws a card case from her rear pocket. She extracts a card. Taps it against my chest then slides it into my shirt pocket. She sniffs, saying, "Your shirt smells like me, nice."

She glances back to Jill, "Sorry dear, couldn't help it. So, yummy. But you wouldn't know that, would you? No? I thought not."

Nadia brushes her lips over mine before walking out. "Bye all."

The door slams behind her.

I lift the door's window curtain. Princess walks to the 'G' car. She leans down to speak to a well-dressed man in the driver's seat. He asks a question. She shakes her head in the positive.

The man nods, asks another question. Nadia shrugs.

The man smiles with a bit of a leer, asking a third question.

Nadia exaggeratedly shakes her head negatively, shrugging her shoulders.

They share a laugh.

He repeats his question, nodding in my direction. Princess laughs once more, then swipes her palm back toward me, derisively pushing something away from her. Nadia focuses over her shoulder on Gaby's door. Sees me watching. Her face falls. The man smirks, says something with a laugh, shaking his head.

Nadia responds sharply, steps back. He pulls away, waves goodbye.

Refusing to look at me, Nadia walks quickly down the block. At the corner she turns to the east, disappearing from view. Moments later an agate-gray Porsche Carrera with its visor down turns a quick left following the route of the "G" sedan toward Archer Avenue. Is there anything that woman does or has, which isn't top shelf?

She sees me watching. It's raining. Why put her visor down? A six-year-old knows that putting their hand over their eyes isn't hiding.

For that matter, why all the drama-rama? I turn to ask them what they think.

I'm alone, my friends are gone. Started the day by myself, must be that kind of day. Nap time.

3

BOOKS AND THE CARRYING THEREOF

The Greek barged in early this morning, came to get me before dawn. We had meaningful work to do.

That is, right after I cooked breakfast. The Greek doesn't like to cook upstairs because cooking stinks up his penthouse. Apparently, it is OK to stink up my place by cooking the Greek his breakfast. He tells me that he went down in the pre-dawn hours to find the humidity of our oak keel sections just right. The wonders of joinery and joint scarfing awaited us.

So, I heat olive oil in a large frying pan. When the oil smokes, I add chopped onion with some red and green sweet peppers, and freshly cut potato squares. The Greek likes fresh.

I chop lean corned beef slices into thin strips, adding corned beef to the cooking potatoes, pepper and onions. In the process Potatoes O'Brien are born.

I spray an old Corningware dish it with butter flavored PAM. Then dump my browned Potatoes O' Brien go into the Corningware. I break whole eggs into dents in the hash. The casserole dish slid into the oven warmed to 350 degrees Fahrenheit.

As breakfast baked, we drank coffee at the breakfast island.

Joe lectures me on my shortcomings, which I discover remain both many and varied.

In the past, Jill had expressed an interest in me. Ever helpful, always playful, Karl decided to play a joke on the poor girl. He implied the Greek and I had a love nest on the Chicago River, which is called Bubbly Creek. The river, not our nest.

I am informed that the Greek views Jill as a nice girl. Knowing me as he does, He's become certain I should leave Jill alone. He knows that I am nothing short of an aging deviant twitching with lust for Jill Ryan's innocent body. Occasionally the Greek and I agree.

He insists Jill is far too young and sweet for me.

The Greek notes after all the trouble I caused at Gaby's, Jill had become worried for my safety. She merely stopped at my lowly hovel with the purpose of checking on my well-being. After all, I was last seen fleeing from two fat guys in denim jackets. How was she to know that when seeking to commiserate with a friend in need, she would not just see how her gay friend decorated his hobo camp.

The Greek noted that, perhaps the poor child was merely intent upon discovering whether I was as gay as I dressed.

Now in addition to being an aged lecher, I am guilty of appropriating lifestyles and clothing styles. Today, the Greek is a whirlwind of helpfulness.

"BUT," he adds.

The poor girl had no way of knowing that I'd be entertaining a biker slut. Although, the Greek noted that my trampy FBI Agent, was possessed of a gorgeous rack and a bodacious ass. The Greek likes to be specific regarding a woman's qualities even as he disparages bad life choices. He felt Nadia extremely attractive for a soiled dove. The Greek would know.

As we finish breakfast, he needs one more cup of coffee. Being Greek, he suggests I make him a Cappuccino.

One might ask what being Greek has to do with my making him a Cappuccino? I have no idea, but he considers the connection significant.

Surfeited, he says, "Come on, kid enough dickin' around, we got work to do. You have to stop malingering. Up and at 'em, lad."

Damn, I took too much time making the Greek breakfast. I'll have to get up earlier

Like guys, boats run from stiff to pliable. One would expect stiff to be fast and sleek, pliable slow, just bobbing along. It all depends on design, though. A stiff roundish cockle-shell flies. A long slender Viking ship flexes all along its length, knifing through heavy seas. Different designs built for particular uses.

We are perfecting our design. Today we scarf, which is a tedious all-day sucker. We are joining oak sections with secure scarf joints. The joinery, scarfs, span easily more than 7-inch joints. In the process of cutting, gluing and screwing we meld them into a strong, tight keel. Done well, these will be the foundation upon which our vessel rests.

We'll get it done, make a killing. Hope springs eternal

Needing help lifting a large plank. I call for Joe. No Joe.

By the wall clock it is 11:30 AM.

The blackboard below the clock displays a note, reading, "Gone to lunch, Gaby's. I'll buy, wash behind your ears."

Joe never buys lunch. If I don't hurry, he'll leave me the bill.

My 6-foot 10-inch Greek bee is buzzing around Gaby's much of late. If I work the keel this afternoon, I'll be by myself. Mother Galvan did not raise a fool. I clean up, put on fresh clothes. Entering Gaby's, I smile at Gaby. She is having none of it, she's all business.

Gaby says, "Cher, I need a favor. One of my girls is in need of a ride to the university. I can't take her. Help me out, I'll buy dinner."

Gaby gives me her sad, huge-eyed-waif look, "The girl is desperate, take her to university. She's got the one day off."

Some game is afoot, Am I being sent out to play with the other children.

Glancing to the Greek, I say, "Buddy, can you hold down the fort for me while I help Gaby this afternoon? "

Agreeably, with a big smile he says, "Buddy, I got it. Help the poor girl out.

Gaby smiles at me maternally.

I'm in trouble, no doubt about it. Did they sell me to the gypsies or are they going to move out while I'm at school and not tell me where they went?

I catch Gaby raising an eyebrow to the Greek. The Greek smiles, at ease inside their plot. I hope these people are nice gypsies.

I fear our skipjack is safe from framing today.

I say, "Gaby, send the lovely lady down, I'll be in front in my SRX."

Timeo Danaos et dona ferentes', means, 'Beware Greeks bearing gifts.' On the other hand, Homer might've meant, 'Beware gifts bearing Greeks.' I'm certain somebody is sure to have moved the words around every thousand years or so.

I daydream sitting in my SRX. For some reason this SRX is my favorite vehicle. I've decided if I have to wait in the car, a Cadillac SRX is just the car in which to wait.

The neighborhood is changing. Bridgeport is gentrifying. I'm not a good example, but the hood is in moving forward.

Chicago has a lot of universities. Either they are situated near Chicago Transit Authority train lines or lines are situated to serve college traffic. Gentry and college students seem to live in clusters along mass transit lines. Bridgeport follows the trend. The new CTA elevated stations running along Archer Avenue's Orange Line just to the south changed things for the better.

Gabrielle's Restaurant is located on the first floor of a large rectangular building which was built in the days just prior to the Columbian Exposition of 1892. When Gaby bought the building it was run down. The Greek and I, with the help of a few friends, rehabilitated the building including the upstairs apartments. The builder's style mimics an Italian palazzo.

Interior apartments are enclosed by an outer enclosed gallery-walk. The center of its structure in Italy would have been a small garden courtyard, open to the air. Here, winter is long and cold. The open-air palazzo was a non-starter. Thus, there is an interior sitting room.

Gaby's restaurant, bar and various small businesses are down at street level.

We rehabbed Gaby's upper rooms as rooms to let to female college students from various local universities. Gaby has a European world view, under my roof under my command. It's her building, students accept her standards, or they can choose another building. Gaby's residents are all female students. Gaby is a fan of female education and liberation. Her premise provides a secure refuge for the educational process. Residents are free to fraternize off site whenever they want, not onsite. To say fraternization is not encouraged in the building, is an understatement.

Upon coming to town, Gaby had a rough time. Gaby's maternal side shows when she helps residents obtain part-time work in the area. Home away from home is an apt description.

Woe-be-tide local lads who mistreat Gaby's residents. They have in the past disappeared, eventually turning up on the menu in the more unsavory restaurants along the river.

Sitting daydreaming, I lower my SUV's windows enjoying the cool Lake Michigan breeze. People stroll the sidewalks. A few young women I recognize, some I don't.

As I sit, I realize any important thoughts I had today are gone, must have forgotten to write them down. The view is just fine, though. I contemplate possibilities, perhaps there's a woman around here I haven't alienated.

I wonder which of Gaby's girls I'll be chauffeuring. Class must have let out somewhere, a lot of college aged people are strolling from the El' Station on Archer Avenue. Individuals, couples and groups disperse into the neighborhood. Young women stroll past with arm loads of books. Year end? Some walk with companions, some walk alone. Serious faces predominate. Exam time?

I'm really getting old, exams already?

Exams. Spring is here to stay. Unless it snows.

If you don't like Chicago's weather, wait five minutes, it will change.

A blond with an armload of books is about to walk past. I don't know her. She smiles.

She smiles my way. I must clean-up better than I figured.

Is the blond waving at me?

No, she's focused over my head. Is she waving at a bird?

My passenger door clicks open, I turn. Standing in the open doorway is a long-legged female form in blue jean cut-offs. Dynamite build. She's wearing a scoop-necked sleeveless shell, as she leans on the roof of my Cadillac.

Being male I'm staring at her cleavage, nice indeed.

The woman says something to the blond across the street about, "Later, maybe dinner time." My radio volume distorts the rest.

My passenger is tall, athletically slender. Bending at the waist she glances in. I am caught studying cleavage. Lovely, the waist bend enhanced my interest. I can't break my gaze, her body is enthralling.

Feeling foolish, I force my glance to her face saying, "Hi, my name is Galvan. Gaby says you need a ride to a bookstore."

As I focus on her face, she responds, "Galvan, we've already met. Are you done looking down my blouse?"

I say, "No, lost my head. Simply wonderful. My heart be still. I wasn't aware of that side of you. You're safe, I won't do it again, Kid. I try not to ogle girls your age."

"Galvan, are you nuts? Is this little drive your idea? Or did Gaby and Joe dream it up?"

"Gaby asked me to help you out. I didn't realize you was you. If I upset you, I'm sorry. I didn't realize they had a campus bookstore at cosmetology school. I mean cosmetology college.

"Galvan, you are really different. Cosmetology college? Really?"

We drive in silence toward Archer. At the light I realize I have no idea where I'm going, so I ask, "Where we going?"

"The U of C campus?" Jill answers.

Confused I ask, "The U of C has a cosmetology school?"

She looks askance. "You're kidding, right?"

"About what? I don't know which campus bookstore I'm supposed to take you to."

"Ohhh? It's the one at the U of Chicago Medical School. Cosmetology and medicine are related sciences. This month I'm in the cadaver lab, practicing French manicure and nail colors on cadavers. I'm having problems with the half-moons in my French manicures."

Bobbie Brown's new book.

I ask, "Does he have more than one?"

"Oh yes, this is the newest text.'

I'm being toyed with, "What's the title?"

Jill answers**, "Cherry on Top: Flirty, Forty-Something, and Funny as F**k."**

She asks, "So, how is your giant FBI girlfriend? I didn't mean to interrupt proceedings. Did you two have a nice evening? She came across trampy. A fun tramp, though, huh? You saved your FBI Agent from a fate worse than death. I'm sure she was extremely grateful.

I say, "She did most of the fighting. I just spirited her away. She didn't have much to thank me for."

"Whatever? You're a guy. I hope she took care of business. Doesn't matter to me what you sleep with? Guy's find easy peasy best I hear. I hope you don't come down with the plague. After having fun with Ms. FBI so recently, why were you eyeing my breasts? I mean, I caught you staring down my blouse. Something wrong with Agent Hussy's?"

"No, you caught me flat-footed. I'm a fan of yours. More so after staring down your blouse just now. I'm sorry, I'm a little old to be corrupting the morals of college girls. You have a wicked sense of humor and you are as smart as they come. I'm not your kindly old grandfather, I'm not above laying hands on you, young lady. "

We pull to the curb in front of the university quad. I turn to Jill. She has a wicked smile," You are not laying your paws on anything at present. Galvan, do you actually have a driver's license?"

I say, "Why? Yes, I had to renew it when I came back. They made me do the whole test."

Jill says, "You drive like you are nuts. Show me the license."

I hand Jill my wallet. She checks the license. Then riffles through the photos. I reach for the wallet, only to get my hand slapped.

Jill says, "I'm not done."

She stops at one, taking the photo out. She glances at the back. Distracted, she asks, "Who is Farthingale Dashingworth?"

I respond, "Me. that is Mary Beth Burke's photo. She and I were partners on the 'Job'."

Slapping away my hand once more, she says, "She looks awful young for you, old man. What's the job?"

I say, "We went to high school. She nicknamed me Farthingale Dashingworth, III, because she thought I was a stuffed shirt. The 'Job', is being a police officer."

Jill says, "She's a smart girl. You are full of nonsense. Who are these people in the group picture with Gaby's boyfriend? They have more guns than the Wild Bunch."

I take Jill's hand in mine, conveying the hand and wallet to view the picture. I forgot the Greek was in the team-photo of my last summer in Afghanistan. The Greek's holding his scoped M-4 with an under-barrel 40 mm under-barrel M203 grenade launcher. The team is armed to the teeth. Funny, the things you'll come to see as normal.

I release her hand, saying after a pause to think, "They were part of the team I was imbedded on in Afghanistan. I took the picture using the Greek's camera. He must've borrowed the weapon for the photo."

Jill snarks. "Did he borrow the flak vest with his name on the ID panel, and the pistol and all the bullet clips?"

I smile, "Box magazines, not clips."

Smiling sweetly. "How many guns and bullet things did you borrow to take the picture?"

I answer as I was directed, "I was a journalist, not a soldier. I'm a civilian. Sometimes we were armed, Afghanistan is not a nice place. There were prices on our heads, all of us r-really. "

Jill flips my wallet onto my chest. Its contents spill in my lap. With a raised brow she asks, "Is it the lying, or the lying to a poor innocent girl like me that has you stumbling over your own tongue, Galvan?"

Jill exits, slamming the door, leaving the window down.

I call to her, "Flip down the visor, it's a parking permit."

Jill reaches back into the cabin to flip the visor down. Looks at me through the windshield. Sticks her head and shoulders back in. Damn, her cleavage distracts my eye again.

Jill asks disapprovingly, "It reads Chicago Police Detective Division-Official Business."

I respond, "Shameful, is it not?"

"What are you looking at, Mr. Galvan?"

"Hazel."

"My boobs are not hazel? You are nuts, you know?"

I say, "Your eyes are hazel. You told me, 'Brown hair, brown eyes, brown shoes. I don't come in a smaller quieter size.' You have hazel eyes. Are you in the habit of lying to me?"

"How observant you are, Mr. Galvan. I won't lie to you any more than you lie to me."

I say, "You do have lovely breasts."

We stare eye to eye intently. Jill says, "You're right, Galvan, they are. Eventually I may give you more opportunity for further study. But I thought I was a young innocent. You're not much older, Mister."

"Okay, let us go to a bookstore."

As we stroll across the quad, Jill asks, "What should I call you, Galvan? Is your name Tray, like in dinner tray? Francis? Or, is it the Bear? Who you be, boy?

"People call you Trey. Gaby told me the Bear was waiting out front in the Cadillac. Are you 'the bear', as in hairy forest creature, jaws and claws?" Jill snarls primly, swiping her red clawed hand across my chest.

I laugh. "Most people call me Galvan. Bear is what my mother called me when I was being stubborn. Gaby knows my parents. My name is Francis Patrick Galvan, III. Mystery over."

Jill growls a little. "Oh, I see, Trey as in 1, 2, 3." Jill stops, grasping my beard between thumb and forefinger.

Jill drags me to her more closely. "So, your grandfather was what? Uno? You father duo. You are what, Tres?"

Exasperated, I say, my Grandmother was French Canadian. In modern French they would be -Un, Deux, Trois. Then it could come from Middle English where trey is three. Or it could come from the old French Treis. Then again, Grandpa Silky was a gambler who called out card value as he dealt cards as in, 'Ace, Deuce, Trey, the kid has a possible straight."

Jill says, "Enough, Galvan, you are giving me a headache."

Holding me tight, she watches my eyes, "Is this an Operator-beard? Do you operate? Nothing to say? What a surprise. Alright, Fuzzy Bear, this is my bookstore.

Over her shoulder she says off-hand, "Oh, I'm studying medicine this summer. I took the summer off from cosmetology. Come. Do not tarry, boy. Try not to look so shocked."

Medicine? I thought she was an upwardly mobile bartender."

She calls back, "Come, Silky Bear number three; I am a busy woman of many parts."

"I've noticed."

"Yes, you have. I'll allow it, for now," she says coyly. "Did anyone ever tell you that you have sneaky green eyes. While you were noticing my eye color you seemed to notice a lot more. Did you have a nice time looking down blouses today?"

I dutifully respond, "Yes, doctor. Although the view from back here is swell too."

Jill arches her back, glancing over her shoulder at me. She tugs the hem of her jeans down over a millimeter of tanned thigh. Modesty, first and foremost.

"You picked the right place to park, Galvan. I was wrong, you've been around a bit. Now who is a person of many parts?"

Inside, Jill shops for books, peruses some and not others. This is work, she's very serious.

Noon becomes afternoon. We hike through various hallways in the old buildings. Some familiar, some are a mystery.

Many of the first U of C buildings started life as homes in the 19th Century. Over time, homes became classrooms. Walking between them always feels weird, akin to climbing up and down a series of small hills.

Jill is carrying an ever-larger armload of texts. I am not. During our tour, I renew my acquaintance with this place. Seems unchanged, however much I have changed.

I become fixed, frozen in a time void. I've been here before, but from a different angle, in a different time. Deja-vous all over again. Who I once was collides with who I've become. Then Jill collides with me, her warmth penetrates the chill enshrouding me, bringing me back.

Contact with this woman makes we want to settle into life. In her time, distance loses meaning. Damn, I'd like put my head in her lap on the grass somewhere on a warm spring day.

I turn to her. It is a warm spring day. I glance at her lap, she catches me, blushes nicely. I feel warm, caught again but I don't care. I'm done drifting in dead water without a paddle or the capacity to use one.

We quietly contemplate each other in a new way. Yeah, Jill, I'm looking for safe harbor and know where to find it.

Reality intercedes, dropping a book on my foot

I pick up her book. I place it on the top of her text pile. She frowns.

"I'm your non-union chauffer," I say. "I won't carry your books. That would make me a stereotypical chauvinist, being nice just to curry as yet unspecified favors."

Jill considers my remark, tapping her toe impatiently, "These books are heavy, I could use some chauvinistic assistance just now, Galvan. So, what do you plan on doing to curry my favor?"

I shrug. "I'll reason with you for a while, then you'll invite me to ravish you."

Jill glares, mumbling, "OK. I've decided I prefer the chauvinism. Carry my Goddamned books. We're going to tour the entire campus.

Jill dumps her book stack into my arms. "Here, be all manly; I'll bat my eyelashes and breathe deeply with a heaving breast admiring your manliness."

As she strolls off, I ask, "Where you going?"

"I'll be back. Your manliness has caused my brow to lightly perspire. I feel faint. Maybe my bustier is too tight."

"If you have a bustier under that outfit, I want to see it right now."

Jill smiles innocently, "Not today, you'll get light-headed. Another time. Be good."

I look for somewhere to sit while waiting. I find myself gazing into a familiar auditorium, recognizing a voice from my past life.

The auditorium windows stand open in search of a breeze on a warm afternoon. This is an 1980s building--then catching a breeze was the only air-conditioning available.

Lower the upper and raise the lower, hot air rises and exits, sucking cool air in the lower as I consider the wonders of 19th Century architecture. I spot the judge in the front of the auditorium skimming notes arrayed before her on a rostrum.

The judge veils one side of her face with a long jet bang, arranged in the manner of Veronica Lake. That bang covers her right eye. A beautiful Black woman of great intellect and elegance.

The judge stands 5-foot 8-inches, but she appears taller. In black four-inch-heels she is taller.

Lost in thought, Judge Standish pivots her right foot on her 100mm heel, its toe slashing a sharp arc in the warm air. Like a sprinter in the blocks she's coiled to lunge. Her toe pivots sharply. She's ready to pounce.

She'll drop a question that will be on the test, then extracts the answer from the class. Best put pen to paper. When she gets the answer she wants, she'll contradict you, make you fight for it. Then require you to fight against your own defense. Law is tougher than it seems.

The judge wears Christian Louboutin heels. Always Louboutin, for things important.

I clerked for her just before Christmas during my days as a wanna be lawyer. My Christmas Eve duties included finding a pair of Strappy Half D'Orsay Pumps, with gleaming black leather uppers, in a size 10.5 US/ size 40.5 EU. I did.

My error was to be found in the box, not the shoes. The judge snapped on seeing what I had acquired, "Good Lord, Galvan, 10.5? Do I look like I play basketball?"

I wouldn't dare respond. The judge did play basketball in college. Then, few ladies are comfortable to being referred to as Big Foot.

I was already late for work at the tactical office. Mickey Menendez skinned me alive when I called. But in the end Mickey was far less terrifying than the thought of facing the judge without her party shoes.

I went back to Saks Fifth Avenue with a plan. I just ran a short con. I played the shell-game with three pairs of Strappy Half D'Orsay Pumps. In the process I left with the original 10.5 US/ size 40.5 EU ensconced in a size 9US/39EU box.

Joy to the world. The judge was happy with her 10.5 heels ensconced in a size 9US box. The happy clerk got her last-minute sale. I got to work, eventually.

Today the judge is wearing a tailored skirt, and contrasting blouse with a matching tailored suit jacket. The jacket is carefully arranged, NOT HUNG, over the back of her draftsman's chair. She demands that chair for the auditorium classes, never sits on one.

I study the judge at rest. A modern master should paint her in oils.

The judge has a smooth complexion and fine bone structure which reminds me of my French-Canadian grandmother's 'Café au lait', coffee with cream. Grandma's phrase is very much politically incorrect, but so is the judge.

Better for me not to be seen, just slip away. My move attracts the judge's eye. Her vision is never obstructed by her raven bang. The judge always lies in wait, anticipating incoming challenges. She uses the bang to distract, camouflage for her next move.

The judge turns en'quatre step toward me. She fixes me in place with her emerald gaze. She acts as if she had been patiently awaiting my arrival. The woman can cast a spell.

She says, "Galvan. Word was that you died."

Maybe she hasn't been waiting on my arrival.

The judge considers my armload of books. "You're a few years late for class, Galvan."

I bumble, "No, Judge. Not late. Not dead. I was. But not at present. I'm helping a friend with textbooks."

The judge sweeps her left hand to hip, skeptical. She replies in the vernacular, "Helpin' a friend. Not dead. Was. Not late for a class you don't have. I give up. Where you been?"

"Gone. Been back in country a year or so. Mostly in Bethesda. Before that, I spent a couple of years overseas visiting strange lands and people."

"Mountains or desert?"

"Mountains, mostly. Some high desert."

The judge, "That would explain the neck,
'When you're wounded and left on Afghanistan's plains,
And the women come out to cut up what remains,
Jest roll to your rifle and blow out your brains
An' go to your Gawd like a soldier.'
Kipling wasn't one to commiserate, Francis."

"Wasn't with the Brits much, judge. I ran into them at times. Handy to have around in a gunfight."

"Thank you for your service, Galvan. Come visit. We'll talk."

The judge smiles. "Ah, I see your friend has returned. Today is far too nice to be indoors, Galvan. The lovely, half-dressed young lady's expression indicates you have some 'splaining' to do."

The judge fixes Jill under an emerald-eyed perusal "Young lady, law school?"

"No. Medical school."

"No lab-coat? Obviously, you are not dressed for rounds. Galvan won't mind. He is a bucolic soul. Galvan, buy the girl a coffee. I'm sure you'll have much to speak of."

As we walk away, the judge faces the auditorium. "Ms. Pomerantz, please forgive the interruption. A former clerk who's been traveling to faraway lands, meeting strange people, no doubt blowing things up and shooting innocent Salafists who were in need of shooting at the time. Continue, your riparian rights brief."

I glance back. The amphitheater is filled to capacity, silent as always, when the judge is at the podium.

Jill and I walk to the northeast end of the quad, where we settle into the lower level, four steps down into the earth. We sit in the cool English basement level just outside the ice cream parlor. The 1890s ice cream parlor sports an intoxicating scent of old seasoned wood and fresh ice cream.

Is this a date?

I find myself telling Jill stories. Am I trying to introduce myself by way of stories on our first date? Is this a date? I think it is. I haven't had a date in years.

Here goes, time to begin to 'splain things. I look around in search of a thread to worry. We sip coffee.

I got something, if not 'IT', I speak from a hoarse start, "Up those four steps in the cafeteria are the paintings of a bunch of old, white guys. One painting is not of an old white guy.

I say, "That august group are all ex-university presidents. In their midst is a white woman who was also university president. The last I saw her she was above the mantle-piece."

Jill sips her coffee. "The president or the painting?"

I ignore the jibe, "Her portrait was painted by Philip Pearlstein. At the time this story takes place, it was valued at around $80,000."

I explain, "My father and the Greek were partners at the time. They were investigating an involuntary sabbatical of the painting. At the end of each school president's term of office they sit for a formal oil painting. Each retiring president chooses the painter for the portrait. The lady in question chose Pearlstein. Pearlstein is a Modernist. He seems to paint only on hot days. My opinion is that his subjects seem to be melting in the heat."

Jill frowns. "Galvan, when an artist works in the school of Modernist Realism, the human figure is painted as inherently imperfect. The human body is viewed as being in a state of plastic reality. The object of the artist's study is not centered on the horizon of the piece. It's placed off center, maybe in a corner at the edge of the canvas. Poses are not idealized. The artist's work displays the mass and weight of the body. They display the body in an unstudied pose."

I argue, "That's what I said."

Jill smiles wanly. "Kind of, in a limited way, maybe, a little."

She explains, "I studied art undergraduate, and later when I was on plastic surgery rotation. I've studied the human form with my focus on clinical application. A plastic surgery patient benefits from a physician's understanding of the human body and from the physician's artistic appreciation of both idealized body form and of the body at rest."

I say, "You're beginning to fascinate me, Dr. Ryan."

She smirks a little. "Beginning?"

I say, "This is new aspect of you to appreciate."

Then I add, "Back to my story. Fraternities around here, like many coming of age organizations in most environments support some societal norms. They also have a history of doing weird counter-cultural things. Here, each year some fraternity or another absconds with a portrait of a school president during pledge season. The selection process remains a mystery. The theft is usually accompanied by clues left behind, which explain both the choice of subject, and where the painting might be found. Usually they move the painting to someplace strange on campus. Clues are used to taunt campus police into joining their scavenger hunt."

Amazingly, she was still listening. I decided her attention was so rare I'd test it to the limit. "The entire student population here is made up of kids who were #1 in their high school class. The student population is convinced that they are flat out smarter than the average peasant. The thefts originally involved just fraternities. Over the years, I think thefts rotated among fraternities. Later, sororities may have become involved. There were also years when social groups joined the rogue's gallery. The year the Pearlstein went missing the miscreants were from a social group sponsored allegedly by some faculty member or administrator who advised the group. The Pearlstein painting was also unusual because when it flew away, it flew off campus. One clue led the Greek and my Father to the bell tower of the Rockefeller Chapel bell tower at 11:56 on the Monday after the theft. There, they found a selfie of the painting propped on a bar stool with its favorite drink before it on the bar."

I expect snores out of Jill. Instead she says, "I bet they thought that was funny."

I smile. "Not when the bells started ringing."

"Most of the subsequent clues were also in locations the police couldn't identify."

"My father and the Greek arrested a con-man named 'Bug', who saw the selfies mounted on a mission board in their office. Bug solved the puzzle."

"How?" asks Jill.

"The selfies they came upon during the investigation were all from famous spots in the community."

"Which ones?" she posits.

"One was found in the Japanese Tea House from the Columbian Exposition. It's a famous meeting place. But it was the first selfie that solved the case."

"How would that single selfie solve the case?"

"The photo was taken in a famous gay bar on Van Buren inside the Loop. Deuce and the Greek went to the bar. They asked the bartender to call the owner. Legend has it the bar had mob connections."

"The 'Boys' arrived shortly. After conversing with the detectives, the 'Boys' extolled collaboration. The bartender, who had refused to assist in the investigation, became cooperative. He revealed the name of the regular patron who had come in with friends carrying the painting to take the selfie. The boys later produced video of the guy and his entourage taking the selfie.

The photographer capturing the image turned out to be the campus advisor of a student group. Deuce and the Greek interviewed the professor, noting that although the theft of the oil painting was very humorous, the university was out $80,000. The good professor was informed that the powers that be were now only interested in the oil painting's recovery in good condition, or a pound of flesh, and a felony charge for the $80,000. It was noted that his assistance would be much appreciated, and the educator was left with a copy of the aforementioned selfie taker.

The professor denied everything until informed that the proprietors of the photo scene (the Boys), had tendered the video. More importantly, said Boys were gonna break a few legs if they were forced into the middle of this bull-shit.

Later my Dad, Deuce, received a call. The painting turned up that afternoon wrapped in a waterproof tarp, sitting on milk crates in an alley during a thunderstorm. The prof was watching from his parlor window.

"Deuce would be your Father? The Greek is Gaby's Joe?"

Gaby's Joe? I'll have to get used to that. Some detective I am.

Jill is drinking black coffee of not-too-exotic origin. I drink mine with cream, I'm a wuss.

Jill says, "Galvan, are you a man of mystery or just nuts? Who are you? Are you a factory worker? The judge implied you were a lawyer? You told me you were a detective. Then you were a newsboy in Afghanistan. Then you were in a U.S. Naval hospital out east. Who are you?"

"I was sworn to secrecy, taught to lie believably, and stick to my legend. Your legend is a biography--real or imagined. That legend is supported by documents and witnesses who will support the story you are selling. It's a variation of who you are. I lied about the steps I took as I strolled through life. I was indeed in Afghanistan. My stepping stones are solid facts in a concocted pattern of lies.

So, I say, "I studied the Law. I was a lawyer for Judge Standish."

"While in law school, I worked the tactical team nights, until I made detective."

"How does that happen? Do they just heavyweight politically connected officers?

"The department announces an exam. Sometimes you get months to study. Answering your question, usually study time is truncated to serve the needs of the powers that be You take the test. You wait."

"They promote in dribs and drabs with 16% reserved for merit promotions. Thirty fit an academy classroom. Six or eight in each class are merit. Criteria for merit are held closer than the Ayatollah's hat size. I was academic, as opposed to merit."

Jill says dryly, "Sixteen percent would be fourish."

I reply, "Welcome to the City Of. When I finished the school, I partnered with Joe. Er, a Gaby's Joe. Joe has doctoral degree in journalism from Medill School at Northwestern. I wrote a number of published articles on Salafism in academic journals. We wanted a change and took a leave of absence, becoming imbed correspondents with a Naval unit in Afghanistan. The unit we reported on was stationed in Gardez, which is north and east of Afghanistan's Shari-Kot Valley. "

Jill asks, "Was that Operation Anaconda? I had a patient who was injured there."

I answer quickly, "Definitely not. That was long before I ever came near Afghanistan. Those were real guys; we came bumbling along a lot later."

"Were there a lot of battleships in Afghanistan?"

"No, the valley sits way up in the Hindu Kush at high altitude. It has been a place of refuge for dissidents since the time of Alexander the Great. We wrote articles on narcotics and terrorist financing among the Taliban and al Qaeda."

Jill is laughing, "Galvan, if you told that story to a mule, he'd kick you in the groin. I assume you were wounded while in military service?"

How can I explain what I'm not allowed to speak of? My field of vision shrinks, tunneling down to porthole size. The flashback is coming. I have to gain back control.

I want Jill to see me, not flee me. I don't want pity. If she sees me as a crippled stumble-bum she'll bolt. The truth of what I've done and who I am are game-stoppers. She'll bolt.

I say, "I wasn't in the service. I worked as an imbed with Navy personnel. The Navy winning hearts and minds. All I did was write about boring community service stuff. Important, but not interesting. Definitely not glamorous. You know, aid deliveries to villages, meet with tribal leaders. I was a stringer reporting to papers, journals, news services..."

Hell, I don't even believe me. I sit across the table from Jill, focused on her face. My vision keeps tunneling, shrinking in around her face. If I'm going down the rabbit hole, I'd rather do it looking at her. Why? Jill watches me patiently, intently observing...

It's getting hard to hear what she's saying. I hear the explosion coming. Got to run away.

My tunnel to the world is collapsing. I am suddenly back in the Kush. I know this place. I'm outside the Shari Kot. I feel the heat, smell the stench of death. I see bad things. Who am I talking to? Am I talking to anyone? I feel like Mitchum narrating Tombstone.

I drone on, "We were walking up some wooden stairs in an old concrete building. The stairs were curved polished wood, too British Colonial. I should have caught it, just too tired, too many runs. I got sloppy."

I continue my soliloquy, "The stairs imploded, collapsing under me. I left Big Bob to die, I've got no excuse, I ran. The falling didn't hurt, landing was a bitch. Whiplash got my neck, down into the shoulders. Afterward, I dragged those twin ass-hats out. I guess the others died. I ran away, so I wouldn't know. I just ran."

I tell my audience, "My 20-inch neck kept me going long enough to get us all to the doorway. Two years with nothing to do between gun-runs but lift weights paid off. The constant competition between us, and those Speedo-wearing, frogman, movie stars was intense. The D-boys call that bunch 'the Movie Stars'. It was one big pissing contest."

Jill's voice drifts into my head, "Was that one of the fascinating human-interest stories, that you forgot to tell me about, newsboy?"

My tunnel vision spirals away. Jill's leaning across the small bistro table between us. Her face is very close to mine. Her lips are lush and lovely. She reaches forward to cradle my head and neck in her palms.

She's close enough to kiss. Tiny freckles across her nose and cheek bones mesmerize me. Her warm, hazel eyes are flecked with sparks of green. My God, I want to kiss this woman

I move my lips toward her. She draws back, calmly. She just dropped into doctor mode, assessing the nut. I must be the nut. I don't want to be the nut. She knows exactly what I want. But I won't be getting it anytime soon.

I've gone from being terrified to barely being able to keep my hands off her. She knows and seems not to care. What I've been terrified Jill might discover of what I did overseas, she's gotten out of me in five minutes in an ice cream shop.

Jill's warm hands remain on my neck, her touch is light. God, I hope she doesn't go all clinical on me. Her fingers are probing the scars on the front of my neck.

I continue my story about how I got my team killed. It will be better when she knows. Time to get it done. Then she'll know and stay away. I can go back to being a hermit.

I say, "When I was dragging those SEALS out by their flak vests, our vests had drag handles at the shoulders. All the blood on the floor made the floor slippery, so I just slid them along. I blocked the doorway with Red Elvis's body when I shot him."

Jill snaps, "Shooting? What shooting, Galvan? You were a journalist. Did you shoot the doorway with your junior newsman camera? Don't hide from me, Galvan. I need to know."

My head is spinning. Now, I don't believe me. My cover legend is indeed a slender reed to hide behind. It appears I've moved Jill and me into doctor/patient roles, trying to conceal things no one likely cares about anymore.

Being a weak-minded mess is a place to hide. People don't expect much, I don't have to do much. I just sit ensconced in my hermit's cave along the river not dead, nor much alive.

I want to be closer to Jill, but I'm lying to her over what? It's stupid to try to keep my word to people who left me for dead. Outside of the Greek, I can't think of anyone from that outfit that took the time to find out what happened to Trey Galvan. I got blown away carrying their water.

The mental dam in my head holds back dark waters accumulated during my tedious, stupid trip to Afghanistan. Just cracked. Not broken, but leaking and it's undermining my sense of duty. I'm not in the mood for a good cry. I want to pursue something with Jill. The truth will kill that at birth. She deserves the truth. It's best she knows and is free to leave--now.

I begin, "No, I didn't have a camera. I was carrying the breacher; that's a shotgun loaded with a frangible copper shot. We use them to smash door hinges. They got us with an IED. I got hurt. I fired until my shell bag was empty. My M-4 was crumpled into a pretzel."

"It was run or die time. I ran away, like in Monty Python. 'Run Away, Run Away'. Only, the Holy Hand Grenade of Antioch got me."

Jill appears confused by the allusion, so I say, "It was a comedy movie. A killer white rabbit tried to kill the knights of the round table. The only way to stop the rabbit was the Holy Hand Grenade in Antioch. I guess you had to see it."

I continue, "My eyes kept whiting out from the pain in my neck and shoulders, I fell a long way. The impact whiplash broke my neck."

I inhale raggedly, like a child on the verge of sobbing. What a mess. I thought getting blown up was bad. I was wrong, there's always worse."

I chuckle sourly, "Then a fat somebody jumped on my back. My chin was forced back, lifting it to expose my neck. An icy cold blade was drawn sharply across my throat."

"I smelled lanolin, He just killed me with a sheep butchering knife. Great. The blade was chilled in the night air as it traveled inside my neck.

"It was time to do something. I had about twenty seconds until I was dead."

"I moved fast, counter-rotating my attacker's arm to kill the fat-ass with his own knife. Only, it wasn't a him. It was a her. A very pregnant her. She'd killed me. I killed her and her baby with her butcher knife. She was dead in an instant. I pushed her away. She fell.

"I used up my remaining seconds dragging those evil Twins to the light. Really dragging them into the rotor wash. My use-by date arrived. Blood everywhere, mine hers, theirs.".

"I flopped flat on my face. I came back several times. Dead, then not. Commander Deveraux stepped over us from the chopper's landing skid, glancing at me with indifference."

"It was a lot of laughs each of the times I came back. One time, Doc Braxton had stuffed her fingers into the new hole in my neck. The finger probe must've brought me back."

Jill is manipulating my neck, totally focused on her sense of touch as she studies me in clinical aspect, "When did you awaken and stay awake for an extended time?"

"There were many intermittent periods of consciousness. When Doc Braxton forced home a tracheal tube. I saw Commander Devereaux give me a disdainful glance as I lay on the helicopter deck. From that expression, I knew I was one dead puppy."

"Doc Braxton pinched off something on the left side of my neck, then I was gone. Later in flight I felt a fierce cold wind blowing over me. We were moving fast. I woke as we topped a mountain ridge and hit an up-draft from the morning sun as we entered Tajikistan."

I laugh bitterly. "The story gets comical here. At one point I found myself walking up and down sand dunes, on a cool summer's night moving away from a large dark body of water. It felt like the Warren Dunes in Michigan. Underfoot was cold, loose sugar sand.

"Abruptly, I felt no pain. Pain and I were done. I lost what I had to lose. I was dead."

"The night is dark. Distant light is dim. Around me people holding lanterns wander. Everyone seems lost. They don't know where to go. I walk away from the crowd, struggling up an enormous unending sand-dune.

"In a clearing at the top, I find a medieval crusader turret tent. The tent is brightly lit from inside. I go to peer inside. I guess getting to the end of the trail is better than becoming lost along the way.

"No one stops me, so I cross the threshold. I glance around. A group of older men stand around a map table. They all listen to a tall young man explain something important. God knows what he was saying.

"The young guy is big, bigger than the Greek. The man was lean, too. Maybe six feet ten, longish hair, beard. The guy has strong veined hands, thick forearms like Pop-Eye. When I see him, I think right off, the dude's a carpenter."

"It hits me, I've gotten my bacon fried or am just about to. The young guy wears loose pale blue clothes. The clothes are the color of Lithuanian-Blue Christmas tree lights. Damn, they've been right all along, pale blue."

From far away I see Jill watching me through the haze. I say, "The Lithuanian version of the 'Infant of Prague' wears powder blue robes. Prague got it wrong, the robes are blue, not red, guys.

"It gets crazy. The carpenter waves me in. Reconciled to my fate, I become convinced I've made it. As usual, I guess wrong. The carpenter holds up his open palm in my face, stopping me flat-out. He smiles sadly, shakes his head, then points behind me."

"I turn to look."

"A substantial, heavy compression impact hits my chest. Pain, my eyes pop open. People wearing surgical scrubs are clustered about me."

"Pain is back big time. I hurt everywhere. I'm in a white room. Bright lights. Men and women are pinning me to the surgical table. I must have been struggling. An unmasked dude shouts, "Fiber-optic tube. STAT you useless jit."

I continue, "The scrubs guy wears what looks like a Russian surgical hat. Where the hell am I? The scrubs dude is straddling my chest pinning my biceps with his knees, saying,' 'Hello American Frog-Man Guy. Open 'vide for Chunkie. In went a fiber-optic tube. I gag, choke, spew blood."

"The last thing I see is the word S-O-L-I-N-K-O stenciled on his breast pocket and his hat. The scrubs look Russian. How do I know what Russian scrubs look like? Maybe Discovery Channel? I think Solinko just killed me."

Jill is close now, sitting knee-to-knee with me; I have no idea where Solinko went. Jill's hands cradle my head. Is she going to kiss me? She makes a small smirk, then rolls my head through its orbit, seeking stops. Jill now holds my jaw. With a teasing look in her eyes, she says, "I've worked with a lot of returning vets suffering from injuries as bad as yours, many with much worse injuries. You have a whopping dose of Post-Traumatic Stress Syndrome, but I think you'll live. That was my primary diagnosis. Physical trauma in a war zone, aggravated by PTSD. If I'm going to help you, quit lying to me, Galvan. If you're a news correspondent, I've been training to be a pole dancer, not studying medicine the last four years."

Smiling brightly, she says, "What are you laughing about, Galvan?"

I say, "I'm not much for pole dancers. But if it's your favored art form, I'd be happy to watch one of your routines, so as to better understand the art form."

"Galvan, I think I actually like you. If you are a very good boy, I'll show you."

"I'll do my best."

Jill says, "I rendered my professional opinion. I expect payment, get me an ice cream cone."

"One scoop, or two?"

"Make it a rainbow cone. I'm on a diet, but it's OK. Someone didn't buy lunch."

I start to rise. Jill, continuing to grasp my face, forces me to sit once more.

I sit. Jill leans in for a quick kiss, flicking her tongue lightly over my lips."

As she releases me I ask, "What was that for?"

Jill smiles wickedly. "I needed a taste test." Her eyes sparkle.

"So?" I ask.

"You pass, for now. It might require further testing."

"The last time I saw her, the secret agent girl at Gaby's that morning, she was furious. From your expression when I embraced you a moment ago, you didn't get lucky, did you?"

I avoid the question. "May I take you to dinner?"

Jill laughs. "Thought you'd never ask. Where? When?"

"Gaby's. Tonight. She's buying."

"You're not buying me dinner after my free diagnosis? Are you not out to impress me?"

"I've been out to impress you since the day we met in the snow. I've asked you to dinner before. You weren't interested. I'm already buying you a very expensive rainbow-cone.

I ask again, "May I take you to dinner, Jill?"

"Yes, I'll take a dinner from you, Galvan."

I reach out, touching her hair, "You can get a great deal more than dinner out of me, Dr. Ryan."

Jill smiles a moment before saying, "YA think?"

4

WAITING ON A FRIEND

As the sun sets, I sit fidgeting on my bar stool. It appears I'm waiting on a lady, hopefully a friend. Hope springs eternal. First dates never change. Jill can't fool me. I've waited on women before. Seven PM is elastic when waiting on a lady.

At 7:30, Gaby calls me into the kitchen. "Galvan, go upstairs and get Jill. Hurry her up. Jill wants my soufflé for dessert. I don't have time to wait, I too have things to do."

Gaby thrusts a key ring at me. "Hurry, Galvan."

I remain in place with a blank expression. Gaby shakes her head, "Proceed with haste. Take my keys, go up and bring Jill down before dinner spoils."

In my hand rest the keys to the kingdom of women, do I have time to make copies? How will Gaby kill my juvenile ass?

Gaby gives me a skeptical glance. "Third door on the left, Galvan. Bring those keys back, Cherie."

"Yes, Mom."

Gaby says, "I'm not your mother, Galvan. I'm too young to be your mother. You have a mother. Don't forget to bring back those keys. Out. Go get Jill."

Exiting the restaurant, I unlock the outer door to access the palazzo staircase. Filled with sudden energy I sprint the stairs. The mysterious and sacred apartments where Gaby's lovelies reside 'en cloister' beckon. If I get lucky, the ladies will be bathing together, combing each other's hair. Guys and their fantasies.

I knock at the hall door. No answer. The second key opens the upper door.

Opening the door, I bound into the perimeter hallway. Darn. No ladies naked in tubs, combing hair. Merely a hallway lined with secured doors along its inner wall. The inner doors are spaced alternately, spaced between alternating outer windows in balanced 1890s style.

Good at following instructions, I turn left, counting doors as I go. The doors are deep broad-framed, made in a century when framing wood was abundant. The hallway is clean and quiet. It smells of women. My God, I've forgotten how nice they smell. The warm woman's scent has been gone from my life for far too long.

As I walk toward Jill's closed, third door, I lean forward to glance into each shadowed alcove doorway. Midway to her door, light streams from the second doorway. I glance in and am surprised to see the blond from this afternoon seated and facing me on a cranked back recliner. She wears shorts, which display long muscular legs. That is a lot of leg, lovely to see.

In the course of my seeing, I was caught looking. She doesn't seem to mind being appreciated. The woman holds my gaze, then glances from me down to her legs. She smiles. "I'm Dori. I told Jill you aren't gay. She wouldn't listen, Pandora just had to go look."

With a wicked smile, she says, "Next door, Galvan. Just walk in, Jill's waiting for you. I was in there just a minute ago. She's trying on shoes. Just knock, and go in. It's open."

I turn to Jill's door, knock and walk in," Jill, Gaby said to come get you. She can't make the soufflé, we're too late."

I'm struck dumb, a lamb led to the slaughter. Dear sweet Dori got me.

Jill is almost ready. She stands before me wearing a cropped dark-blue sweater, shiny black tights over high black heels. That's it. Engaging, lovely, arousing. Dressed? No.

A wraparound skirt is spread for wrapping between Jill's hands. She is standing with her back to me in tights, sweater and heels. I find Jill long, slender, captivating.

Jill stops, glances coolly my way, as she sorts out her skirt, "Galvan, you should see your face. You've had your look, out. Dori, I'm going to kill you."

My face feels warm and red as I turn to leave. As I exit, I can't help looking back. Jill faces me with a resigned smile as she slams the door in my face. Looks as good walking up as turned away.

In the background, Dori is laughing.

I take a deep breath.

I retreat to lean on the intervening window frame. I lean, waiting. In a moment, Jill struts out. She closes and locks her door. She laces an arm through mine, asks, "Devil got your tongue?"

I say, "No. An angel in black tights."

Frowning Jill says, "You aren't thinking anything about angels, Galvan."

We start down the hall, passing Dori's open door. Jill says, "I owe you, Doris dear."

Dori says, "How'd things go? Did the man find what he was looking for?"

I glance at Jill in profile. Do I detect a smirk? We enter Gaby's through the bar door. It seems Gaby's is closed for spring cleaning. The restaurant is empty, save for Gaby, Jill and I.

Gaby isn't wearing pearls and apron over a dark dress. Gaby wears a blue and white horizontally striped Chanel fisherman's tunic over dark blue cargo shorts. She sports red canvas boat shoes with a bulky white cotton sweater knotted loosely about her shoulders. Fourth of July? Bastille Day, maybe? Nah, too early.

Her eyes done casual, smoky even. I think the Greek is in trouble. Gaby says sternly, "You two--It's about time. Jill, I left you my quiche in the middle oven. There are cooled pea-salads marinating in red wine vinegar in the refrigerator. There is chocolate mousse with Grand Marnier in there also. Wine's in the cooler. No soufflé, dawdlers."

"When you are done, make him help clean. He needs domestication. Jill, take my keys back from Galvan. Lock-up. He looks Irish, but has enough French blood; don't give him his head, he might put it in your lap, Cheri.

"Joseph and I will be walking along the river. If you can't be good, be careful."

Gaby points a red-nailed index finger, "I'm warning you, Galvan. She is a nice girl."

"Don't worry, Gaby. I can manage Galvan."

Exiting, Gaby says, "See that you do, Jillian. I warn you, he's as slippery as an eel."

Jill watches Gaby leave. "Those cargo shorts are perfect with that Chanel tunic. Your Greek better watch his step."

She favors me with a knowing smile, "Spring is in the air, Galvan. You're not the only guy thinking about a half-dressed woman."

With a pot holder, she opens the oven door. "Come on, open the wine the quiche is ready. I'll get the salads."

I open Gaby's Riesling.

The quiche is tasty, light. Seems a breakfast food, but does just fine for a light dinner. The wine is better than Gaby advertised. Then, it might be Jill, not just the wine.

Jill asks, "How did you end up living in a boatyard?"

First dates give me the jitters. When I'm nervous, I tell boring Galvan stories. It's a family tradition to act foolish on first dates. I'm very good at it.

I tell a favorite, "When we got back in the USA, my uncle told us the boatyard was for sale. In the process, we got treated to my uncle's version of local history. My uncle told us the boatyard sits on a big flat rock shelf."

Having no sense, I go on, "When the last glaciers cut out the lake's south end the bed left on this side of the river was mush for maybe a mile underneath us. Later, the mush was backfilled with wreckage from the Great Chicago Fire."

"Before the fire, the city was all wood-frame buildings. Afterward, they were built with fired Chicago Brick. The mountains of rubble were barged and dumped in the swamps."

I note, "There are several primordial reefs in this area. The river once flowed out into the lake along here. The boatyard foundation sits on a reef's highest point. In spring, the pool in our inlet bubbles like crazy. The inlet turns into seltzer water. Carbonation gets so intense narrow boats lose enough buoyancy to sink."

Jill cuts in. "Introducing a lighter than air gas into water steals the ability of traditional hull shapes to remain buoyant. Archimedes Principle only goes so far, Galvan."

I add, "Yes doctor. My uncle insists that the Miami tribe once lived on our rock shelf. He says the tribe moved to Florida. Business was too good, forted up here on our rock. My uncle claims the tribe, gave us Miami Beach. He said the tribe was the best at ripping and running. Smart and safe on their rock in the river, they kept the world at bay."

Jill is stern. "So, you live safe on that rocky point protecting yourself from the world? Might you just be hiding under a rock? If you hide well enough, people will quit looking for you. Where'll you be then?'

"Safe?" I answer.

Hands on hips Jill says, "No. Alone, old, and cold under a lonely rock. If a girl offers you her hand, take it. While you play mind games, be careful she doesn't move on." She's come close to home. It stings.

Rather than return to a subject that worries me, I return to the silly story, "My uncle insists the tribe up on our rock was in the habit of chucking prisoners into our effervescing spring, testing for improved buoyancy."

Jill asks, "Was your uncle convinced there's some river god sitting at the bottom of that pool? You think the Miami used captives as ant-acids to settle the river god's stomach?"

I say, "You're more skeptical than my family."

Jill reaches a palm to my cheek, "You know, I can see you, right? If I ever come to want you, I won't be looking for a clown telling apocry-phal stories."

I lift her hand from my face, turning it up to kiss the palm, "Come ahead, girl. I have done awful things to awful people. At times I've probably done bad things to people who were less than awful. War can be like a gunfight in a closet with the lights off. Everybody gets hurt. It just happens: good and bad, young and old die. There's no logic. I hurt people and got hurt by people. Shit happens. I lost most of my mind when I was penned up as a gorker ward working toward vegetable. Before you get involved, realize it may not be loads of fun hanging around with some old fart just out of the looney bin. As soon as you learn the things I've done, you'll walk. I understand, you might be better off if we enjoy the evening and walk away.

Jill smiles coyly. "Will you be watching me as I walk away?"

I smile as I agree, "Damn straight. I haven't been able to resist so far. You walk nicely."

"I noticed. Does your long story have a moral, Galvan?"

I say, "Does it have to have a moral? Maybe waste not, want not. Still water runs deep."

Jill says, "Yes, it does. Your uncle is a troubled soul. You just have troubles."

I answer the question unasked, "Consider my sojourn at the War on Terror before you take a swim in my dark waters, my love."

She laughs. "My love, Galvan? Give that some thought, honey. We're closer in age than you think, I just look young. I think you ought to wait for developments before you throw that love nonsense around because I might not be around, sweetheart."

Jill holds my gaze, "You have sharp edges. I'm not afraid of you.

Edges aren't going to protect you from me. And there is no guarantee that I won't have to leave town--soon."

I respond, "We can just go upstairs and have wild sex, you have the keys to the kingdom."

Jill frowns, "I do. Take me for a walk, Galvan. I need to think. Did you scare me off or are we going upstairs? Are you worth the trouble? Maybe the fog will help me decide. Do I have prospects?"

"Fading, but some. You have a few good qualities. To be worthy, a man requires a certain steadfastness of character."

I say playfully, "Have I a steadfast character?"

She shrugs. "You're kinder, more considerate than anticipated. You make a girl feel wanted. To play, you need to get in the game. Your decision. I'll decide what we play."

We stroll through the fog across the playlot north of Gaby's. On the playground's low ground. Jill shivers, appears chilled, walking with arms folded across her breast. She kicks a pebble from our path with the toe of her shoe. Glancing north in the fog, she asks, "Are conditions propitious for us, Galvan?"

I answer truthfully, "I hope so."

In the cooling fog, I remove my suit coat, draping it over her shoulders. On impulse, I reach out to touch her hand. Jill glances down at my hand, then grasps my hand."

"Jillian, I like just being around you."

Jill says a bit sharply, "My name is Jill. Remember that, tall, dark and troubled man. You're the one with more names that a Spanish Grandee. Only Gaby calls me Jillian when feeling motherly. Remember, because I'm deciding your fate as we amble along."

"Since we met, I've been fascinated."

Enjoying herself, Jill says, "Were you? I hardly noticed. Was it just my vivacious personality that enchanted you? You did a lot of staring."

"Might have been your lovely features, or perhaps your authoritative stride."

Jill laughs. "Not my legs?"

I shrug, "That and more. I guess it's your totality. I appreciate new fine notes each day."

Jill smiles with wicked intent, "Leg-man, huh? I get that a lot."

My gaze sweeps up to her waiting eyes. "Well deserved."

We circle the path around the small park in companionable silence, then slowly circle the park holding hands.

"Lost in thought, Jill?" I ask.

Jill is serious. "I'm trying to decide if you being a little crazy will affect the kids."

"What kids?"

"Our kids, silly."

My face flips through a variety of expressions.

Laughing hard, Jill chokes out, "You should see your face, Galvan. You freaked out. Don't worry, I'm a new MD. I have a three-year internship and residency facing me. The only babies I'll be delivering will be my patients'. I don't have time for babies, especially not yours, if they're going to be as crazy as you are."

I am annoyed by Jill's cavalier attitude. My God, I thought myself eligible. Jill's not interested. Who is chasing whom off? Who's not interested? I step close, studying hazel eyes.

Behind Jill, on the far side of the playlot a sports car darkly trembles at the curb, lights dark. I hear its motor murmuring. Vibration causes a huge water drop to cascade down the vehicle's highly polished agate-gray hull. Nadia's Porsche Carrera?

Why is Nadia tailing me as we walk in the park? I need to get that woman off my back.

"Fascinating," Jill responds

"What?"

"Did you really just spot the bitch? Really?" She sighs, "She's been sitting there watching Gaby's since early this evening. Before that she was lurking around the university quad this afternoon. While we talked in the coffee shop she was up in the cafeteria looking down at us."

We stop at a park bench on the walkway. I position to watch Nadia's Porsche. Neither of us sit, leaning against the bench back.

I place a foot on the bench seat, leaning toward her. Jill leans back nearby. Thin fog air separates us. I edge in. Jill steps toward me. Facing me, she rests her palms flat on my chest, playing with my collar points. For the moment we're paired against the night. I feel heat from her long, elegant fingers warm on my chest. I lift her palm to my lips once more. Jill's thumb and index finger close around mine.

A mild tectonic shift occurs between us. Jill releases my hand. Her chin rises, as her hand drops. We lock eyes.

She steps in pressing herself to me. "If you're out for a welcome-back from the war hook-up, you're out of luck. A long-term relationship may not be in the works, either. We might have to settle for a summer romance."

Behind Jill, Nadia's windshield wipers flick on in counterpoint to our growing proximity.

Jill says, "We haven't much time. It will take an effort by both of us to find each other. If you hide in your boatyard, it might not work."

Ignoring Nadia's presence, I reach over to brush a lock of hair from Jill's eyelash, "I'll take what you can give. It seems I'm at your beck and call. Will you be gentle?"

Jill says, "No."

I say, "Good."

"Up front, you need to know I'm not mommy material at present. I may never be. I became a nurse to fulfill someone else's dream. Becoming a physician, I followed my own dream. When I left nursing my mother called me an ungrateful little jit."

"Your mom saw you as a little prison, bitch thug?"

"Is that what jit means?" questions Jill.

"In prison it means a juvenile-in-training, a punk in need of correction," I say.

Jill laughs. "Ooops, Momma's gone gangster. She hesitates. "I like you more as I get to know you; I never know what you'll say next."

"I may have fried a few filters when I got banged up."

Looking wistful Jill says, "I grew up Southside Irish. We lived between the Nabisco and Kool-Aid factories. In the summer when the north wind blew, my world smelled of Vanilla Wafers and Kool-Aid. At night, from my upstairs bedroom, I could see the light of the giant pink Kool-Aid Man peeping at me over the horizon."

My hands settle on Jill's hips.

Behind her, Nadia's Porsche Carrera inches forward. It still has its lights off. She's on her cellphone, the screen back-lighting her face in the dark. Is the witch stirring her pot?

Jill grasps my beard, draws my face to her, "Pay attention to me, not her. I see Ms. Bitch." She releases my chin, spinning her body back into my arms, which I wrap about her, drawing her in to me. I interlock my fingers over her waist from behind, drawing her back to me.

Jill struggles, just slightly. Turning toward me, molding herself into my grasp, Jill's not escaping; she's making herself at home.

We stand close, almost touching. She says, "I'm all but done with medical school. The national match is what remains, now. It's like the NFL

Draft. We all match to programs based on skills and training. It occurs next week. Students and faculty are headed to a tavern in the Loop to celebrate good and drown bad luck. We're to await results in Mulligan's.

"I wanted to match in emergency medicine. I had a good interview in Tacoma. I had one in Dallas that was iffy. That bitch was afraid of competition. Most programs are outside the area. I wanted out of Chicago. ER is an action field, spots are tight."

"I interviewed internal medicine residencies locally," Jill says, lost in thought.

I note, "I understand some of it. My mother is a doctor."

Jill says, "I'm not your mom, honey. Otherwise, your response to our proximity would be problematic."

Resting my palms on the curve of her hips, I lean forward to kiss her, "Thank goodness."

Jill smiles, we part. "Goodness has nothing to do with what you have in mind."

Jill presses against me, "On reflection I think I might like internal medicine. You get to know patients. I'd be part of the community. Emergency medicine is more, wham, bam, thank you, maam."

She laughs. "Ooops, sorry. I'm usually more ladylike. You bring wicked out in me. Sooo, will you be my date for match? Scandalous things have been known to happen. "

Having a vested interest, I ask, "Are you inclined to scandal?"

"You'll have to be there to find out."

I say, "I enjoy being with you. I'd be happy to be with you at the match."

I don't want her to slip away. My hands draw her back to me. I don't want to drift out of her future. Even if she may drift out of mine after this match.

Her life may carry Jill to Tacoma. The course she chooses probably won't jibe with mine. I'm coming back, she's moving on. I roughly understand what she needs to do or why she has to do it. Best to enjoy the evening and see where it takes us. When she leaves, I can always crawl back under my rock.

I'm startled. Jill places a light kiss to my lips. The kiss is barely there. Losing my resolve, I draw Jill more tightly to me. She relaxes her torso into my advance. Moments pass as we embrace in the fog.

A ripping screech breaks out.

Nadia.

In the distance her tires spin out with a loud ripping noise on the slick pavement, spitting water back into the fog. I wish she would just leave it alone. I'm a little busy at the moment.

Nadia's lights pop on. The racket isn't enough, she really wants to be seen. Her engine roars, the Porsche Carrera slithers forward quickly, slinking swiftly around the corner heading south toward Archer Avenue. The Porsche loses traction several times before snapping into a straight-line course.

Don't leave mad, just leave. Why is she tailing me? Nadia's been upset since the first time we ran into each other. With small exception, things haven't improved. What is in her head?

As I glance toward Jill, she's already staring back. She swings her gaze after the disappearing Porsche, then asks, "What just happened? One minute you're trying to bend me over the park bench, in an instant you're gone. What's up?"

"When Nadia flew out of here, she was talking on her cell. The screen backlit her face. It wasn't good trade-craft. She should know better, but was mad. She's going to do something bad. And wanted us to know. Why?"

"Why? Knucklehead. You are with me, that's why. She has convoluted plans for you, Galvan. You shouldn't have slept with the girl in your great big, giant bed."

"I didn't sleep with her in my bed or anywhere else. How do you know how big my bed is?"

"Or she's mad because you didn't try to sleep with her when you had a chance. The girl knows she's gorgeous. Refusing your big chance, may be as big an affront to that woman as trying to take advantage of her. Or, she might be out to arrest you, and I'm in the way."

"For what?"

"I don't know? Maybe placing your hands on the bottom of an innocent medical student in the playlot. That might relate to my earlier argument about her convoluted plans."

I suggest, "On that note, I'll walk you home before whatever Nadia plans comes to pass. You don't want to be involved in this, whatever it is. The 'G' is relentless and vindictive. Apparently, it's a crime to lie to them. Be polite, admit nothing, deny everything, demand an attorney was the rule among the police."

Jill smiles, a little perplexed, "Where did you get that pithy phrase? Do the cops sit around Dunkin' Donuts saying stuff like that?"

"About as much as you do during your Wednesday afternoon golf outings."

I take-up Jill's hand in mine. We walk back toward Gaby's. I stop-- Jill up on the concrete stoop, I on the sidewalk. We stand eye to eye, her abdomen pressed to mine. I contemplate another kiss as she lifts her lips to mine.

Abruptly I hear something and decide I need to create distance between us. I dig out Gaby's sacred keys to open the outer door, handing Jill the keys.

If I walk her upstairs, I'll do my best to stay there with her. Until I know what Nadia has done, I need to keep my distance from Jill. I can just barely keep my hands off her, which makes keeping a distance difficult.

"What is it with you? Did you do something overseas that has the FBI investigating you?"

"I have no idea what Nadia is doing. She doesn't seem to know what she wants either."

Jill and I stand on the stoop in the fog looking at each other.

She asks, "What do you want, Galvan?"

"When you are around, I'm desperate to come back in from the dark. You implied if I come in from the cold and dark, I have to be ready to play. I spent a lot of time over the last few years locked out by injury with my nose pressed to the window, looking in. If I come back in, I have to accept the risk that I will lose you. That makes it harder to give up the hermit life. I'm working on it."

Jill says with a nod, "There's no guarantees in life, Galvan. Life has its costs. Do you want to live or wither on the vine?"

I hear motorcycles out in the fog. Motorcycles? The thrum comes as a slow roll out of the south.

Nadia went south. What're the chances? She's an awful bitch. If Nadia has stirred that pot, I have to get Jill off the street. Bubble, bubble toil and trouble. Nadia stirs the pot more that Macbeth's witches. What does she want?

Unexpectedly, Nadia's Porsche swings into view, flying inbound from Archer Avenue heading toward us at speed. The grey sports-car slip-slides around the corner on our side of the railroad viaduct, then quickly disappears to the east not much south of us.

Taking Jill by the arm, I usher her quickly into the palazzo's staircase, telling her, "Go inside. Lock up behind you. If it gets out of hand, call the cops. Don't come back down."

Jill resists as I close the door behind her, I again admonish her, "Don't get involved. Go, girl."

Jill's eyes flash with anger. I shoo her on her way up the stairs then turn my back to her.

The commercial wall of structures leaves me nowhere to run. The playlot to the east is wide open. There'll be no hiding tonight. I've had enough hiding and cowering, anyway. I'm tired of running. Can't hide from myself. No time left, too late and foolish to flee for the boatyard. I'd just die a coward. Almost did that before. Didn't like it

Multiple engines rumble, closer now, out in the fog. The throaty roar has Harley written all over it. The roar bores into my clouded mind. Today is as good a day as any. Waiting for a better day merely delays the inevitable.

Coincidences occur rarely. Nadia flings it into the fan to see where it splashes. Crazy girl didn't like what was happening in the park between Jill and me. That woman can be a bitter pill.

Now, she's made herself scarce. The bikes are slow-crawling in her wake. The woman has a sense of drama. She led the wolves to me, knowing I was in the open. Such a sweet girl.

Paying attention is always important. I got wrapped up in Jill. I let my guard down, and didn't pay attention. Too bad, so sad, bye-bye. Nadia pimp-slapped me. Must want attention. Nadia has no idea what she wants. She's crazy beyond belief.

The bikers file in, forming a semi-circle before me. Played with fire, gonna get burned. I lean against the cold wet door frame behind me. The lock is secure.

The door handle pulls from my grip. Great. A glance tells me Jill is pulling the door open. She wants to join me. That's all I need. I force the door shut behind me, against Jill's resistance, I call to her, "Thank you for the lovely evening. Go to bed. Don't get involved."

Getting this done is a good idea. God, I need to let it all out here. Hard to resist. There's the weird copper taste of blood in my throat. I've been slack and torpid since I came back. Haven't fought for my life for a long time.

We had a nice dinner. We talked about nice stuff. I can't remember what, but nice. Just no time. Too bad.

Time for the coffee grounds to settle. Jill needs a new playmate for match. Get your licks in first, Galvan. Won't be a later. My feet glide over the sidewalk onto the gravel. My hands and arms surge with energy. They rise of their own volition. Hit 'em, while they're sittin'.

Over the motor roar, I hear a voice, probably not an angel from heaven, though the guy it looks like Laughing Jesus, he's saying. 'I thought you were dead.' The voice rises above the cacophony, commanding, "Shut 'em down, ladies. I can't hear myself think. Turn off the god-damn headlights."

Then Laughing Jesus says, "Francis Galvan, let us have speaks." It dawns on me: Doug is Laughing Jesus. Doug the Mogadishu Marine transformed to long haired, bearded Laughing Jesus. Life is strange. Doug was my sparring partner when I was in high school studying martial arts with Uncle Old-School. I guess Doug was a biker before Mogadishu, now just less squared away. Doug was a friend, maybe mentor. That is if bikers can be mentors.

Hell, my Father, Deuce, had a group of aging bank robbers out of Leavenworth as mentors when he was a kid. His mentors were in prison so long they went through the entire automobile repair course three times. The crew taught Deuce to tune-up cars, change the brakes and oil. I guess the world is like that.

At the distance of a few feet we have speaks. Occasionally, Doug revs his throttle to throw off listeners. Who? Probably Nadia and company. It's hard to record a conversation with all the shake, rattle and roll. We do some lip reading, employ body gestures, there are even a few audible phrases.

Nadia comes around that corner on foot, left hand in her jacket pocket, holding something black along the tight black legging of her right thigh.

She's trying intently to listen. Waste of time on her part. Doug and I have known each other for ten years. We're speaking a foreign language, police. It's like gangster, but different, almost a patois. Besides, in the din of sticks clashing on sticks in an Escrima studio one quickly learns to communicate in gestures, nods and expressions.

Doug asks, "What is Nadia doing? You know, Galvan, that one, has a hard-on for you.

Surprised, I ask, "Why? I'm not her type. She's 'G'. Nadia was bird-dogging your pigeons before the squawk."

Doug asks, "Why the conflict with you?"

"Ruffies. Your pigeons slipped her some, then tried to take her to the playlot."

Doug goes glum, "That's why you put the boots to them?"

I glance at Tweedle Dee and Tweedle Dumb, who are looking

sheepish astride their Harleys. I say, "Well, really, she did most of the putting of boots to them. I tossed them around some."

Doug concludes, "So, J. Edgar's niece put it to the lads?"

"Yes and no, did it to themselves mostly. They were dancing when I cut in."

I add, "Nadia was weakening from the ruffies, didn't want to see her hurt."

Doug shrugs, "Sorry, can't watch the children all the time. Date rape ain't our game. I didn't know Nadia-girl was G. Figured her for corrupt practices or IAD from the job. I'll make it right. Won't happen again.

Doug says, "J. Edgar's niece baited us to you tonight. She's trouble, kid. Showed up on Halsted at the club, wagged her tail to get our attention. Then she led us to you. Please tell Slenderella up in the hallway I won't hurt you. She looks like she's gonna gouge my eyes out with those house keys."

I glance through the plate glass at Jill. I give her an OK, waving her up the stairs. Jill stands firm, watching. I turn back to Doug. He wears an amused expression. His eyes flick between Jill and Nadia.

Nadia is closer now. The women glare at each other.

Doug chuckles, looking at me. He asks, "You are aware that these two are fighting over you? Right?"

I say, "Not likely. Nadia's investigating me for God-only-knows-what. Jill, will be leaving town for a new job soon. I'll probably return to being a boatyard bum."

Doug laughs, "Get real. Women are still women. Neither may keep you. But, from this scene, neither wants the other having you. Your wishes are secondary. Doug says in a low tone, "I don't care why the 'G' is investigating you, Galvan. The club has an in-house issue. Rohypnol and other things have popped up around the club. As the war on terror slows down, we are seeing a lot of new friends-of-the-club, and hang-arounds. As always, guys coming back from war, lost structure and they need to find something. Belonging, I guess." He shrugged. "Things got out of hand, too many new guys mixing with retired or fired coppers. Get her off my back, I'll fix things, but it will take some time. A Dun-and-Bradstreet for all of them takes time."

I ask, "You do Dun-and -Bradstreet backgrounds on prospects now?"

Doug smiles wryly. "We have standards, but for you I'd make an exception."

"Not me, Doug, I'm scared to death of bikes. Whenever I get on a bike, I fall on my head. I've broken all the bones I want to in Afghanistan."

Doug raises his eyebrows. "How long were you in theatre?"

"Just under two years, outside of Gardez."

"Uncle Old School told us. He said, you got dead."

"The report of my demise was premature."

In the background, Nadia is shutting down her phone. I wonder what she's done now? Doug follows my gaze to Nadia.

Doug asks, "Who do you think she called?"

"Nadia baited you to interfere with what I was doing. Now it's time to lower the boom on your people. Probably called the cops to punish the bad motorcycle gang."

Doug asks, "You figure they'll come?"

I answer, "They'll come with bells on if she didn't tell them she was the 'G'."

I ask, "How long you been in the hood, Doug?"

"We moved into a wino-bar on Halsted a year ago. Urban re-development got the last one. With all the new prospects, the brothers needed more room anyway."

Doug announces, "What did you do up in the mountains?"

"I was a civilian working the hearts and minds thing."

Doug chokes, laughing, "Ain't no civilians when the assholes are in the wire, kid. You can't bullshit an old bull-shitter."

I nod, "That would be my observation."

The tenor of noise in the fog is changing. Something dangerous comes. Blue lights in the fog.

Now, sirens in the milky distance. Maybe Nadia did tell them she was the G. The police dispatcher sent a couple of cars for a look-see, but they aren't coming very fast."

Doug shakes his head. "Who calls the cops on the cops? Most of us were the cops. Very unfair. Call her over, we'll make peace."

I catch Nadia's eye, wave her to us. Nadia is triumphant. She walks over, hands on hips. Deer in the headlights, her face freezes momentarily with a confused, questioning expression. She shrugs pointing back to siren roar, where did that come from. Now all cheshire cat smile, she saunters over. I'm standing with my hands in pocket. Nadia slides an arm through mine, settling her body against my side. Nadia can't help herself. She glances behind me up the staircase, her smile broadens. With a satisfied expression, Nadia lays her cheek on my shoulder.

"Hi, Doug. You miss me?" she asks.

Doug says, "Agent Dimitrieva, how can we be of assistance to the bureau this evening?"

Horrified, Nadia shoves my shoulder sharply away from her, "You told him I'm a Federal Agent, Galvan? I'll have your badge. Revealing the nature of my investigation is a Federal crime."

"I don't have a badge. I don't know anything about your investigation. I told him you were in the FBI and are investigating me. He thought you were IAD, I told him you were much more important. Before you brought Doug to visit, I haven't seen him for maybe a decade. I didn't meet the other fellows until I helped you beat them up. Now, Doug and company know it is wise to stay away from me if he wants to be a citizen in good standing in this community."

Doug says, "Agent Dimitrieva, it will help me in maintaining my squeaky-clean reputation, if you stay out of the club. We'd like to keep up appearances."

I catch Nadia's eye. "From your expression, you're surprised I know you are investigating me. Are you investigating these gentlemen, as well?"

Nadia has an annoyed frown. Her arms fold across her breast. She scribes a crescent line on the sidewalk between us with the toe of her boot.

I say, "Is that a 'no comment'. What did I do? I saved you from a fate worse than death."

Doug looks up into the hallway to wave at Jill, asking. "Agent Dimitrieva, Slenderella up there on the stairs is white knuckling a handful of keys. I think she's gonna use them to gouge my eye out. As a law officer, will you protect me from harm?"

Studying Nadia's deepening frown, Doug says, "NO? Well, then you need to know one thing, agent ma'am. If you don't nail this boy down one way or the other, Slenderella will have the boy buying pampers by Christmas."

Doug adds, "Damn, Kid, your parents would love that. Slenderella is as pretty as a picture when she's mad. I'll bet she's lovely when she doesn't have murder in her heart."

He switches subjects. "Uncle Old School told me your parents thought you were dead."

Blue lights at Archer. Here comes the cavalry.

"Varlets do not lie to the FBI. Lying to the FBI is a crime. If you feel threatened, consult our legal counsel. If you think of doing something bad, don't do it. Don't talk about bad things. Crime is crime, do not commit crime. I am not a priest, I do not hear confession."

I don't care what sins you have or have not committed. Live clean, be free. If you do or have done bad things, you may be in trouble. Drink beer, if you think the water is bad. Do not eat yellow snow." Do not under any circumstances bother these people. In fact, stay away from all of them. The police are coming. Be civil, leave quietly when they tell you to go. We live in this community. We are stakeholders."

Doug winks at me. Do I discern a note of inherent insincerity?

Doug says, "If there is any way we might help you, Agent Dimitrieva, please feel free to ask me. I will be glad to help if I can. We are always glad to be assistance when we can, but we reserve the right to consult legal counsel as we deem necessary."

"Kid, stop by if you're up for Sinawali; it's been far too long. Go see your parents, they are probably worried to death about you. They know you're back in town, the Greek told them."

Nadia's eyes flick back and forth between Doug and me.

Doug clears his throat, "I didn't visit my parents when I got back after Mogadishu, Kid. Years passed. My mother got sick and died. Let it go, you may not get to set things right."

Doug kickstarts his bike, "Uncle Sugar eats up true believers. What happened in those mountains is over. Nobody cares. Sooner than later, those who were there will be the only ones who remember. Those who weren't already do not understand. Let it go, it's done."

Doug turns to an avidly listening Nadia. "Agent Dimitrieva, ladies of your pedigree should not mingle with men of our ilk. Please stay out of our clubhouse; it's a private club. You're banned on account of your history of playing with fire. You are welcome to enter. If you have a warrant, we'll gladly cooperate."

Nadia demands, "Do you have the authority to make that decision, Doug."

"There was a vote of the membership. Ours is not a public place. Please stay out."

"Who voted, and under what circumstances?" she snarls.

"Get a warrant, Agent Dimitrieva."

Indicating the two men we fought at Gaby's, he says, "These two knuckleheads won't bother you again. If you feel you've got to bag them up and take them to the Bastille, do what you think is best. You should not poke brutes with pointy sticks, they'll do brutish things."

Nadia's crowds in against me. Seeking warmth, Safety? Who knows?

Doug smiles sagely as he backwalks his bike, "Whoa, Galvan. You got sexual tension of the first order. She's inserted herself between you and Slenderella. Good luck. Remember, Kid, you get to choose. Hammer your sorrows out on the hips of the lovely, but duplicitous Nadia. Or, ascend to heavenly bliss with yon Slenderella. "Nadia will break your heart before she's done. Before that, she'll lovingly break your back. You might even find she's just a nice girl, acting badly.

"Slenderella on the other hand is filled with resolve and righteous fear for your well-being. She stands ready on that staircase to sally forth to do battle on your behalf armed with a handful of keys. The heart of a good woman can make you happy, but you'll buy the diapers. Choose wisely, kid. I know I didn't. But then if I hadn't made the choice that I made, I would not be the success that I've become." Doug gives us his Laughing Jesus imitation.

Sirens sound out somewhere along Archer. Thank goodness we're not in dire circumstances as Nadia can't do directions. The fog is thinning as cold air seeps in from the lake. Fog still lingers over low ground near the river. Fog remains firmly nestled, like a thick cotton ball stuffed beneath the low black viaduct south of us.

In the viaduct the fog swirls. Something comes. A glistening wet, black Chevy Suburban bursts from the ground cloud. Homicide, maybe? Who was killed? Did I do it? Even if I didn't, is Nadia convinced I did? Homicide's engine growls with serious intent. No siren. Run silent, run deep.

As Doug glances at the oncoming SUV. Its blue grill-flashers pop on. Fancy.

Homicide's siren sounds once announcing arrival. It echoes back from the fog bank.

Show-offs.

The driver drifts the large SUV across the wet road surface, stopping broadside just short of us. A dark skinned, powerfully built black man of moderate height with rugged good looks emerges. His scalp seems polished to a high sheen. Must one use a car buffer to get that luster?

I'll be damned. Incongruously dressed in a crisp white shirt, red, white and blue rep tie. But it is Vito Gennaro. Vito's in Homicide. Gennaro's gaze pans the crowd, stopping his survey at Nadia. Recognition? Yeah.

Looking at Nadia, he says, "You said you had an emergency, agent."

Nadia smiles sweetly, "It's okay, detective. Things settled down. Thank you for coming."

Gennaro holds his hand unit to his face keying, "Give a slowdown, squad. We don't want anyone to get hurt out here in the fog. Slow them."

Gennaro adds, "To answer your complaint, we try to please. You owe me dinner, Agent Dimitrieva, mine's lying on the floor at Connie's."

As Nadia nestles in to me possessively, her breast warms my damp arm. Gennaro blinks in shock, snapping his eyes back and forth between Nadia and me.

I glance sideways at Nadia for her reaction. In the dark and foggy night air, her blue eyes luminesce. They glitter with what? Triumph, I guess? Nadia slips her tongue delicately over her lips. Damn that looks like fun.

Nadia can't wait. She asks in an intimate voice, "Did you do it, Mr. Galvan?"

Mystified, I ask, "Do what?"

"Did you kill the pregnant girl? When you did it, did you know she was pregnant? It was so early in her pregnancy. Did she tell you? Is that what made you fly into a rage?"

Nadia's tone remains intimate as she continues her barrage, "Is that why you ran? You must have known we'd find you. Don't cops say, 'the truth will come out'? Face facts, mister, get it off your chest. Tell us why?"

What is this crazy wench talking about? How would the bureau know about the Afghan woman? The Afghan woman wasn't early in her pregnancy she was at the end of her pregnancy. How could Nadia know about her?

Footsteps sound behind me. Jill quickly descends the stairs.

Unable to resist, I tumble longways, "He grabbed me before I saw him. I was trying to run away. I panicked. It happened, then the blade was in my throat. I reacted. In a blink he was dead.

Sad recollection settles in. My nightly flash-back rolls, I smell explosive. An explosion roars. Big Bob's body disperses, ripped into red mist. Blood spatter everywhere. Pain is incredible. I probably squeal as I flee. The fat guy is on my back, slashing my throat. As I go down, I reverse my killer's knife, driving it into his abdomen, killing the fat bastard with his own knife. Only, it's not a fat bastard. It's a very pregnant woman that I kill.

Someone is mumbling. Oh, it's me. What am I mumbling about?

What was I talking about? I babble on, "I was concussed. That fat guy killed me. It was all a stupid mistake."

I doubt anyone is listening. I tried to explain. I was a big, cascading foul-up."

"Why did you do it?"

I just stare at Nadia. "Do what?"

Nadia announces, "Mr. Gennaro, I need you to bear witness. You heard this man confess to killing your victim."

Gennaro looks at Agent Dimitrieva. "He confessed something. Maybe his sins. I have no idea what he was confessing. Can you link him to the scene by blood evidence? I didn't find gouts of extraneous blood at the scene.

Nadia snaps, "Why would there be? Besides I didn't have a chance. I was involved investigating this ongoing criminal motorcycle gang conspiracy."

Gennaro runs a hand over his damp scalp, staring at Nadia, "Listen, kid, try to finish one thing before you run off to do something else. Please start closing up all your loose ends before traipsing off into the fog."

Doug interjects, "She's talking about us."

The young Marine who spoke earlier says, "WTF. Half of us are the cops or were."

Doug shakes his head," She's FBI, trained from birth to see all cops as the locals and all Chicago cops as the local crooks."

My mind wanders, I ask, "Confessed? To what?"

Gennaro studies me. "Who are yo, dude? I heard you were dead. I have documents from the Navy that say you died in combat. Where the hell have you been? You look like death warmed over. You sound like you been drinking whiskey and smokin' cigars for twenty years.

I say, "Yeah, it's me, Gennaro. My voice has been fouled up since I got my throat cut. It was worse. I lost about a hundred pounds."

Genaro has a pained expression. "Did you really do it? Did you kill her, Galvan?"

I say, "Yes, I killed the Iranian woman. Maybe five minutes later I died. Went flat on my face, gushing blood like a fountain."

Doug shakes his head, "Agent Dimitrieva, you should listen more and play with your cell phone less. If you listened to what we were saying when you were peeping around the corner, you'd know what he's telling us."

Doug faces Gennaro, "And you, Gennaro, shouldn't jump to conclusions when a rookie is asking leading questions of a subject suffering from a PTSD."

Nadia snaps, "WHAT? I wasn't on my phone."

I say, distractedly, "Your screen backlit your face. I pointed you out to Doug."

Doug asks me, "Where did this pregnant woman you speak of get killed?"

"In Afghanistan, northwest of Gardez outside Tud Ghar at the foot of the Shahi-Kot."

Nadia is aghast. She yanks my arm sharply, snarling, "You confessed. You can't take it back. You confessed."

Taking in her response, Doug says, "Anyone know where Gardez is?"

One of the younger bikers speaks out loud and clear, "It's outside the Shahi-Kot Valley. I was in Operation Anaconda up there. It's a hellacious place. Gardez is the provincial capital with one of our bases. I was Force Recon humpin' a ruck to the high ground. Who were you with, dude?"

Spaced out, I answer, "I was with the Navy movie stars, down in Gardez. I was a civilian embed."

"You alphabet soup, dude?"

"No. I was an embed correspondent."

"Right, that's the ticket, asshole. Sure as shit it is, Mo-Fo. And I was in an outreach program selling Girl Scout cookies while I was wandering around up in the king's lap. I hated that fucking valley and everyone in it."

Confused, Nadia asks, "What's alphabet soup mean?"

The young biker responds, "You ARE a newbie, agent. YOU are alphabet soup. If he was with the movie stars, he was with the CIA. Embed correspondent? Really, man? Blow me."

Doug shrugs, "From the lips of babes to God's ear. The kids are so impulsive."

"He admitted to murdering our pregnant woman, Detective Gennaro."

Thinking for a second, Gennaro says, "He admitted to killing a pregnant woman. My victim wasn't killed in Afghanistan outside of some hole in the ground called Gardez. You are jumping to conclusions, agent."

She says, "He lied to a Federal agent. I'm going to arrest him. Put your hands behind your back, Galvan."

Doug says quietly, "He didn't lie to you. You are looking foolish. Galvan was talking about another time, another person, and another place. Build a case if you have one. War is awful, people die. Why did you kill the pregnant woman, Galvan?"

Like Pavlov's dog I blurt, "She slashed my throat."

Nadia roars, "BULLSHIT."

Jill steps between us, pushing Nadia back. Nadia staggers a little on her heels of substantial height. Gennaro catches Nadia's shoulder bracing her.

Jill pulls open my collar, points to my throat and its long, jagged scar line, "I've been treating Mr. Galvan for PTSD. He told me about his injury yesterday. The scar extends roughly from below the left ear lobe almost to his right ear. The wound depth was variable."

"BULLSHIT. You're a friggin' bartender, biotch," snarls Nadia to Jill.

Jill smiles benignly at Nadia, "Yes, dear, I worked as a bartender part-time while I went to medical school full-time."

"BULLSHIT," yells Nadia.

Gathering her wits, Nadia tries to seize control, "Obviously, honey, you'll be coming into the office tonight to give a statement."

Jill demurs saying, "Only when I get a subpoena, cupcake."

"Only after you receive a subpoena? What gives you the right to demand I get a subpoena?" shouts Nadia.

Jill answers calmly, "Because you are an out-of-control cupcake."

"You're coming in, Missy," says Nadia reaching for Jill's arm.

Out of the blue I hear me say, "As result of your aggressive posture, my client will only submit to an interview, and/or deposition incident to the issuance of a subpoena. Our response comes pursuant to your strained demands and lack of familiarity with HIPAA rules and regulations."

Nadia actually stomps her foot, "What is this HIPPO BULLSHIT?"

I say from far away, "Not hippo, honey. H-I-P-A-A, which is the

Health Insurance Portability and Accountability Act. In particular, patient privacy provisions forbid my client from revealing patient care data without a court order, or a subpoena from a seated grand jury."

Nadia snaps, "You're a fired cop, Galvan. You're a nobody. You live in a god damned empty warehouse along a sewage canal. You pretend to make row-boats. BULLSHIT."

"She sure says that a lot," Doug says.

Regaining my focus, I say, "Madame agent, I am an attorney at law recognized as a member of the Illinois Bar Association. I am also licensed to practice before the federal bench. When I came back, our opening of our boatyard along Bubbly Creek was an ecological recovery venture, not an empty warehouse along a sewage canal. I saw Dr. Ryan as a patient at the U of C this afternoon. I am also retained to represent Dr. Ryan."

Doug laughs, "Galvan told us about something that happened to him in Afghanistan, Agent Dimitrieva. As far as the lawyer thing goes, I have been a family friend since he was a little kid, so I can fill in the blanks if you like. Galvan is a lawyer."

Nadia steps further away, resting her fists on her hips appearing confused.

Jill leans in, touching the scars on my neck with gentle fingertips.

"People argue round us. Our horizons shrink." Jill smiles, "Don't worry—you haven't sprung a leak, your head isn't falling off. You'll be alright."

Jill gives me a light, brushing kiss on my neck. "Thank you for such a nice day. Remember we have a date. Call me." She hands me her business card as she strolls upstairs."

Damn, she strolls well.

Confused, looking for something to say, I ask Gennaro, "Did you make detective with Mary Beth, G? "

Nadia breaks in, "She didn't make detective, Galvan."

I see a predatory glare in Nadia's eye. How does this Nadia know Mary Beth?

Gennaro speaks into the cloud in my head, "Galvan, we need to talk. Mary Beth is gone."

"Did she leave the job?" I'm confused. "Is she with the bureau now?"

"No, stupid, that girl didn't join the bureau. She was a Chicago cop," Nadia responds.

Panicked, I ask, "Did she get in with the state's attorney's investigators, Gennaro?"

Gennaro's cold as he asks me, "When did you last speak with Mary Beth?"

I think for a moment. "I stayed at Mary Beth's just before I left town. Brenda had already moved out. Mary Beth and I spent the day in court testifying in the sentencing phase of an old case. She cooked us dinner, then gave me a spot on her couch. I left in the morning."

Gennaro appears shocked. "When was that, Galvan?"

I answer, "Late August, early September, I can't remember. Been a long time. My marbles got knocked around in the interim."

Gennaro says in a tone growing skeptical, "Galvan, focus. Mary Beth has been gone for more than three years. She couldn't have been here in either August or September of last year."

I snap back, "How would I know? I wasn't here last August or September?"

Gennaro asks with interest, "In the fall two years ago?"

I'm annoyed now, "More like three years ago. I don't think it was more."

"What kind of injury are you talking about?" asks Gennaro.

I say, "I got blown off a staircase. Explosion. My neck and back were all fouled up. I was in the hospital a long time. Maybe a year, maybe less. Seemed longer."

Doug spits. "God damn it, Gennaro. You are being an ass. You were his partner. Just tell him, he doesn't know. He's got PTSD. He just got out of Bethesda, you jerk."

I say, "Tell me what?"

"Mary Beth is gone, Galvan," says Gennaro.

Doug says, "She's not gone, she's dead. She was murdered in early winter of the year you've been talking about.

Dazed I say, "After I got back, I tried to call her. Her phone was disconnected. I stopped by her apartment building. The building is even gone. Did she and Brenda finally buy the dream townhouse in the suburbs?"

Angry, with a mean look, Nadia holds forth an open palm to stop Doug and Gennaro, "She's dead, Mr. Galvan. But you know that already, don't you? Who would know better than you?"

"Lost," I say, "Gennaro, what is she talking about?"

Gennaro says softly, "Galvan, Mary Beth has been dead for over three years."

I feel sick as her words land. My legs feel uncertain beneath me. I sit on the wet concrete stoop.

Doug shakes his head as I drop, saying, "Gennaro, you and your lady-friend strokes. We weren't ever gonna be friends, but at least I respected you before tonight. What you're doing is a disgrace."

Doug turns to his troops, "Scatter boys. If you ain't got a home, go to the club. If you get stopped, be respectful. Go. Admit nothing, deny everything, call Levy."

Someone asks, "Who the fuck is Levy?"

Doug says, "You remember the giant guy with the 1958 metallic mint-green Duo Glide? That's our lawyer, bonehead."

As his boys depart, Doug continues, "Galvan doesn't know what you two ass-wipes are talking about. Not once did I hear you read him his rights. You know better, Gennaro, even if Nadia, the teenage FBI witch-girl, doesn't. He was obviously the focus of both of your investigations. No rights? Really? Gennaro, you two were partners. To Nadia he says, "You, Lady, are just a disgrace. You blew your own case witchy-woman. You didn't tell him that he was under investigation? You say he confessed. You knew he was the focus of your investigation, but did you give him his rights?"

Silence.

Doug continues, "No, witch, you did not."

Nadia says loudly, "He's the police. We don't need to do that stuff with him."

Doug and Gennaro say in unison, "Oops. Cops got no rights? Everyone who becomes the focus of your investigation gets their rights."

Gennaro sighs. "You have the right to remain silent, Galvan. Anything you say can be used against you in a court of law."

Doug says, "Etcetera..."

As Gennaro finishes he asks, "Do you understand your rights, Galvan?"

My mind totally fogged, as I say, "Yes? What am I accused of?"

"Mary Beth was murdered in November three years ago. Where were you?

"In the mountains during November. I left here at the end of summer. I haven't been here for years."

Nadia snapped, "BULLSHIT. What mountains? Where? You were hiding in what mountains?"

I fight down a feeling of nausea. I still sense a lack of strength, as I say, "We landed at Fort Carson near Pueblo. From there, we were transported somewhere by helicopter. That night it snowed after midnight as we arrived at a ranch in the mountains. The weather was bad until we left. We transited overseas in early January, into Afghanistan. The weather sucked there, too."

Gennaro asks, "Agent Dimitrieva says you admitted to murdering, P.O. Mary Beth Burke. Did you kill Mary Beth, Galvan?"

"No." Confused I say, "What are you talking about, G? She's not dead. She's back with Brenda. I just haven't found them yet. I went over to their old apartment, but the building was torn down. Come on, G, don't even joke about that. This isn't funny, dude. You are all kidding. Right? This is a bad joke. You are all messing with my head. I need to talk to her. Where is she?"

Nadia says with a cruel lilt, "Short of visiting church or dying, you aren't talking to Mary Beth Burke anytime soon. She's long cold and dead by your hands."

Gennaro focuses on me, "Mary Beth is dead, Francis. I inherited the investigation when my partner retired. I'll need to talk to you. Come over to the area in the morning. Bring a lawyer if you need one. Remember, a lawyer who represents himself has a fool for a client." Gennaro hesitates before saying, "It's just a fact-finding interview for the moment. If you can prove you weren't in town, you have nothing to worry about. We'll work it out, but we need to know what you know. "

Nadia sweeps down beside me focusing tightly on my eyes. Mocking Jill, Nadia kisses my neck, slips the tip of her tongue over the scar. Says insincerely, "Thank you for a nice, odd day," Nadia smirks, stuffing her business card in my shirt pocket, saying," Call, lover. We can do a deal."

Nadia says to Gennaro, "I expect to hear from you, I'm sitting in on our interview."

"You want to sit in when I interview Galvan? Assuming there are federal issues?"

Gennaro appears skeptical. Nadia snaps, "You heard me, officer."

Nadia strides away from us on her long lovely legs. Before she reaches the corner, she stops to smooth the left thigh of her leggings.

Then looking at me, before scanning the other two. I watch her face in that moment, not her bottom. She has a lovely, desirable bottom but I don't like her. Her gaze darkens, then sweeps in triumph over the other two. She glances coldly back at me before she sweeps around the corner. Something at the last moment, her chin drops in uncertainty.

Her gray Porsche roars around the corner, flying through the fog southbound.

5

DREAM A LITTLE DREAM FOR ME

Doug says, "Damn, Nadia walks away nicely. Crazy mean biotch, but legs she has."

He looks down at me, sitting on the wet stoop," Galvan, you better hope Nadia never wraps those legs around you. She'd have you confessing to most anything."

Gennaro says, "I would, and I'm getting married."

I ignore the pair as I sit thinking. How can Mary Beth be dead? We need to talk. I always figured we had time. We didn't. Sad. The others don't care, Mary Beth has been dead three years for them--just died for me.

Gennaro shrugs. "Nadia isn't all bad. The bureau sent her here for seasoning. The bureau has DNA telling them cops are corrupt, and Chicago's are the worst. I think 'crooked cops' is a mandatory class at Quantico. They'll overlook our vile odor if they need our help."

Doug asks, "Is she convinced Galvan killed Mary Beth? Why? Most days we practiced sticks at Old Schools, the girl was in the peanut gallery. She'd come before the women's class early to watch us--well, to watch our boy.

"Old School separated the sexes? Chauvinism lives."

Doug says, "Ladies wanted it that way. Personal issues develop abruptly that need airing. They liked the privacy. If he needed villains, he'd call us back. Collegial, but no pussy-footing."

Talk clichés, I asked Mary Beth out to a movie for a first date after class. I had a new license, and wanted her to think me a man of the world.

Doug laughs, "Old School couldn't separate the pair. If one showed, the other popped-up.

With a shrug, Gennaro says, "Young love's that way. Nadia claims her confidential informant fingers Galvan as the last one to see Mary Beth alive. For Nadia, Galvan's a murderer."

Doug asks, "Who pitched the snitch."

Gennaro says, "The informant has a code name. Sounds like 'river mud.' Where do they get the names? She talks too fast, ya think she's trying to con me?"

Doug nods, "If her lips were moving, yeah. Doesn't explain Nadia's third-degree. She's filled with fire about him. Why so furious? She shows her hand. Was she like this all along?"

Gennaro appears perplexed, "Nadia was all business until she got slipped a date rape drug. Kid Galahad here jumped in, saving the damsel and nursing her to health. Then she got furious."

Doug states emphatically, "Nadia went out of her way to pick that fight with Slenderella. She finished by mocking Slenderella's interaction with him. I know I'm the oldest tool in this shed, but I was shocked when Nadia planted that kiss on Galvan's neck. You don't plant an intimate kiss on a serial killer. She was doing a taste test."

Gennaro says, "Nadia's rage is new, seems directed more at the doc, than at Galvan. Red flag there. Bureau girl is competing. They bully. First time I saw one neck-lick a suspect in front of me. "

He continues, "For them, all is in black-and-white. Nadia's worse than a 22-year-old Tac-Man low on pinches at the end of the month. Nadia claims she's assigned to assist me to get a UFAP warrant for Galvan. Until tonight, she's been trying to run a local murder investigation. Nobody told me anything about that at the area, so Mary Beth is my case still."

"Galvan's back in town. So, you need her for what?"

Gennaro says, "Diddly. Galvan's sitting in front of me."

"I think we all need a drink." Doug walks back to his saddle bag where he extracts a large silver flask.

Doug taps me in the side of the head with the flask, saying, "Take it, kid, you need a drink. We should talk. "

I take the flask, opening it to drink. Sweet but with a bite. I ask," What is it?"

Doug says, "Wild Turkey Liqueur."

I answer, using Nadia favorite phrase, "Bullshit."

Doug takes the flask, handing it to Gennaro, saying, "Wild Turkey Liqueur. I keep up pretenses, but I haven't been really nuts in a long time."

Gennaro says, "Not bad."

We pass the flask. We talk. Eventually, they leave. I walk home lost in thoughts of Mary Beth as I wander through the slowly dissipating fog.

Eventually, I find my way to the sail loft. There I locate a bottle of Jameson Black Barrel, deciding each to his own poison. That drink does not soothe the troubled mind is a truism, held true once more.

Drunk, my mind just skips across the surface of sleep. My life has been gapped in many places by wasted opportunity. But none more than my time with Mary Beth. Gone stays gone.

I return to full awareness. I find myself sitting, looking out over the river. How long?

Imbibing a moderate amount of alcohol can induce sleep, but as in other things, moderation is the key. I look at the wall clock. An hour has passed since I lay down. I feel so well rested, what will I do with all this spare time?

Not long ago, I was infallible. Suddenly I found myself fallen far short of master of the universe. Now I wander the place, unsure of what I am. Youthful verve never ends, until it's gone.

I am eminently fallible, no master of the universe. Things gone wrong, need put right. Mary Beth and I have, or is it had? a long history. A first passion here then all gone. Passion is funny. It has a life of its own. Passion grabs you. You don't grab it.

First love rarely becomes first lover. We often get side-tracked. Tossed together, time and again we permit people and events to rip us asunder. We happily find each other for a moment, make plans. What could go wrong when you got it right?

By coincidence, the world was momentarily our oyster. Suddenly lovers planning a further exploration of unexpected passion when I returned from the Hindu Kush. I almost didn't, returning to find her absent, now departed.

You get what you get. You get it when you get it. No guarantee it will be waiting for your return. Shit happens. Diana is the goddess of the hunt. She's an eternal virgin. On occasion she provides a hunter with what he needs. Reject her gift to your regret. A goddess will bust your chops. Diana is beautiful, lithe and forever nubile. She is ephemeral, a slip of a girl just beyond reach. I guess perpetual virgins need to be just out of reach. Mary Beth resides in my memory as my Diana. Elusive, unattainable. Rarely touched.

Hardly ever held. She remains my riddle, wrapped in a mystery, concealed in an enigma.

Later, I doze lightly. She opens her door to me, eyes are intent, focused and bright. The next day I depart for the Hindu Kush.

We long put off melding to find disaster looming over each of us. Offered the gift of the goddess, I allowed pride to carry me elsewhere. Hard to beat stupid.

In my fevered dream, Mary Beth drifts ever erotically closer. The embodiment of sexuality, Harlow leaning against her doorframe. Deciding. She wears a loose, silky white peasant blouse. In cotton it would convey relaxed domesticity. In silk, over black palazzo pants she conveys more serious intent. I try to caution myself she is off limits. Just a high school girlfriend, now a fellow cop deserving respect earned. I'm in a relationship with another woman.

I was a friend. Beyond that, insulting male foolishness. Unwelcome, uninvited. Stay out.

I switch my travel bag to my left hand, offering my right hand to be shaken. At worst I'll get a one-armed buddy-hug. I get neither. Instead of steady body contact, an eye-to-eye hug, Mary Beth is usually in blue jeans, wearing a pullover shirt, an off-limit fellow cop in female form.

Mary Beth has been with Brenda for several years. My reaction surprises me enough for me to swing my go-bag up between us as we part, hoping Bren' doesn't walk into view.

Mary Beth's eyes are bright. She smiles, no surprise.

Ha, Ha, you got me girl. I'm the guest. I can take a joke. It is what it is.

I look around for Brenda. Mary Beth walks to the kitchen, donning an apron over the silk blouse and pants. She must be cooking. When did female domesticity begin to arouse so?

I place my bag near the door for a quick exit, in the morning. Then follow her swaying hips toward the kitchen. Calm the hell down Galvan, you idiot.

I sit at the table, anticipating Brenda's pending arrival. They are arm's-length friends.

I'm not in her kitchen to interlope. I'm an invited guest, borrowing a night's rest on their couch and a morning's ride to the airport. A friend's place to rest on my last night in Chicago.

I glance at my bag sitting at the door. Traveling light into the wild blue yonder.

Surprised, I turn to discover Mary Beth studying me closely. She laughs, "Are you really running away to join the French Foreign Legion? I hope it isn't love lost. If it left, it isn't lost."

"Give it up, Calah is ambitious, onward and upward, mister. You always chase climbers. Relax, Calah will marry one of her own. Relationships with the locals is a career killer. Spend yourself on someone closer to home.

Annoyed I snap, "I'm not joining the foreign legion. We engineered a contract with the Secret Service. We're off to battle the criminals financing the war on terrorism. We'll be in Afghanistan a couple of years. Neither of us has much holding us here. There's easy money to be made, a good fight to be fought."

"The Greek is at the farm already. I join the team after my morning flight."

"What do Deuce and the Doc think of your trip, Francis? Did you even talk to them?"

"Low blow, Ms. Officer Mary Beth Burke. They are still mad at me for letting you change your orientation. Mommy and Daddy have always felt those Burke hips perfect for child-bearing. They are still looking for our grandchild. Afghanistan is just the straw that broke the camel's back."

"Now who's throwing low blows. You bedded your red-head. I wasn't quite ready to dance yet. Don't blame me for your older woman."

Mary Beth lifts her blouse from her midriff asking, agree or disagree?

I stare at the flexing muscle of her abdomen, at a loss for words."

Tone coy, asks, "Need a better look?"

Her blouse hitches upward, exposing the lower curve of her breasts. Great. In a moment Brenda will smack me in the side of my skull.

Suddenly hoarse I say, "Be fair, you know what I think, you always have."

Smiling triumphantly, Mary Beth says, "Galvan, are you staring at my breasts. You are such a guy. I should have figured it out years ago. Don't worry, Bren' isn't here, we broke up. Look all you want, she won't beat you up, I'll protect your six-foot-seven-inch body." She shrugs, "To get even for the red-head, I let Monsanto Man jump my bones. When I realized that disturbed bastard was in my head, I was in deep trouble. The guy was disturbed beyond belief, stuffed with steroids and growth hormones 290 pounds of dynamite with a quarter inch, flaccid wienie."

Mary Beth jabs her index finger at me, "Monsanto Man turned me sour on guys. You turned me sour on red heads."

Dispirited I say, "Sorry, she was a force of nature."

She replies, "Don't need to apologize, Galvan. We were seventeen and you ran around with a perpetual erection. I know that for a fact because it was pointing at me. I wasn't ready, you were. Maybe red did me a favor."

"You were just swayed by the charms of an older, more experienced woman. Happens to all of us, eventually." Mary Beth laughs at me.

She adds, "We went our separate ways. I'm not offended, But you're doing it again."

Mary Beth returns to her cooking, "It's OK, a girl likes being noticed. Bren' and I are through. Bren' moved in with the little princess."

"Amelia?"

She smiles sadly, "Figures you'd smell a rat. Guys know right off with that one. How? I thought she was after you when she was training with the office."

"Amelia comes across as girl who'll come across. I get the impression it might cost one to experience her favors. She hovered around Brenda as a clerk. Bren' has always appreciated a worshipful young lass among her admirers.

Mary Beth says, "Don't worry, I knew the way Brenda was when I met her. I just expected better of her. Brenda went back to type. So, I put her out."

Mary Beth is hurt, remains quiet for a time. I extract and open a Sterling Cabernet to go with the steak she mentioned, handing her a glass.

Over dinner we talk of high school and college. We've known each other half our lives. Scary old people say, 'half-my-life.'

During dinner, I discover Mary Beth cooks well. Being my blockhead self, I assumed 'they' ate tofu and lettuce. Apparently, I mistook anorexic fashion models for lesbian women.

We finish one bottle, sip some of the second. Things wind down. Mary Beth is a planner. She has my morning travels organized for efficiency. My flight is a 9:00 AM flight to Baltimore. She suggests, "We go early. TSA is only, what, four hours?"

I am slow, but get the message, she's saying, 'Bedtime'. I best don my jammies.

Luckily, I manage to keep my hands to myself. Good not to make a fool of oneself.

Mary Beth starts the dishwasher. I grab basketball shorts and a t-shirt from my bag, heading to the bathroom.

Mary Beth calls after me, "I've got a spot for you tonight."

I return momentarily, wearing my basketball chastity-suit, finding a darkened living-room and kitchen. I feel my way couch-ward in the dim light.

Clumsy, I bark my shin on the coffee table.

In the darkness, laughter. Mary Beth sits on the couch. I stumble.

Mary Beth rises from the couch, taking my hand before I plant my face on the floor.

She has such small hands. Small, warm, soft. Educated by prejudice, I expect hands rough and callused from all the golf.

The things I don't know could fill a very boring book. Too many broken noses, I have no sense of smell most days. It's a great benefit in homicide. This evening, in the dark, isn't most days. I catch her scent, elusive and arousing.

I reach for her waist, stopping my hand at the last moment. Careful, moron, don't insult a friend with boorish advances at this late stage. We play on different teams.

Mary Beth's hands sweep to my shoulders, turning me toward the bathroom. She slides across the tight hallway, gliding past me in the darkness. In the process, her breasts brush freely across my chest.

She steps past me. In the soft light from the bathroom door I study the arch of her spine beneath a lavender gown.

With my hand held in hers, we walk into the darkness at the rear of her apartment.

Mary Beth draws my hand to rest at the base of her spine.

I was last in her bedroom carrying Mary Beth to bed after she had one cup too many at our team Christmas Party.

Mary Beth spins back into me, her eyes huge.

We stand close in narrow space. Her breast rests lightly on my forearm, apparently, my hand has found the warm curve of her hip.

A last futile step back, Mary Beth draws me back. So be it. My eyes adjust. I turn my palm, caressing the curve of her breast.

Mary Beth trembles slightly as I make contact. With a smile she closes my hand about her breast. Her body is warm and firm beneath the sheer lace of her gown's lace halter.

Am I pulling her to me, or is she pressing her hips to mine? Both it appears. Things aren't getting out of hand. They are well out. My arms slip about her. I ask, "You sure about this? If I have an idea that we don't share, tell me. Couch sleeping is hard enough. Change your mind, it might be harder."

She laughs softly, pressing her cheek to my chest. She says, "Galvan, it's time."

I ask, "What you laughing about? I'm losing my battle for nobility. It's not funny."

Mary Beth asks playfully, "If you want to return to the couch you have to unhand my breast. You'll also need to let go of my bottom. If I'd known you were still this interested, I'd have done this sooner."

She wraps her arms around me, kisses my neck, "You're not sleeping on my couch. You're not putting me in bed and kissing me good-night like you did after the Christmas party."

Serious now she says, "I brought you here because I want you here in my bed with me tonight. Settle down, Galvan. I need you inside me tonight. Come to bed."

I did. Then I was. It took both us a long time to settle down.

I ache for her touch. She's dead. Good is gone, gone for good. I've been so crazy for so long. In Bethesda, dreams felt more solid than reality. In my dreams Mary Beth's body is vividly alive to my touch. Reality's become a nightmare. Feverish, dry, awake I sit alone. Yeah, I'm awake. I feel like shit, too much Black Barrel. The sun is up. Its glare hurts. What am I late for?

Got it, I need to talk with Gennaro at the area. A place now called area central. Good grammar? No, feels wrong. It's fifty-two blocks off city center, which is a lot for even the city-that-works, a place off center and forever out of plumb.

Need coffee, food. I'll see Gennaro after breakfast. I look at the time, we'll talk after lunch.

6

BABY'S DADDY

Eventually, I park my SRX in the area central parking lot. This parking lot is very similar to the previous area one parking lot. Oh yeah, it's the same one. Different sign.

Police Parking. I'll move later if I don't get indicted upstairs. I don my retired detective I.D. lanyard, which is the old ID incised with the word retired. In the old lanyard. I walk up to the front desk. The 2nd District known as the deuce is on the first floor. Central detective division is upstairs.

At the front desk, the desk sergeant is signing bond slips, which makes him both busy and cranky. I'm ignored.

I stand across the high desk from the sergeant. The desk sergeant eventually looks up, asking, "May I help you, sir?"

Strangely the sergeant seems to be saying, 'What the fuck do you want?'

I know the sergeant, worked tactical with him. He doesn't recognize me. On 'the Job', two years is a lifetime, three years an eternity.

I say, "Sergeant, I'm here to see Detective Vito Gennaro on a case. Hearing my voice, he looks at me. His head tilts right, then left.

The desk sergeant asks, "Galvan? I heard you were dead."

He always had a mind like a steel trap. I broke him in when he was new. Must've made sergeant after I left. I reply, "I was dead, but didn't like it. I came back to haunt Gennaro."

The desk sergeant grasps my lanyard, stares at my ID, "You're retired? You're younger than I am."

I reply, "Didn't have a say. I was dead. Later, I wasn't. By then, they'd technically buried the body. Listed as dead, I came back. They didn't know what to do. So, I got retired."

The desk sergeant shakes his head, "You have always been a lot of trouble, Galvan. Take the elevator up. I'll call Gennaro; he'll have to buzz you in through the air-lock. When you're done stop back, your rat-partners may want to welcome you back from zombie land."

I enter the open elevator, punch 2. I don't press the heliport button on the roof. No heliport up there since 1960. The new copter is downriver in the suburbs, too heavy for the roof.

My one floor ride feels ridiculous.

If I don't take the elevator, I won't get in. I'll just stand outside the door forever. It's a tradition. Tradition is important.

I trudge to the 'stand here' rug which is printed upside down. EREH DNATS, tax dollars at work. I stand under the light of a single bulb in front of the armored door panel, press the bell.

I see a loose wire protruding under the brass edge of the button's frame. I become quickly bored, and ring the bell, again. Disconnected the buzzer, I can ring all I want. No one 's coming.

A window port slides open. Gennaro's black face regards me skeptically.

The speaker sounds, "Did you ring the bell?"

I say, "No, are you guarding the door?"

Gennaro says, "The bell doesn't work."

We stare mutually, he asks, "What do you want?"

"You told me I had to visit."

He says, "That was a morning appointment. Have you been out here all morning? Should have looked, I guess."

I ask, "Should I go away?"

He says, "It ain't morning, you were late, I arrested somebody else."

I answer, "OK. I'll go home." I turn to leave.

The door bolt electrically unlocks loudly. Abandoning all hope, I enter.

This is my first-time visiting area central. Funny way to say it. Why not just CENTRAL?

I get a huge white Gennaro smile. Eyes don't match smile. I'm still the bad-guy.

Should I have brought a lawyer? I am a lawyer, but a lawyer who represents himself is a fool. I'm the suspect. I must be a real fool, I just reported for my beating. Fool-Boy in the house.

A fool enters where angels fear to tread. Mary Beth is dead.

Questions need answered. Surprised, I look over a work floor covered by 8-foot tables with computers sitting on them. When I left, the computers were in cubicles. When deuce was up here, they had these long tables set end to end north and south. Now the tables are back running east to west in tiers. Modernization, point the tables in a different direction.

Two detectives wave to me as they walk out through another exit. I don't see an air lock visible. We're safe if the bad guys attack the airlock.

Gennaro leads me to the mission team office. We face each other sitting in desk chairs. Predictable, my thug chair has a missing wheel. It wobbled when I worked here.

Gennaro shuffles paperwork. To break Gennaro's spell, I open my old desk drawer. Most of my junk stares back at me. I initiate the recorder and mic kill switch. Kill switch to off. I put it in to give arrestees attorney client privacy. Can't fight city hall, but one can fuck with them.

In the drawer I find candy. I unwrap it. It looks good. I pop it in my mouth. Tastes good. I offer one to Gennaro, he agrees. We consume hard candy sitting staring at each other.

Gennaro looks in the drawer, asks, "What is all that shit? "

I shrug. Reaching into the drawer, I shuffle candy over the 'record interview' switch. Its red record light is off. The kill switch shuts down the camera on the wall, the sound recording system and the overhear mic in the boss's office.

I look quizzically at Gennaro, "Who knows. I was looking for candy. You want more."

Gennaro doesn't know there's a kill switch in my drawer. He says, "I'm going to tell you what I can. I won't leave out much. Officer Mary Beth Burke was our partner. Apparently. you two met at her apartment just before you disappeared."

I say, "Didn't disappear. Went to Afghanistan."

Gennaro change-time, "Galvan, that's Coronet's candy. She'll be pissed about you eating it."

I respond, "Tell her you had to feed your suspect."

"OK. Give me a peppermint, asshole. No, I can't stand spearmint. Do I ever do spearmint? Jeez. Give me a red one."

"Sorry. I must've forgotten we were once partners."

Gennaro regards me, nods as if seeing me for the first time in a crowd, "Point taken."

He asks, "Where you been for three years? Why did you leave suddenly? When did you get back? Why come back now? Where were you at?"

Gennaro's questions drone on. I stop listening as I search the dance floor. I spot a young guy who appears to be about twelve years old sitting in a small office staring at me. He's sitting at a desk, writing on a yellow legal pad.

I slap my palm flat on the desk. Gennaro jumps, yelling, "What did you just do?"

The young guy doesn't flinch, but he looks over. He opens his desk drawer, fiddles inside. The youth just realized his bug isn't working. Found my audience.

Gennaro taps my wrist. "Feel free to say something at any time."

I say, "Testing: One, two, three.

The young guy is management. Management likes me for Mary Beth's murder. Game never changes.

Gennaro drones on, he's playing it out.

The listener removes an ear bud. Shakes it. Back to playing with something in his drawers. He fishes around. I turn the kill switch off rolling volume to full blast. I point to my ear saying loudly, "SORRY, GENNARO, I'M HARD OF HEARING. BIG EXPLOSION. BAM." I slap the desk loudly over the intake mic. Feed-back squelch.

My listener jumps. Yanks out his ear bud, throwing it down.

Gennaro says, "Funny."

I shrug.

A button on an old black desk phone next to me lights up, the old dial phone doesn't ring. My listener went to old time technology, listening in through the intercom. The earpiece is a pick-up mic now.

They should send this guy to the Northwestern Traffic Management Institute, he's a born technologist.

Gennaro says, "I'll give it to you straight, buddy."

That will be novel. I look up at Gennaro, trying to appear soulfully grateful, "Why, thank you so very much, detective sir."

Gennaro blinks.

I snap, "Get your intro over, Gennaro. You haven't given me my rights, so I'm here as a good citizen. Keep the bullshit up, I leave. If I'm a person of interest, I don't find the bullshit very interesting."

We eye each other, I say, "What do you want? What happened? When did it happen? I drank a bottle of Black Barrel last night. I feel like I'm gonna die. Either you tell me what happened to Mary Beth or I'm leaving."

Gennaro silently focuses on me, shakes his head, then says, "You stink like a brewery. You look like shit. This the new you?"

I answer in a testy tone, "You surprised me last night. For me, Mary Beth died last night. I drank myself to sleep, detective sir. I lost a woman very close to me last night. I don't have a lot of friends, I lost one last night and I am in the process of losing another this morning."

He can't give it up, "Do you drink a lot now, dude?"

I respond, "So far only after listening to you, asshole. I've been gone for years. When I left, Mary Beth was alive. I was wounded and hospitalized while I was away. Those injuries froze me in place for a long time, on foreign soil, then later in this country.

"I've been trying to get up the nerve to go see Mary Beth since I came back to town. On returning here, I was debilitated by injuries. I could barely walk, spent a lot of time in physical therapy or flat on my back. I wasn't going to show up at her door in that mess. I've been staying away from friends and family. I was not ready for prime time. I was almost a basket case."

My voice reflected complete sadness. "I went to Mary Beth's apartment when I finally got back on my feet. I was on an aluminum walker, but wanted to leave a note. Her building had been torn down. The world kept turning while I was gone."

I say, "Gennaro, there's a lot you don't know. Mary Beth and I finally got together before I left. When I was in training, I got a lot of snail-mail from her. Later, I stopped getting letters."

I shrug, "I got access to a phone. I called when I could. I left messages until her mailbox was full. I got no response. Eventually, her phone was disconnected. I have a hard head, but I'm not a total fool. My eventual presumption was that Mary Beth brushed me off. I'm an adult. I assume Mary Beth could and did go back with Brenda. I gave up."

Gennaro says, "Enough melodrama, came back from where, Galvan?"

"Afghanistan."

"You keep saying that nonsense. How on earth did you get yourself in Afghanistan? When were you there? Who were you with? What were you doing there, buying dope?"

I say, "The Greek gave me your wedding invitation from the

envelope you left in Gaby's mailbox last night. I can make it really easy. Ask your fiancé where I was and what I was doing."

I suggest, "Your bride knows exactly where I was. I was with her."

Gennaro snaps, "You were in Afghanistan with Emma? That was a Secret Service operation, Emma ran it. She never mentioned you being there."

"So, what, Gennaro. Em' never mentioned you while we were there. Could we be rivals in love?"

Gennaro is furious. "OK, smart ass, I'll call her.

I pick up his phone first, dialing from memory. Emma Wainwright picks up quickly, saying, "What's up, baby?"

I answer, "Not much my love."

Emma's voice asks, "Trouble, this you?"

I say, "None other, beautiful. Here, I'll let you talk to Gennaro. Oh, by the way, congratulations on the upcoming nuptials."

Gennaro snatches the phone, shoving me back into my chair. "For Christ's sake she's pregnant, jerk. Why the fuck did you just drop that on her? You are one insensitive prick, Galvan."

Gennaro walks off, talking softly into his phone.

Gennaro returns, speaking in a soothing tone, "It's OK, baby, don't cry; he was always a mean prick. I have to ask. Did you have any other Chicago detective with you over there? Other than this asshole."

They converse on the phone, "The Greek? Any other cops? New York Narcotics guys? Any other cops? Yeah, I consider the DEA and ATF cops. How about your people? Them too? No, this asshole is working up his alibi. Was there a bus load of nuns, Mother Teresa? The Navy SEALS. Great. Why were they there? Did they all make it back? Can I interview them, was he around them?"

Emma must've responded, Gennaro says, "So, the DEA guys didn't. What about the Bobs? The big guy's dead. Sorry, you didn't tell me. What do you mean Galvan got killed with Big Bob, he's sitting here glaring at me?"

She asks something, he answers "What do you mean? He looks like a crabby underweight Galvan. Skinny, maybe 170 or 180. Needs a haircut, has chin beard, walks with a limp. His throat? It has a long, ragged scar running I guess ear-to-ear, now you mention it. Very weird, the women were there both kissed the neck while I was watching."

He answers again, "Dealing with whatever, I assume. What do you mean, 'Is he with somebody?' Because they like the asshole.

I'm investigating him for the murder of our partner. YES. OK. He was with a tall pretty brunette when I was there, looked like a date. Yeah. Both did. The other was that pain in the ass FBI Agent that was bugging you. I know, too weird. Yes, she meant it. I think it's a kind of a cat-fight. No, it's very complicated--with the asshole, it always is. YES DEAR, women often like him.NO DEAR, not the dumb ones, the smart ones."

Gennaro responds to further questions, "Yes, I know him very well. We were partners with Mary Beth before I met you. No, I know the Greek through Galvan. I never worked with the Greek. What you mean, 'Why didn't I tell you?' You were sound asleep, snoring up a storm when I came in. I let you sleep."

Family talk, "Yes, you do snore. You snore very loudly." She does snore. Snored like a bear in the Kush.

I say, "Does she ever!" No sense being here, if I don't start shit with an ex-partner out to lynch me.

I apparently annoy both of them—phone conversation stops. So I say, "Excuse me, Mr. Detective sir. I just remembered that Special Agent in Charge Emma Wainwright did mention you once when we were feasting on Campbell's franks and beans with hot sauce in cream of mushroom soup. Add it to your dinners; it is a favorite of Emma's."

Gennaro stares, jaw agape. So, taking my opening, I say, "Emma says they remind her of that nasty Soppressata sausage that you cook-up in your garage. Her only complaint was she felt your Soppressata was disappointingly small, under-spiced, and floppy soft. She asked if you were Irish."

His cell emits a loud, audible roar. Heard me, I suppose.

I remove his phone from his hand, saying into it, "Hi, Em', Miss me? Yes, dear, it is mean, but he's fitting me for a noose. No, dear, he doesn't know about Mary Beth. Yes, you do know, we talked about her enough. Tell him if you want. No. They aren't giving me a date, but I think she was murdered when we sequestered. Yes, I am that dumb. I trusted you, White Girl, silly me."

We continue, "No, the snail-mail I got from her stopped when we were at the ranch. I mentioned the snow. She said they had none when she wrote. Yeah, I know we were sequestered. I should have figured you were reading my mail in sequester.

Gennaro snatches his phone back, "I know, honey. Yes, he's just being an asshole. He does that. He's having fun pissing everyone off. They were a couple. Bunk, Mary Beth was a lesbian. He had a crush on her? Good, all the more motive, considering. What do you mean take it easy? Why? He doesn't know? Yeah, I'll go slow."

He says, "I'll call you back in a bit, dear. If you can squeeze a few moments out of your duties guarding our beloved President. Could you please send me an official Fax listing the time period you took custody of this moron and when you last saw him? Yes, I need to know. We are looking at him on a murder charge."

He shakes his head, "Yes, a FAX, it has to be official, Snookums. Because he's using you as an alibi witness. It needs to cover the period you were in training at someplace called 'the ranch' and a place called 'the farm'. And the dates he was with you?"

Exasperated he says, "What do you mean, talk to higher authority? Withhold inculpatory or exculpatory evidence, there will be court orders and consequences. Murder's like that."

"No dear, He has a federal judge for his attorney, gave me her card. He clerked for her when we were partners. Oh, you knew about the lawyer thing. He's admitted for practice at the Federal bench."

Gennaro says, "HOW? His name came up. The Feds were looking for him. Yes, our girl was out for blood. Says she still is, I wonder. He's a person of interest, that kind..."

No, dear I can't let you speak with him again just now. No dear, I have to tie him to his chair now and beat him with a rubber hose. It's a tradition."

He concludes, "What do you mean, 'Don't you dare.' No dear, I'm kidding, we haven't used our rubber hoses since last week. You'd get a Habeas Corpus Writ this close to the wedding to free this jagoff. Send the FAX, you know something, tell me."

Gennaro says to me, "OK, Galvan, I get it. Fuck you, too. Just so you know, you're listed on the books as a person of interest in Mary Beth Burke's murder. Welcome home, asshole. Why 'd you do it?"

I ask, "Do what, Gennaro? What happened, where did it happen, when did it happen?"

Gennaro's spiel, "Was it an accident? Explain what happened, I can help you, but we've got to get your version on paper. If the G gets involved, they'll fry you. They think this might be a serial murder thing. No more bullshitting, buddy."

I stare back coldly, before saying, "Fuck you, asshole, wait for your fax, you might get one you don't expect. I think EM' has the conscience that you've lost, GOOD BUDDY."

My argument continues, "Gennaro, you prick, you told me Mary Beth was dead. You did not tell me she was a serial murder victim. Knowing me for years, you think I'm a serial killer? You are really nuts, dude. From information I've heard about your goofy time-line. I wasn't in town. I was with your bride-to-be and her team.

Resigned, smug, Gennaro confronts me, "We have your prints at the crime scene."

I ask, "What scene? Where in that scene?"

With portent weight he says, "In Mary Beth's apartment, in the bedroom, on her door frame, on her night table by the bed, in the bathroom. All over the place. Galvan. She was a lesbian. You might have gotten into the kitchen or the bathroom. I find it difficult to believe she let you wander around her bedroom."

I sigh, "Gennaro, how long have you known Mary Beth and me?"

"Since the academy, smart guy. The only male company I ever saw her keep were us and on the team. I tried, she wasn't interested, dude."

I nod, "In detective work, there's always something you don't know. To hear, listen."

Testy he says, "You aren't my mentor, Francis."

I shrug, "OK. You don't know Mary Beth and I were a couple in school. Doug told you. Did you hear him? I went to the Naval Academy, hooked-up with a friend of Em's."

Gennaro freaks. "You expect me to believe that you dated Mary Beth? She was gay."

I answer, "Lesbian, not gay. There's a difference, Gennaro, but I'm not an expert."

"Regardless. How did you end up in her bedroom the night she was killed?"

"You're being a lunkhead, Gennaro. Fingerprint evidence is based on dust, oil content, heat humidity and surface quality. It doesn't have a clock timer. Presence does not indicate guilt. It proves I was in her bedroom. It doesn't in itself demonstrate whether I was welcome, what we were doing or when I was there."

Gennaro's shoulders drop, "I give up. Why were you there?"

"We slept at her place the night before I left for the Kush. She'd broken up with Brenda. Bren' was cheating. I was invited to sleep at her place the night before I flew to Baltimore. She gave me a ride to Midway Airport the next morning."

"Call your fiancé. I lied earlier. We had a long conversation one night in the Kush about people we thought might be waiting for us in the world. Ask Em' if I mentioned anyone."

Gennaro demands, "You were talking to my fiancé about your love life?"

I say, "Were you ever on a surveillance, Gennaro? One gets bored. We were all sick of talking about food and cars. You get lonely, hope for a better future."

Gennaro speed-dials Emma, "Em'? His alibi goes all over the place. Why do you have to get clearance to tell me when he worked for you? What do you mean it's a secret? This is a murder case, you're a witness. I know. Okay. Okay."

He asks her, "Can you tell me if he ever had a conversation with you about a woman?"

"No. One he had a relationship with? Did he mention a name? Mar', Mary Beth? Did he give you a last name? Why didn't you say so?"

"I know there are a million women named Mary in Chicago. It's a Catholic town. I'm Italian-Catholic. Well, there's that, so are you. You too, only you're Yankee Church of England."

Gennaro nods emphatically, "So he said she was a police-woman he worked with? A relationship? Sexual? REALLY? I doubt that, the woman was lesbian. What do you mean people change? I know people are fluid these days. OK. Listen, I need that itinerary. Try harder. Did he leave your command at any time?"

"What do you mean he was KIA? He's sitting right here. Where did they send the body? You have to check, Ms. Wainwright. Yes, let's manage the release as much as we can."

He asks me, "How long were you in the hospital, Galvan?"

"More than a year."

He inquires, "Did you come back here during your convalescence?"

I shake my head, "I was in a hospital bed. They thought I was in a vegetative state for a long time, Gennaro."

He smiles, "You've been a vegetable since I met you."

Sadly, I ask, "What happened to Mary Beth, Gennaro? I can't believe she's dead.

I didn't get back to Chicago until late last year. When I did get back,

I was a few steps away from a body bag. I spent a lot of the winter scurrying around on an aluminum walker. You know, one of the ones with little wheels and lime-green tennis balls."

He smiles.

I tell him, "I didn't look for Mary Beth until well after Christmas. I was in nasty shape and did not want to plead my case like that. I was a scarred-up, crippled mess. I punked out recently. I rationalized that Mary Beth went back with Brenda. Eventually, I figured Mary Beth was better off being done with me. "

Gennaro asks, "You're saying you weren't aware of Mary Beth's death until I told you?"

"When I was away, I got blown up. They put me in a coma to aid healing, then they forgot. The medics were overloaded and didn't talk to each other. They lost me in the system. Tell Emma I said, 'fuck secrecy.' Ask your bride-to-be to check on where I was, and what we were doing. Hell, Emma was commanding the insert team the night I got killed."

Gennaro's surprised. He says into the ether. "Lieutenant, come on over, you need to hear this." He disconnects the intercom microphone.

The kid is a lieutenant? It appears I've gotten old.

"Gennaro, three years ago I hired out with the secrets for overseas contractor duty. Joe and I both went. We were sort of bank inspectors in Afghanistan, but listed on the unit manifest as embedded, freelance writers. We were assigned to a naval unit, way up in the Hindu Kush near a place near the provincial capital of Gardez."

"Isn't that a little far from the ocean, Galvan?" asks the lieutenant, sardonically.

I ignore him, turning to Gennaro, "Talk to your bride, she thought it all up."

The boy-lieutenant is perplexed.

I say, "A few days before I got killed, the DEA team and the New York Narcotic Team got ripped to pieces when they inserted. We were extremely short of warm bodies."

Gennaro's phone vibrates. He listens, then hands me his phone saying, "It's Emma. She wants to talk to you."

I ask derisively, "Hello, is this to whom I am speaking?"

Emma Wainwright's voice, "WHO IS THIS? Who the fuck do you think this is, Trouble? It's Emma God-Damned Wainwright. You were supposed to be dead, why didn't you stay dead? Never mind, you got your FAX. I can't believe you have most of law enforcement as your alibi–Secret Service, DEA, NYPD."

I ask, "How about the NBA?"

She says, "Out! Vito back on the phone."

I hand Gennaro his phone, He listens intently, answers, "Later, Emma. Right now? I'll get the FAX, hang close a moment."

He walks to the FAX printer, comes back with several pages. He reads his papers, You owe me a story, Baby. I'll call."

I say loudly, "My thanks, White Girl. I needed the help."

Gennaro snarls, "Carry on blithely, Asshole. What's this White Girl bullshit?"

"White-Girl was her radio call sign in the Kush."

"What was yours, Galvan? Twerp?"

"NO. Trouble was my call-sign, Mr. Detective sir."

He says, "That figures. Did you read that invitation I left at Gaby's? If you're not indicted, we'd like you to come." He looks shocked. "You prick. You weren't even going to come to our wedding, were you?"

I say, "I think it inappropriate, as the groom was railroading me for the murder of a woman I loved."

Things are rarely more fun than having a crazy-jealous, Black-Italian Homicide Detective in charge of your fate. It just doesn't get any better.

I say, "When I got hurt, signals got crossed. The Russians had me up in the 'stans. After they stabilized me, they sent me westbound in a Christmas basket. I eventually woke up in a hospital in Landstuhl, Germany. Later I woke again in Bethesda.

"Along the way, I was paralyzed, non-verbal and on a ventilator. Too many wounded. Wasn't staff or space for putting us. We were warehoused."

"During out-processing, my combat air surgeon returned to Bethesda to close out assigned cases still in hospital, accountability. If she failed to document her plan of care, she anticipated them extending her tour. She agreed to complete delinquency on patient care notes. Surprised a dead guy was on her roster, Doc Braxton looked me up. I was listed and she became incensed as my physical condition was deteriorating from neglect.

Motionless and mute, I watched her read my chart and prayed she would turn off the vent so I could die. Recently, I had gotten to the point where I could move my right hand and index finger slightly. She leaned in with her short cardiac stethoscope to listen to my heart, I caressed her breast.

"Doc leapt back, freaked out. What the fuck? I was dying in a few minutes. Gotta take what you can get. She raised her fist to belt me. Then settled on my eyes. I was watching.

She tapped my forehead with her index finger asking, "You in there?"

"I blinked."

"She nodded. Did you just grab my breast?" I blinked. She recached for the vent switch. Then looked at me. I blinked. She said, "No way. You're coming off the vegetable shelf."

"In time, I finally got back on my feet and came back here."

"The Greek and I set up a boatyard on the river. I couldn't get around for a long time. Driving didn't come back right away. I kept a low profile."

"When was Mary Beth murdered?" I ask.

Gennaro says, "Mary Beth was at home on December seventh, the year you got an approved leave of absence for unspecified reasons, then disappeared."

"December seventh, is Pearl Harbor Day, Mary Beth's birthday. The things you remember."

Gennaro purses his lips in debate before saying, "When attacked, she was painting the spare bedroom. She had drying paint splotches on her clothes at the time our first contact got there. The first responding officer got paint on her uniform trying to resuscitate Mary Beth."

He glances to a general progress report, "As near as we can tell looking at the scene, she answered the door for a pizza delivery at about 8:00 PM. Her elderly landlady timed a banging door to the start of her favorite TV show."

Skimming the GPR he says, "The pizza appears ritually positioned, upside down on the dinner table. Two places were set with a mat, silverware, and wine glasses. One upside-down, one right-side up. There was a candle burning in a holder. Footprints indicate that the offender traversed the scene several times arranging his display. Then stepping away to view it. He left bloody footprints. The bureau says he was wearing size nine Navy-Oxfords."

I say, "Look at my feet, Gennaro."

He looks over, "Sixteens, like me?"

I answer, "Fifteen, but the difference from size nine is obvious. So, we know it ain't us."

Gennaro says, "Obvious now, huh?"

With an apologetic expression he goes on, "Mary Beth sustained defensive wounds on her forearms and hands. She fought him. There's blood spatter around the doorway. Blood spatter is arrayed in a cast-off pattern around the doorway. The pattern indicates he blocked any escape, leaving a body outline shadow where he was standing. The G thinks the guy stood five-foot-eight to five-foot -ten. Yeah, I know you're six-foot five, Galvan. Sorry."

Gennaro continues, "The underside of the pizza box is scorched. The scorched area has gunshot residue over the underside of that box, as well. The doorframe has back-blast spatter on its inner edge. The theory is he camouflaged his gun under the box. When she opened the door, he was locked and loaded, ready to go. He came to kill." The first rounds drove her back into the room. Blood spatter evidence indicates initial abdominal wounds."

Gennaro looks up, saying," Mary rushed the door several times. At some point, it appears she got hold of his hair. She cracked his head hard, at least twice, leaving a bloody hair transfer imprint the second time. There was blood on the right knee of her jeans, where it appears she kneed his face. The related blood evidence was submitted for DNA comparison. We harvested spatter from Mary Beth and that of an unknown-and-flown who wasn't in the Bureau CODIs Index."

The lieutenant moves in, "We know that blood samples are from a male, likely Caucasian. We established his primary position using the string kit. We'll need a sample, Galvan."

I ask, "What type you got?"

LT says, "The blood from the door is B-negative."

I respond, "Mine's O-Positive, I'm a universal donor. Get a warrant, lieutenant." I say as I pick up the phone on the desk and begin dialing out. Yes, it is a very old rotary dial.

The lieutenant reaches for the phone, "What do you think you're doing?"

"Calling my lawyer," I reply. "Gennaro, despite unending evidence to the contrary, you still like me for Mary Beth's murder. Your killer's blood B-. Mine is O+. I was out of country. I'm six-foot-five, he's at most five-foot-ten. I was a couple of thousand miles away, on a US Military Reservation. He was here. It wasn't me. Choose a side, look for the killer or railroad me."

Abruptly, to break their timing, I ask, "Why are you fixated on me?

Something's missing. Who is pulling your strings? You look like a pair of bumbling carpenters building a frame that does not fit the picture. Let me guess, inexperienced Agent Nadia Dimitrieva, because her confidential informant has the weight to push her into committing a misprision of justice? That is a felony, guys. Better hire you a good lawyer, I got one."

Gennaro lowers his gaze, saying, "Nadia's informant is code named River Mud or something like that. She showed part of her file to the commander. I haven't been allowed to see the file."

The boy-lieutenant says, "The 'G' wants you for the murder, I haven't seen the file, either. Neither of us are allowed to speak with the informant. When we thought you were dead, their informant insisted you killed Officer Burke because Officer Burke got wise to your sexual liaison with a Columbian narcotics princess."

Gennaro takes it, "The 'G' informant insists you met with the Columbian woman in Washington, just before you disappeared. The Columbian is described as tall with a skinny build like a model. The woman is pale, with long wild, curly bleach-blond hair."

I think. He probes for my weak spot, "You met with her in a restaurant in DC. She was wearing a bright orange, short waisted blazer with one big black button when you were cozying up to her over lunch at Bistro Bis in DC."

Gennaro smirks as he asks, "Did you at least get a quickie after lunch, Galvan?"

It clicks, Bingo. Smiling I stare at Gennaro a long second before saying, "Ask your bride to be, Gennaro."

"Why would my fiancé know about that, smart-ass?"

I ask disingenuously, "Does your beloved own a couture, red-orange Armani woman's suit similar to what you just described, Gennaro? I know that, you see, because she was wearing that suit in her DC office when she interviewed me for the mission to Afghanistan. Then Emma took me to lunch at Bistro Bis after the interview. Call her."

The youthful lieutenant says, "The woman in that restaurant was a blond white woman from Columbia. I mean, your fiancé is a black woman from Chicago."

Gennaro folds, "Emma is a woman of mixed-race, lieutenant. Her family owns several small states out-east. She's the Chicago Secret Service Chief of Station. I think I've seen the suit Galvan just mentioned. I can't verify just now, She's in a meeting with the United States

Attorney for the Seventh Circuit for the Northern District of Illinois. I'll ask later."

I pick up his phone from the desk, saying, "I have a funny number, she'll answer."

The operator says, "Yes?"

As the operator answers I say, "Priority call. This is 'T-R-O-U-B-L-E', patch me through to 'W-H-I-T-E G-I-R-L'."

The operator notes, "Your clearance for connection has an issue noted on the file."

I answer sharply, "Yeah. Well, I'm not dead anymore. Connect me as a priority caller, I escaped."

The operator says, "Yes sir. Connecting, 'Trouble' with 'White-Girl'."

A single ring, then Emma Wainwright's voice speaks sternly into the receiver, "Why are calling me at this number, Vito? How did you get it?"

I say, "Hi, Em' dear. Would you hold for a moment? Your beloved has some questions you'll just love. He's discovered our tryst."

I hand the phone to a glaring Gennaro.

Gennaro snatches his phone from me as if it was hot potato, "This is Detective Vito Gennaro, Chicago Police Homicide. To whom am I speaking?"

A loud inaudible voice answers him.

Gennaro glares, then snarls at me, "Funny, asshole."

I respond, "I hope I haven't created family discord, Gennaro. Let's go back a moment, you were accusing me of the murder of Mary Beth Burke. Here's some more shit you don't know, you traitorous fuck. I have been very close with Mary Beth most of my life. When you diverted our conversation, you were wondering if I banged a certain blond whore after lunch. Ask the lady, asshole."

Gennaro asks her, giving me a fisheye. Then says, "Who? You? Is the blazer bright orange? What do you mean it's red but it looks orange? Did you ever take this moron to lunch at Bistro Bis in DC? Yeah. When? After he signed?

"Who were the bookends with you? Two of your agents. Who are Big Bob and Little Bob. Can I interview them? Oh? Why not? Then it appears you are his alibi, dear. Yes, sweetums. I'll explain later."

"She doesn't even look vaguely Columbian, Galvan."

"Appearances can be deceiving. In the right light it's hard to see you as Italian, you prick."

"Funny," says Gennaro.

"Funny as a crutch, Mr. Detective sir," I answer.

Gennaro rapidly scribbles notes. He looks at me closely, then says, "Why did you leave town with her?"

"We committed to it because Emma asked. EM' is a square block, the service was going to hammer her into a round hole. Em' had to get away before they broke her down. The Greek and I were convinced Emma would get herself killed if it got down and dirty in the Kush."

It is Gennaro's turn to bust my chops, "Something you obviously do not know, Mr. Galvan. Mary Beth was painting a baby's room when she sent for the pizza."

"Come on, Gennaro, are you telling me Brenda let herself get pregnant? That I'll never believe." I laugh at him.

Peeling back an edge of my hide, Gennaro says, "No, Brenda remains Brenda. Mary Beth was pregnant, Galvan. On the desk in the other bedroom was a letter addressed to some Forward Operating Base to some unnamed dude. The address we couldn't track down."

Gennaro says, "The letter was addressed to you. Mary Beth was telling you she found out what she was waiting for since she last wrote you. The letter wasn't finished. We think she was writing it just before she answered the door. "

The boy lieutenant says, "Her autopsy established she was pregnant.

Gennaro says in ominous tone, "Didn't know that did you, smart guy?"

The boy-lieutenant continues the thought, "Did you kill her out of jealousy, because a rival got her pregnant?"

The weight of knowing settles on my chest. Recognition dawns. In her letters Mary Beth kept saying she did not know if I could cut the mustard. She was waiting to see if I got her pregnant."

Did Mary Beth just want to be pregnant? Was she looking to have my child? Or did she just want to have my child? Why play games? Why did she let me walk away to play soldier?

And like a fool, I walked. I left Mary Beth alone to work her way through developments. In that process, she was murdered. The straw that breaks the camel's back is always a surprise. You think things are tough, but you can manage. Suddenly you can't and down you go. If I'd been around, could things have been different? Will I ever know what she intended? The air we breathe has weight. Eventually, the weight of the world will crush us all, I can think of no reason to keep going. Why keep trying, things won't get better.

I'm not gonna do this anymore. So, I decide to stop breathing. Paralyzed in hospital I had time on my hands, I learned the difference between breathing and not breathing. After months on the vent I became ventilator-lazy.

When the staff removed my vent for cleaning, I had to tell myself to breathe. With the breath reflex supplanted by the vent for months, breathing required conscious effort.

One day I realized I could choose to breathe or not. The knowledge brought terror. I feared to sleep. I might stop breathing if the electricity shut off. Eventually, the reflex returned. But as in many such things, I'd acquired wicked knowledge. I had the knowledge I could stop. When depressed in hospital, I'd get stubborn. I decided to scare the staff; I'd reject the breath reflex. I suddenly had a power over my life. If they pissed me off, I could always kill myself. On occasion I'd allow myself to become woozy, waiting for the staff to panic and rush in with the crash-cart. The brat in me had something to do on a boring day in the vegetable bin. I reverted to pouting child. I could get even for being ignored. I showed them.

Mary Beth and I made a baby. Sex is like that. Mary Beth was coy in her letters. She was waiting to see whether I had gotten her pregnant. Did she want to see how I'd react, or just want the baby? I guess I cut the mustard. A very different mustard than I anticipated.

We ran into each other. I was running off to play soldier. Did she want the baby, but not me? I've had enough, I'll never know. She's gone, the baby's gone. Time for me to leave too. So, I get done. I stop breathing, I set my mind, telling me to not breathe. I reject the impulse for air.

My last observation was of the long sequence of stupid things I did to get here. My sequence lasted well after my head cracked the marble-aggregate floor. Thunk. Marble aggregate lacks the give of concrete, it's really hard.

So much for a noble passing. Smacking my head on rock adamant blasted aggrieved nobility right out of my skull. Damn, it hurt.

Someone's rolled me over.

Head wounds bleed like crazy. Mine always do. The pain is piercing, far worse than brain freeze from cold ice cream on a hot day. If Deontay Wilder hits this hard he'll be Heavyweight Champion forever.

A voice in my head roars, "You, gutless wonder. Get up. Go find this prick, strip him of his humanity, and kill him. Shoot his horse. Kill his dog. Burn his home. Drive his family before you with great lamentation. Get it done, Galvan. The voice, sounding very much like an angry Mary Beth Burke, says, "No dying. Get up and find him, Galvan. He killed the baby and me. You are crazy-nuts, this is right up your alley. On your feet, do something awful. Find him, kill him slowly."

My chest is getting pounded fiercely. Then five chest compressions. Damn, that hurts. I have to stop them or my ribs will break. I roll onto my side, inhale painfully as my lungs burn. Mary Beth is gone.

Gennaro is kneeling at my side with palms doubled on my chest doing compressions. No wonder my ribs are breaking, Gennaro is built like a tank. The boy-lieutenant kneels opposite Gennaro. I'm flat on my back. I gag, "Enough with the breath of life shit. Stop the compressions, I'll live."

I find it difficult to sit up, but force myself to sit on the hard floor. I look around me from floor level. Central is as depressing from floor level as any other. Resolved to my fate I say, "Get a Buccal swab kit, Gennaro, Mary Beth's child. It's mine."

Gennaro, kneeling on the aggregate floor beside me, pales. Being pale is difficult for Vito Gennaro. Having swabbed my cheek pockets with several stemmed cotton tipped wooden swabs Gennaro seals the package and removes his face mask and gloves.

Gennaro gathers up the sealed packets from the sterilized surface of the desk, saying, "I should have just swabbed your forehead, Galvan. I can't believe you swooned."

"I didn't swoon, Gennaro. I was being dead."

"You held your breath until you passed out?" he asks.

"I was on a ventilator so long I can shut off my breath reflex."

Gennaro shrugs, becoming thoughtful, "How long were you on a ventilator?"

"A year, maybe longer."

"What did you do, carry the ventilator around in a shoulder bag?"

"No, I was paralyzed, laid out flat most of the time. The staff dragged me around with the vent attached. We were kind of inseparable."

Gennaro stares intently my way, "Mary Beth came-out when she and I were still in Marquette, Galvan. She and Brenda were inseparable. What were you, a sperm donor?"

I respond, "They broke up before I left. Brenda took up with Amelia."

"Amelia is scary." Gennaro says shaking his head, "Scary. Ruthless. Ever self-serving, but always lovely."

He says, "While you were gone, Brenda became a supervisor over state's attorney. Amelia works for her."

Funny the way things turn out, "Mary Beth and I dated in high school. Then I went to the Naval Academy for a summer session try-out. I got involved with a friend of your fiancé while I was there. When I got back, Mary Beth and I broke up.

I say, "We saw each other occasionally during college. I had screwed the pooch; we were through. She had bad luck or bad taste in guys."

Gennaro smirks, "I'd agree with that, considering the fact she dated you."

I shrug, "We all make mistakes. Mistakes leave marks. Mary Beth's 'freshman-mistake' believed in better living through chemistry. The boy was a weightlifter trying to build giant muscles on a small frame. He used a lot of d-ball. With the muscle came side effects."

Gennaro laughs. "Dianabol was bad, Guys who used ended up with shrunken testicles, impotence, heart disease. Not counting rapid mood swings, and the mania of anabolic steroids."

Gennaro continues, "Mary Beth hated that stuff. She worked up warrants on a manufacturer after you made detective. On the raid she broke her flashlight on the guy's head. The guy used his own product, wanted a fight. She gave him one. At one point, I thought she was going to kill him."

I say, "Mary Beth learned to detest her d-ball freak. She called him Danny Dupont. Things degenerated fast for her. Danny boy blamed Mary Beth for his inadequacy, He beat her."

"Mary Beth got an order of protection against him. He violated, and half-killed her. Before the police showed up, Danny got into it with some country-dude, who escaped."

"After his fight with the farmer, the police found Danny crawling around in a blizzard with his own knife sticking out of his thigh. Cops arrested him."

I conclude, "Mary's testimony got Danny Dupont three-hots-and-a-cot for a term of years."

Gennaro agrees, "They are serious about orders of protection downstate. Which thigh did he get stabbed in?"

Dazed from bouncing my head off the aggregate floor, I have to think. I look at my right hand, noting a thin scar along the back of my hand from Danny's knife, I say, "Left thigh."

As I speak, I realize Gennaro just bagged me for stabbing Danny. The air seems to thicken as we engage in a mutual stare down.

Gennaro shoves my shoulder roughly. "Galvan, after that last team Christmas party, you left for detective school. That January on a night surveillance, Mary Beth told me a different version of that story. She added a part where you drove through the blizzard from Omaha after she called your cell. She said you drove from Omaha to confront Danny Dupont. She thought you and Danny both got cut. The way you are looking at the scar on your hand, she guessed right. Your Grandfather Silky told her that you were in deep shit with deuce for $400 car rental on his credit card in Nebraska. She said you rented a Yukon and drove to her rescue and then back to Omaha through the blizzard to cover your tracks."

I say, "So?"

Gennaro smirks, "Mary Beth told me that you should have stayed long enough to be thanked. She realized you just weren't into her, so she let it go until the party. She thought you had a change of heart, then you left. That was that, shit happens. When my partner retired after I made detective, I was assigned the follow-up on Mary's murder. I checked on Danny Dupont's whereabouts on the theory he might have come back for revenge. Danny died in prison. He never got out, died of domestic abuse in the joint."

"Such is life," I answer.

Gennaro makes a decision. "Just so you know, Galvan. She and I talked about your weird ways. She stayed furious for years about your tryst with that red-head from Annapolis."

"The Irish hold grudges, Gennaro."

Gennaro says, "By the time the three of us partnered-up, she had revised her views on you. You had your chance at that Christmas party when she curled up in your lap for the team picture. You blew it, dude. She was death on guys afterward. You do have a way with the ladies. From what you've said this afternoon, I gather she was not completely done with you.

I say, "Neither of us was done with the other, Gennaro. The night before I left town for training, Mary Beth offered me a couch to sleep on and a ride to the airport in the morning."

"In the process, I discovered Mary and Brenda broke up. In retrospect, what I saw as a serendipity was her intent. Mary Beth intended for a baby to be conceived that night."

We drink coffee for a time, lost in thought.

In time, Gennaro speaks again of the murder. Or maybe he'd been speaking as I sat thinking. Maybe, I wasn't listening.

I hear him saying… "Well, I think this guy took his time, he got to know his target, laid his trap carefully. He cornered her in what she saw as a safe haven, her home. Then he went all in. She willingly opened the door. He was looking forward to pizza. Maybe she knew him. Mary Beth wasn't afraid of him. Went down fighting."

Gennaro postulates, "We think he waited for Friday. Watched for long enough to establish her pattern of ordering Pizza Hut on Fridays. Her killer approached the pizza guy from over his left shoulder. He popped the guy with a couple of .22 bullets behind his left ear. He parked a car near his entry door, then propped the door open with a pizza box.

He continues, "The killer dragged the delivery guy into the bushes, getting a blood transfer from the dead driver on his own gloved hand. The killer's bloody gloved left palm left an impression on a railing in the hallway. Pretending to be the pizza guy he buzzed in."

We read reports sitting at the table.

Gennaro reads from notes, "The attacker fired a total of seven rounds from his weapon. Maybe a minute went by."

The detective in me sparks, "If he panicked it would take less than two seconds to empty the pistol. A second to see her, less than a second to fire seven."

"Why do you say that?" Gennaro asks oddly.

"Training. I overloaded my father's automatic which held nine .45 caliber rounds with one in the chamber. In .95 second, as timed on a chronometer. SEALS told me I was dead slow. The original drills were set-up for revolvers, requiring six rounds in one second. I argued nine holes was more than six. They said I cheated

Gennaro says speculatively, "The scene indicates he used a .22 caliber semi-automatic pistol. He fired 9 rounds. He used two to kill the pizza guy. The wounds overlapped, looked a little different under a scope.

I say, "Describe the difference."

Gennaro says, "One is tattooed and stippled, the other had a soot ring. "

"Old school detective work, Gennaro. You came up after the old-timers retired. They didn't have the benefit of science we relied on since the turn of the century. I had to learn scenes from the oldsters. The Boom wasn't dumb, they trusted in observation."

Gennaro says, "Explain, dude."

"I think he rushed up on the pizza guy. The driver noticed his approach. The killer hurried his first shot as he closed to medium proximity. That one left more soot from partially burned powder around the first wound. The guy was probably dead or dying, but the attacker was in the frenzy of his kill. He continued into closer proximity. Maybe the barrel came into contact. Close proximity and contact forced the expended powder under the skin, creating stippling and tattoo imprints inside the skin. He was having fun, wanted to make sure with a double-tap. Then I think the killer was aroused by the killing and hurried upstairs to get into Mary Beth's murder."

Gennaro asks, "If you were doing the deed, what would you have used?"

I shudder. "I'd use a Ruger .22 Mark-IV, the assassin's weapon, easily suppressed. Readily available, inexpensive."

"The landlady only heard a door slam. How much is the sound suppressed? I've never heard one in use."

I say, "Today, the Ruger SR-22 has an unsuppressed decibel reading of 140dB. Suppressed, it maybe has 40dB."

Gennaro looks confused, "What's that sound like?"

I answer, "About as loud as a bird call in a quiet library. The cartridge firing is suppressed enough to hear hammer strike firing pin, the pin strike primer."

I add, "He killed the pizza man; that kicked things into motion. Once he started, compulsion took over. A serial killer is not merely driven to kill, he has a ritual to complete. It is not about getting it done, it is about getting it done right. Psychotics don't brook interference with their rituals. They react violently to challenge, losing control. Interference shakes their sense of omnipotence."

Running up the stairs, he was committed. Assuming he had a standard 9-round magazine, he emptied the magazine when the door opened. Didn't reload, ran the Ruger dry."

I continue, "If he was trained, he'd have switched magazines on his way up the stairs. When she opened the door, she either recognized him or counter-attacked. She upset his ritual, so I think he panicked. He feared her. I think the guy that shot her knew her. I'd bet Mary Beth was boring in when he was empty. So he went to the knife."

"How did you know that?"

"Mary Beth told me there was never going to be another Danny Dupont who could make her cower. She was never again going to take her beating. She said she would die trying."

"She did," answers Gennaro glumly. "The weapon was a .22 caliber. It was a semi-automatic, the ejector scored each of the casings recovered on the scene. We bet it's an SR-22. We couldn't find a witness who heard shots. I think the weapon had a suppressor. There are powder-burns on the pizza box consistent with silencer-cans gas vent perforations on the SR-22 suppressor. The firing left a faint, gold colored fan impression in front of where he stood and on the underside of the box. The State lab's mass spectrometer identified the fan as having a copper content similar to that used on .22 bullet jackets. Your bureau friend has identified the copper as commensurate with a copper alloy used in the jacketing of expensive .22 match ammunition."

Gennaro says, "Anyway, Agent Dimitrieva informed me her lab insists the killer's .22 automatic is new, or had a new barrel of match-quality. Match barrels are carefully made, the tools and dies are fresh and sharp when they cut the lands and grooves into barrels. The sharp edges in these barrels shave off jacket material from bullets, creating the copper fan."

My voice sounds faraway in my head as I speak, "There's a market for integrally silenced weapons. I'm familiar with the weapon. I've used it overseas. The armorer told me new cans bring sound levels below 60 decibels for at least the first five rounds."

Gennaro asks; "What's 60 decibels sound like?"

"Like an intimate conversation in a restaurant over a dinner table. At 78 decibels it has the volume of the dial tone on your phone when it is close to your head."

"You learn that stuff as a bank inspector, Galvan?" asks Gennaro.

I eyeball him with my right eye, studying his face. "We used them during audits, when dealing with total jagoffs. The U.S. Commercial Code advises its use when dealing with them."

Gennaro says, "With no shots heard, the suppressor theory flies."

He adds, "The driver was still warm to the touch when the first beat car arrived. Everything happened at once."

I started to drift, lost in the realization of Mary Beth's last fight. If Gennaro said more, I didn't hear it,

Eventually, I gave them contact information for Dr. Braxton,

The Greek, Lt. Commander Deveraux and others to check my alibi. National security, career endangerment, politics, plausible deniability be damned. They left me for dead and went on with their lives."

I see Mary Beth looking at me. It's time to stand up. My team, friends or not, are my alibi in a murder case. I need to be out looking for this guy, so I need the alibi. This guy killed Mary Beth and our baby. She's right, I need to do something awful.

As I rise, I'm told not to leave town. On release, I walk down the back stairs to the lot. Spring. It's still sunny. Hot, humid with thunderheads to the west. Gennaro walks me to my SUV. He tells me to get something to eat and quit drinking.

Out of the blue he hugs me, telling me to hang in there. In where? Then, he orders me to come to his wedding, "If you don't Emma says she will come get you."

Gennaro leaves me trying to fit a key into my door lock. After several minutes I think to press the remote door opener, don't have a key. At least the car doesn't blow up.

Gennaro calls back to me, "Bring Slenderella, she had your back with just a hand full of keys. Don't let that psycho FBI bitch run her off. Don't be stupid, stay away from Nadia."

7

SAVE A HORSE, RIDE A COWBOY

My afternoon with Gennaro has worn me down, the recognition of reality tore what was left into shreds.

I tried to escape. There are no easy exits. Mary Beth blocked my escape. As in that tent in the dunes, it's time to carry on, firm in my resolve. Apparently, there is no rest for the wicked. Of late, noble resistance to the slings and arrows of outrageous fortune has been a bitch.

I forced myself to sit through Gennaro's presentation of the murder scene. It horrified me, then numbed my mind, absorbing even rage. I tried to harbor my resolve, only to see it wash from under the pressure of what happened.

I need to man up, creating a vessel to contain my animus until it is ready. In the process, I visualize a large pot. Into the pot go the components of my rage, set to simmer until they become soup. Reckoning, like revenge, is a dish best served cold.

I'll need help to work through this. Plunge like a crazy man, I'll be stopped or ignored. I need to drift slow and steady until I know. Then? Then I'll understand exactly what to do, and how to do what is to be done.

I think, I drive. Emotion has emptied me, leaving me exhausted and starving. None of this will gel quickly. I need to eat, to separate myself from the crime scene with time. What to do? Eat, rest, let my subconscious worry the threads of this Gordian knot.

Life requires sustenance. Things take time. Enough philosophical thought, I stop for Ricobene's. Better living through greasy French fries.

I return to the boatyard with a very greasy bag. It contains a large

Breaded Steak Sandwich dipped in Marinara Sauce, a 'Big' (as opposed to large) fries and a large chocolate shake. In essence, hangover food.

I trudge up my concrete stairs, halting at my concrete landing to open my door. I fumble for my keys, only to discover the door open. Did I leave the TV on? I am getting goofy.

Stupid, stupid, stupid. I missed the tell-tales. Instead of falling sleepily across the threshold, I sweep into overdrive. I surge inward in a crouch, hands out. If I'm gonna die, I'll die trying.

There stands no raging-bull before me.

Jill lies at rest in my recliner. She lounges sensually looking up at me. Her eyes bear a droll expression as they sweep over my silly combat stance. In the background Neil Cavuto is addressing some pending disaster lurking just over the administration's horizon.

I look foolish, feel foolish.

Jill has been running. Her hair is rain-frizzy, her clothes gently rumpled. Wet, frizzy hair, slightly rumpled, languid beauty, my heart swells. I must be alive.

I can't believe I'm lusting for the woman after this afternoon. Am I just a self-centered old fart eyeballing a pretty young woman? Or am I fleeing the aura of death, through lust for Jill. She catches something in my eye. She smiles and straightens her clothes a smidgen. "Gonna splash me with that chocolate shake? I'll make you lick it off."

Seeking to regain my balance, "How did you get in here, Jill?"

"I climbed up the wall. Very poor security, typical imbedded newsman. You left the sliding doors open when you got drunk last night."

How does Jill know I got drunk? I set the food on the kitchen counter. The empty Black Barrel bottle rests on top of the garbage in the kitchen can.

I gaze about my domain. It has been officially straightened-up. Subjected to the inspection of a woman, and found wanting.

I glance up toward my loft, fearing Nadia is about to strut out in her undies.

Jill smiles, rising from the recliner. She takes the food from me, saying, "Don't worry, I checked. Nadia, the succubus, isn't up there waiting to assault your loins. I might."

Stunned, I ask, "Might, what?"

"Assault your loins."

Enjoying my consternation, Jill whispers, close to my ear, "Don't you wish?"

I'm ashamed, wanting exactly that.

Jill cuts off my musing, "After what I heard last night I went to the Greek; he told me about Mary Beth."

Carrying dinner, Jill walks to the counter, "You look awful, Galvan. Come sit here at the island. Tell me about what went on while we have dinner. I'm starving."

"Jill, I ordered one sandwich, fries, and a milk shake."

She smiles, "That's fine, I enjoy the idea of sharing your stuff. You, I'm not for sharing."

Jill goes all domestic, setting places on the counter. I strive to be miserable. I try to project a sour lack of desire for company. My mind drifts to the texture of her hair. I find myself wanting to touch Jill's hair. I do. She smiles across the counter to me. I smile back at her, losing the dour thing. What's going on? Mary Beth is dead. Gone.

Jill sits watching. Ricobene's serves a hammered flank steak, breaded and deep fried, then dipped on delivery in sweet marinara sauce on Italian. Jill cuts the sandwich, 1/3-2/3. Catching my eye, she picks her 1/3 sandwich. She takes a bite. Sauce spills a blob of red sauce from the opposite end of her sandwich onto mine.

Chewing happily, Jill gives me a big, closed mouth little girl smile. A thing nice to see.

She accuses me of making a mess. Now I'm a sloppy eater. I haven't eaten anything yet.

Lucky, I ordered a large everything. Jill has a healthy appetite.

People around me have the habit of being broken or destroyed. For her own good she has to go. Very quickly I've come to enjoy her proximity. Better I chase her off before she gets hurt."

It's bad not to enjoy being with Jill.

As I stare Jill raises her arms over her head to slip a scrunchy onto her hair, creating a pony tail, saving her hair from the marinara sauce. Cute with her hair pulled back.

She sits gazing skeptically back. I startle, I wasn't staring at her breasts. Now I discover I am. She shakes her head. I say, "I wasn't."

She says, "I noticed, pay attention."

Face it, Galvan, Jill is nice to see. If you chase her off, you won't be able to look at her and that is something you truly enjoy.

I still need to scare her off. How? I'll tell her about the murder, that should do what needs done. As a doctor she isn't squeamish, but she'll realize I am far more trouble than I'm worth.

I'll tell her about Mary Beth and the baby. If I don't someone else will. Time for her to abandon ship.

I relate the story to Jill. Bad choice, she becomes more interested.

Along the way, my inner-detective takes over. I've begun organizing facts and information in my head as I speak.

Time passes swiftly.

I look up.

Jill watches intently, her brow furrowed. I must have lost my place in our conversation.

Jill speaks, "The Greek said when you two went to Afghanistan, he thought you were out for vengeance. In time, he realized a difference, you were out for a reckoning."

She chewed on her straw studying me, "I'd guess you are one hard-to-live-with cowboy."

Seeing my opportunity, I say, "I am very hard to live with. Free advice, lady, stay away from crazy hermits along Bubbly-Creek. Flee immediately. I'm way too complicated. Mere proximity can be the cause of headache, confusion and stress."

Innocently playing deer in the headlights, Jill asks softly, "Are there lots of guys like you I should stay away from? I'll just bet you scare off everyone who lives with you."

I smile. "Nah, I scare them off before they get a chance to move in. They wilt and disappear when they discover the assumed bad boy is a cream-puff. Voosh, they're gone. When I run into them, they pretend we never met."

Jill says, "Voosh? What is Voosh? Do you flush them down your water slide into that spring out there? As what, virgin sacrifices? You must have long, lonely spells between Vooshes with the current virgin shortage."

I laugh. I shouldn't be laughing. Laughter lifts gloom. I was enjoying my gloom. Jill's wicked sense of humor breaks through.

Jill says, "According to the Greek, you are a three quarters Irish and one quarter Spanish-American Princess. I assume your Irish genes account for the gloom and doom. I just love your pregnant pauses. The dire warning stuff is so cute."

Jill snatches my chin turning me to her, "You don't scare me. I'm a big girl. I'm a Ryan, not a Milquetoast."

Jill changes the subject, or maybe does not, "I've spent a lot of time working with patients at the VA. Many experienced post traumatic stress disorders in Iraq or Afghanistan. Some are crazier than you are, Mr. Galvan. Not all of them, but most."

She says, "Detective Gennaro talked with the Greek. He told me that Mary Beth died three years ago. For you, she just died last night. He told me, you already carry a load of survivor's guilt and have seen a great deal of trauma from your injuries. Ten months of paralysis in the hospital wasn't meted out to you as just punishment for what you did in Afghanistan; it was a consequence of injury."

She adds, "Now you fine yourself for grieving for lost loved ones."

Flicking her long brown pony tail over her shoulder, she continues, "I know about the baby, Galvan. Gennaro told the Greek, he told me. If you want me to go, I'll go. If you want me stay, I'll stay. I'd like to stay, but it's your choice."

Her warm hazel eyes capture mine, as I say, "Stay. I went into a tail spin last night over Mary Beth. I got plastered. When I drink like that, I have crazy dreams. Last night's dream carried me back to Mary Beth. It then spun me into a recurring nightmare during which I always acquire my injuries, become hospitalized. When I got home, I told myself that I'd look up Mary Beth, to straighten out whatever had gone wrong. Last night I learned Mary Beth was a murder victim. This afternoon I discovered she was pregnant when she was murdered.

"I've been telling myself I was headed to her place to talk since I got back to Chicago. I never got there, always found someplace else to be. My grandmother often told me that the path to hell is paved with good intentions. It is. I put my visit off, wanted to recover before visiting. She was dead before I left the United States for the Kush. I've spent my life wandering around looking for my next goal to achieve, without a destination in mind."

Jill asks, "Did you love her?"

"We loved and hated each other on alternating days. We met in school. We dated. We were a couple. Later, partners on the tactical team. We were each capable of anticipating the other's next move on the street. We rarely were able to sync our feelings. Sad."

Jill asks again, "Did you love her?"

Angrily I admit, "We couldn't get in sync emotionally. We acted like kids."

"You're hedging. It is a simple question. Do you think you loved the woman?"

"Yes. But." I am unable to complete my sentence,

"You say 'Yes, but...' Neither ever carried the friendship into a relationship. Then it appears you did. Hard Question: Do you think the baby was yours?"

I say, "You need to know. I do think she was carrying my child. Gennaro submitted my DNA for cross reference. We'll know soon enough. How do you feel about that?"

With a skeptical look Jill says, "Why should I care? I don't need proof that you can make babies. I'm not doing anything like that soon. What? You got her pregnant before we met. I didn't know her. I know of her demise because, but we never met. Not my business." She raises an eyebrow as she regards me, "That was cute, I dug you and you came back fighting. Are you claiming a checkered past? You don't have to scare me. I offered to leave."

Jill rises from her chair, then looks to her forearm. My hand rests on her forearm as my thumb gently brushes her wrist. Jill raises her eyebrow, "Ah, you'd like me to stay, after all?"

I release her arm. "You're welcome in my home. I'd like you to stay. I've enjoyed being with you. I enjoy speaking with you. I enjoy looking at you."

After a moment, I lower my chin breaking eye contact. "It might not be wise for you to be around me. I'm a few bricks short a full load. There is a murderer out there. The FBI likes me for a suspect in a murder case. It might not be a good career move for a young doctor."

Jill enjoys my discomfort. "Are your intentions honorable?"

I answer, "Mostly. Such nice legs. I may be overcome with lust at any moment.

"I've noticed. You have possibilities yourself, mister."

On impulse, my lips move to Jill's. She moves lightly with me. We share an embrace. We move gently, each exploring the other, a getting to know you kiss. Jill glides into my lap as our embrace continues. My hand slides to her hip.

Jill rises smoothly from my lap.

She laughs brightly, "That confirms my suspicions. You like girls in general and me in particular. Nice to meet you."

Jill continues, she straightens her running clothes, "I'll have to keep an eye on you. Watch those hands, mister." She laughs, "Don't look so crestfallen. It isn't time, yet. I wouldn't have slid into your lap if I wasn't interested in sitting on your lap."

Jill steps away, clearing the remains of our meal. Why do I find myself aroused by her abrupt domesticity? I focus on her intently. For better or worse, I'm falling for her.

She pauses with a swish of her ponytail between my knees, a hand on either side of my face, to say, "I like you, Galvan. A girl has something to work with."

I gently grasp her hips. Drawing her to me.

She sweeps my hands away, laughing, "Enough, you're like an ocpusa. I suggest we do something other than wrestle. I don't know you well enough to let those hands near me just yet."

I ask, "What is an ocpusa?"

She replies, smiling gaily as she escapes my grasp. "My tiny niece can't say octopus.

Jill walks to the bow rack to pick up the bow she handled on her previous visit, "You promised to show me how you shoot. Show me."

Being a large, not overly bright fish, I rise to the bait.

Confident in my manly skill, I choose and string a brown recurve. I lay my strung bow like a set of elk horns back onto the bow rack above a work bench. I select two sheaves of arrows from the shelf under the bow rack.

A sheaf of arrows is twenty-four by 'Olde English' reckoning. Two dozen should be more than enough. She'll get sore and tired before we fire a dozen, but by giving Jill the chance at a full sheave I duck chauvinism charges while allowing her to make me look good.

I set an arrow-sheaf in front of Jill, roll two X-frame target stands into each target lane before the south wall. A river-reed target bale, is set on each stand below the loft balcony.

The targets are beer 'barrel' sized cardboard cement-form tubes, filled end-on with river cane reeds. The reed filled tubes absorb arrow shock, while saving the fletching-feathers.

I tell Jill, "I made the archery tackle, the bows, fletched the arrows, and the Flemish-twist bow strings as therapy for my hands when we got back.

"This bow is different. It was my father's. I learned to laminate bows from fiber-glass and cherry-wood when I was a child."

My father and I then baked each bow. We pressed the laminate strips in a framing jig which sandwiched them tightly together with a sealed, inflated fire hose. We baked the sandwiched forms inside a coffin-oven. Baking was accelerated with the light bulbs. A thermostat provided an emergency dead-man switch. The epoxy stunk. The stink seeped into my mother's kitchen. "

"Mom was furious. We mollified her by making her a white recurve that Christmas. My bow draws at forty-six pounds, which explains the roman numeral and plus mark on my grip. The draw- weight on your bow is about 30 lbs., if you draw the string to your ear."

Jill steps through the arch between her bow and string. She strings her bow, as I had mine. Jill may not be the novice to archery I anticipated. Few do this stuff, especially women.

Jill points to her face. "Galvan, I'm up here. Don't stand there staring at my bottom. Archery time, shoot arrows, boy."

I laugh in surprise. Jill has the capacity to pull me back from the edge? She makes me want to be alive. Since returning to Chicago, my mind has wandered from place to place. With Jill I feel grounded, smiling and enjoying her company.

The loss of Mary Beth weighs on my soul. I need to know what happened. My thoughts meander through a world of what-ifs. What if Mary Beth told me she was pregnant? What if I quit my Afghan folly to be with her? What if I'd come to that door that Friday night, could I have stopped him? What if I'd just stopped those, giving her time, could she have stopped? What if I can't find this bastard? What if I find him, then what?

After just a few minutes with Jill, I know I have to find my way out of this oblivion. I have to escape stasis. I need to figure out what needs to be done. Jill gives me a way forward. Am I rising steadily, following a thin string of bubbles toward the surface?

Maybe I'm just using the last of my air, only to break through into a cold, dark airless void. What a nice surprise that would be. Maintain discipline, I may get somewhere, or not. If I panic I'll definitely lose my mind. Let my mind wander, I may remain hopelessly lost.

To break the spell, I step to the firing line. I draw an arrow from the sheaf.

As I turn to my own bow, I observe Jill spin an arrow by the nook, positioning the paired feathers spread at the arrow shelf with the odd-man-out feather perpendicular to the bow. She knows, surprise.

I relax, time to teach. As I release my arrows, I speak calmly, so as to reassure Jill in an intimidating new environment, "Jill, this all has a natural flow. It is a kind of by the number(s) thing. Fit the arrow nook to the string, resting jaws of the nock on that brass ball clamped to the string, as you lift the bow and arrow. Hold the string above and below the nock. Nice and easy, draw to the ear, sight down the shaft, release. Do that a few times you'll feel right at home with a bow."

I drone on, "Don't worry about missing the target. This is an old building. The wall is made of oak logs that must be a hundred years old. The arrows have field tips, they'll stick without damaging the wall."

Eventually I shut up, so as to allow Jill to become at home with her bow.

I get into the rhythm of my own draw and release. After a time, I reach down for another arrow to find empty space. I look at my target. I'd placed most of my arrows well.

I turn to Jill to encourage her shooting, "Go ahead and try a few more shots. Relax, there's plenty of time."

I glance toward Jill. She's gone. She isn't shooting, because she out-shot me. Behind me there's a popping sound. Jill is strolling from the kitchen, opening a cold frosted Perrier bottle. Jill's arrows found a home in her barrel target before I finished.

I may be immersed in a cloud of burnt ego.

Jill sits, posture erect. She's smirks a little. Was my long-winded lecture funny?

A twinkle in her eye, she asks, "How'd I do, Teach?"

Embarrassed, I say, "I thought you wanted me to show you how to shoot a bow?"

Jill laughs brightly, "Wrong, what I asked for was you to show me how you shot. I've been drawing a bow since I was five. I wondered if you could draw a bow, or if your fancy bow range was a decoration to impress women."

"Just women?" I ask.

Jill is coy, saying, "You told me you weren't gay on my last visit. I discovered how happy you were to see me when I sat on your lap."

I ask, "I take it you have demonstrated the foolishness of male overconfidence before?"

"This isn't my first rodeo, cowboy. But you were so easy."

"Okay, cowgirl, let's gather our arrows. Want to see who rides best?"

"Oh goodie, save a horse, ride a cowboy."

Jill's gaming me. Looking at her it's hard to concentrate. Jill enjoys my consternation.

We shoot two more sheaves of arrows. I'm more competitive.

Falling ambient light announces the dinner hour. Jill glances at the wall clock, startles and says, "I'm off to work." She reaches the door, stops, saunters back hands on hip. She stops close in front of me. We stand toe to toe. She says, "I need a night out, take me to Gennaro and Emma's wedding? You need a date, women often think you are gay."

I gently place my hands on Jill's hips, drawing her to me. "Gennaro told me I have to bring you. If I don't go, his bride will drag me. I don't drag well. Be my guest?"

I need to explain, "It's a weird kind of wedding. In part it's a 'cop' wedding. There will also be a bunch of rich people, leavened by the bride's secret service cadre. Maybe some SEALS and DEA people. There will also be some local color."

Jill asks, "Local color? Is that a cheap joke at Gennaro's expense because he's a Black?"

I respond, "I'm shocked. You think Gennaro's black? Whoa. We're not talking melanin content here. Gennaro doesn't see himself as black. In his mind, Gennaro is Calabrese. The Calabrian Mob is known as the N'drangheta. Gennaro's Dad is a man of respect in the community. His father is a presence if not a participant."

Trying again, I bow to waist level, "I would be honored if you were to be my guest at the Gennaro wedding. What I'm telling you is to be prepared for people acting out. There will probably be overwound watches just back from overseas. Some may be tighter wound than I."

Jill says, "I haven't met anyone lately, more interesting than you, Galvan. Can I see your suits? I have an outfit in mind, but it won't work with the wrong suit."

"I have suits, I just need to go get them."

"Good, I'll come with, we can save time."

"Jill, my suits are at my parent's home. I haven't been there since I left for Afghanistan. If I walk in the door with a girlfriend on my arm. They'll have heart attacks."

Jill places palms flat on my chest, giving me a light shove, "Girlfriend? Do you think your mom will think I'm pregnant?"

"Why would she think that? Don't we have to have sex first?"

"Mothers are like that, sex or no sex. They all assume we want their little boy."

She continues, "The Greek went to them before he brought you back. The psychs were worried about the way you were refusing to interact with others in Bethesda. Apparently, you were refusing to speak with them."

I shrug. "Psych wanted to play croquet in my head. I didn't like the sound of the wooden balls clacking around inside my skull. They were convinced that I couldn't have survived a year of isolation inside my head without benefit of their acumen. I was surrounded by Freudians in search of a sexual pathology to analyze. It wasn't about sex. I'm stubborn, I survived in spite of them. Psych held onto me like a favorite plaything. Listening to them made me crazier than isolation."

Jill says, "Psych was afraid you'd act out badly if you were allowed to leave too early. The Greek took custody of you with the help of a doctor named Braxton. Psych talked your parents into slow and steady. With the Greek's help, eased you back into society. Time to go see Mom and Dad, Galvan. If you ever get a girlfriend you can introduce her to them. I'm going with you for moral support. We don't want Mom and Dad strangling your crabby ass."

I surrender. "And to see my suits? Are you free Saturday afternoon? I lost some weight. I may need to see a tailor. Maybe, we could go early enough to be invited to dinner. I'll talk to Gaby to get you a night off."

"Gaby gave me the wedding off. Dorie's working for me that Saturday. In exchange, I have to work dinner this coming Saturday. Can you get me back in time for my shift?"

"Planning ahead?"

"Girl Scouts and cow girls have to be prepared, Galvan."

I place a hand to her waist as she steps to the door, "Save a horse, ride a cowboy?"

Jill nods with a languid smile, looking back over her shoulder, "If you are very lucky."

The Greek Joe is descending the hall stairs. He stops at my landing to greet Jill. She tells him about our trip to my parents' house.

The Greek gives me a skeptical fish-eye, "Finally getting your shit together?"

Jill asks him, "Give me a ride to Gaby's? I'm late for work."

He says, "Sssh, he doesn't know about us."

Jill takes his arm, "Then we won't tell him. They start down the stairs.

Late, I think to offer her the ride.

She laughs, "No. You need to take a long shower. Preferably a cold one, all the exercise has you sweaty."

"What's with the 'horses and cowboys'?" said Joe.

Jill snaps as my door closes, "None of your own bees-wax tall, dark and handsome. Take me away to safety, Galvan is feeling frisky."

I sprint to my deck and glance around the brick corner-wall at the parking area.

In the lot, Jill strides arm-in-arm with Greek to his car. She lays her head on his shoulder after saying something to him, Joe hugs her. Laughing, Jill shoves him away.

A gurgling sound emits from the direction of our spring, drawing my attention. I'm mesmerized. At the center the spring is up-surging, rising above the pool's surface.

Sixth sense, I sense human movement, a man is across the inlet in the bushes. I've seen him out there before. Now, he's intently watching the Greek and Jill. The small motion of the spin-casting rod being reeled in quick spurts caught my eye

A quick serpentine glance sweeps my way.

He shrugs at me, finishes his in-reel, and attaches his over-large hook to the lowest eyelet above the reel. A worm wiggles on the hook. The man watches. The man gathers his gear, turns and departs to the south in the direction of last night's playlot. The impaled worm writhes.

I'm disinclined to touch the five eyed fish that come out of the Chicago River. Rumor has it they dumped the bricks from the Manhattan Project's nuclear pile along here somewhere.

Are worms the proper bait for Uranium irradiated, five eye carp? I haven't run into a guy who's gets sadistic with worms before. What should one do with weird guys who lurk in the vicinity of playlots?

I look back to the lot, the Greek has driven off.

I return my gaze to the point, worm torturer gone. Curious. Dusk. Night still comes quickly in early spring. I douse the sail-loft lights. I change into loose, well-worn black jeans, a charcoal grey hoodie and black ball cap. Last, I step into well-worn black-suede Morrell Continuums--suede absorbs light.

Hooded up, I've become a shadow.

I clip a small Protec flashlight inside my jeans pocket.

Being hopelessly paranoid, I slide a black plastic IWB holster onto my belt where it rests comfortably concealed in my jeans. The holster contains my Springfield-XD .45. With a round in the chamber and 10-rounds of .45 caliber, 230 grain, core-bonded, Ranger hollow points staggered in the magazine it should suffice. Unless I'm attacked by a rogue elephant.

I walk from shadow to shadow until I reach the east side of my deck. There, I trace the path Jill ascended. Not exactly Mt. Everest, but looks slippery for my descent. I don't like heights, but I clamber down the wall anyway, trying to stay out of view of the fisherman's former perch.

I walk the inland curve of the river-walk toward the playlot. Our inlet terminates short of the playlot. The park is empty. Street lights just coming on. I lean my back against the honeycombed climbing structure. Cool to be a kid, except for the presence of worm torturers. I study the weeded area of the point, searching for a foot path among the tumbleweeds.

Other than a mild breeze and the gurgle of the upsurge in the inlet, there is silence. No one is out here. I scan the park around me. Nobody.

I stroll softly to a nearby break in the tumbleweed wall.

Entering the brush I find a small path winding through the thick weeds to the inlet. There's a small mound of dirt. The mound faces our boatyard.

Another wider path parallels the river. Behind the tumbleweed wall sits a concealed parking area? In the lee of the tumbleweeds, I find muddy tire tracks. Seems my new acquaintance hides his car in the bushes.

Tread shape and wheel base seems to indicate a small cross-over sat here. The guy backed in here through the fresh mud from last night's rain. Plant damage indicates he backed in carefully. Then he drove out suddenly, spitting mud on his perch in the bushes.

I follow the tire tracks back inland. I find the spot where his cross-over jumped the curb, His right rear tire left the impression of a large unique scar on its tread on entry and exit. A small muddy pool at the curb-line is fogged, indicating his recent departure.

I use my yellow small pocket-tape measure as a scale to take photos with my phone of the ruts and the fisherman's sparse perch. I have a pocket tape-measure, I'm becoming my dad. The fisherman used an overturned bucket for a seat. Did he notice that it is a used roof tar bucket? Tar bucket contents are smelly, messy and indelible. The top has blue jean stud impressions in tar on its closed lid. He sat in the tar. Is he paying attention?

Science time, I measure impressions in the mud around the bucket for shoe width and length. I take scaled photos of the clearest foot-prints with my cell. The soles look like Navy Oxfords with glued on Vibram replacement half-soles. Haven't seen those since I was a re-cruit some years ago.

Our watcher isn't a smoker, no scattered butts. He is a eucalyptus cough-drop addict. Twenty wrappers are scattered in the mud around his bucket. With enough eucalyptus cough drops maybe he didn't smell the tar?

It appears he's gone for the night. I flash the tiny 10,000 lumens flashlight over his hiding place in the bushes. Nothing catches my eye. I walk back to our building, pondering events. He's been watching us for days, but I only just saw him. If I'm going to stay alive for the sum-mer, I need to pay attention. Hopefully I can get my head out of my ass before it gets blown away.

8

ROLLING THOSE DICE

J ill called at dawn to remind me of 'the Match'. That is so frantically so not-Jill, Then, I'm not matching, she is. I'm so sensitive I forgot what day it was today. I made myself ready, getting us to the required location on time. It's mid-morning. I'm sitting in a bar with a large group of very nervous people. I have awaited jury verdicts in murder trials with a lower level of hysteria.

I have listened. I am getting the gist of things. This is a matter of life and death. We're all gonna die. The entire community of fourth year medical students throughout the known universe is participating in this single 'match'. We're all gonna die.

Someone has explained that prior to 'match day', med-students everywhere have interviewed for residencies in hospitals in the field in which they most want to practice.

Each student takes up his or her entire pile of chips that they earned in twenty years of education. Then one steps up to the roulette table and places one's entire poke on a single numeral embossed on the baize table cloth. Then we sit and watch the roulette wheel spin.

Beyond that, these medical students are frozen in a world unknown to mere mortals. Things are more complicated, each student hedges with multiple side bets on 2nd-choice residencies that will form the rest of their lives. The air is indeed charged.

Jill has a friend named Paula who is destined for OB/GYN (obstetrics and gynecology). Paula, who as a Mormon is a non-drinker, sits before me drinking her third St. Pauli Girl (German beer must be non-alcoholic.).

Paula earnestly explains to me, "OB/GYN involves the care and maintenance of women's baby-making equipment." Paula gestures toward her lower abdomen, helping me comprehend where that is in the female form; I always wondered where they kept the fun stuff.

I restrain myself from inquiring if the equipment location might vary from girl to girl. Now as I feel better for having the technical issues explained. I wonder where Jill went. I'd sure like to show her what I've learned today.

Jill set the tone early, by informing friends I was a 'cop'. Ergo, her friends speak slowly and loudly to me, as all cops are apparently slow witted and deaf.

As we await developments, Paula has a growing string of empty St. Pauli Girls martialed before her. She has several times explained that a good Mormon girl doesn't drink. I think today she is enjoying not being good Mormon girl.

Paula is in a, hopefully platonic relationship, with Fitz, whom she describes as a 'real' Irish guy. She asks me skeptically if Galvan is a 'real' Irish name. I say it was, she's skeptical.

Fitz plays Gaelic Football, which 'Fitz' tells me, "It's a lot like Rugby, for sure. But a bit rough. You should play, Boyo. A lovely sport." Knowing a little of Gaelic Football, I demure, "I've become attached to my teeth."

Fitz born in the 'Old Sod'. His Irish brogue can be cut with a knife. Which seems odd, seeing 'Fitz' is a petro-chemical engineer just finishing a Masters in petroleum science.

Her fellow communicants describe Paula as very smart when Paula gets 'matched' quickly in OB/GYN in the distant land of Nebraska. Fitz asks me, "Would that be a wee bit west of Chicago, now?"

I had to think about that a moment. Did they move Nebraska while I was gone?

On being informed I am Irish Catholic, Paula and Irene break in with a number of compelling 'Catholic' questions which are in need of immediate answers.

Irene is not a good Mormon girl. Rather Irene is Jewish. In addition to her medical degree Irene she has a doctoral degree in earth science. Irene is older than all of us. While in medical school, she has been teaching earth science at undergraduate level.

Apparently, the ladies are unfamiliar with Catholicism. They do not wish to offend, but they have a few opinions. They crowd Fitz and me, seeking the secrets of Papism.

Our papist eccentricities seem to bestir inquiring minds' need for knowledge.

Paula asks bluntly, "What do Catholics sacrifice?" She uses the two finger air quotation marks," The 'sacrifice thing' means what animal is killed on your altars during rituals? You call it a 'Mass', does everyone kill something or just the men?

Fitz sits behind the ladies stone-faced, watching me. Fitz winks.

Ahhh, a fellow-traveler.

I attempt to answer their questions to the best of my ability, "These days we use a single dove, but in times of scarcity a pigeon will work."

They swing to Fitz. He nods, sagely, "Ta sacrifice varies. At home. we're more traditional. Sheep and bullocks went out during the second Vatican Conference."

Paula and Irene nod sagely. Beer encourages nodding, as one becomes ever more sage.

I continue, "So, because of the large number of doves available in this country, we use the white ones."

Fitz suggests that, "We use dah morning doves, don't yah know. We get up to catch before Mass. Yanks put on airs. They can affard the damn white ones. I say too showy by half."

It's a good thing Fitz has recovered his Irish brogue. If the petroleum engineer had lost his brogue, Paula might have had to operate here on the table to save him.

Fitz slips his arm around Paula's waist, his hand rubs Paula's right flank companionably. Paula does have a shapely flank. Paula leans, kitten like, into Fitz. I certainly hope their residence arrangements remain as platonic as Paula suggested in her 'good Mormon-girls don't do' monologue. What with her taste for St. Pauli girls, I have my doubts. Then, I know less of things Mormon than the ladies know of a quality sacrifice.

Irene changes the subject, switching to something really significant, "How can you stand to write all those parking tickets? Is that green ring from your high school?"

Irene has many more questions that need answering immediately. Apparently, Paula has lost interest in our conversation as she squirms into Fitz's lap for a rest. Now, she is looking for a warm spot. What a nice man, offering himself up to succor the poor lady.

I respond, "In homicide we limit ourselves to five or ten parking tickets a day. You know, what with all the dead bodies and what not."

Fitz nods sagely. Irene nods sagely. Paula is warming her hands in Fitz's lap.

I realize these are Jill's friends, so I better cut back on my sarcasm, "I went to Marist. My high school ring there was a red stone. This ring is from grad school."

Fitz notes, "It's a whopper, Boyo. Would you be usin' it to drive nails?"

"Funny, where I'm from it is known as a 'door knocker'. It came from a military academy."

Paula, although somewhat preoccupied, wonders, "Why did your family make you go to military school? Were you a discipline problem, Galvan? How did you become a cop, if you went to reform school?"

I startle. Jill slips up behind me, wrapping her arms around my chest. She rests her chin on my right shoulder. Her breath is warm on my cheek, as are her breasts against my back in the air-conditioned bar-room.

Jill was listening to our conversation, so she says, "Here's the deal. He has a law degree, but doesn't practice law. He has a masters in terrorism studies, but hasn't shot any lately. He builds wooden sailboats, but I haven't seen one."

Jill bumps me with her hips then chest from behind, shoving me forward, "He claims, once upon a time, he was a foreign correspondent in Afghanistan, but I think he was a spy."

I ask, "How'd you know about Norwich?"

Shaking her head Jill says, "That was a tough one, Galvan."

She lifts my ring-hand to the light. "It's written in huge letters on your big ring. Can I have it?"

I offer a deal, "Only if I can see that dance routine."

She hugs me again, "Be good, we'll see. Maybe later."

She gives me the fish-eye. "Funny you should remember that one little tidbit of conversation, Galvan. Are your impure thoughts all that brings you around?"

"I'm a fervid patron of the arts. But the impure thoughts encourage me. I'm also drawn to your form."

Jill slides a palm to my forehead, "Fevered maybe, but not about art, honey."

Jill frees me from her bear-hug, stepping back. She spins my stool around to her. She gazes into my eyes. The corners of her lips rise slightly. I receive a tight, barely perceptible leer from Jill, disguised as an innocent glance.

Jill says, "You stay here, secret agent man. Rest, gather your strength. Don't tease my friends."

Jill strolls blithely off, the walk holds my attention.

Jill wanders back to the match table, studying the screen. She stops abruptly, noting the latest entry. Upset?

She stands lost in thought. I walk up behind her, returning her bear-hug at waist level, asking, "Trouble, kid?"

Jill sighs, relaxes her back against my chest. Jill is listening intently. Comfortable, I rest my chin on the top of her head, enjoying the scent of her hair. My hands are chastely wrapped about her tummy, above the waist and below the breast. One hot stud, be I.

Jill places her hands over mine, sealing my grasp in place over her abdomen. Cradling my palms to her abdomen is suddenly erotic on many levels. I absorb tension from her body. Jill relaxes against me. "I didn't get ER, not in Seattle or Dallas."

Trying for a neutral tone I ask, "Is that good or bad?" I can't admit it yet, but I'm not looking forward to Jill leaving town.

She tells me, abruptly, "Wait."

I distantly hear, "Jill Ryan, internal medicine."

I murmur in her ear, "Good or bad?"

"It appears I'll be doing a residency in Chicago for the next three years. I'll be in adult medicine. Medicine, not surgery. A lot of deductive and inductive reasoning. I like the idea. I'll be in town. Come visit me?"

Jill whip quick, spins in my arms to me. She presses herself to me, reaching her hand up to caress my cheek. She reaches up grasping my face, tilting my head down. She locks on my eyes, saying, "Good or bad?"

I pull her hips to me saying, "Good. Best news I've heard lately."

Smiling brightly, Jill kisses me for a long minute. She hasn't kissed me in public before.

Surreptitiously, she glances about to see who's watching. Her eyes go serious. She edges back.

Jill stares up at me, probing. Is she wondering what I am thinking?

I'm a guy. I'm thinking about her eyes, the warmth of her body pressed to mine. I'm falling for her.

With a knowing grin, Jill breaks contact.

Control yourself, Galvan. Jill is an attractive woman attending a mandatory event with me as her date. This is a required professional informally formal function. Jill has earned her place in the line-up. I screwed up on that issue by being overly careful with Mary Beth. I need to proceed cautiously. If given the chance with Jill, I don't want to walk away willingly.

Jill's joining the doctor club. She's entered their hierarchy at start. Getting her chance, involving privation and effort I likely will never understand. Her effort to arrive here far exceeds my efforts to get myself back here. I best go easy. Maintaining one's status in hierarchies, requires adhering to rules and proper decorum.

Jill is the only stake I have in this crap game. People see me as Jill's traffic cop. Friends and colleagues are watching to see how Jill behaves today with her traffic-cop. The peanut gallery will gladly render judgment on her.

How she acts, how I treat her, will affect how they treat her.

I need to behave. Jill needs to be in the driver's seat. The ball and court are hers.

As a result, I decide to concentrate on being good. I make nice conversation with people who think me to be both deaf and slow. Jill circulates, congratulating some, consoling others.

I'm able to position myself as an outsider in the group. A consistent rule in life suggests that about the time you feel comfortable gawking, shit happens. Thus, I meet Evanoff. He has close-cut, curly hair. Evanoff was born to be annoying. He matched early in a psychiatric residency. They say that indicates he's smart. As a psychiatric resident he quickly seeks me out. He glances repeatedly between Jill and me. The boy is up to no good.

Several times he tries to enter conversations in which I am engaged. I don't want to play, I walk off, he follows. As I depart each time, Evanoff tries to engage Jill in conversation. Each time, he reaches to touch her. At each contact Jill rebuffs him, breaking contact.

An unrequited admirer? Who would guess?

Evanoff wears horn rimmed glasses which are perched on the tip of his nose, an odd thing in a guy of 25. Is he seeking to display academic gravitas?

As Evanoff flits about, he removes his glasses. When he gets a classmate to converse, he chews on the ear-piece of his glasses. His posture indicates he is holding that person in judgment. He has few takers for his conversations.

I watch his eyes, which tell the lie to his pretense. He merely waits for a chance to snap back in attack as people respond with their view of his premise. He's just looking for a fight.

Evanoff is using his glasses like a blade to fence with his opponents. Removing his glasses, putting the earpiece in his mouth is his en garde position. On a classmate's response, he lunges forward in a riposte, driving his slobbery ear-piece at their eyes. Having made his point Evanoff flees each encounter. I think Evanoff the psychiatrist is a nut.

My grandfather, Silky, wore horn-rimmed glasses. His glasses were also stage props. Everything comes back, even 1950s prescription eyewear props.

I glance across the room to Jill. She's watching me. Evanoff has timed his latest conflict perfectly. As he flees his most recent encounter, Evanoff collides with me, blissfully watching Jill as he stumbles into my space.

Out of the blue, he asks rhetorically, "As a detective, do you feel there is any chance that a family which produced a serial killer might have to be resigned to producing subsequent compulsive malefactors."

He falls back into his en garde position, off come the glasses, earpiece plops into mouth, as Evanoff says, "Either in the same generation, or 'lineally, so to speak."

To annoy him I respond, "Sure it could be some genetic inherited compulsion, if it isn't learned behavior. Who knows, see one, do one, teach one? Right doc?"

They don't like to be called doc.

I'm perplexed, could Evanoff be the only one in the room who has seen through my traffic cop disguise? Darn.

Here it comes, Evanoff lunges in for my eyes with the slobbery ear piece. He's saying something about nature and nurture. I brush the outside of his wrist from my face as I tap the inside of his wrist to release his radial nerve. Evanoff's wrist folds inward. His thumb, index and second fingers go numb, releasing his grip on the glasses.

I catch his glasses as they fall.

Oblivious, Evanoff verbally continues his attack, informing me, "My research has not established that cases of lineal or familial serial killers exist. What say you, Old-Boy?"

I must be Old-Boy.

Jill is sitting across the table from me, eyes brimming with innocence, as she watches my interaction with Evanoff.

He still doesn't realize I have taken his glasses, as I respond, "Of course, I don't have your experience, Doctor Evanoff. You're probably right. I did meet a father and son pair. There was also a weird grouping containing two brothers and a cousin. But there, the cousin was raised as a third brother."

Evanoff appears shocked, both by my assertion and his lack of chewy glasses as he tries to fall back to his en garde position, only to realize he has lost his foil. He stares at his empty hand, then looks around the floor for his glasses. I take the opportunity to slip the folded glasses into Fitz's half full Guinness glass.

I blithely continue, "With father and son. Dad was a rapist who got caught because his victim lived to identify him. Afterwards, Papa killed all his subsequent victims, following his release from prison."

Evanoff jumps back into his argument, forgetting the glasses as he asserts, "Obviously the pater-familias exhibited superior intellect by his concealment behavior. Recognizing the existence of his uncontrollable compulsion, became ashamed, and made a reasoned value judgment to hide his unacceptable weakness."

Nodding at his own brilliance, Evanoff says, "Yes. I would hazard that was the case in the instance you cite. Startling, isn't it? It must terrify you to confront those of higher intellect who are among these apex predators you attempt to catch. How do you cope?"

I say, "When we met, I hit him in the head with a honeydew melon."

Evanoff asks, "Why?"

I respond, "It was there."

"To what purpose?" asks Evanoff with a smirk.

I say off-hand, "To clear his sinuses, knock him on his ass."

He asks, "Do you think that accomplished something?"

I say, "I assume so. He was fleeing, waving his arms over his head, screaming, 'Don't let the police get me.' The melon knocked him down and it shut him up."

Seeking to recover his initiative Evanoff lunges in absence of blade, saying, "Your man, Old Boy, sounds remarkably like Loeb and Leopold speaking reverently of the Nietzschean Ubermensch, who blithely wanders a world with no God, deciding the fate of each deserving Untermensch. Superior intellect excused any behavior. Always consider the crime from the view of the smart one, detective."

I say in response, "Or perhaps, Nate and Dick were just reminiscing for shits and giggles, not even trying to justify the murder of their unfortunate 14-year-old cousin Bobby.

I continue, "Eventually your pater-familias and I established our priorities. I asked him about the dead girls. He got all dreamy, saying they were too loud."

Jill's eyes are incandescent, watching my interplay with Evanoff.

Going on in the interest of annoying Evanoff, I add, "Later I arrested his son for sex crimes and aggravated battery."

Not caring for an answer, Evanoff asks, "Was it a date rape, maybe a little rough handling, Hmmmm?"

"No, Junior stabbed each of the women with a rusty steak knife several times. You know, those serrated knives with black Bakelite handles. Sonny enjoyed stabbing the girls during the assault."

Having lost his blade, Evanoff puts hand to chin saying contemplatively, "Rusty knife, you say. No doubt, a poor man using what came to hand. Like the melon thing you know. What, just another common bumbler seeking something handy, Old-Boy?"

I say in answer, "No. We talked, Sonny mentioned he loved raping young girls in white shirts and black pants and stabbing them with his rusty steak knife, just like Dad's."

Evanoff snarls, "One instance of pathology in a population does not a theory make. Why white shirts and black pants? Fetish?"

I am reaching my limit with Evanoff, as I say. "The girls were middle-schoolers. He hunted for the uniforms they wore. He was after young girls from private schools because those girls were from more sheltered backgrounds and often terrified of him. Terror thrilled him."

Seeking to end our conversation, I add, "The semi-fraternal bunch all killed prostitutes. But one brother killed three girls riding bicycles after school and then attacked a small woman wearing her teenage daughter's school clothes at the laundromat. The mother put on her daughter's uniform as she washed her own clothes. Mother stabbed the lad in the groin."

Jill walks away with a smile. Evanoff apparently annoys many.

Fitz examines his glass, containing Evanoff's glasses. Evanoff reaches for Fitz's eye-wear. Fitz palms Evanoff's arm away. Fitz says, "Guinness Stout on tap, fresh glass, Boyo. Come back with my stout, ya can have the swim googles back. Chop, chop, BOYO, I'm thirsty."

Evanoff scurries off toward the bar.

That was fun, but I need to escape before numb-nuts comes back.

Wow, the deep thinker didn't even ask how his glasses got in Fitz's stout.

Abruptly, an awful shiver runs up my spine. My eyes sweep the room for a source. I coil, ducking in anticipation of an attack. Suddenly, things ain't fun.

Fitz is staring at me strangely, as he asks, "Someone just step on your grave, Boyo?"

I refrain from an answer, shrugging. I think, someone, somewhere did. Bad jolt, that.

I make my respects to the table, then I go looking for Jill. When things wind down, I take Jill by Uber to Smith and Wollinsky's along the Chicago River at Marina City. Jill clapped her hands in surprise when I walked her past the Hard Rock Café. The afternoon sun warmed our evening on the patio over the river.

The steaks were much appreciated, the wine good. Busy day, after dinner Jill announced she was exhausted. We wandered back to my SRX. I take her home, Jill's home not mine. At the door, I receive a light kiss. I do not receive an invitation up for coffee. Didn't anticipate one.

9

AN EARLY MOTHER'S DAY

I sit, waiting for Jill in Gaby's barroom.

Jill flew by me maybe 45 minutes ago. I received one of those looks men have received from women since the beginning of time. She told me she was running late, and she would be right down.

She mentioned something about needing a minute to freshen up. Then she was gone.

The Greek sits smirking down the bar from me watching me squirm. He finds me amusing. "Bet you wish you went to see them sooner. I won't say I told you so, but I did. Maybe they won't kill you in front of Jill, but I could be wrong.

After a long time sensing I've been hiking in mush, life is quickly picking up speed. Time to return to the real world. I can't hide in my sail loft much longer by myself thinking. I have to get out there, or I will never get out of there. There are things that need doing. Good things and bad things. Hiding like a crazy uncle in my attic won't get much done.

The Greek is wearing his purple Northwestern sweatshirt, boat shoes and jeans. He says he'll be sailing out of Burnham Harbor in our 'nutty professor' boat. I bet I know who's crewing.

The barometer is high today. A steady breeze is sweeping off the lake, carrying the scent of that giant immensity of fresh water. That scent draws people to the lakefront like fish to the base of a waterfall.

Chicago spreads in a long ribbon, north-south on the west shore of Lake Michigan 100 miles all the way to Milwaukee. Summer may be just over the horizon, or it could snow.

I have heard visitors, new to town, refer to the Michigan ocean. It's not an ocean. One whiff of that breeze tells you there is no salt in its depths. Trillions of gallons of fresh water has a scent of its own.

A tall glass of Guinness Stout appears before me as if by magic.

The bartender, Karl, regularly spends his days ignoring me. The end of a day must be coming, Karl just placed the Guinness before me, unbidden. He beams beatifically down on at me. A smiling Karl is a scary sight to behold.

Gaby, her hair in loose disarray, sashays into the bar with a navy-blue sweater knotted about her neck. She wears a long sleeved white and red striped top over tiny khaki cargo shorts. Looking all of twenty.

Gaby stands a statuesque five feet zero, in stark white canvas deck shoes. Tiny and cute, the Greek's crew has arrived.

Gaby hands him a hooded Patagonia jacket. Pinioning us in place with her pointed index finger, Gaby instructs me, "Have Jill back by 7:30, Galvan. She's got the bar by herself tonight. Tell Nicky and Deuce I, we send our best."

Gaby runs an arm through the Greek's. They exit, as he calls back, "Take it easy, but take it, kid. Remember, you're taking the girl to meet your parents. She'll use every second she has to get ready. Sit down, take a deep breath, drink your beer."

I turn back to the bar. Karl winks. Karl is having fun. Karl is scaring me.

Jill steps into the barroom, from somewhere. She strides purposefully up to me, lifts my Guinness to her lips delicately sipping. Her eyes reflect internal debate. Deciding, she takes another sip.

What a weird feeling, Jill is drinking from my glass. Carl smiles at her, nods to me. Indication of proprietary interest? One can hope. Jill is meeting my parents. We're staying for dinner. I feel civilized. How strange?

In the car, Jill sits primly beside me, without a word. Perhaps meeting a guy's parents induces terror, terror inducing speechlessness? She seems poised and erect in her posture. Nerves, for sure. This afternoon has that vector-feel. I could have faced this homecoming myself, but ever the coward, I face it by bringing a woman home with me to deflect judgment. Maybe Jill came along for the ride out of some sense of pity.

I've been bouncing between choices: life or death. Is taking Jill to my parents' home my vote for life or just an effort to defuse their scorn for my behavior? Or am I merely overthinking?

When you come to a fork in the road, should you take it? I'm planning for my life based on Yogi Berra baseball metaphors, I have lost my mind. Or I might just be in love. Nah, I have more sense than that. Maybe?

Glancing toward Jill, I notice she has acquired a faint tan Guinness Stout mustache. I offer her my new, Egyptian cotton handkerchief. I know it's new because it still the little gold tag stuck on the stark white fabric. Egyptian cotton, I'm so suave.

Jill smells of shower, and French milled soap as the distance between us shortens.

Puzzled, Jill takes the handkerchief, picks off the little gold adhesive rectangle. She sticks the rectangle onto my shirt pocket like a tiny gold medal.

I point to my upper lip. She snatches my rearview mirror, hopefully a Mack truck isn't bearing down on us. She then produces a make-up compact glancing in the mirror. She frowns, swipes the evidence away with fine cotton.

Jill places handkerchief and the compact in her purse, saying, "Come on, we're late. Let's go. This was your idea. It's a long drive." So much for my classy acoutrements.

We are lucky for a Saturday on the Dan Ryan. Road's open, nobody shooting at us. We arrive at 3:00. She snatches my hand quick marching us to the door.

Jill's eyes dart nervously about. Does she fear ambush?

I have been away from home without a word for a long time. Fears of ambush may not be paranoiac. I spot my parents sitting in the front-room. Seated, they appear as casually postured as an 1890s wedding couple posed for a daguerreotype.

Jill's hand feels cool and dry in mine. She displays little tension in her arm. I'm enjoying the sensation of her hand held gently in mine. The real Jill surfaces, as her palm nervously closes tightly over my thumb.

I knock on the door. Jill gives her stiff-upper-lip smile. Her smile is capable of brightening a cloudy day--at the moment it merely shows anxiety. Maybe just courage in the face of danger. Meeting a guy's parents is like that.

My father opens the door, startles as he catches sight of Jill, welcomes us in.

My mother says hello. Trying to avoid tears—doesn't. Bear-hugs me.

My father is of two minds, lost somewhere between strangling me for making my mother's life one of hellish sadness and being glad that the report of my death was premature. His expression flickers between poles considering diametrically opposed responses.

We exchange perturbed glares.

Jill breaks the ice by stepping forward to introduce herself, "Hello, Mr. Galvan, I'm Jill Ryan."

My father smiles at her. "Call me Frank. As a child my son declared he was Francis. My wife only calls me Francis when I foul up. The lady in tears hugging Francis is his mother, Nicole."

My mother extends her right hand to shake Jill's.

Jill says, "It's nice to meet you, Dr. Galvan. Trey, er Francis, tells me you did your residency in emergency medicine, but ended up practicing internal medicine."

My mother digests Jill's comment, as she considers Jill.

My turn. I explain, "Jill is just finishing her medical degree. She matched in internal medicine earlier this month. It was weird."

The women ask jointly, "What was?"

Careful Boyo, so, I say, "The match was weird; I was gawking at things I didn't quite understand."

The both respond, "OK."

Then they exchange a glance and a knowing shrug. Will they exchange the secret female doctor handshake, now?

I stand between my mother and Jill. My mother glides back a half-step, watching Jill and me with an altogether different eye.

Jill half-steps toward me, gently gliding her hip to settle against mine. My mother smiles through misty tears."

Father leans back to the wall watching the three of us closely. He shakes his head slightly, as his glare softens into a wry smile. How the world turns.

Nicole smiles at Jill. Jill opens her purse. She hands my mother the bright cotton handkerchief I gave her earlier. Pointing at me, she says, "His."

Mom uses it for make-up damage control, then pockets it. What is it with the kerchief?

Mom, now, gives Jill a hug of greeting, saying, "The Greek was right, you're gorgeous. I hear you're staying at Gaby's convent for female students."

"Yes. Gaby said to say hello. Thank you for the compliment. Your son obviously gets his good looks from his mother."

I watch the exchange transpire between the women. A divide bridged.

Deuce says to me, "The Greek kept us up on your progress. He's been stopping by since Doctor Bragg found you in Bethesda. He and I buried the hatchet after he got back from Afghanistan. The three of us talked about what happened, rough time for all of us. In comparison our feud seemed small bananas, after you were reported dead."

Later he stopped by with some secret service guy and a blond Secret Service Agent in Charge. The SAC was broken up, she told us you died dragging two wounded SEALS out of an IED blast zone."

My mother cuts in, "We thought we lost you, Francis."

My father hugs me, "It's good to have you back, son."

My mother says, "Joe suffered a lot of survivor's guilt. He was convinced that you died because he didn't have your back in the action."

"He told us you were working for Deveraux. Said Deveraux forced your hand, while the Greek was off the base. We've had nothing but trouble from the Deveraux clan."

My mother diverts our conversation, informing Jill, "When Dr. Braxton found Francis in Bethesda, he was a mess. He was non-verbal. They lost Francis in Bethesda because he wasn't in the military. Bethesda was on overload of IED casualties. Hot war transformed into insurgency. The staff couldn't fit him into the template. So he got less attention. Welcome to modern medicine, Jill."

"Dr. Braxton arranged for surgeons to repair his airway, close the tracheal-tube by stages. Braxton located Joe through the police department."

My father said, "Doctor Braxton knew a bit about the pair of them but because of secrecy issues she wasn't aware of the whole background story. Joe identified Francis. Prints got compared. Then he contacted us."

My mother adds, "Francis had slumped into his stubborn phase. He was acting-out, pretending to be a catatonic little snit. Be forewarned Jill, Francis sulks. He was like that as a baby. As a child, he'd get mad at me for being on-call. When I finished my residency, I did twenty-four-hour ER rotations. ER had just become a residency. The hours were awful. Francis was furious with me for not being home. He likes things orderly. Kids are always trying to control their environment. He acts all relaxed and laid back--now. He can be very stubborn, Jill." Laughing, Mom says, "When I finally did get home, he'd wander around in his diapers pretending I wasn't there. When I talked to him, he would stare at his father."

She says, "I headed out east to Bethesda when I found out he was still alive. I was frantic. Dr. Braxton stopped me from running in. We went to a viewing room and she let me see him through a two-way mirror. I remembered his turtle behavior as a child. In response to my absence, he pulled himself into his shell for protection. I explained my observation to Psych, noting he wasn't going to come out to play until he wanted to come out. We concluded that his isolation from others was a learned behavior from childhood applied in response to the PTSD incident to the violence of his injuries. They set up a regimen to get the turtle to come out of the shell. It's been a long process."

Jill says, "He can be truly awful."

Jill places her palm on my chest, shoving me back slightly, "Such a brat. Look at his face, we're embarrassing him."

My mom laughs, "Joe served as bad cop to Braxton's good cop. The Greek laid down the law, getting Francis on his feet and into therapy. Our son went cursing and swearing, but he went. In the end he worked harder than they expected, and made progress quicker."

She says, "I hovered a little, but I had to stay out of sight. I didn't want his hostility to focus my way. Been there, done that. It was still hard to do."

Silence.

To break the spell, Jill says, "When Joe first started bringing him into Gaby's I thought Francis had suffered a traumatic brain injury. He was so skinny. Looked frail. Never said much. Then out of the blue I realized he spent a lot of time joking with me."

Jill stares me in the eye, "Then I realized your son wasn't out for laughs, though I was a little confused."

Jill explains, "I asked Gaby about the Greek and your son when Joe brought Francis back from Bethesda. She told me that he and Joe were partners and had been overseas together. I saw that from a millennial perspective."

Jill says in explanation, "I know you won't believe this. When I met the two of them, the Greek was surprisingly gentle with your son. Joe Greek is on the gruff side generally. When I met them, he was always solicitous of Francis. When Gaby introduced them as partners, I thought she was telling me that Joe and your son were partners, as in life-partners.

"I thought them a gay couple. It dovetailed with his absolute silence with me. In the face of no real explanation, I made up my own. I didn't grow up around the police. The partner thing was lost on me."

Nicole and Deuce are laughing. My face has to be beet red.

Jill continues, "I caught Gaby in her office one day sitting on the Greek's lap. About that time, Francis had started to make small talk with me at work. One day as I came back from a run along the river walk, I saw Francis pounding a speed bag like a fiend. He was up on the second floor of their warehouse."

"I watched him pounding away, then I decided it was time to get an actual answer. So, I knocked on his door. My arrival broke his concentration."

Deuce said, "I imagine that wasn't difficult for you."

My mother says sharply, "Frank."

Jill interjects, "I called up to him. He invited me in, offered me breakfast. When I got up there, I found out for sure they were not a gay couple."

I tried to keep her from explaining further, hoped she was going no further in explaining. My face feels red enough. I say, "It's a long story. A young lady fell asleep at my place after getting in trouble with a couple of bikers at Gaby's. I was letting the girl sleep off the evening's effects in my loft. Jill misunderstood."

To Jill, I said, "You didn't eat your breakfast, nor did you give me a chance to explain."

Jill says, "Secret Agent Nadia was wandering around in her underwear. I thought it was a liaison. I was embarrassed. I left. She stayed, hopefully she got dressed at some point."

In the face of continuing embarrassment, I change the subject, explaining that Jill and I are visiting partly so she can pick one of my suits to go with a dress she plans on wearing to Gennaro's wedding. My parents invite us to stay for dinner. I relate we have to be back by 7:00PM. Jill is at Gaby's tonight.

My dad and I head for the kitchen to start dinner or he may strangle me.

Jill walks upstairs with my mother. They are talking medicine, shoes, residency, Alfani tops—things somehow much related. I smile at the sight of them with their heads together. Why am I more invested with this visit than a casual dinner?

When they reach the landing, Nicole places an arm over Jill's shoulders. That makes me feel happy. Have I been holding my breath?

I turn into the kitchen, where I find Deuce leaning on the island watching my behavior.

He says, "You like her, don't you? You also seem to enjoy the fact that your mother and Jill are getting along. Jill's a nice girl. I think your Mom is trying hard, considering all that happened."

I ask, "You still looking for a fight, Dad?"

"Are you?" Deuce asks.

I respond, "No, I'm not. I didn't choose well on a lot of issues before I left. You and I are a lot alike. Sorry I put you two through it."

In the same vein, I say, "I thought I was making the right decision by going overseas. We were offered a chance to make a big difference. For a time, we did. While we were successful it was a good thing, later when it wasn't, the whole thing lost its luster."

Deuce nods, saying, "When you're fighting the bad-guys, they get to hit too. I had to learn that the hard way myself. I got shot, developing a collapsed lung that almost killed me. Your mother put me back together, saving my life in the process."

To the topic I add, "We experienced something familiar, al Qaeda and the Taliban figured out our game-plan, then ambushed us. We established a pattern with choke points. They were waiting for us. I caught my lunch. They did the same thing in Mogadishu a generation ago. Afterward, I had plenty of time to think about my mistakes. The worst part was knowing Devereaux. I let myself be railroaded when I knew better. It almost got me killed."

Deuce says, "At your age, I knew for sure I was smarter the everyone else. My big over-complicated plan got the Rev and I shot. Your mother put me back together. Son, we both got shot doing what we thought right. Neither of us turned out to be Superman. Nobody gets out of life unmarked. The trick lies in learning from our errors. Time to make dinner."

While we cook dinner, Dad says, "Before you go, talk with your mother. She's been worried about you for a long time now. We missed you, then lost you. It wasn't easy for her."

It has been a long time between family dinners. Time to come home.

My mind wanders, Jill is having a good time. When did her happiness begin to matter? Lately, happy meant enjoying the ability to do small things. Planks on the skipjack snuggly fitted. A stiff breeze off the Lake. Watching the cold north wind build snowdrifts. Then one afternoon, I saw Jill wading through a snow drift, that changed things. I went from dabbling a little in life to actively seeking a role. Enjoying the happiness of others is far more sublime. The sensation does make your heart ache. Sometimes the ache is good, others painful. Perhaps I might become the killer-poet?

As we cook, Deuce recites a recipe he's been telling me about forever, "Slice the steak into thin strips while it's slightly frozen. That allows thinner strips. Place the steak in a large plastic bowl. Slice a large onion into very thin vertical slices."

"Why slice the onion like that?" I ask.

Deuce says, "I decided it looks cool, while you were away."

He hands me green peppers, "Here, cut the ends off, slice vertically, the way the fiber grows. The long fiber in the pepper keeps it together in the sauce. Pile it all in the bowl with the sliced strip-steak and onions. Now, sprinkle Sea Salt, Black pepper and chili powder over it. "More. Remember your mom is Spanish. That's it, brown sugar, garlic powder, cumin, basil. Shake some olive oil and Worcestershire sauce in. Squirt ketchup in, nobody will notice."

When satisfied he says, "Now. Put a dinner plate on top for a lid. Get a tight grip. Shake that mixing bowl up and down. Gently, Trey. Let the marinade mix seep in. Put it in the refrigerator. Cool marinades better."

He says, "Form a big piece of aluminum foil into a shallow dripping tray shape to fit the grill. We're going to shish-ka-bob it all then spear tiny tomatoes before we grill it a nice brown."

"Before we're done, we'll make up Spanish Rice. Get a can of refried beans from the pantry. Make that two."

"Now what?"

"Beer. We must drink cerveza. It's traditional. Tell me of life in the Hindu Kush.

I start at the beginning, "We signed on with the secrets as a partner-team. The plan was to follow the money. They originally derived funding from personal fortunes. It takes really large money to keep soldiers in the field. Under pressure, they began diverting monies accumulated through Zakat, which is a pillar of Islam similar to the giving of alms for the poor."

The U.S. Secret Service helped to dry up those funds after al Qaeda tried to assassinate key members of the Saudi Royal family. In the process, al Qaeda and the Taliban, the decriers of the narcotics trade, became willing masters of that business in pursuit of a way to make the money to finance terrorism.

The Secret Service chose detectives and investigators from different locations and from among personnel they had success working with. There were two teams working in with us. One was made up of New York City Detectives out of their narcotics unit, and two DEA agents with a SAC supervising. The Greek and I worked with two Secret Service agents supervised by our SAC Emma Wainwright. Each pair had four Navy Seals assigned with them. A SEALS Chief Petty Officer coordinated the two teams with Commander Devereaux in over-all charge."

"The Secret Service contingent on our Team were the Bobs, Big and Little. Most of my team was blown with me. Big Bob tripped the IED that got us. I think Little Bob was behind me on the stairs. I took the pair working tail-end-Charlie with me when I fled. I assume Little Bob stayed with his partner and died with the other two SEALS.

"The blond who came here was probably Emma Wainwright.

Deuce asks, "She looks and sounds WASP-y. She's marrying Gennaro. Is she aware he's Italian?"

"Emma is a proud black woman. Her great, great, grand someone came over on the Mayflower. She refers to that forebear as a person living in reduced circumstance. Maybe that's Yankee for slave. I have no idea. She seems to accept his being Italian."

Deuce shrugs, "Ms. Wainwright who has very distant black relatives and looks like her name is Olga Swenson identifies as a black woman. Gennaro who is one of the darkest-skinned men I have ever met, identifies as Italian. Do I understand?"

Deuce thinks a moment. "Does Emma Wainwright know Gennaro is an Italian?"

"Dad, I think Gennaro even knows Emma is leavened by Pilgrim ancestry."

Appearing confused, Dad shrugs, "Go on with your story."

"There were four SEALS with us. Kelly (call sign-Machine Gun), and his partner Amos Floyd (call sign-Pretty Boy); Blackmon who is white (call sig-Black) and his partner Tanner who is African American (call sign-Tan). The latter pair are called, 'The Twins'.

Deuce says, "I'm surprised. I didn't know The Navy SEALS were Irish."

I smile. "I thought that when I heard all the antonymic call-signs."

I agree, "Call signs are bestowed upon one. Yes, they are often diametrically opposite of the person. They think of it as low-level security and of themselves mnemonic. Anyway, a SEALS Master-Chief ran logistics for us. I think his given name was, 'master-chief', which is all I've ever heard him called."

"Emma Wainwright, was our Special Agent in Charge (SAC). Her call sign was White-Girl."

"Obviously, why didn't I think of that?" says Deuce.

"I'm pretty sure Emma's parents own a few small states out east. They consider Kennedys to be among the nouveau rich, really just Irish-gangster, rum-runner, trash."

Deuce says, "Some of our rum-runner ancestors ran whiskey to Chicago from Canada. Joe Kennedy's Somerset Importers held American rights to Dewar's Scotch and Gordon Gin. He also owned Canadian distillers through Schenley Industries. Family legend says we stored a lot of unspecified import goods for later distribution inside the merchandise mart. Police never raided the mart. It was just legend, but Joe did own the building. Our Canadian ancestors thought its central location with water and land access ideal."

I nod, then return to our topic, "We were contracted to track narcotics on the way out of Afghanistan to gain sufficient financing to implement their war of terror. It was a complicated web. Dope shipped out of country to obtain funds which matriculated back to them to be used to buy weapons and supplies that wormed their way back in to support the terrorists. Since 2004 heroin sales have been supporting local terrorists under the al Qaeda and Taliban banners. Prior to that, the Salafists were death on the heroin trade moving along the Silk Road. When we cut off funds, they became dealers for the cause."

Shaking the marinade bowl, Deuce nods. "Efficiency begets survival."

I say, "The law on unintended consequences set in. In the beginning Al Qaeda was run by a group referred to as the 'Core', which was made up a group of intellectuals and highly educated leaders religiously and idealistically committed to a restoration of the Caliphate."

"Their movement is patristic. In its view one sees Islam as a holistic entity referred to as the 'Ummah', which is 'the community of Islam'. Fundamentalists want to turn worship and the practice of Islam back in time."

"They want to turn the world back to the 600AD?" asks Deuce.

I say, "No, they want the worship of Allah to reflect its practice at the time of Mohammed. Like Christian Protestant Fundamentalists, the Salafists want their Ummah to return to a personal relationship with God which mimics the teaching of the Prophet Mohammed. In the Salafist view, Islam success circa 700AD is proof of Allah's favor."

I note in explanation, "That fundamentalist form of Islam prospered during the lives of the prophet's four companions, who are known as the righteous caliphs. Those caliphs worshipped properly. The Salafists believe that since then the quality of worship has fallen off."

I say, "For the Salafist, state is religion and religion is state. If the faithful return to the form of worship from the time of the caliphate, Islam will be restored to its purest religious format. If proper worship is restored, the Ummah will reclaim its lost lands because the Allah will come to look upon the body of Islam with favor.

I further my point, "Al Qaeda originally had a highly educated 'core' management group. The cadre was made of rich, highly educated men with doctorates and masters degrees in the hard science like medicine, engineering, finance. They don't deny science or medicine. They want all of Islam to worship in the manner of their righteous caliphs. They are religious fundamentalists. They are not luddites. They watch TV.

"In al Qaeda's early days foot soldiers were made up of radicalized, reformed juvenile delinquents from the Maghreb along the northeast coast of Africa from Egypt to the Atlantic."

"Many of those recruits speak their own dialect of Arabic. Most were criminal delinquents, who found Islam in jail or detention. A substantial portion lived in and traveled through Europe. After experiencing exclusion and discrimination in Italy, France, and further afield they came home knowing who to hate. The United States winnowed the 'core' leadership after 911. Then we hunted down middle managers in areas adjacent to the CORE and then worked outwards from the management team.

Deuce squints at me out of one eye, his other is tearing from the onion slicing, "There can only be so many bosses in the boat--someone has to row.

I nod. "The law of unintended consequences set in. They started to form ever-more-isolated islands of al Qaeda. Natural selection promoted new leaders from among the foot soldiers to fill vacant command niches in functioning localities. The new leaders weren't educated in international finance but knew how to make money by moving product. Their biggest potential income source lay in the growth, harvest, manufacture, smuggling and sale of narcotics. They also understood how to enforce their will through violence. Dope got many of them in jail in the first place. Because of FinCEN strictures they suffered an abrupt decline in religious donations. When FinCEN killed Zakat funds, drug dealer wisdom prevailed. By bringing in lots of money the kids gained access to real power. That led to the secrets recruiting us to assist in applying pressure against gangbanger financing. Suddenly it was the Roaring Twenties. The secrets played Elliot Ness to our Untouchables. They adapted the techniques for tracking narcotics money to tracking narcotics money used in support al Qaeda and the Taliban. We rewarded the loyal, punished the disloyal. Afghanistan was a floating Mongolian crap game. Local tradition is to sell out enemies and friends with equal fervor. The tribes have been selling each other out since Alexander the Great was a tourist."

Trying to describe the effects, I add, "Inflation got out of hand. Bundles of $10,000 in one hundred-dollar bills were flying around like confetti. Status came to be measured by the height of one's ben-bundle. Things got personal, fast. Military and political managers couldn't decide what they wanted to do. They quickly decided loyalty purchased had better stay purchased."

I recall sadly, "We spent the rest of the year runnin' and gunnin' from pillar to post. Deveraux and Em' conducted over-watch with the long guns while we worked entry teams. We got up close and personal. We ambushed bad guys. They ambushed us. Deveraux was riding the helicopter skid in bound, looking at me like I was four-day-old chopped liver as I got medevac'd out."

My father asked, "What was the admiral doing in combat? He must be in his sixties, maybe his seventies. I mean, he was Viet Nam."

Surprised I answer, "I thought the Greek explained. We were working for the other Deveraux, the one from Annapolis is now a Navy Lieutenant Commander."

Deuce is visibly shocked, "I'll bet that went swell. I assume you were recognized?"

"Not at first, toward the end I was."

Deuce's fatherly admonition, "Francis? Please tell me you had the sense to get away from that family."

I shrug, ending my story. "Not really."

Deuce shakes his head sadly, watching me closely, "Son, tell me it's done."

I shrug. "I got killed. They all think I'm dead. I spent ten months in the hospital paralyzed. When I got out, I met Jill. I think I've fallen for her. So, I brought Jill here.

"Do you intend to tell Jill that?" asks Deuce.

"No, Dad, she's gone out with me once. That ended a mess. I think I'll need a little time showing her I'm not crazy before I tell her."

Deuce raises an eyebrow, "You just told her. Nicole and she have been standing behind you for several minutes."

I glance in the kitchen doorway. My mother leans against one side of the doorframe wearing a motherly smile.

Jill's leans on the other side of the doorframe, her eyes are huge with hazel tones. Jill rests her hands on her hips, saying, "Finally. The true story. Nicole, he told me the version where they were war correspondents. I heard one where they worked for a relief agency. In another they were like bank clerks. But he admits to Frank, in fifteen minutes, what they were doing."

Jill pokes my chest with her index finger, "Francis, I told you, 'if you told your crazy stories to a mule, he'd kick you in the head.' Don't lie to me, mister. It won't work out well, especially when you're falling for me."

Jill runs her fingers through my hair, snatches a handful, giving it a tug. "I don't think you are crazy. I don't think anything is weird about you. What bothers me is trust. I'm happy that you're falling for me. Be careful, you may be caught."

My parents have disappeared. I wrap an arm around Jill's waist, as she slides onto my lap. The taste of her lips on mine in the family kitchen is nice. She tastes of home.

Eventually, dinner gets cooked. The Bistec is excellent.

We leave early to get Jill back for work. My parents ignored our kitchen time. Family secrets? I see a knowing smile pass between them. They both hug Jill as we leave.

As we leave, they smile at us, we at them. A lot of smiling going on. The mysteries of life.

As we take our seats in my SRX, Jill launches at me. Maybe we launch at each other. We wrestle about the small cabin of the SRX. Things get heated.

Jill breaks away, settling back into her seat, "Take me to work,

Galvan. I'm getting overheated. Don't be so feisty in front of your mother's house. Geez, you're like a fifteen-year-old in heat."

From her reaction, my enthusiasm was appreciated. No sense embarrassing her. I ease up, string the car. Taking a deep breath, I drive Jill to Gaby's.

10

SAND FLEAS AND FIZZIES

We were steaming, drilling and securing hull planks to the skipjack's hardback frame before dawn. The skipjack no longer looks like a giant insect sprawled on its back with its legs pointed to the ceiling. It has the shape of a vessel.

Tired, I climb the south inside stairs to my loft. My throat is dry, my voice hoarse. I need beer. Before I shower, I head down to the kitchen for a Corona. Distracted, beer in hand I perch in the shade of my deck.

My shoulders ache. Forcing the springy, steamed wood to the skipjack frame progresses in millimeters in tight quarters. Five hours standing on concrete sucks the life out of you.

Before dawn I pre-positioned a lawn-chair to cut a pie-wedge slice of the tumbleweed-strewn point. As I sit drowsing, my vision drifts.

Something startles me. I scan for trouble. There is movement in the western edge of the tumbleweeds. Northwest wind; some brush parts to the northeast. Our lurker lurks once more.

His blue-black dyed hair waves in the breeze over the tumbleweeds. My pie-wedge cut places me in his blind spot. The tumbleweeds may be man-sized, but his cartoon quail's top knot hair dances above the tumbleweeds.

The city must've opened the sewer drains into the river during last month's heavy rains. All the high-quality fertilizer has given us 6-foot tumbleweeds.

Our lurker's movement is erratic. What is he doing? Do I really want to know?

Breath on my shoulder. The Greek stands silently behind me. Must've followed me. He remembered I bought beer yesterday. A bottle pops, he found it. He's a God damned blood hound. I hid it in a cabinet.

The Greek whispers, "Why did you put the beer in the cabinet, again? You been watching this asshole? He's been around for a couple of weeks, maybe more. The goofy prick is wearing shiny, metal-rimmed glasses. The light-flash off the frames caught my eye up in the penthouse. Does he ever stop fidgeting?"

I murmur, "I doubt it. Weird guy. Does he look familiar? I almost recognize him but can't place him. He ran off the last time. He drives a cross-over. He parks it in the mud under the poplars back by the playlot."

The Greek nods, "I'll put up out a game camera when he leaves later. Every time the electric eye catches movement we'll get pictures. The way he fidgets, we'll need the 32G memory sticks. I'll put a second viewing where he parks the cross-over. We'll get him coming and going. I hate guys who hide in the bushes around playgrounds."

He points, saying, "Look, there he goes. The dud's slithering down the hill backwards. He playing ninja."

"That's dude, Joe."

"No, kid, this one is a dud."

"Dud, my mistake."

The Greek points to a growling sound, "That's his car starting. Sounds like he screwed up the exhaust driving over the curb at the playlot. He's a determined little devil. What's he about?"

I answer, "Whatever he's up to I don't like it. I caught him watching you and Jill a couple of times. He hides in those bushes most days. I'm going to put a kink in his tail and mark him, in case we run into him in public.

When I leave, the Greek is lounging on my balcony, drinking my beer.

I open the overhead dock door to snatch a strip-built kayak from the wall-rack. Mounting the baidarka, I paddle out into the river. The Baidarka is a kayak common to the Aleutian Islands. It is a sleek style built to be quick and responsive in the tight spots among ice floes. I like using the Baidarka rough in the surf along the shore of the lake. The challenge of the agile kayak rebuilt atrophied shoulder muscles.

We developed a penchant for kayaks early in our contract with the Secret Service. When we were assigned to the fast course at the farm. Everyone was in a hurry then. Toward the end of our stay, we trained on Klepper folding kayaks out on Chesapeake Bay. At the Farm old timers take the kids to the beach to blow off steam. These kayaks are modern versions of the WWII Cockle Shell. We were trained to assemble the kayaks or make them disappear in under eight minutes. When our assembly skills were good enough, I came to enjoy paddling rough water.

I'm sure 'the Farm' staff were aware of our assignment to Commander Deveraux's Seal team. SEALS and water are joined in legend. What water there is in the Hindu Kush is usually frozen or too rough to paddle. Kayak usage in Afghanistan is rare. I figure, our trainers were committed to reliving glory days whether we blew off steam or not. Kayaking stuck with me.

Strip-built kayaks carry well with one hand--thus the name Ultralight. I carry my Baidarka and double paddle out on the dock from which I paddle downstream, west toward the Ashland Avenue. There was a popular shrimp restaurant on the little bay south of the bridge. Their shrimp was good with house hot sauce and a cold beer. The odd part is that the restaurant sits upon a body of water where the last shrimp swam during the Paleozoic Era.

Can't stop for lunch, awful things to do this afternoon. Along the south bank, I spot crumbling driftwood lying along a weedy peninsula east of the bay. I paddle past several dead-wood piles looking for movement. Eventually, I see one half in the water. Wet pulp makes a lively home for sand-fly larvae. I lift a section of bark with my paddle. Juvenile sandflies nap in the shade as a cool breeze skims over the water. I have found what I sought. I don a lovely pair of yellow Playtex living gloves. Sand fly bites leave welts. Using my lovely gloves, I harvest a large batch of the sand-fly larvae, placing them in a black garbage bag. I seal the garbage bag tightly.

Time to get gone, wouldn't want to deal with vengeful swarm. I paddle back upstream toward the point west of our boatyard. There, I disembark onto the rubble at the shoreline along our spring's inlet. I return with my garbage bag to find the water-filled tire I'd seen earlier in the tumbleweeds near the watcher's tar-bucket seat. The larvae will be comfy there until he returns.

If the Greek thought he jumped around a lot, wait 'til the watcher meets my little friends. Not only meant as a suggestion to leave, my effort will mark him with sand-fly welts. Again, I dislike guys who hide in the bushes around children's play-lots.

I glance down at the spring. It has been gurgling louder and more persistently, lately. The up-well has begun to swirl above the surface of the inlet. I slide into the kayak's cockpit, planning a quick glide across the inlet. I shove off, settling into the seat, gliding near the outflow. The Baidarka snaps about. My balance falters, I just avoid a spill. The current's snap shocks me.

As I hose the kayak, watching water surge above the spring. Odd, I felt like it grabbed me. I rack the kayak before I return to my loft. The Greek's in my lounger, drinking my beer.

He swallows the beer, extends the empty too as he points to the refrigerator. I think he needs a fresh one. I go for the beer. He says, "That bastard down there almost got you, Galvan."

I ask, "If you mean the guy in the bushes, he's long gone."

The Greek shakes his head no as he takes the beer, "I mean whatever lives down in that ice water. Whatever our playground creeper plans, that thing down there wants to eat you, kid."

I ignore him, opening my own beer. He asks, "What'd you do, Kid?"

I respond, "I put sand-flea larvae in the old tire alongside his perch."

He shrugs, "Damn. When we're rid of him, I'll have to kill the nasty things. You think DDT will work?"

I ask, "Where on earth would you get DDT? It's been outlawed since Viet Nam. It was killing Bald Eagle chicks by making their shells too thin."

The Greek says, "They said that about Agent Orange, too. Tell the DDT story to the sixty bald eagles in Lake Calumet. It didn't hurt them. The opium growers in Afghanistan were using it to kill capsule weevils when we were there, Galvan."

I ask, "Where do Afghans get the stuff?"

"India."

"Where did the Indians get it?"

"California until 1985, then the California company moved the process to India."

I give up. "The one place DDT won't screw up the ecology is the Chicago River. "

The Greek belches, "What ecology? The Chicago River has the ecology of a nuclear reactor. It won't have one for another 2500 years. I read somewhere that they dumped refuse from the Manhattan Project's original atom bomb pile out there in the river as a flood barrier in the 1950s."

"Where did you read that? Who dumped it?"

The Greek shrugs, "I forget. Probably the scientists who made it. At Northwestern we always figured they weren't very bright in Hyde Park. Anyway, would you want that crap sitting outside your lecture hall? Who else could've gotten away with it?"

He burps again, "You cheapskate, this gassy beer makes me hungry. Some host. Make me a sandwich for Christ sake."

I go to make sandwiches, "Don't drink it if you don't like it."

He smiles, "It's free, free is good. Make me the sandwich. If there is enough left, make yourself one. In the future, buy quality beer. This swill is bad for my digestion."

Later, we sit drinking my gassy beer and eating ham sandwiches, even though it made the Greek burp.

He says speculatively, "You don't seem to be mad at this guy yet. Otherwise, you would have done something awful to him. Then, putting bugs in the tire is humorous and much more civilized than when you put the king cobra in that Taliban sniper's lunch box. His shocked expression was worth humping our rucks up that mountainside. He was one very surprised dead dude."

The Greek continues his line of thought, "You are your papa's son, Galvan. Grandpa Silky told me a family story once. In it he and your crazy uncles sat at the dinner table watching your papa in the alley. Deuce was fighting six of his contemporaries. As they watched, Deuce spun them into a pile, beating the shit out of them.

The Greek adds, "Silky eventually went out to rescue Deuce before they got him on the ground. By the time Silky got to the alley, Deuce was standing in the middle of the alley with flotsam and jetsam scattered around in the dirt. Silky told me he didn't help Deuce earlier because the kid needed to be able to handle himself. When Silky got to Deuce, flotsam and jetsam were trying to pull Deuce down by his ankles. Silky told me the family decided right then Deuce was the 'mean one'."

Joe asks, "Have you seen Uncle Old School since you got back?"

"No, Old School and my father were feuding for years before we left for the Kush. I saw him in Home Depot when I was buying those cargo boxes we took to the Kush. I looked up to find Old School loading tile cases on a hand truck. I gave him a hand. He said thanks and walked off. He didn't recognize me. I haven't talked with him since high school.

The Greek says, "How did it go with your parents, Kid?"

"Good. They like Jill. I tried to explain Afghanistan to Deuce. Maybe he got some of it. My mom and I talked some. She's upset with me. It will take time. I really screwed up."

Looking at me through one eye he says, "Kid, you do awful things to awful people. I think you inherited your father's worst traits."

"I let awful people do themselves. Occasionally, I give them a nudge."

"How's that work?" asks Joe.

"I let them choose. They can leave it alone, or not."

"How did you nudge our sniper?"

"The guy crippled a lot of young Marines, then used the wounded as bait to snipe Corpsmen coming to help them. That was sadistic. He could've stopped sniping, gone on a diet. He didn't. Instead, he got complacent, set a pattern. He brought lunch. I spotted his cooler inside the hide. I found Mrs. Cobra in some roof thatch. I put her on a diet, then set up the introduction."

The Greek asks, "What was his choice?"

I ask my own question, "Did he deserve one? You know, sometimes I lie?"

We sit in silence for a time.

Eventually, he says, "I got results on the water sample from the spring's up-well. I used a fifteen-foot boat hook to take it. I am not going anywhere near Him."

"Him? Who him?" I inquire.

The Greek's intensity surprises me, as he says, "I'm talking about that thing down there on the bottom of the spring. My buddy at Northwestern says the water sample I drew from the spring is from Lake Huron. Mineral content proves the connection. My buddy told me a subterranean river runs along the basalt beneath us. Deep down there are rivers crisscrossing under the south end of Lake Michigan.

He's on a roll. "During the spring floods, our spring level rises in reflection of the water level in Lake Huron. As Huron drops in summer our upwell will drop off.

"If that's the case, why is our spring carbonated?"

Joe shrugs, "Who knows. Maybe our demon has a sense of humor and he passes our water through a Fizzies deposit. They got the name Bubbly Creek somewhere."

Laughing I say, "For a guy with a doctorate in journalism from Medill, you remain a Greek fisherman."

As he speaks, I see him clutch the matiasma black, blue and white eye pendant which hangs from the silver cross chain his aunt gave him before we left for the Hindu Kush, "You'll learn. Some judgment, when it comes from a guy who wore a Celtic cross and Shamrock overseas. I quote one Vito Gennaro, who once said to you, 'Look who's calling the kettle black.' Are we going to the wedding?"

I say, "Do you think he knows? Yeah. Jill and I are good for the wedding. Want me to drive?"

"You drive for shit, Galvan. We'll take my Lincoln. We'll leave from Gaby's."

"Good, we'll sit in the back so I can talk dirty to her."

"Kid, you're Irish, how dirty can it get? If you get too dirty for the sweet young thing, I'll reach around and slap you. Now, I sound like my father."

11

ROUGH MEN AND WOMEN IN THE DARK

To paraphrase George Orwell, this evening the rough men and women who normally stand in the darkness ready to do violence on behalf of people sleeping peaceably in their beds have taken the night off.

Contingents drawn from the local law enforcement communities will be the wedding guests. At the Gennaro-Wainwright wedding twains seem to have met. The stature of the Gennaro family will draw the elite from the Bridgeport community. Some drawn to the festivities may even be denizens of other less reputable families and crews. You are on your own tonight, sleepers.

We arrived in a timely fashion at 'the hall' as in banquet hall. Progressing through the reception line, I introduced Jill to Gennaro's parents, who are Italian, as in from Italy. Gennaro's father has thick greying hair, an olive complexion, and is a sconce under six feet. His mother is a beautiful tiny woman with pale, creamy skin. They adopted Gennaro, after discovering they couldn't have children. Gennaro, as an orphan lacking parents, was lucky in finding good ones.

If you ask Gennaro where he's from, he responds with a twinkle in his eye, "Calabria." Don't push. Don't ask stupid questions. Vito Gennaro will likely play you, or he might knock you down. Playing is preferable; from experience I know he hits hard.

Gennaro, before I met him, played football for the Chicago Bears. In his first season he blew out his knee. On recovering, he became a police officer. We met in the academy as recruits.

Mary Beth Burke was in our class. In the Academy people train to become police officers.

With time and experience, some not all, become 'the cops'. First comes the goal of successfully completing the academy's long, hard course of study. The latter is a quality judgment bestowed by fellow practitioners.

Many are called, few are chosen. (Matthew 22:14, King James Version).

The bride comes by her blond hair from both sides of the family. Her father resembles the actor, Sterling Hayden, Yankee right down to his socks. Mother, like her daughter, is tall, slender, and blond, with features favoring Somali heritage. Emma is a mixture of both. She inherited the peaches and cream complexion of your average Victorian heroine and the ferocity of an African warrior in battle. The Greek once described Em' as disconcerting; she is.

Both sides of the family rose to prominence in the era of the 'Nantucket Sleigh Ride'. Preceding the sleigh ride, brawny sailors rowed a long narrow boat toward broaching whales on the open sea. One of their number perched in the bow, a wicked barbed harpoon close at hand.

If successful, a large, harpooned, mortally wounded whale dragged the sailors and their whale-boat to incredible speed over open ocean, skimming and skipping across the surface. The 'Nantucket sleigh ride' was an incredible thrill of speed and danger in the era of horse and buggy, if it didn't kill you and the whale.

In the modern world the Wainwrights strongly support Green Peace, abhor whaling, and are regretful of the manner by which their ancestors carved the family empire from the 19th Century.

Times change. Today there exists a minimal taste for the harpooning of whales. Yet, I have noted as they decried the family's whaling heritage, occasional flashes of pride pass among family members under the influence of demon rum. Emma once told me her mother's family crossed the Atlantic on the Mayflower, in 'reduced circumstance'. Emma inherited mother Sara's curly hair and fine bone structure. They look lovely in the reception line.

I've known Gennaro's family since around the time we joined the police department. I met the Wainwright family on a family property not far from Nantucket. Her parents threw Emma's team a going away party just before we left for Afghanistan. At the time, I inquired after chances of a Nantucket sleigh ride. My comment drew frowns. No sense of humor I guess.

At Emma's going-away-party, Wainwright viewed the Greek and me as a necessary evil. We were cops (small c), sort of a native levy drawn from those people (small t, small p) At one point early in the party I leaned, drinking beer against a garden wall, thinking thoughts.

Squire Wainwright walked up saying, "Come, Galvan, eat-up. Too early for all that beer. Come. Don't want you to morph in the archetype of the drunk bog runner. Need you sober on the morrow to look out for my daughter, say what?"

At least Wainwright didn't pat me on the head, and scratch behind my ears. Later, Wainwright told me to call him William as he got into the rum. He let me know he'd dealt with cops before, finding the lot of them to be racists capable of sordid behavior. Tonight, I wonder if Wainwright's view of the cops in general includes his new son-in-law.

At her daughter's going away party, Mrs. Wainwright viewed us with suspicion and hostility. Sara Wainwright was leery of our sort of large Catholic heathens (The Greek being of the Orthodox sort was close enough and I being of the Irish-Catholic sort suited the bill just fine).Sara did not appreciate the idea of our sort traveling in the company of her unmarried daughter. Young ladies of Emma's quality must needs be careful around our sort as we are regrettable brutes prone to lusty and unseemly behavior when in the company of young ladies of her daughter's status.

Standing in the receiving line I take out time to slobber and drool, quietly. This evening, Mrs. is gracious. She seems to recognize Joe. I'm a mystery whom Sara Wainwright pretends to know. Mine is not a memorable face. Then maybe I've changed, since we first met.

The Emma's marriage to an Italian cop has gentled Sara. This evening, Squire Wainwright suggests we call him 'Bill'. My, my, might we no longer be thugs? More likely, Em's parents are happy to have their daughter back from Afghanistan, alive. And they are merely greeting wedding guests.

Glancing to their daughter, I realize Emma has used her time back in the World to good purpose. I think she might be a little pregnant. Maybe that is making her parents happy. Sara turns to her daughter, brushing her palm soothingly over her daughter's abdomen.

A mother and daughter moment, I shift my prying eyes away. I think of Mary Beth pregnant with my baby. Sara's moment of intimacy with her daughter settles in.

The last few weeks I've lost my indifference to life. I find myself acting again, rather than being acted upon.

Someone presses my hand. My eyes are fierce as I snap toward unexpected physical contact. Jill smiles softly. My hand is warmed by her grasp, as she guides me back into the flow of the receiving line, or is it life?

The Gennaro family beams at the Wainwright ladies. No doubt about it: Emma's pregnant.

When we approach, the Gennaros extend a warm welcome to Jill and Gaby. Vito, Sr., embraces both women warmly. The Gennaros are a warm Mediterranean family. I think that Gaby and especially Jill look lovely this evening. Perhaps that is why Vito, Sr., hugs each woman a few moments too long.

Mrs. Gennaro shakes her head, apparently she's familiar with Vito Sr.'s hugging traits from previous experience? Emma is a beautiful, smiling bride. She doesn't recognize me as I walk up to offer my best wishes. Have I changed that much? Reality slips a notch.

In Bethesda, psych gained insight into me when they discovered I once surfaced unexpectedly beneath a swimming pool liner. The wet plastic stuck to my face and body suffocating me. Terrified I panicked. Rather than die, I dropped back into the deep water.

I forced myself to descend smoothly back into that pool of water. Short on oxygen, I swam seeking then finding the pool's side-wall. I peeled back the pool cover allowing me to burst into the night air. At Bethesda, psych told me to act, rather than continue to allow myself to be acted upon.

I told my parents when it happened. I had told no one else of the event. Who told psych? Being so much smarter and more worldly than psych, I've regularly ignored their advice to my detriment. Psych told me that in time my panic attacks would become few and far between, but that stimuli might trigger PTSD episodes at any time.

Standing in the receiving line, past blurs present. My perception of reality alters. Emma in her wedding gown morphs into Em' in digital pattern camouflage BDUs as I last saw her. Instead of a bouquet, Em' carries her Heckler & Koch MP5. The submachine gun judders at full auto. The acrid scent of burning propellant pervades the banquet hall, night air closing about us. The smoke of smokeless powder halos her face as her weapon cycles a magazine into a charging man in a dishdasha blazing at me with his AK-74. Emma keeps me from dying in some little arid Afghan gully.

In the, now silent, reception line I hear the clacking echo of Em's

MP5 over my head as she drives my killer-to-be onto his knees, well short of his goal.

Suddenly back in the world, I feel the squeeze of Emma's strong grip on my bicep as she asks, "Trouble, where have you been? You don't even look like you, boy. Come on, talk to me."

Jill squeezes my other arm to get my attention, as she introduces herself to the bride.

Hey, do Emma's eyes challenge Jill over her forced smile. Jill only said hello. Why does Emma take offense regarding well wishes from a woman she's never met?

Emma is openly hostile to Jill, abruptly. Why? Continuing to glare, Emma draws me from Jill's side into a hug, whispering, "We need to talk, Trouble."

The happy bride of moments earlier studies me with cold eyes. I embrace her, my suspicion of pregnancy seems to be confirmed, "Congratulations, Em'."

Warm-eyed bride is back.

Gennaro leans in from Emma's side to receive my congratulations. Jill speaks with the bride. Gennaro gives me a bear hug, saying, "Looks like I might have someone to teach the family Soppressata recipe."

Gennaro whispers, "Your DNA swab came back fast, too fast. You were a busy little beaver, Galvan. You are Mary Beth's baby daddy, for certain. Emma got notice this morning that you also were on very friendly terms with one of her secret service agents."

He steps back saying, "Watch your step, my brother. My wife calls you Trouble. Well, Trouble, you got big plenty of trouble. The bureau has the knives out for you, son. Special Agent Dimitrieva won't be in a mood to listen. I gave her your alibi. But Nadia is a Russian blockhead. She's locked on you tight, Galvan. Talk to my bride when the crowd thins. "

Unexpectedly concerned for my immediate future, I locate our table as Jill and Gabby seek out the ladies' room. I sit to ponder developments. I don't come to a satisfying conclusion.

Taking a moment to think, I seek out the bar. In time I return from the bar with two merlots. Jill crosses before me walking in wide, firm strides back to our now crowded table. Jill strides well. She is wearing a loose black, white and grey Alfani handkerchief-silk top that rides low her over her hips in back, higher in the front. The silk drifts above black, silky form fitted leggings. I marvel at the woman's balance and grace on those black strappy heels as she weaves through the crowd on the dance floor. At the sight of her, my heart skips a beat. I fear I'm smitten.

People in general and women in particular are quickly aware of being watched. Jill, catching the heat of my gaze, turns toward me. Her eyes assume a deer-in-the-headlights expression. Her gaze spellbinds me. Then she smiles at me, confident in her effect. She sits next to Gaby.

Holding my gaze, Jill winks at me. She knows. The bunny is trapped.

Captivated, wholly focused on her, I stroll to our table. Hopefully, I won't stumble and pour our wine in my shoe. Jill has sped up the pace of life around me. It feels good to be back in the world. Anticipating being with Jill, I ignore the other guests at our table. I'm looking forward to the evening with her.

Silly me, I forgot. One can only do happy in short spurts for a few fragile moments. Keep your head up and moving. Never let yourself be distracted for long. Sooner than later, something knocks the bottom out of your bucket.

Blackmon's voice sounds. I should have left him on that staircase in the Kush. I wouldn't have gotten my throat slit, I wouldn't have gotten killed, and I wouldn't have lived life as a pancake, flat on my back. The fog of recognition settles on me. The arrival of happy should've made me prepare to duck. Happy is usually a leading indicator that it will rain assholes, shortly. It just started raining. Blackmon is on a roll, "What is this, Joe? When you sent your pet boy for drinks, he should have known to bring drinks for all of us. We are the COMPANY, we get served first, after all. How about a little hospitality, Greek?"

Another county heard from, Tanner's voice cuts in, "Galvan, how about you scurry back to the bar for a couple of Tequila Sunrise's while my man here chats up your date? By the time you get back you'll be an unfortunate memory."

The Greek says, "Being dead knocked some of Galvan's wires loose. He got killed saving you two from a fate worse than death. They've been getting bombed up in those cold mountains for a long-time, lads. The Taliban would have found a lot of joy in a SEAL boy with his brains knocked silly. Think they'd have gone for twins? When I got back you two punch-drunk assholes were still on queer-street. He saved you two. Why he did that I'll never fathom. I'd have let them have you, not get my throat cut dragging you two to safety. I'd have expected at least one of you to thank Galvan for saving your useless lives before you tried to move in on his action."

Blackmon snarls, "BULLSHIT, Greek. You weren't there. Galvan ran away and abandoned Big Bob on that staircase. Bob died up on that staircase. We didn't have enough of Bob to out in a Tupperware bucket and bury. We had to put what there was in a coffin with several cinder blocks, so his family would think there was a body in the coffin."

Speaking in a distraught tone, Blackmon says, "Big Bob's father was a local powerhouse. He contacted his senator. His dad got an order from the Secretary of the Navy for us to let him look at his son a last time. We were in formal uniform as an honor guard when they opened the coffin, Galvan. A boot, some bones, and the Tupper Ware box and the cinder blocks, so this asshole could prance off to safety."

Tan snaps, "Bob died because Galvan ran. This coward stumbled over us on that staircase, trying to run away. I admit we were a little out of it. It was us who carried this coward to safety before we collapsed. He killed some pregnant bitch, trying to get out on the first medivac."

Black won't shut up, "Yo, Galvan. Thanks for bringing this fine young thing. Emma told us you had hooked up with some gorgeous little thing, but this girl is a true stunner. She doesn't look old enough to be tending bar. You definitely don't need this jerk, honey, why don't we just leave him here and take a spin around the dance floor."

Black reaches out, lifting Jill's right hand in his as he sneers my way, "You are one sweet little thing, girl. I've been looking for a girl like you my whole life. I'll take it from here, stick-boy. Why don't you sashay back to the bar, Galvan? Get us some man-drinks, and a pink squirrel for yourself?"

Jill snaps her hand free from Blackmon's saying, "My grandfather was a Navy torpedoman. The reason you haven't found yourself a girl was because you spent all your time taking new recruits down to see the golden spike that held the keel together. Women had the sense to run when they saw you two coming. Come in to visit early some night, I'll introduce you two to my day bartender, Karlie. Karlie will really love you two."

The Greek chuckles, Gaby smiles.

I actually am considering killing both of them here at the table. Maybe I might split up and I can kill them one at a time.

Jill settles against my shoulder, "Look all you want, Mr. Blackmon, I'm taken."

She rises, taking her purse in one hand, my hand in the other. We walk from the table toward the bandstand. Jill fishes around in her purse, comes up with a red ribbon.

Jill says, "Give me that enormous green ring-thing."

I hand her my door-knocker. Jill makes a double loop, handing the loose ends to me.

Jill pivots smoothly, pressing her back into my body, saying, "Tie the ribbon around my neck. No. Let it hang down. Not like that, silly. Let it rest between my breasts. You know where they are, you've been staring at them for months. Dangle the ring right there, where the moron can see it when he's hawking my boobs."

Jill spins back into my arms, saying, "Don't worry; he's a few bricks short of a load. Don't worry, Galvan. I don't believe the story about your running away. I believe you were all injured. All of you had concussions. That pair remembers parts of what happened and have confabulated memories around the explosion from what little they remember, their large egos and their antipathy for you."

She says, "Concussions damage the brain. Memories on either side of the impact are blanked. Over time portions return. Parts of what was wiped may never return. It is a lot like the Korsakoff's psychosis which develops in long term alcoholics. What was there in terms of memory is just gone. We see the confabulation as I mentioned among alcoholics speaking of the past. But it also began to show up a lot in the War on Terror among military personnel exposed to traumatic brain injury from the concussive effect of explosives like IED's Everyone inside the blast radius loses memories. When together, they try to reassemble what happened from bits and pieces--spaces between each other's remaining memory. Sometimes, people injured like these two confabulate a common memory, building it from real bits and pieces, preconceived notions and personal prejudices."

She presses her torso to mine whispering in my ear as she lightly kisses my neck, "Wasn't my lecture nice? It seems to have gotten your attention. Is that your gun, detective, or do you really like me?"

The ring sways gently between us as we dance. Do all women have red ribbons in their purse? If I needed a crescent wretch might there be one in her purse? She was right, I really like her.

Jill molds to me. We dance until the music changes, going up tempo. Time to grab a seat before I start grabbing her bottom.

It has been a long day, I'm dragging my right leg. Broken backs are so fun. The world is good tonight. Black and Tan are guests sitting at our table, who cares? The twins aren't with us, they're seated near us.

I'm with a beautiful woman. I may be limping. Then I'll have to limp my way through this. Jill and I walk hand in hand back to our table. The Greek sees something, frowns at me. Then chuckles. Gabby smiles in a motherly fashion.

Abruptly, the Greek's expression clouds. Gabby startles, surprised by the change.

I seat Jill, then sit facing her with my back to the dance floor. The Greek is on point, intently focusing on something coming up behind me. Jill follows the Greek's gaze at what is coming. Her features take on a confused expression. Jill frowns.

Black and Tan pop to their feet like toast from a toaster. These days, I am slow on the uptake. Oh my God, the shit just hit the fan.

I tuck my chin, rising into the coming blow. Every little bit helps. Entering the zone of impact shortens the angle of attack and weakens the force of its torque. Drive into the wave, weaken the impact.

Hands grasp my shoulders at the base of my neck. The hands clamp strongly down, locking in place. I freak out. Having been mostly beheaded, my neck is an incredibly mental weak spot for me. I will kill this prick.

My hands reach back, snatching my attacker's hands, pinning the hands tightly to my shoulders.

The attacker hauls me backward to break my balance.

Now standing, I step back between us, pivoting to face my attacker. I crisscross my opponent's forearms before me, locking the attacking arms against each other. I brace to dislocate my attacker's elbows. His only exit is a full-forward front Judo roll.

OR she can reverse fold her body into my arms, settling her torso into mine.

I should have known from the tiny delicately-boned hands.

She rests her head on the tawny fan of her long hair on my shoulder, looking up at me as she says, "Miss me?"

Women do the unexpected, this one nestles her back into my hips with only the thin blue silk of her dress between us.

Dazed and feeling foolish, I stand, my arms crossed over the warmth of Eva Devereaux's breasts. Eva scoots her bottom back into me. Eva has had some practice over the years doing just that type of thing. She knows well how to scoot and when to best get my attention.

I stand dumbly in place being of two minds. Either I will get an erection and Eva will pick that moment to hip lift me, judo throwing me over her shoulder, or I get the erection and Jill strangles me here on the dance floor. What could go wrong?

Eva relaxes smoothly against my body. No hip buck, no forward throw. Jill is gonna kill me. Eva presses my arms down over her breasts, sighing, "You did miss me."

Lifting her chin, Eva kisses me with open lips. I'm in very big trouble, now.

Lt. Commander Evangeline Deveraux is hard not to miss, and hard not to kiss. This is not the first time I kissed this United States Naval Officer. Not the first time by any measure.

Eva turns her body to face me, nestling in warm and tight. She wears a blue silk gown. Her body is warm, almost hot in my grasp.

Yes, I missed Eva. Paralyzed from the neck down, I have awakened in the dark of night reaching for her with hands that were no longer able to move. Sometimes in fevered dreams I have reached out to strangle this woman. More often, I ached to touch her. The relationship was always complicated.

We have issues. We met in high school, sort of. Passion dragged us onto her couch. More likely we dragged each other. The delightful deed done, violence exploded around us. Violence has dogged our relationship ever since. Weird, but fun, issues remain unsettled.

After I met Jill that snowy afternoon, I haven't thought much about Eva. She left me dying, bleeding out on that medivac deck. Was I glad to be discarded? I suppose so.

Tonight, Eva wears a navy-blue silk sheath, which feels more nightgown than dress. Navy blue, what a surprise. Her soft dress matches the warm, crystal blue warmth of her eyes.

Eva glances over my shoulder, giving Black and Tan her as-you-were gesture. The pair settles into their chairs. As usual the twins are glaring at someone. My goodness they're glaring at me. What a surprise.

As I attempt to step away from my own personal demon, Eva snatches and twists my thumb into a thumb-lock, saying, "Come with me. We need to talk."

I mentioned the unresolved issues.

We walk toward the dance floor. How I hate being bullied by a Glamazon in a silky evening gown, with perky tits and a bodacious bottom. Jill has likely already departed on her way to burn down the boatyard.

Stupid. I should have known that Eva would be lurking nearby as soon as I spotted Blackmon and Tanner. They are her favorite bookends. Like an American Express card, Eva rarely leaves home without them.

If life were a fantasy, I'd describe us as stalking on the floor like jungle cats. Life isn't a fantasy. I am being dragged by my twisted thumb in front of everyone onto said dance floor by a Female Navy SEAL Commander. It is reassuring to realize Eva hasn't changed.

The last time I saw Eva Devereaux she'd just gotten me killed. The last face I saw was Eva's. Well, the last one I saw in Afghanistan. On the flight out I saw Doc Braxton puffing air into my improvised airway. That was scary. Then I saw Solinko sitting on my chest telling me to open wide for chunky. That, was really terrifying.

Eva treated my demise as somewhat unfortunate and distasteful. Not to mention the inconvenience caused by my dying. The mission remains the mission inconvenient. Yes. Significant? Hardly.

Having been disdained for failing to do Eva's bidding, I died and was forgotten for a couple of years. When did her sudden, very public interest in me develop? I hate this bitch. No, it's a guy thing, I want to storm the castle and take the princess. Having been checked off Eva's roster on account of deadness, I was troubled at first, then came to feel relieved. Too bad, so sad, bye, bye. Oh well.

Now, Eva's back. We're waltzing around the floor, rubbing tummies. Rubbing tummies has always been fun for us until the floor falls away beneath us. Eva Devereaux is a woman truly liberated. She's on a mission tonight. She's always on a mission. One mission was to be a fighting admiral, whether or not the Navy likes it. Her mission this evening worries me more, she'd make a great fighting admiral.

U.S. Navy Admirals have run in the Devereaux family since the War of 1812 when one of the Devereaux clan at the Battle of New Orleans quit Jean Laffite's pirate crew for a career in the Navy. He was a gunner for Beluche and Youx. The family has been Navy since. Until Eva was born, Admiral Grandpa are the last of the line.

I once strove to change her destiny, but was found unsuitable as a mate. Truth be told, Eva allowed me to try out for the role on occasion, only to decide I was socially insufficient. Could you see me serving finger-sandwiches at a brunch for officer's wives?

No. This is done. I'm not doing this again. I have to get back to Jill. I reverse Eva's thumb lock. Slipping away, I search the room for Jill.

In the Bible Lot's wife looked back at Sodom after having been told by an Angel of the Lord not to. The Hebrew phrase has complicated meaning. Lot's wife looked back debating the wisdom of the Lord's decision. Her heart was still back in the perversions of Sodom, so she was changed into a pillar of salt. The Angel told Lot's wife to run. She didn't, I didn't either. I also looked back. Eva's face is sad, vulnerable. Her eyes in the dim light of the dance floor now troubled midnight-blue. I've never seen Eva so sad and alone. Right there I turned myself to a pillar of salt in Jill's eyes.

I'm lying to myself. There's something undone between Eva and me. A manly man could make it all right for her. Somewhere in Eva's crazed head, I'm a safe harbor on stormy days. In clear weather Eva has no need of me. She soars on her own power. In troubled weather, she cleaves to me. Somehow Eva believes I won't hurt her.

Eva's forlorn visage dissolves into a look of the satisfaction she now feels in her triumph over my resolve.

To the rest of the guests, it's just a wedding reception. Eva has lived a decade in the eye of the hurricane, spending half her life protecting George Orwell's peaceful sleepers. Then one day, the storm moved on. Storms always do.

The War on Terror began as a Special Forces war and has devolved back into a Special Forces war. Eva's fought that fight. She is the first Female SEAL Team leader. She had the clout to get herself into the experiment, the will to drive herself to compete, and the luck to succeed. Then she lived through a decade doing what had to be done.

Now, life has gone on. Looking at Eva I've seen her attack, plunge into depression, and become elated in triumph in what, may be fifteen minutes? She looks mostly lost and desperate. Moving between emotions swiftly. I fear she's seeking to re-enter the world by returning to a life that has since gone its own way.

Home is a strange, alien place for those returning from this long, long war. She's having a hard time being back in country. Consider that she brought two body-guards to protect her. Chicago is a rough town, but perhaps not that rough.

The kettle in Eva's head is still at full boil. She remained overseas leading her SEALS into battle while I napped at Bethesda. I am bound to Eva at a primal level. She's a former lover and has been a comrade in arms. She led us in war and brought in the medivac that carried me out. Though it may finish my relationship with Jill, I need to hear her out. Eva is sad and lost trying to adapt to a life out of kilter with the one she left behind. The things one does to help a comrade?

Eva's blue eyes are crazier than my green ones. I've finally found someone crazier than me. Eva is always a delight to behold, but she definitely has issues. I take Eva in my arms in a clumsy effort to comfort her. I am familiar with holding Eva, comforting this self-sufficient leader of men is something new. She's trembling like a leaf.

Somewhere before I came along, society decided women needed to do it all. No one can do it all. This war has run longer than any other war in our history. During that long run, women have occupied more combat roles than ever before.

I hold Eva close. Eva's skin seems to vibrate at my touch. My superwoman is approaching the end of her capacity to cope with her world at war. I can't save her. Maybe I can help her a little tonight. My days of being a willing vacation destination for Eva died with me in Afghanistan.

I'll do what I can. Eva and I go way back. I met little Eva of the tight blue-jean cut-offs when I was seventeen. We were fighting for nomination to the Naval Academy at Annapolis. We met at a summer sessions in Annapolis.

Eva and I were in D-Squad under the supervision of a female lieutenant. I note this because, female warfighters were still a rarity. Our lieutenant had just returned from Iraq.

At the time I knew everything. I was a seventeen-year-old after all. I saw our lieutenant as a martinet. All piss and vinegar, lacking common sense. The woman trembled with nervous energy. I had much to learn about myself, women and the stresses of modern war. Commensurately, the LT barely tolerated us. She took her duty to preventing fraternization among squad members somewhat cavalierly. LT expected us to act like adults, police ourselves. Fat chance of that. Suddenly we were down to the last days in Annapolis, what trouble could we get to in a couple of days?

Almost anything.

Detective testimony begins two ways. The first, "On the date and at the time in question..." The second, "My investigation revealed..." Been there, done that.

I recall that on the date and at the time in question, LT worked us all day, convinced all that exercise would exhaust the children. Silly girl, at seventeen marching, running, exercising is how you start your day. The rest of one's day is devoted to eating and thinking about sex.

The Navy delivered us to the Marines at a Severn River embarkation point. We traveled to their compound by a vessel looking more Conestoga Wagon than launch. The Corps ran us through a course of overhand pull-ups, calisthenics, and obstacle course dashes before they sent us back across the Severn for more fun and games.

On return we ran in formation from the de-embarkation point near the submariners monument, We crossed the academy grounds in the noon heat to the old football field. There we were turned over to the SEALS at the Small-Boat Ramp. The ramp sits in the shadow of the new stadium, except it was noon and there was no shadow to speak of.

The stadium thermometer read 103 degrees Fahrenheit, a very humid 103 degrees.

The SEALS did their fire hose thing to cool us down, while we did sit-ups on the pitched concrete launch ramp. That sucked; I can see why many trainees ring-out on the ship's bell.

Under the low-pressure hoses, the cold water was momentarily welcome. The water got cold fast. I looked around for a bell to ring out. The SEALS must've left the bell at Coronado. We were frozen and soaked. For shits-and-giggles, the SEALS then crawled us through red clay mud trenches around the old athletic field. The SEALS constructed the trench maze with a back-hoe. If we popped our heads up, we got blasted with the aforementioned fire hose.

Exhausted, right?

Wrong, were you never seventeen?

I couldn't keep my eyes off the shape of the cold wet Eva's breasts in her muddy T-shirt.

The Eva of those days was on her way to becoming an icon. Earlier in the summer she had been certified as a National Match Distinguished Riflewoman.

She did more sit-ups that day than I have done in my entire life. When we went for a run around the field Eva lapped me. That was OK with me. I got to see Eva dripping muddy water as she passed. She looked amazing. Yeah, I had a thing for Eva Deveraux. I wasn't completely sure of what I was supposed to do, but was committed to doing it immediately.

LT's mistake that day was letting us attend the dance celebrating our stay. At the dance, LT had eyes for the Marine Captain in charge of Squad B. Theirs was an unrequited thing from their academy time. Love was in the air. Dereliction of duty ensued.

Eva and I slipped away. We ran, laughing across campus to Porter Road. I had no idea where we were. Eva headed us for Captain's Row.

I didn't know Captains Row from a park bench. That side street had old large gothic homes. Later I discovered that academy command staff and top educators reside there.

I could've cared less. I was following Eva's little blue-jeaned bottom in the dark.

When we arrived at Eva's house, she informed me that she lived there on Captain's Row with her Grandpa. Admiral Grandpa was away for the evening, visiting her Aunt Evangeline. Grandpa wasn't expected to return until just before our graduation ceremony the next morning.

We flew up the stairs into the darkened house. I slammed the door behind us. We embraced in the doorway. Locked in a grasping, gasping embrace we staggered across her living room where we eventually tumbled into a tangled ball of arms and legs. Clumsy but fun.

It could have been a bed of nails. I don't remember, didn't care. Buttons popped. Clothes dropped. I fumbled with the front clasp of Eva's bra. Inexperience stymied me. I welcomed her assistance in loosing that Gordian knot. I was enamored by every naked square inch of that girl. We both got a little wild.

Later, I sprawled on my back proud and manly, Eva lay naked, draping her leg over me. One of us was purring. Peace and happiness reigned through the world. Lights snapped on. Grandpa come from the sea, early.

Admiral Grandpa is wearing boxer shorts. He holds a lacrosse bat in his right hand, his left holds the hand of an attractive blond woman. The woman is dressed in bewitching black lace. She vaguely resembles Eva. Aunt Evangeline?

Being from the inner city I am both young and quick. At the time I planned on doing this stuff again shortly. I had a strong desire to survive the evening to do so. I leapt to my feet, surprising Admiral Grandpa by snaking my arm over his arm, stripping the lacrosse bat from his hand. It sailed through the air to stick handle-first in a nearby wall.

Enraged, Admiral Grandpa drops the lady's hand in an effort to choke me senseless.

My ass is grass. I agreed with the ladies, who are yelling, "Stop it. You're gonna kill him."

The lady in lingerie pulls at Admiral Grandpa saying, "Steve, he's a kid."

Alas, 'Steve' really wants to kill me for doing to his granddaughter, what he had been doing to Aunt Evangeline.

Silky's words sound in my head, "Break his nose, the taste of his own blood will slow him down." Silky, a man of many wise, grandfatherly sayings.

Admiral Grandpa lets loose a right cross.

I slip his punch, only to receive Rolex gouges to my forehead.

Grandpa is a Naval Officer and an adult.

I am Deuce's son, Old-School's protégé.

Admiral Grandpa, miffs another right.

I land an overhand-right, hooking Admiral Grandpa's left temple. The blow lands square.

Admiral's Grandpa's eyes roll back in his head. Doesn't go down, but wobbles.

Body weight will tell, eventually. Time for a Galvan to flee.

I crack Grandpa's jaw with an upper-cutting rising elbow. The admiral slumps against the wall.

I flurry punches, stepping back, to drop into a low crouch before spinning in a reverse circle to sweep his feet out from under Admiral Grandpa. My Iron-Broom slid Grandpa down the wall, sitting him hard on his ass.

Grandpa oof's as he lands on his keister.

Quoteth Lynyrd Skynyrd, 'Give me one step mister, just one step toward the door.'

In the middle of the fist fight, Eva somehow got dressed as we fought. How do women do that so quickly? Another mysterious thing I'll never understand. Eva stands beside the somewhat naked blond lady. Yeah, this Aunt Evangeline that has her arm over Eva's shoulders. In perspective their resemblance confirms the family relationship.

Eva definitely inherited those long legs from her mother's side of the family.

This woman is Eva's namesake, Aunt Evangeline, her mother's older sister. The lady in black is smiling as she gives me an appraising look. She whispers in Eva's ear. Eva smiles brightly and hugs her aunt.

As I slip from Admiral Grandpa's grasp, Eva slips up to me for a quick kiss. Her eyes are lit with a new bright light. Tonight, I discovered many things, and for the first time met a woman who enjoys being fought over. I mumble something about loving her and apologize for getting carried away.

Eva shakes her head slyly in the negative. She pushes me toward the front door as she hands me my pants and shoes.

Admiral Grandpa is unsteadily staggering to his feet.

So, I take that one step, Mister, That one step toward the door. Feet don't fail me now. Out that door, naked I run, jeans over my shoulder, shoes in my hand.

I don my jeans as I flee, hopping from one foot to the other. Looking back for pursuit, I slip my running shoes on, and I'm off. Dressed in what I have, I find myself at Bancroft Hall.

At Bancroft, my roommates already initiated their abandon shit drill. Their stuff is gone. The rats have left the ship. Sitting on my bunk I eventually drift off. I dream restlessly of a sea of swimming rats, and vaguely familiar figures swimming desperately from my sinking ship.

So much for lasting friendships and academy bonds.

The Navy mantra, swim as hard as you can away from a sinking ship. They say that a lot in the Navy. I was never in the Navy; once visited their academy. They must have a lot of ships sink.

The LT strides in and boots me in the rear end. She announces that I am one colossal fuck-up. Because I'm now a man of the world I readily notice that LT's uniform blouse lieutenant's blouse is misbuttoned. Visible is the pink lace and the pink skin of a new hickey adorning her cleavage. Apparently, I'm not alone in my fraternization, this night.

I wonder? Am I in trouble for having sex, or for getting caught?

Staring at LT's breast-hickey doesn't help my case. LT and her captain are considering love, I guess, at twenty-three. Eva and I are seventeen. Obviously, I screwed the pooch.

By dawn's early light, or maybe a little later my parents arrive at the main gate for our session graduation. From there, my parents were escorted before Admiral Grandpa.

LT personally escorted me to the same meeting, later. The only reason I wasn't in shackles was because LT couldn't find any. Judging from his fierce expression, Admiral Grandpa is out for blood. Mine.

My mother is worried. My father is studying paperwork the older of the two policemen just handed him. He looks up at me with the icy cold Silky eyes. He grasps his chin with his index finger over his closed lips. During the whole process she is staring me in the eye. He sighs loudly, then looks down at the paper.

I've just been told in the unspoken language of my Grandfather

180

Silky to shut my lip and keep it zipped. I've also been told that Deuce just read something on the paperwork that will affect proceedings.

Admiral Grandpa appears to see himself as being in charge. He looks to be proceeding over a court of the star chamber. The younger police officer almost gets to read me my rights from a card when Admiral Grandpa waves the surprised policeman to silence. My parents will be informed of my sins. Having shamed my family with my misdeeds, I will be carried bodily to the nearest, rope-draped yardarm.

RHIP (Rank hath its privileges).

The older policeman frowns, looking Admiral Grandpa up and down. Then takes the Miranda card from his partner, before reciting my rights from memory, while holding the card before him.

The Admiral splutters. Apparently, this is a police investigation of events between civilians, not a sailor's summary court martial. Striving to assist Admiral Grandpa in regaining control, an aide appears from the ether to hand the officers and my father a formal Navy summary listing of my many indiscretions. Deuce reviews the allegations

The older officer glances at the paperwork then tosses it to a side table near his chair. The aide's list of my indiscretions is thicker than I expected. Eva and I must've had more fun than I remembered. I wonder if the summary mentions the admiral's lacrosse bat, Aunt Evangeline in black lace and stockings or the consensual nature of what happened between Eva and I. Probably not.

Deuce looks up from his document to stare at me. He shrugs and points out something to my mother. She startles. Deuce squeezes her arm before she speaks, shakes his head. She nods.

As well as being the mean one, the father of the other mean one and an evil sorcerer, Deuce is a detective to the bone. Deuce shrugs, leaning over to say something to the older Annapolis Police Officer. Admiral Grandpa leans forward in an effort to hear the conversation. By his expression, Admiral Grandpa regrets placing the police chairs so far from his throne that he can't catch what Deuce said.

The older officer says, "It's the same."

The older officer says, "And?"

Deuce responds, "My son isn't seventeen, yet."

The officer asks, "I noticed. Does he have a driver's license?"

At Deuce's nod I hand my license to the officer.

"Oh. Ah. OOPS," the older officer says in reply. He hands my driver's license to the younger officer. They both study my academy application, then take what looks to be Eva's from Admiral Grandpa's battleship-sized desk. Admiral Grandpa misses a grab for the paperwork.

The officers smile at each other. Apparently, they aren't fans of the Admiral's RHIP attitude.

Deuce asks, "Any other allegations?"

The officer says, "None to us, nor was one made to the victim's advocate at the hospital. The sole allegation is statutory rape, on the theory that the victim can't consent because of being of tender years."

Deuce glances around the room before saying, "As the officer just noted, the allegation in this case is that the victim cannot give consent, therefore the alleged offender and the victim cannot have consensual sexual activity."

Admiral Grandpa says, "Enough legal poppycock. I order you to perform your duty and make an arrest immediately."

The officers shake their heads in the negative at Admiral Grandpa's outburst. The older officer says, "Nope, not gonna do that. This happens with kids their age. It would ruin the kid's life and ruin the victim's Naval career."

Admiral Grandpa roars in outburst, "I don't give a shit. Do your duty, place the charge. He ain't got no Navy career. He's going to the brig."

The officers look at Deuce. He nods, "Admiral, our son is soon to be seventeen. Currently he is sixteen. Your granddaughter is currently eighteen. There are two years between these kids at present. The underage person is the victim in a statutory rape case. A gap of two years aggravates the offense."

Deuce says, "I think I speak for my family when I say we don't want to press charges against your granddaughter for statutory rape. I understand your being a by-the-book naval officer. We don't want to ruin her promising future by having her arrested for a sexual assault on a child. Let it go. I'm not making excuse for them. They're young, maybe they are in love.

It ain't right. I feel so cheap. I don't feel like a victim. Eva at 18 to my 16. Eva is technically the miscreant.

The admiral appears confused. Deuce assures the admiral that as my parents they do not wish for Eva to suffer for our youthful indiscretion. He advises the admiral that nothing further need be said of the unfortunate incident. Our family has no need to teach Eva a lesson. She deserves her U. S. Naval career.

Later in the day, my summer session and my nascent naval career ended ignominiously.

When called by name at graduation ceremony, I received a certificate of attendance in a plain cardboard folder. Indeed, rank has its privileges.

Down deep I think my parents might not have wanted their only son to enlist in the War on Terror. They never said. Being as I am, I willfully chose to participate in the War on Terror. It was my way of pretending to be a warrior. Being a genius, I almost got myself killed. Parents rightly worry about their children, especially the dim-witted ones like me.

As I passed Eva in line for my certificate, she grabbed my ass. Yes, I jumped. The D-Team laughed.

Eventually, Eva became Midshipman Devereaux. Midshipmen and Midshipwomen go on summer 'cruises', sometimes on actual vessels. Don't know, wasn't there. Somehow Eva, who has girl-parts, got herself into an experimental SEALS rotation. RHIP? It appears clout remains clout the world round. At some point during her first 'cruise', Eva, being Eva, found adult companionship copasetic with her new lifestyle.

Bye, Bye Eva. My wounded heart healed, broke again until it acquired the texture of Formica.

Eventually Greek and I signed our employment contract with the secret service. We were assigned to a Fire-Base Shudarski in Afghanistan with our secret service team. We fought U.S. Currency Infringement. In the process, we found ourselves under a SEAL-Special Operations Command in Gardez, Afghanistan.

That endeavor placed us under the command of the by then Lt. Commander Evangeline Deveraux, USN. Little Eva was back. When I explained the situation to the Greek he commented, "Galvan, when you screw-up, you really screw-up. You are more fun than a barrel of monkeys."

Luckily, Galvans grow late in life. I added six inches in height between sixteen and the present day.

With six additional inches in height, a beard and shaggy hair Deveraux didn't recognize me. Being a 'guest in her house,' I kept my mouth shut, only telling the Greek. Partner-thing. I was hale and hearty, with 50 additional pounds of back and shoulder weight, cop arms and a 20-inch 'cop neck'. My new appearance concealed my identity. Eva was no longer the prom queen. She was my boss and a SEAL Commander. I'd have been a long time walking home from Gardez.

As a SEAL team leader, Eva is scary when she's just doing her rounds.

Subtle quirks of fate don't register in Devereaux clan, there's no sense of humor there. Life is a carefully guided tour to the top.

Everything goes swimmingly in Afghanistan. Eva never notices me. Until, one day we hump our rucks up some endless mountainside that felt like Everest. Catching our breath, we position in the shade of an overhang on the long trail from where we had been to where we arrived.

Being judgmental, Lt. Commander Eva Devereaux stalked past my position. Eva's was strutting well that day. Exhausted, in a moment of weakness, I allow myself to intently admire that strut. As mentioned earlier Eva has an effect on me, regardless of our past history.

So, I sit there, in the shade, on the side of the mountain, in the middle of nowhere hawking Eva's ass. The girl is possessed of one bodacious bottom. Even when the Commander is exuding martial vigor. I do not do so in disrespect. I am recognizing a long-past lover, saying nothing to anyone. The only thing moving is my eyes. Then I get caught. From Eva's return glare, I am certain that staring at the backside of a lieutenant commander is a hanging offense in the Uniform Military Code of Justice (UCMJ, 64 Stat. 109, 10 U.S.C. §§ 801–946).

Weakness on my part. Shouldn't have done that. Bad move. Eva spins on me. I rise to my feet. With hands on hips she charges up to me. Can a civilian be brought before the mast for ogling? Awaiting my fate, I exchanged glares with Commander Devereaux for the first time since coming to Afghanistan. Outside of my control, I may have allowed an eyebrow to rise as my best crooked bad-boy smile formed.

With her fierce glare Eva holds my eyes. Suddenly her expression changes.

I expect to be slugged, or taken to the nearest wall to be shot. Eva's eyes soften. A shy smile of recognition forms on her lips. Self-consciously Eva sweeps a loose golden lock from her cheek, tucking it beneath her black ball-cap.

Eva's eyes pop in recognition. Trouble. Eva sweeps her eyes over me, down then back up to mine, saying, "Where on earth did you come from, Galvan? My God you've been eating your Wheaties?"

Eva and I stand silently facing each other on a narrow mountainside goat trail. Eva's blue eyes are bright. She reaches out her right hand to brush the stubble on my face. Trouble, trouble, boil and bubble. She quickly draws her hand back looking left and right. Her eyes settle left.

I follow her gaze to Emma, sitting on a rock watching the inter-play between us. She drolly rolls her eyes at me. Eva and I step away from each other, former lovers in the process of appraisal and reappraisal. Eva smiles, then turns continuing her rounds. Nothing much was said in the days that followed.

I think Eva was finally war-weary. A decade is a long time. The satisfaction of command carries with it the weight of responsibility. Troops and resources need doling out, objectives need achieving, mission successful completion. The process ground good men up, and these days it grinds up good women.

I've become part of Eva's system. I become committed to my squad-bay. I don't like Black or Tan, much, I've protected them with my life more than once. We've wandered out on many a limb togeth-er. Operate at the pace of do or die. Pay attention. Bide your time. Contemplate the contract's end.

Then? Then, get the fuck gone. No matter how hard you fight, things won't change the people of the graveyard of empires unless the people living here choose to change.

The days pass. Occasionally I feel eyes on me. People shooting at you on a regular basis gives you eyes in the back of your head. You develop vibrant sensitivity for being watched. Watchers kill. My eyes would dart about under my Oakley's seeking the lookout, only to find Eva studying me. Sometimes Eva would remove her Oakley's. Her eyes had a predatory cast to them.

In the real world, I'd say she wanted me. This is something more, Eva needed to absorb something from me. I felt then too that she wanted me to give her back the past. The past is gone, I'll listen, but the past, like our dead won't return any time soon.

Emma is wise to the change between Eva and I. Emma Wainwright is Eva's shadow. They are female friends when no other American women are within a hundred miles. As a result, Emma becomes hostile to my presence. In that period, Emma starts referring to me as Trouble, which is awarded me as my call sign by her buddy, Eva.

Emma would say, "Trouble, quit distracting her. Trouble, you'll get us all killed."

Eva's walk began to sway with her SEAL swagger when I came around. I think I came to represent unfinished business out in the world. In our core we all held in focus something of what we wanted on homecoming. Thoughts of a warm place at some distant place in our futures sustained us on dark days. If we don't get killed in the cold reality of the present.

No matter how I fantasize about Eva, I don't understand Eva. What I've come to understand is Eva's low level of regard for me. Loyalty runs deep in Eva. Loyalty to the Navy. Loyalty to the SEALs. Loyalty to family. Loyalty to country. Beyond that?

In the desolation of Afghanistan, I think of putting right past wrongs. For some uncontrollable reason, I must have reached a certain age, I really want to pop a bun in little Eva's oven.

That may not be a good idea. Unfortunately for me, Eva remains Eva. I doubted then and I doubt now that I am listed on the wall of Eva's loyalty as a keeper. In Eva's world my purpose appears transitory. I must be a dandy fellow. Eva wants me but does want to keep me. Every guy's dream. Why does that bother me when I pause to think of it? Does sex have a higher purpose, say it ain't so.

Since we arrived in Afghanistan the Greek and I have become the personification of the failure of military discipline. Our very existence may destroy the universe. Adversarial? Sort of.

Eva's warming demeanor toward me turns things downright homicidal. Her Rottweilers begin to array themselves to protect Eva's honor. Does she want it protected? No.

Curiosity kills cats. Eva's got curious. She'd been through three tours before I showed up to study her dusty little bottom. The callow lad she dumped is now back as a man grown. Eva is appraising me as she did years before. I may like to consider Eva for the potential for an us in the impact of our collision. Eva's version of an us is most likely not the same concept at all. Eva wants to play games. At ten years Eva is Navy and sailors on leave are notoriously short-term thinkers. Passion overwhelms, but subordinates itself to the limit of shore leave.

As the heat rises between the twins and I, the Greek is having a picnic, smirking malevolently at the pair. The Greek enjoys smirking at the twins, as much as messing with them. They get so pissy.

Our Secret Service partners, Big Bob and Little Bob are southern gentlemen of a certain quality, they choose not to see. While having all this fun in the wilds of the Hindu Kush, operational tenor tightened.

The bad-guys begin to anticipate our moves. When they manage to pattern us they'll be waiting. They get a vote, too. One might think them out to kill us. It was long past time to change our game plan. We need to modify our game and stay away from repeating past success.

The military is a bureaucracy. The first function of the bureaucracy is to keep the bureaucracy intact. It does so by creating fixed dogma. The novel, workable plan is transformed into dogma. Dogma gets you killed. Eva was preoccupied, then. She was cocky from years of success, but tired down into her bones. As a result, Eva let the bad guys pattern us.

My old sparring partner from the park, Doug the biker, told me that he was tormented at times in his sleep with memories of being patterned by the forces of Mohamed Farrah Hassan Aidid in Mogadishu on the day the Blackhawks went down. Do the same thing one time too often, they'll be waiting for you.

A controlled delivery took us one day to an isolated village southwest of Gardez on the edge of a mountain valley. The Shah-i-Kot Valley has been known as the seat of the king, since Alexander the Great was a pup.

Eva Devereaux is a competitor. She needs to come out first in every fight. Therefore, Deveraux is our sniper. Emma Wainwright is her spotter. Above that dusty village Eva, Emma and a protection team positioned first, as always, is done to be our overwatch. Eva positions her team above the town on the highest point. As usual her sniper skillset at the tip of the spear. If you take over-look, you can't be command and control. Eva didn't feel much like coaching. She wants to play, too.

Unfortunately, Eva has done this village the same way previously, twice since I'd been in country. Both times from the same perch. Bad move, that.

On the day and at the time in question, Eva sets her a sniper overwatch on the same lopped off hill. The local map name of the village sounded like Tudeha Gar.

In honor of a guy I once worked with, I rename Eva's hill 'Tud" Ghar. The guy whom I'd worked with on the docks called my crew a bunch little 'tuds'. When pressed for a definition of a tud the older guy related that a 'Tud' was a little dick with its head cut off. I fear he was prone to make things up.

Tud Ghar straddles a Silk Road choke point. Opium cakes are processed there into non-water-soluble Heroin#1. Heroin weighs less than opium cake and is more easily smuggled. Less bulk, fewer pack animals less attention drawn. Smuggling, growing and manufacturing in the opium to heroin trade are solid career choices in the wilds of Afghanistan. If they had high schools, it would be in the curriculum.

The Greek and I, accompanied by the twins, enter the low end of the village via the Gardez road after Eva announces the overwatch is in position. Rubble had been heaped in the streets in odd places since our last visit. New walls had been built. Throughways now lead to blocking rubble strewn, high walled dead ends.

We pick up our pace, re-route through an alley, losing time, making forward progress. As we approach the headman's house, we are greeted by a roar of gun-fire, not good.

The crescendo rises around the Tud itself. The overlook team is under fire. We force our way through the rear of a blacksmith's shop. Deveraux's overwatch team is surrounded on the Tud and they are being bum-rushed by a small army.

Raccoons aren't very smart. Dogs tend to run them up trees. Devereaux has got treed. She's in the process of getting her eyes bloused. Then she'll look like a raccoon. Eva, Eva, Eva.

We emerge perpendicular to the al Qaeda assault column assaulting Deveraux's trapped overwatch team. Somewhere I snatch up a blacksmith's cutting hammer, on which one hammer face is 'V' wedged. The wedge is used to cut lead-soft cherry red heated bar stock.

I break the lock hasp to exit the street gate. I glance up the tud. Snipers usually pick their roost for its multiple exits. Don't enter a hide you can't back out of. Made lazy by repetition, Eva places them on isolated high ground where entry is exit. Good field of fire, poor place to hide. Hard to escape through a blocked exit.

Eva is up there on scope with her Sako TRG M10 Sniper Weapon System, calmly sending .338 Lapua rounds screaming downhill. There just aren't enough of them With Eva on the rifle a rhinoceros is doomed. Eva just faces an army of Rhinoceri.

She knocks fighters down as fast as she can work the bolt. Stalin was right, quantity has its own quality.

As unit roles changed, psychological warfare was the ticket which allowed women to be attached to the Green Berets. Eva is better at sniping than at psychology. That skill, and changing times, opened the BUDS door. Skill and determination got her into the SEALs. Clout may have played a part on getting her high on the waiting list.

Considering Eva's homicidal demeanor and red hair, the call sign bestowed on Eva was originally 'Blood-Angel'. Over time, the double syllable effect of the two words created on air difficulties during emergencies. Someone reduced Blood-Angel to Bang.

I couldn't get the team to revise my call sign to something simple like, 'Hero-to-Multitudes' but the Team stuck with 'Trouble'.

Somehow, from a leak, or by monitoring air traffic, or maybe from the radio units taken off our massacred DEA team, al Qaeda became aware of Eva's call sign. Coming over our team frequency they deduced Eva was on the Tud again that morning. Al Qaeda wanted 'Blood Angel' and 'White-Girl'. Soiled or unsoiled by the wear and tear of war the women had big bounties on their heads. So, al Qaeda kept coming and kept talking on the radio about their plans for our female partners.

The enemy's plans for the women are sexual, depraved and sadistic. Al Qaeda and the Taliban have an eighth-century mind set, but they act like high school kids on the telephone. Talk and talk and talk.

Being Irish I'm a sucker for a forlorn hope, so up the Tud I go. Abruptly, we are in the middle of their assault column, as we rush out of the blacksmith shop screaming like Banshees. Surprise, extreme violence and large volume noise work wonders. Sometimes that's all it takes to break a narrow over -ocused attack plan. Enemy confidence melts to dread, luck evaporates in the hot sun and it's time to run like hell, abandon ship, every rat for himself.

The Greek realizes we are delaying the inevitable. Sooner or later the bad guys will get wise to there being only four of us. He calls the cavalry. At that point our cavalry is a Marine Force Recon quick reaction force. The Greek tells them to come, now or not come at all. They came.

Things get messy, anyway. It is a very close thing.

Superior tactics and weapons go a long way, but sheer numbers have a quality of their own. Very soon, we are black-on-ammo, down to one or a partial magazine.

I had picked up that 40-ounce hammer in the blacksmith shop. Empty, I slung my M-4. The battle goes eighth century. Hand to hand we aren't going to last long. I lay into my opponents with the small 9mm runaway gun from my go-bag and my new hammer.

My world becomes small and medieval. How can one hold the enemy close by the belt when they don't wear belts? Then the Marines *save the day. The Marines are like that. Their Stryker Combat Vehicles send the enemy reeling. We survive for another day.*

At the onset of darkness, we laager with the Marines high on a hill-side road looking down on the village we abandoned. Darkness falls, as our enemy re-occupy Tud Ghar.

In deepening darkness, her AC-130 gunship comes on circuit. Over the distant thrum of giant engines, the very female voice of the Angel of Death speaks into the Valley of Tud Ghar. The Angel announces that she will not tolerate those who attacked her sisters.

Silence follows as gun crews marked their targets in the darkness. The Angel electronically seizes the local airways. With loud speakers blaring and over the airways she chastises the Taliban and al Qaeda in a sad voice. A yellow tongue of flame flicked from the darkness splashing fire over Tud Ghar. Moments later, the whirring endless roar of Gatling gun fills the dark night, raining death and magic upon those who surge into the village.

I assume the survivors, if any, are frightened out of their wits. The Angel of Death and her dragon-tongue scared the living shit out of me. From above expended casings rain down, spewing spent brass upon us during one pass. The air stunk of burnt brass. I think I still have a burn scar where one went down my vest.

Eventually, we withdraw back to Gardez. At our base-camp we are debriefed to the point of insanity. Who fucked up? Why? Our role was documented, hashed, rehashed, likely ignored. I assume they swallow what we tell them.

Upon being released from the debriefing the Greek and I retire to our quarters. Nap time.

Our quarters are a converted cargo box.

We cut out doors and window openings. Then we meshed and screened those windows so as to keep out grenades and rocks. All sides of the container house had firing ports. Afghanistan makes for a collegial atmosphere. Beneath the floor we built in an escape portal and concealed a tunnel out of the vicinity. To the whole we attached our lovely covered, shade porch. Home would've looked stylish in 1930s Appalachia.

As I approach, the Greek sits on the porch sipping a mint julep out of a tin cup. Inside our steel shack, I hang my bail-out bag on its hook over my bed. I then spray-clean the action of my M-4 and 9mm pistol. I reload magazines for both and rack each. Pay attention, be ready. Count the days. Shit happens.

I try to peel off my grubby, black Chicago Police 'Homicide' T-shirt. The one bearing the slogan, 'My Day Begins, When Yours Ends'. Behind me, the porch door flies open.

Between sweaty shirt and big head, I find myself stuck. The sunglasses on top of my skull do not help. They jam against the bridge of my nose. Ouch. No wonder it seems so dark in here.

The door slams closed. I turn my t-shirt ensconced face to the doorway, "For chrise sake, Joe. If you break the god-damned door, we'll be up all night fixing it."

Small palms smashed into my chest. A slender ankle wrapped behind mine. Trapped, I fall flat across my bunk.

Eva's voice announces, "Tud Ghar huh, a dick without a head. Really, Galvan? Playing games? Did you think I wouldn't remember? Do I look stupid enough to forget the first guy I ever made love with?"

Recognition dawns. Too late now. Eva pins my arms over my head. She slowly extracts me from my t-shirt trap, tossing the shirt in the corner on top of her BDU jacket.

Eva drops her gun belt on my desk, then pulls her SEAL T-Shirt over her head. My turn. I snatch her belt to me, releasing the buckle and dropping her blue jeans to the floor. Grasping her pale hips, I settle Eva onto my bunk. As I finish disrobing Eva draws me down on top of her. A struggle of one sort or another fills what was left of the night.

I rise early, Eva, the infamous Lt. Commander Devereaux sleeps late, must've been tired. The Twins are sound asleep on the Greek's porch swing, don't ask. The Greek has a finger in many pies. The Greek sits across the porch from them with a double-barreled coach gun across pointed sort of at the Twins from under a camouflaged survival blanket. I signal him to wait one. The Greek shakes his head sadly. Would have been a waste of time talking; the Twins sleep leaning on each other snoring and drooling on each other on the swing.

I return shortly from the general's mess. The Greek has friends there who appreciate capitalism. I leave all but two coffees on a table near the Greek's rocker.

When I enter Deveraux rises shyly, leaning on one arm. Her red hair loose about her shoulders, her small breasts perfect in the dawn light. She sips inky, mud black coffee as she dresses in silence. Eva has duties. Her t-shirt was shredded during the night's activities. She dons my black one, wears the camouflage BDU jacket open over it.

Without a word she kisses me lightly, rises to leave, then returns for a deep bright-eyed, happy kiss before strolling out into the cool morning air with her BDU jacket flapping open over my Homicide T-Shirt. Eva gives me a wicked smile, blows me a wicked kiss, heading to her quarters.

By that time the Twins are up and drinking coffee before falling into step behind their commander. I shake my head. They sat outside on the porch all night guarding Eva from me. I hope we didn't disturb their rest. A new item added to their list of reasons for killing me.

Across the porch, the Greek rises stiffly from his rocking chair. He sits out here on watch for us, watching the Twins watch us.

The Greek glances at me with tired eyes, "Kid, you are somethin' else. That pair was ready to kill you. The racket you two made kept half the camp awake."

The Greek goes inside to sleep.

Me? I'm hungry, exercise gives me an appetite. I go to breakfast twice.

Two weeks later, Eva gets me killed, when the Greek is in Kandahar scheming up a shipment of God knows what.

Now Eva wants to rub tummies again. That has always turned out so well.

Eva remains a hard to resist woman. I think Eva needs to stay in my former life. Eva and I are neither teen lovers in heat, nor survivors escaping death in need of violent love to efface the presence of imminent doom. That was a mouthful! Like the rest of us, Eva needs to work at saving herself.

Time to get back to Jill, and away from my wayward past.

12

WE ALL GOT ISSUES

I glance at Eva in her blue silk dress standing close against me. So much for the days of yore. Time to exit stage left. Just then, Eva settles proprietarily into my arms. A major problem, that. On some levels I feel as though she belongs in my arms. Breaking with Eva will be harder than I anticipated.

Eva decides that in dancing, as in all other things, she must lead. Maybe it's genetic. Maybe if they used it as a final definitive exam for leadership school, we'd save money. With one dance, the nation would definitively know if one was leader material. You got what it takes, or not.

Eva's assertion of that one small control warns me. In that instant Eva marked the page, folding the corner back. I stand motionless. As bony as I am, I'm hard for a woman Eva's size to drag around the dance floor.

Eva's eyes snap to mine. I've displayed the temerity to challenge her dance management skills. Tension sparks. I say, "Let me lead, Eva. It's boy-girl. Lt. Commander Devereaux, we are not on maneuvers, we're dancing"

Eva's balks, stops tugging, her face tightens. "*Commander* Devereaux, Galvan. After you left, I was promoted."

Left? Difference of opinion. I left because my body was no longer operating.

Rank is the definitive characteristic in Eva's world.

"I didn't leave, Eva. I died," I snarl, having lost capacity to subtly make my point.

I release my grasp on her, creating enough room for a slight bow, "Congratulations, Commander Devereaux."

Turning about, I initiate my escape. Eva sighs audibly as she yanks me back into contact with her whipcord tight torso. She assumes a bored, languid expression draping her arm over my shoulder.

Eva softens her body, forming to mine. Relaxing, she lays a cheek to my chest, "I thought you were gone, baby. I'm glad I have you back."

She tries out a sultry tone, "I couldn't imagine life without you out there somewhere waiting for me. I have been wandering around lost. I thought you dead, baby. Then out of the blue Emma called me in Annapolis. She was making sure I was coming to her wedding."

Devereaux continues, "Emma was weird, all girly conspiratorial. She was all, 'I got a secret.' Girls get so like that. She asks me if I'm bringing anyone, 'special'. I told her I was bringing the Twins."

Why on earth did she invite them? Anyway, they make excellent bodyguards.

Eva asks, "I mean, do I look like I'm hiding a gun under this dress? If you want, you can search me."

Never vacuous before, Eva drones on, "I set up the Twin's shore-leave so the Navy will pay them. After all, this wedding is in Chi Raq. My God, these people are all killing each other, aren't they? You'd think Emma would find someplace civilized."

Eva molds her body tightly against mine. Seeking warmth? The air-conditioner may be penetrating the single ply of silk over her abdomen.

Eva continues coyly, "'Em' told me she meant 'special,' like an important male friend. I said, 'I hadn't planned to, but when I got back to Annapolis, I expected to hear something significant from a former beau."

Eva lifts her head from my chest to look at my face. Seeking my reaction? She is absolutely crazy. Eva's already playing me off someone.

Eva says, "My old beau is a full bird colonel in the Marine Corps. I told Emma I couldn't bring him because he was otherwise engaged."

A frown appears on Eva's delicate features. She does not like the something else to do part. Said he had something he needed to do, "Do you believe that? My best friend is well, I think they call it jumping the broom. Kevin can't even make the time to come."

Why all this dancing and squirming with me when she has a suitor?

Eva continues, "In our conversation, Emma mentioned that Vito ran into you. He told her you were living in an abandoned factory. You're living in an abandoned factory? Really, Galvan?"

She continues, "Vito Gennaro, what a strange name for a Black. How does that work? Was there a Gennaro Plantation or something?"

Annoyed I answer, "He's Italian. His family is Calabrese. His father's name is Vito. It's a family tradition for first sons to take the father's name."

An arch of eyebrow from Commander Eva, "VITO told Emma that you were starting a gang fight with a bunch of bikers. At least you could have called before getting yourself killed."

A silence ensues, which I no longer wish to break. .

My lack of response makes Eva's tone sadden, "When I heard you were alive, I couldn't breathe, I hyperventilated. I DO NOT GET GIRLIE, MISTER. You already made me cry twice, don't do it again."

War fucks up all comers. Nobody gets a pass. Even Commander Eva Devereaux.

Eva has a good heart down inside her navy armor-plate. Her heart is hurting. Ease up, Galvan. Let her get it out of her system before you go.

Eva says, "Emma freaked. I'm sitting in my academy office wailing away with tears running down my face. Boogers everywhere. Suddenly, I was choking, crying, laughing." She grabs my shoulder, "One of my mid-shipmen rushed for a medic. He thought the 'Old-Lady' had a heart attack. Do you believe they call me "the Old Lady", outside of my presence mind you? Are we old enough for heart attacks, baby? Anyway, I was rocking back and forth and making awful sounds."

Eva is crying freely, forehead pressed to my shoulder. "Do you still like me? Even a little, baby?"

Pressing herself tightly to me she smiles. Asked, but not interested in an answer?

Why tell this? Eva's awaiting an offer of marriage. Why massage me with her heaving bosom. I'm not on the agenda?

Do I want to be on her agenda? I begin to doubt it. Maybe I've been designated for her Chicago bachelorette party? That would really disappoint ladies in attendance.

Eva is an emotional wreck. I fear she needs a shoulder to cry on. I'll listen.

Eva continues. "When the Twins and I rotated out, I went straight to Grandpa's. As the plane flew over Annapolis, I knew for the first time, I'd made it. home. A weight lifted off my chest."

"Was it like that after you left for home?"

I think, 'No, bitch. I died in route, only to come back trapped in a broken body. No window seat, just a moldy acoustic ceiling to look at in Bethesda.'

With a confused expression Eva asks, "No? Well, I just blubbered. I was just so glad to be out of Afghanistan. Then I ran a threat check in my head of those seated around me. Instead, I saw the faces of my men who had died. All of us who didn't make it out of your damn Hindu Kush."

"You called it 'The Kush', you sounded so Rudyard Kipling. Gardez and the Hindu Kush are a world apart."

Eva's mad now. At me, again? The world? She snarls, "You god-damned romantic. Something is wrong with you. Life isn't romantic. Life is duty, honorably executed."

She soars onward, "We're not in the 19th Century. We're in the very nasty 21st Century. No white dress and veil for me. I'm a SEAL, God Damned Commander, not a wilted memsahib."

As usual Eva is nuts and blowing up whatever bridges we still have between us.

Her shoulders tremble. She chokes, cries against me. "I had all the faces of my dead flashing through my memory. I named all the people I got killed. They all lounged around me, nobody showed the proper military courtesy. They were dead, they didn't give a shit."

Eva's double-palms away from my chest, "I expected to enjoy my freedom flight, but I sat in my damn seat, wearing my dress whites, blubbering like a bitch."

She roars loudly, "I DON'T DO THAT STUFF, GALVAN. The flight attendant brought me some Kleenex. I acted girlie nice. I coped. I stopped the blubbering."

"Then I panicked, I left someone over there. I couldn't recall who got left behind. We bring everybody out with us. SEALs leave no man behind."

"I wrote letters to almost all the families. You know, 'Your Son died bravely in the service of his country, fighting for the freedom of a grateful nation.' Who had I left out?"

Eva knocks my arms from her body, snapping loudly, "It was you, you bastard. You had to call my bluff. You had to prove my battle plan was wrong. Then you got yourself killed to rub my nose in it, you son-of-a-bitch."

Crazy as a bed bug. She says loudly, "I blocked you out. I never wrote your parents the fucking form letter. I couldn't. I'm that Navy slut who tried to put their darling boy in jail. I got you barred from the academy. Then I killed you. I'll never write them. I won't give them the satisfaction."

Eva's eyes look inward, lost in her thoughts, "The plane went silent. The stewardess, flight-attendant, whatever they call the bimbos, said nothing. A moment before, everyone was full of sympathy for the sobbing little biotch. Hysterics are a girl thing. Maybe they thought the little dear was being hormonal, my time of the month. Ignore her, you know, support the troops."

"FUCK THAT, GALVAN. My silence scared the shit out of them. Suddenly they were seeing the dark side. Damn, they got nervous. Fuck 'em, if they can't take a joke."

I think, I'm not the only one with PTSD. In this war, genius prevailed. We sent in the women. Now they are as crazy as we are. Now the nuts can breed together and produce exceptionally crazy kids. Sorry, teacher, my mom can't come to the PTA meeting; she's banned for bayoneting some bitch at the last meeting.

Eva comes back to the present. "Emma and I were the only white women over there. We could cry on each other's shoulder. She told me about Vito, I got a surprise there. I told her about my old beaus and complained to her about the big dumb Irish cop who was ogling me."

She's free associating, "You never said a thing, Galvan. You just smirked whenever I turned my back. I could feel those wicked green eyes gliding all over my body. When did you get green eyes, Galvan?"

So nuts, so unobservant. I've always had green eyes. Too much crazy is weighing down one slender redhead.

Eva picks at the loose flip-knot of my tie. Eva's all Navy. Is she squaring my tie knot? Annoyed, I grasp her hands, to stop the fiddling, "I don't do ties, Eva. It's a slashed throat thing."

Eva's eyes pop, she startles, "It's not right."

"Eva, it's OK. It's too late to square me away, darlin'."

Eva asks rhetorically, "Why wasn't I pissed at you for all the ogling in Afghanistan. Hell, the whole bunch of you were ogling us."

Speaking to herself, she murmurs, "On some level it made me feel safe and secure. I knew you had my back because you wanted me, would fight for me. Even when no one else would. I felt young, carefree, desirable in a rumpled, grungy way."

She snaps, "I haven't felt safe since you died, motherfucker. Damn it, Galvan, I depended on you."

How does she keep her hips pressed so tightly against me? Oh, that's me holding her. Hard to give her up.

Eva laughs, her small breasts dancing lightly against me, her eyes bright and warm. Here she goes again: "Arguing with bikers in the street? I mean really? Why didn't you just call me, or come to see me in Annapolis? I'd have calmed you down."

She arches her eyebrows, "How have you got time to be arguing in the street, and not call me? Em' said you had taken up with some bimbo bartender. Did you go on shore-leave while I was out of town, baby?"

Eva says, "Well, that's over now, baby. Momma's back in town. Is that her at the table with the mousey brown hair? She's cute. Long and lean, but you always like 'em long and lean."

I turn my head to meet Jill's now cold gaze. How long have Eva and I been on this dance floor? It starts to feel like a week.

Jill's eyes go dark, becoming glacial. Then she goes blank. I'm out, for playing footsie with nutsy.

Eva snatches my chin between thumb and index finger, yanking my face to her, "I'm over here, baby."

"I lost you twice, Galvan. Tonight, listening to your heartbeat puts me at peace. I thought you were dead, feared I'd never hear your heartbeat again."

Which is the truth? Had she forgotten my existence until she was on her plane home, or had she longed to rest her head on my chest to hear my heartbeat? There's a strange cast to Eva's eyes. She's plotting. Eva remains Eva, "I froze, baby, when you got into that Medevac. You looked so dead. It was sad. Then your fucking green eyes glared at me. You were mad. MAD AT ME. What did I do? You got yourself killed. The pilot told me you died. I dealt with it. We all deal with that stuff."

Eva exhales, "I was sure I was dead up on Tud Ghar, baby. I wanted desperately to die well, before AQ got us. I wasn't black-on-ammo. I was red on rifle ammo, down to my last few loose rounds. What took you so long?"

"Boom. Then you showed up Hammer-Boy, You, the Greek, and my Twins took your sweet time breaking their flank. At Fleet Operations they still think I planned it that way to max out the body count. They think I used my people as bait. SEALS don't play bait, Galvan. Who said you could call the Marines, Galvan?

"Do you know the Commandant of the Marine Corps demanded the story of what he calls the battle of Tud Ghar from me. He said he was putting his boys in for medals. The commandant says Marines saved us, not you four assholes. He thinks you and the god damned Greek were itinerant Gurkha basketball players."

I say, "Did I ever tell you that you sure swear like a sailor, Eva, when you're upset."

"I am a sailor, Hammer-Boy. Jesus. A hammer? You are one brutal troglodyte bastard."

Eva looks at me strangely, "Baby, you were so dead and gone. How could I still smell you on that nasty t-shirt? I washed it fifty times, Galvan. I can still smell you on it." She frowns, "Then, one day it was over. We packed up, shut down. Politics. New broom sweeps clean."

We continue swaying to the band's music.

Eva asks playfully, "Officer, is that your gun, or do you really like me?"

It is a problem. I do still like Eva.

She coos softly, "You'd think you hadn't been around a girl in ages, baby."

"Eva, you were the last woman I was around."

She roars, "YEAH. WELL, DON'T WORRY ABOUT IT. At least you're back, now."

"Eva, I'm with someone now."

"You mean your slender, bartender-bimbo? That's an Irishman's dream-girl. Lose her, Galvan. What on earth did you put around the bitch's neck?"

Answering, I felt a growling volcanic rumble rise in Eva, "I gave her my grad-school ring so she could hang it on the ribbon. She wanted it to chase your boy Blackmon away."

"WHAT? ARE YOU SEVENTEEN? Are you kids going steady? You didn't give me your ring when I was eighteen. I had sex with you." Eva punches me to the chest, "Really? She didn't haul your ashes, and you gave her your school ring? Asshole."

Eva looks toward the table, "Well, baby, your steady just left in a huff with the Greek and his pet midget."

Shocked, I turn my head to look for Jill. Turning was a mistake on my part.

Eva barraged me with punches. A right cross to my jaw followed by a solid upper cut to my eye. Followed by a left to my heart.

Eva is a woman scorned and on the offensive, "You, asshole. Going steady at your age? What is wrong with you? You gave HERRR? THAT SKINNY BRUNETTE BIOTCH YOUR DOOR KNOCKER? Trey, I can't be-lieve you didn't even call me first."

This is nuts. She didn't know I was alive last week. Now I didn't call her. Call what, where be my crazy SEAL girl? Eva spins, stalks toward the exit. Black and Tan pass to either side of me. Tanner shoves me leftward driving me toward Blackmon, who tries to pin my arms to my sides.

Black swings a practiced low left hook toward my kidney. Such nice boys. Black's hook almost catches me over my right kidney. I would have gone down hard with that one. So, I catch and ride his punch down and forward, away from me. As he passes, I smack a thumb up ridge-hand inside Black's bicep. My thumb-swipe rakes the Heart-2 plexus. I get it, Blackmon's right arm flops loosely to his side. Black is right-handed, and now numb from shoulder to wrist.

Road rage sets in, I'm done with this bunch. They were on thin ice the minute I saw them. I yell after Blackmon, "How's your arm, Black? Does it feel dead? Maybe it'll come back in a day or so. Next time I'll put your doink to sleep for six months."

Tanner yells back, "Galvan, we may owe you, but we don't owe you much."

The Twins bracket Eva's tail. No sense letting her abandon them in the Chicago suburbs. SEALS usually head to the water for their escape. Maybe the three of them can swim up the sanitary and ship canal to their hotel. That is such a nice thought. I yell at their backs, "You only owe your lives, boys. What's that worth that to two useless pricks?"

Gennaro is beside me, "Well, Galvan, that went well. The Greek left with Slenderella and Gaby around the time your nutty redhead called Gaby the Greek's pet midget. The Greek and Gaby, huh? What's going on there, 'Compare'? No answer, my partner?" asks Gennaro. "Go easy on the redhead, Goombah. My bride is female-friends with her. Don't rock my apple-cart. Capisce? Galvan, before you run off to start a fight someplace else, I need you to speak to the new Mrs. Gennaro. She has scary shit to impart."

I walk to the edge of the dance floor toward where Emma is dancing with her father. Em' sees me waiting, says, "Daddy, I promised Mr. Galvan a dance before he leaves."

Em' positions her arms out from her body, to be held, "Trouble, trip me away to the light fantastic."

Gorgeous in the Kush in cargo pants and a t-shirt covered in grime, tonight Emma in white is the consummate bride.

"It's getting warmer, Trey. I chose the chiffon because I didn't want to wrinkle. It's been a long day. Am I wilting?"

"You are a dream to behold, Em'. Gennaro is busting his buttons with pride."

She says, "It's hard to pull this look off, Trouble. Do I look pregnant? I feel like I swallowed a watermelon. Gennaro was so happy to see me when I got back. Now, I'm carrying twins."

"Congratulations, Em'. I'd never guess. You're ballerina trim. He's a lucky man."

Emma smiles happily.

Abruptly, my former boss comes on-line," Stow it. You are Trouble, and you got trouble. Remember Calah Morgenthau? You ought to."

Perplexed I say, "Yes, boss, Calah was in the Chicago office. I worked with her. Does she like the Baltimore office?"

"Worked with Calah? More like plonked Calah. I know you were banging her, Trouble. I saw the evidence."

"Em', you know better than most about female agents fraternizing with local cops. Half the single female agents were dating cops. Cops understand your weird hours, and your weird lifestyle. Female agents get involved with a male agent, your boy-bitches make it office gossip. We dated. She ended our relationship before going to Baltimore."

"When did you last see Calah, Trouble?" she asks.

"We met in the hall at your DC Office as I went in for your interview. After I signed-on, I had dinner with Calah at her apartment. Calah informed me, there was no us. I had served my purpose in Chicago. If invited, I could visit. I might have been able to call ahead and set up a short weekend stay, conditions permitting. Calah's 'reservations-required' thing didn't work for me."

Emma says, "Our office rule is one needs a new guy at each posting, Trouble."

"Thank you for the insight, Em'."

"We all thought Calah was gay."

"Your guys said you were lesbian, Emma."

"No, I was an 'angry Black woman'. Half of the male agents are Southern boys. I got a wide berth from the Mountain Williams. The Black men stayed away from a 'Vanilla-Wasp Girl. Gennaro wasn't having either," Emma says ruefully, hand soothing her tummy.

"Gennaro told me to brace myself," Emma says, laughing.

"Brace yourself Bridgette is Irish foreplay." I laugh

"Really?" asks Emma coyly. "Gennaro doesn't look Irish."

"He doesn't look Italian either, Mrs. Gennaro."

"So, what's the story? I doubt Calah is complaining about my stay. I was a gentleman. A satisfied, if somewhat disappointed gentleman. I stayed the weekend, left at dawn Sunday morning. I was demoted to standby status, I let it go. How's Calah doing?"

"Did you have sexual intercourse with Calah when you were in her apartment, Trouble?"

"Yes dear. When I left, Calah was on her porch in her nightgown to give me a rapturous goodbye kiss. My cab driver enjoyed the wait. Apropos of nothing, my cab was number 1776. I went home a sadder but wiser lad."

Emma says, "I had to ask. Calah was murdered on the Friday after your interview. You logged in to a flight to Chicago. Calah was killed Friday evening. "

"Gennaro submitted your buccal swab for expedited DNA analysis. The results linked you to the DNA of an infant being carried in Chicago by Gennaro's ex-partner, Mary Beth Burke. You are also linked by DNA analysis to bed sheets found in the clothes hamper at Calah Morgenthau's murder scene.

My heart skips a beat. I can feel Emma's warm breath on my cheek as she speaks but I can no longer hear her words. Who is killing these women? Why? Mary Beth died a week ago. Calah died this evening. Both have been dead for years. I don't understand. Who is the monster? Why did he do it? The killer traveled halfway across the country. How? Why? What purpose was served?

Homicide is a game of evidence, motive, opportunity. Working homicide cases is a lifestyle choice, that over time becomes part of the way you observe the world. Unexpectedly, that training effects my thoughts. Why do I feel I saw something? It is not that I know something. Deep down within me I've picked up a scent.

The impact of the facts is making me lose my capacity to concentrate. The hamper. What is it about the hamper? I have it now, "Calah was folding clothes when I arrived on Friday. Calah is hyper-organized. Her mom was a schoolteacher, they always washed clothes Friday evening. End the school week, wash the clothes for the next week's work. I was a family regimen. Having a space between weeks was important to Calah. Friday evening was for housework, that left the weekend was for fun. Calah was about fun. I conclude, "When I finally got back to Chicago I ran into Mary Beth in court. I told her that I signed onto your team.

Feeling confused, I change tacks, "Mary Beth had ended a relationship with Brenda Thalburg. Bren' was the state that handled the airline con-game case, where I met you, Emma.

Em remembers, nodding, "Who'd have thought?"

I answer, "We've all got lives, Mrs. Gennaro."

I continue, "Mary Beth, Gennaro and I were partners on the tactical team in the old Marquette district. Mary and I grew up together. When I was under the team contract, I got rid of my car, sublet my apartment, warehoused my worldly possessions. My last tie to Chicago was the case I was in court on when I ran into Mary Beth."

Reluctantly I admit, "She offered me a couch to sleep on for the night and a ride to the airport in the morning. Things developed. I'm sure Gennaro told you I'm the father of Mary's child. Our baby's DNA apparently linked me to both scenes."

Emma says with derision, "Trouble, you are such a jerk. You repaid the girl by knocking her up, and blowing town?"

I retort, "That wasn't my plan, Emma. The same thing happened to a bride I'm acquainted with. That bride didn't plan on being pregnant for her wedding. We both got a surprise. Maybe I'm the only one surprised. Incompatible became companionable. I thought we were invulnerable to the slings and arrows of outrageous fortune. There was talk of there being an us when I got back. Two years, what was two years when you are in your twenties and gonna live forever? It was all over before I left the country.

Emma says speculatively, "I'll be damned. If I hadn't seen you and Deveraux the morning after Tud Ghar, I wouldn't believe this bullshit. You're a fooler, boy." Tapping my chest with an index finger Emma says, "Much more game than I expected. Do you always fight above your weight, Trouble?"

I respond, "It's not a joke, Emma. I have lost Calah, then Mary Beth to some psychotic serial killer. I lost your homicidal, redheaded girl-buddy to the United States Navy long before I met you. What you heard about in the Kush, is not half of the goings on between Eva and I. We've known each other since I was seventeen."

Emma says in a mocking tone, "You've lost more than that. Tonight, while making love to Eva the Commando Queen, I think you lost your bartender girlfriend. Trouble, the only life you have runs from sort of screwed-up to really screwed-up. Hell, you might as well go after your FBI girl. That one would be glad to let you confess your sins. Then if you get lucky, Eva will have sex with you one last time before the FBI houses you forever for the murders."

I just love working for a good boss, they always have your best interests at heart. I say, "Em', thanks for your suggestion."

"Nadia Dimitrieva is FBI. She says she's been looking for you for the last year. She came to my office with a report containing very few facts and a bucket full of opinions. In retrospect, considering your love life, I should have figured you would end up being hunted down by a Glamazon super-model. So apropos."Emma shakes her head sadly, "Tell me you didn't. Agent Dimitrieva was attracted by your bony good looks? Say it ain't so, Galvan. The only thing in your favor right now she told me during her infiltration of your operation. Said you saved her from a fate worse than death, which she felt was out of character for a serial killer. Pay attention, Galvan. She's a Special Agent. Dimitrieva is out to lock your ass up for Murder-1. She's investigating you as an international narcotics kingpin and a psycho/sexual sadist. That'd make a G-girl shiver with delight."

Out of answers I ask, "Nadia says her informant is inherently reliable. How's that?

"She uses the guy who has a codename that's something like, 'Muddy River'. What she calls her *inherently* reliable informant swears you murdered Officer Burke and Calah Morgenthau because they were closing in on your crimes."

I ask, "What is an inherently reliable informant? I have never heard that term. Does that mean Nadia could take that one before the court for a warrant?"

Emma shrugs shaking her head negatively, "She could try the court of the Star Chamber. I've heard of reliable informants and confidential informants. Inherently reliable informants? Nah. Maybe it's an FBI term."

"Anyway, Muddy River told Agent Dimitrieva that he saw you meeting on the Friday before Calah was murdered in DC at a restaurant with a blond Columbian prostitute who wore a white Armani suit."

My detective mind clicks into gear, again, I ask, "What restaurant?"

Emma thinks a moment. "The DBGB Kitchen. Hey, I've eaten there, Trouble. They have great burgers, the fries come in little silver baskets. I'm always hungry since I got pregnant, I could use a DBGB Kitchen burger and large fries right now."

I smile, "I was in DGBG that afternoon. It's a block from the Grand Hyatt."

"So, you admit being there with your Columbian whore?"

"The lady in white was wearing a white Armani suit."

"You're a big boy, Galvan. I don't care where you park your car. Why'd you pick someone up at your hotel bar? Why meet the woman at DGBG?"

"I actually met her across the street."

"Where?" asks Emma, suddenly intrigued.

"In an office across the street."

"What office?" she asks, now fully into the sordid details.

"Yours. You are the Columbian temptress in the white Armani suit. And you bought me lunch at DBGB, after you swore me in as a Deputy U.S. Marshal, for the duration. Think, Emma, what were you wearing that day?"

"Some old thing." she says with an offhand wave, thinking.

"You were wearing a white Armani suit, Emma, with a large button. Nadia's inherent informant is talking about you, Em'."

She covers her mouth as she guffaws, "Did I really look like a high priced Columbian lady of the evening then? I'm just a sweet, prim little pilgrim girl."

"Nope, you are one hot pilgrim biotch."

Emma smiles.. "Calm down, pale boy. I'm a married woman with responsibilities and commitments. Your love will have to be unrequited. Unrequited is big with us pilgrim girls. We leave piles of unrequited lovers in our wake." Emma hugs me. "Come on, Trouble, you been warned. Walk me to the bride's table. My back is killing me."

"I think you may suffer from that sore back a little longer, beautiful."

13

ON THE ROAD AGAIN

W hat can be completed here has been. I head for the exit at a good pace. It's always good to leave before they toss you out. I stop to get my bearings. I think the exit to the parking lot is on the left.

The reception is in a far south suburb of Chicago. In the distance to the north I can see the lights of I-80. Thus, home is north by northeast. I could get in my car to drive to I-80, turn right and be home in say, 45 minutes. That is if I had a car, I don't. Tonight, a raggedy ride would beat a proud walk. I got no ride. Am I in a foreign country? I am south of Orland Park. Is that even in Illinois? I think so. Thank goodness, I have forgotten my passport. Given enough time, perhaps a few weeks, I can find my way back to Bridgeport." Glancing around, I consider the terrain. No, I'm sure this isn't Bolivia. It's not Serbia, either. Serbia would be to the east on the other side of the lake. I don't remember swimming to get here, but then I've been punched in the head some tonight. I'll just walk north on La Grange Road for fifty city blocks; that will be six and one-quarter miles. Then I can cheat at the commuter station. From there I'll take the train into Union Station. Problem solved. Fifty long city blocks is what, six or seven miles? A mere stretch of the legs. The walk couldn't take me more than a month, unless it snows. Does it snow in Chicago in late April? Or is it May?

I walk along the east side of LaGrange Road. It feels as though I've been at it for an hour. Might have been two hours. I think I should buy a watch.

An occasional car zips by but otherwise it's a quiet spring night. This section of road runs for miles with river cane cattails and reeds.

Businesses have given way to mushy nature and run-off ponds. There really isn't much traffic this time of night. There are bugs galore. What traffic there is changes lanes, moving outward to give me a wide berth, speeds up and zooms quickly away. Perhaps drivers are afraid I'll explode. One must time the passing of exploding pedestrians just right.

In the silence of the fresh, oncoming breeze, I notice flashing mars-lights reflecting their light oddly off reeds and thinning marsh gas out in the erstwhile swamp. The lights are following me at a walking pace.

I stop, extract my retired detective star from my pocket. I open the star case in my left hand. I raise my arms over my head, then turn to displaying my star case toward the police vehicle inching up behind me.

Being shot accidently by the police on a dark road is never fun. No quick moves allowed. A second squad, both State Police, sweeps ahead of me. My goodness, could a concerned citizen have called in the potentially explosive guy in a suit walking down the road? Perhaps they'll tell me.

A loudspeaker tells me to face into the swamp, kneel, cross my ankles behind me. Figures, it has been that kind of night. Kneeling on the damp surface of the moraine I feel the rhythmic bounce as two troopers approach me from behind. One steps down on my ankles, locking them in place. That stings. He takes my star-case from me.

The other officer shines a bright flashlight in my eyes. Considering the evening's events, I assume he has a pistol in his hand to shoot me as soon as he has a moment. Guys in suits, coming from weddings are right up there with ax murderers on the list of people to shoot these days. Or it could just be a quiet night and they're bored. I hope he's a good shot. My brains flying out my ears would be a quick and violent end to a lovely evening. I can see my epitaph, now floating before my eyes, "Following an unfortunate episode in the Hindu Kush, the fool was shot for no apparent reason in the swamps of Orland Park as he infiltrated his way back into Illinois–poetic justice.

I start to laugh. I enjoy my own jokes too much.

The trooper behind me says, "He's a retired Chicago Detective, Hank."

The other trooper directs his million-megawatt death ray into my eyes, "He's younger than me, Morris."

Morris says, "The Golden Arches are younger than you. ID has his picture on it"

To save time I say, "It's a long story."

Morris, steps down on my ankles saying, "Make it short, to the point."

Professional courtesy is not dead.

I say, "I was a Chicago homicide detective until around three years ago. I went to Afghanistan on leave of absence with the secret service. I got banged up bad. The department thought I was dead. I got lost in the hospital in Bethesda, Maryland. This evening I went to a wedding back there to the south. There was an argument. I walked home."

Hank snaps, "We know where Bethesda is, Genius."

Morris says, "You smell like you've been drinking alcohol."

"No. I got one at the bar, but didn't drink it. I may be wearing a couple, though."

Hank studies my face, tilting his head side to side, "He's got a mouse on his left eye, Morris. A littler one on his right. Maybe he got beat up by a Girl Scout Troop."

My manhood challenged, I respond, turning to glance at Morris, "My commander slugged me at the wedding, otherwise it was a swell event."

Morris steps down on my ankles, "Shouldn't turn your head, Mr. Galvan. Were you fooling with the commander's wife? You that type of guy?"

"Maybe it was the commander's daughter, Morris," suggests Hank helpfully.

"The Commander is a she. She's a SEAL. I worked for her in Afghanistan."

"Enough, I'm getting a headache. Where you headed?" says Morris from behind me.

"The Orland Metra Station on La Grange."

"The first train doesn't come until around sun-up," says Morris.

Hank says, "We got time. Let's run his name on the way to the train station. If he's got no stops, we'll leave him there."

"If you got no wants or warrants, you can catch the train," says Morris. "In the morning you can get back to Bridgeport on the Archer Express."

I ask them, "Expatriates?"

Morris nods, "Yeah, we moved out. We couldn't stand all the ring-kissing Chi-Raq bullshit. Come on, give me your hand. Up, lean here on my car, Hank is checking you for warrants."

"Can you take the cuffs off?"

Morris says, "Not until you clear. Hank hates letting anyone go."

A few minutes later, Hank says, "He's clear, Morris."

"Get in the car I'll take you to the Choo-Choo."

Morris sets my wallet in the front seat. At a stop light he flips through the photo sleeves. Where is the group picture from, Afghanistan?"

"Yeah. The woman with the reddish blond hair was my commander. The Black woman, the giant white guy, and the little white guy were secret service. The four guys with sunglasses, who look like movie stars are SEALs. I'm coming from the Black woman's wedding."

Morris asks, "What Black woman?"

"The blond woman is Black. The red-head socked me. The Black lady only yelled at me for fighting at her wedding."

At the commuter station, Morris, the trooper, helps me out of the squad car. He walks me around to the back of the car, positioning me under a street light while unlocking my cuffs. He hands me my wallet and IDs, saying, "Count your money."

Barely over the thrum of the trooper squad, Morris says softly, "Can you keep your mouth shut?"

I nod slightly.

Morris says softly, "The G asked our dispatcher to stop you and check for wants and warrants. We were also to search you for weapons. You're clear. You got no gun. We'll let them know. I didn't tell you any of this."

Morris lowers his window, saying as he leaves, "Don't look now, but there's a black Ford Explorer in the back of the lot with its motor running. Can you guess who's it is? Always with the Fords. Good luck and goodbye. Go, sin no more."

Morris the trooper drives off, shaking his head.

At the train station I check the time, comparing it to the posted schedule.

I sit on a bench outside then spot a Starbucks east of La Grange Road.

The coffee shop is lit inside, getting ready for the morning trade. The black Ford Explorer in the back of the lot has black-out tint. It is also freshly washed. A blacked-out Ford, yeah, it's the bureau? What are the odds Nadia is one of the agents in the Explorer?

I ignore the Explorer on my way for coffee. As I pass, I raise two fingers, pointing to Starbucks. Playing at mime, I offer to buy.

No response from the thrumming vehicle. It's them. I shrug theatrically.

At Starbucks, the barista serves me a Grande Coffee with extra cream and sugar, and a Grande Café Americano. I am served through the drive-up. I request a large bear claw cinnamon roll, which turns out to be the size of a small pizza.

I carry the roll and coffees back to my bench. An anti-terrorist squad has not usurped it.

The SUV thrums softly as I pass. The dark finish glistens. Condensation drips to the pavement beneath it. Returning to my bench, I wave at the Explorer, then indicate an open space on my bench.

No response.

I hold up the two coffees.

Nothing.

I wave the bear claw pastry. The front passenger door opens. Special Agent Nadia of the 'G' languidly exits.

Hip cocked, Nadia leans back, saying something to J. Edgar and Clyde Tolson. Nadia closes the car door cross-over stepping in my direction. The Explorer pulls out of the lot onto LaGrange Road.

I bet they stay close by. It has been an awful night. I'm not even surprised that I have been dumped by two women before sunrise. Abandoned by my friends to walk home through a swamp. The 'G' sicced state troopers on me. I got punched in the jaw. I got both eyes bloused. I had both my ankles stood upon. What a busy night it has been.

I glance up at the approaching Nadia. She wears a waist length black leather jacket, a tailored light blue button-down tailored blouse, and black skinny jeans. She has on highly polished black half-boots with a two-inch heel that is scratching a spark at each step, must be steel capping the high heels. She is, as always, bewitching and quite fetching. The corners of her slender wide lips curl slightly up, just a flicker. She is clearly aware of the effect she's having on her audience of one. As she reaches my lonely perch, she extends a right hand to be shaken. Surprised I take the hand as I rise.

She says, "Let's start at the beginning. My name is Nadia Dimitrieva. I am an FBI agent assigned to the Bureau's Chicago office. I apologize for my accusations, and I'm sorry for your loss. We talked with your former supervisor, Agent Wainwright. We have preliminarily verified part of your alibi. Documents have been re-quested, pending the certification of that paperwork it appears I misjudged your character. I'm sorry."

I think my jaw may be agape with surprise. Nadia smiles with a touch of triumph in her eyes. A man would be a fool not to accept this one's apology.

She surprised me and enjoys her ability to pinion me in place with just a smile. She's doing it because she can. I don't like scary-pretty women to begin with. Rumor has it that the power of a woman's smile can launch a thousand ships. Yes. I suppose it so. When I can, I like to play from a position of strength. Did Nadia choose her ensemble to play from strength? Her casual beauty has a soothing balm to it. Is Nadia's elegantly casual appearance serendipity. Or has luck swept back my way? I find no answer in her eyes. I am unable to assess the level of her interest. Something changed. What? Is this show to lull me?

A pace of humid night air separates us. The thin fog between us carries a static electric charge. The air is alive with Nadia's scent. Her blue eyes seem to glow under glare of the parking lot overheads. Her presence amplifies my senses. For days I've wakened with a scent on my pillow. I was at a loss as to its source. Looking at Nadia, I no longer wonder. Her scent is unnerving. Wishful thinking on my part or chemical reality?

Nadia eyes me shyly from beneath her backswept exaggerated bangs. She's sure of herself, yet seems shy. A totally screwed up night just acquired a sensual texture.

14

NOBODY LOVES ME, BUT THEN...

Nobody loves me. Then it seems I get my first look at Nadia Dimitrieva. Nadia and I somehow are standing closer. Each openly eyeing the other. Damned if we did not just meet. I step back a pace to avoid drawing her to me. I spread my handkerchief across the damp surface of the bench. Those jeans cost a fortune, and my bench takes all comers, including seagulls.

My action causes Nadia to smile shyly. She's surprised, the sensuous lips alter a girl's smile. She settles delicately on the bench, on one side of the coffees and my steaming brown bag. I think it just became our bundling-bolster. The coffee and sweet roll serve as a minor barrier between us. We'll see for how long. Lost in thoughts of Nadia, I sip my coffee. Nadia laughs brightly. Turning, I look up at her face.

She says, "Galvan, you just discovered I'm a girl? You look so shocked. I've tailed you. You fought for me to save me from a fate worse than death by those two idiots. We ran around your neighborhood all night. I slept drugged out of my mind after trying to seduce you in your own bed. I've threatened to jail you for murder. After all that, you just figured out I'm a woman? Priceless. Guys are so weird."

Nadia pokes me to the side of my head with her index finger. "When I met your little bartender friend, I was standing outside your bedroom door in a very nice bra and panties. You barely glanced at me. Tonight, I'm all grungy from following you all day long. I'm wearing a leather jacket, a work blouse, and jeans. I'm carrying a gun and a radio and you're undressing me with those green eyeballs. You are a trip, Galvan. This outfit turns you on?"

I shrug, sweeping my eyes over her again. "You're right, I am seeing you in a different light. I been aware that you're a woman, since the night I first saw you."

She studies my expression tightly for a moment. Her brow furrows, then she decides, reaching out to grasp the back of my head and draw my lips to hers. She tastes of mint. Her tongue flickers, seeking mine. She releases me. Settling back to the bench, reaching under her jacket. She says into the ether, "Shut it down, George. I'll meet you in the morning. I'll take the train into town to my place. Dimitrieva signing off."

Nadia stares openly my way. "What is different tonight, Mr. Galvan, is that tonight is the first time you've treated me as a girl with potential. I think you actually like me as a woman."

I hand her the Americano. Then place the bear-claw between us on top of its open bag. I gesture to a pile of napkins, saying, "I'll even share breakfast with you."

The bear-claw is wreathed in cinnamon steam, rising into the damp night air.

Nadia says in an annoyed tone, "Galvan, Nadia is a diminutive for Natalya in Russian. My father told me it means born on Christmas, or maybe Christmas gift from God? Don't leer, it isn't December and I'm not your present, yet."

I say dully. "A Russian speaker. Educated for it or did you come by it naturally?"

"What should I speak? With a last name like Dimitrieva should I speak Gaelic? I was conceived there, born here."

"Anchor baby?"

"You are a real snot sometimes, mister."

Nadia rips a toe from our bear claw, popping the bear's toe into her mouth.

She chews slowly, eventually swallows with a sip of her Americano.

I wait, placidly watching her sensually consume bear toes Then I say, "Nadia means exotic, not born on Christmas. I looked your name up. Nadia means filled with hope, Nadezhda."

She smiles crookedly, sips coffee. Frowns a bit before retorting, "Did I say I allowed you to call me by my diminutive, Galvan." Nadia becomes playful, "You want me to be your Christmas present?"

My turn, I grasp her at the neck, gently bringing our lips back together, our tongues clash for a bit longer this time. We break apart. She's slightly breathless.

I say, "Christmas is a long way off, Nadezhda. I'm not looking for a present. I'm seeing you, maybe for the first time, though I've been looking at you for weeks. Let's finish the bear claw before it gets cold."

Nadia snatches the last toe, eating it and licking sugar from her fingers. I lunge quickly forward. Maybe for the bear's palm, maybe for Nadia's thigh. She giggles and scoots away smiling.

I pick up our pastry, tearing it before offering her share. She slides back to touch the offering, prepared to flee.

I say, "After a bad night, it is nice to be have an early breakfast with a beautiful woman. Unless I'm to be stood against the wall and shot at sunrise. Will you offer me a blind fold?

Nadia licks the sugar from each fingertip, Then she dries her hand with a napkin. Her arm extends to caress my cheek. She whispers, "I bet that stubble tickles."

I grasp her hand, nibbling the open palm. Her eyes pop. Nadia draws her hand back, clasping it in her lap. She appears startled, "Why?"

I say, "I'm not sure what's going on. But I'm not kidding, Nadia."

She's nervous, now. I might have gone too far. I try for a joke, "Warm buns in the cool of dawn do that to me. Sorry."

Measuring my gaze. She snaps a retort, "You look the type."

"Don't you?"

Nadia asks, "Don't I what?"

"Don't you like your buns warmed in the morning?"

"Galvan, you are talking dirty to a federal agent?"

"No, a man and a woman are sitting on a bench at a railroad station in the dead of night having breakfast. I was just talking with you about whether you enjoy having your buns warmed in the morning. For future reference, I'm inquiring whether you wish me to warm your buns for breakfast. I've been making you breakfast a lot lately, Agent Dimitrieva. I'd like to know your preference."

Nadia smiles brightly, saying, "What a wicked little trap. Yes, I like my buns warm in the morning. Whether you get the chance to warm my buns at breakfast again will depend on how you measure up, Mister Galvan."

I say, "Excellent riposte, Nadezhda."

Nadia's bear claw vanishes between sips of Café Americano. I watch her lick sugar and cinnamon from her fingers. I'm taken by surprise, seeing her as a happy child. Nadia makes me smile. Beauty must learn at an early age how to captivate. She looks up, startled, face clouding with embarrassment. There's a kid down there deep inside her model's body. Damn, I'm getting old. I'm glad she's out of my reach. I'd easily make a fool of myself.

She relaxes, a young woman laughing at her own inelegance. Demonstrably happy to see herself accepted? Glad to be liked?

I ask, "Why didn't the 'G" just come into the wedding and snatch me?"

She leans back on the bench, "We weren't out to snatch you, Galvan. We were waiting on the DNA comparison from the lab. During our surveillance the office called to tell us that documents came back supporting enough of your alibi to move you off target. My partner, George, said I had to apologize. I did."

Choosing her words carefully, Nadia asks, "What happened between you and your doctor-girl-client counselor? When she came out of that wedding, fire was shooting out her ears. Did you do something bad, Galvan?"

"I did," I answer.

Softly, Nadia asks, "What did you do?"

I shrug, "I ran into an old friend."

With a sweet expression Nadia asks, "Was Commander Devereaux that old friend?"

My turn. "How do you know of Commander Devereaux?"

Nadia gives me a Cheshire cat smile, "You are the one who gave Gennaro the alibis, Galvan. I just checked them out, Commander Evangeline Devereaux, USN, was one of them. I called the Naval Academy at a number Agent Wainwright gave me. A grumpy old man answered. He is a professor at the academy. Some retired admiral, with the same last name. I thought him the hubby but turned out to be her grandfather. When I mentioned your name, it appeared he doesn't recall you fondly. Surprised?"

"NO. I am not surprised. The last time I saw Admiral Grandpa. I had to clock him."

Nadia eyes me, "I eventually reached Commander Devereaux and she reluctantly verified her part of your alibi. The commander informed me she was attending the wedding and said she would say hello to you from me. Did she?"

"She didn't mention meeting you. I assume your contact was telephonic."

Nadia looks perplexed, "Why?"

I rubbed my swollen eye socket as I answer, "If Eva saw you, you would have heard about it."

I pull Nadia back to me. Our noses touch as we sway staring eye-to-eye. Nadia asks, "Should I take that as good? You've been a busy boy, Galvan. Should I feel safe?"

In a more businesslike tone Nadia says, "Devereaux provided the alibi, as did Gennaro's new wife. Agent Wainwright says you were under her close supervision on a closed government reservation when the murder of Officer Burke occurred. Agent Wainwright describes you as trouble, but she backs you to the hilt. Her too?"

I say, "No. Emma Wainwright is a professional and a very good supervisor. Trouble is my radio call sign."

Nadia asks innocently, "Why that call sign? Wainwright is such a hardcase. Why Trouble? Does Wainwright-Gennaro look pregnant to you?"

Women always know. I let her question pass.

Nadia says, "I figured. Aren't most brides these days? How long has it been since all guys started wanting a test drive on the first date?'

I study Nadia's face. "You're kidding, right?"

Nadia smiles sweetly, "I'll make a jump in logic. Let me guess, Commander Devereaux played a part in your break-up with Jill Ryan this evening?"

I ask, "Did you have me stopped by the state troopers?"

Nadia says, "Of course, George said I had to apologize. Besides, you were all beat up and looked very glum and lonely."

I soothe her tense shoulder blades by delicately rubbing them with my palms as I respond, "Do FBI duties include the counseling of wandering vagabonds. To put your mind at rest, I got beat up by Devereaux after she saw Jill had abandoned me at the reception. Afterwards I came to fear nobody loved me."

Withdrawing slightly, Nadia asks, "Who beat you up?"

I say, "Devereaux is a female ruffian from my sordid past. She was annoyed that I brought another woman to the wedding. Her two SEAL bodyguards tried to give me the willie-lump-lump. They weren't wholly successful."

Nadia asks, "The redhead was Devereaux, and the Black guy and the pretty white guy with the bad arm were the bodyguards? What's wrong with the white guy's arm?"

I say, "The Twins. Black must've hurt it."

Nadia says, "The white guy has the bad arm. It wasn't hurt when he went in."

Nadia shudders as I slide my thumbs down the outside of her shoulder-blades, saying, "What sharp eyes you have. If you get a chance you should ask him. They are called the Twins in the SEALs. It is a joke of reversals. The frogmen love that stuff. Blackmon is the White Guy and Tanner the Black Guy, thus Black and Tan-the Twins."

The Twins can verify my passing. They were with me at the Tud and were with me when I was passed."

Nadia asks, "What's a Tud? And what did you pass?"

"A Tud is a dick without a head, as opposed to a pud which has one. Passed away in Chi-Town means died. We saved Devereaux's overwatch team at what the Marines are calling the Battle of Tud Ghar. A couple of days later I got killed by a pregnant woman with a great big, curved sheep butchering knife."

Nadia glares, so I speak, "You asked. Don't mention the Marines. It makes Devereaux furious. The commandant of the Marine Corps wants to give a Marine Raider Unit mounted on stryker vehicles a medal for saving her ass."

Nadia snaps, "I thought you and the Twin Guys saved her?"

"We broke the force of their column by attacking the middle of it. Devereaux went red on ammo, I had my 9mm Lady Smith with 9 rounds and a ball-peen hammer. We were a minute from losing when the Greek called in the Marine Raiders, who really saved her little pink bottom."

Nadia's lips curl into a small smile. Try as I may, I'm not quite shocking this poor young virgin. I explain further, "I re-named a mount outside the village of Tudah Gar, calling it the 'Tud'. Tud Ghar is a narrow, erect, vertical, headless shape. Something like an African termite heap. Tud Ghar is outside of the city of Gardiz, or Gardez, your preference."

Amused, with eyebrows rising, Nadia scowls, "Are you fucking with me?"

"Don't I wish? Only in my dreams, Agent Dimitrieva. We're having breakfast. I'm feeling-up your shoulders to relax away a long day's tension. If I was, we'd be smiling more and wearing less."

Nadia drops her eyes slightly. "Pretty sure of yourself on that subject?"

"Empirical experience. Maybe I misread our interaction this fine morning."

After a moment she asks, "Where is Gardez?"

"Afghanistan."

"Afghanistan is over," Nadia snaps.

Angry I snap back. "Tell the men and women who died or are dying there, Nadezhda."

"Cut it out, Galvan. You haven't earned the right to call me Nadezhda. Diminutives convey the existence of relationship."

She pauses, watching my response. "Why did you go over there?"

"I'm realizing you still think I was on the lamb in Afghanistan. I didn't join the French Foreign Legion because of lost love or at the sound of wolves following me, Nadia."

"What does 'on-the-lam' mean?"

I explain, "The phrase goes back to when the Quakers fled persecution in England, Russian Princess. The Hayhurst family fled at the last moment on the good ship Lamb. When authorities came for the Hayhursts they were told that the Hayhursts were on-the-Lam."

Shaking her head Nadia says, "You are genuinely full of shit, Galvan."

I shrug. "I'm not lying to you. We come from different worlds. I say things in my language, not yours. You flared up at me just a moment ago because I used the diminutive of your name in Russian. Obviously, I am looking at you in more depth than your classically pretty face, toned ballerina's body and alabaster skin. Willing to bridge our differences? Give me the benefit of the doubt, Nadia. Your temper flared. You went for my throat. Your research thus far verifies that I've been telling you the truth."

I study her face, "You and I just met. We are obviously in the process of getting to know each other. You taste of mint. We are people with different backgrounds. We are feeling each other out."

Nadia looks down, puts her hand on mine to stop its gesturing. "Why am I to trust you, Galvan? Until not long ago you were my best suspect in a murder case. How do you come to deserve the benefit of the doubt?" "You earn trust by demonstrating you deserve trust. Who was the Columbian wench in DC?"

"I'll spill if you tell me who River Mud is."

She says, "Him? He's an inherently reliable confidential informant."

I shake my head, "No such thing. Your man is either reliable because of his past provable performance or confidential and possibly less reliable. They can also be a concerned citizen. Each is weighed differently in considering application for judicial warrant."

After a moment's delay, "I got one anyway."

I say, "No you don't. I checked. But I'll give you a hint. Re-interview my alibi list in person. Ask the one most likely if they own a designer suit with one big button on the jacket." I pause. "Alright. We take it slow. You are swinging a double-edged sword. Are you swinging it at me to make clear I need to keep my distance? Is it because I lied to you? OR, are you banging me over the head because I won't submit to your demands?"

Nadia's face reddens in a show of anger. The girl has a temper. Regaining self-control, she snaps, "Says who? I didn't refuse to believe you. I gave you the benefit of the doubt when I discovered you were dating some goofy bartender after we spent the night running all over the place together. I hope you don't think I'm incapable of separating my personal and private life? You are definitely no big thing for me, Galvan. I can take you or leave you."

"Agent Dimitrieva, I can lie to you. If you catch me, you can put me in jail. I'm not lying, haven't been lying."

"How is it that you warrant any consideration? Don't even cite that professional courtesy crap. I haven't seen much in cop behavior that entitles you to consideration. Why judge me?"

I answer, "I didn't, I brought you breakfast because I wanted a second chance to meet you."

She sips her coffee then smiles slightly, "There is that to consider. Do I taste like mint still? What happened to you in Afghanistan that could keep you in the hospital for a year? You're up walking around, I've seen you run along the river."

I remove my untied, flop-over tie. I roll it up, placing it in my pocket.

I reach for Nadia's hand. She flinches. I grasp her right hand gently, lifting her fingertips to place them to the jagged surface of the long horizontal scar running across my throat.

I say, "There was an IED explosion that blew up a staircase as I climbed it. I fell into the wreckage breaking my neck in the process. While I evacuated, two of the wounded, a pregnant woman jumped on my back and slashed my throat. I killed her in the struggle. It was that woman I was talking about outside Gaby's, not Mary Beth."

I complete the sweep of her hand, releasing her.

Nadia's eyes close, her expression relaxes. Her fingers return to my neck. Her touch gentle as if reading the braille from the scar's irregular surface. Her lips part as her eyes open, unfocused, large and luminous."

Where Jill's touch was probing and clinical in examination, Nadia's touch has intimacy. She closes her eyes, tilts her chin down, hides her eyes from mine.

The intimacy of her touch binds us in the moment. Nadia closes with me. Something just changed. Nadia glides into my arms. She lifts her chin, kissing my neck's scar tissue. We are eye to eye. Nadia sweeps her hair bang aside. Her eyes glow. She settles to rest softly in my arms. We exchange a light kiss. At close range, each studies the other.

I smell coffee, taste cinnamon sweetness on her kiss. My hands cup her shoulders gently. I draw her to me. She moves to my embrace. This kiss is more intense. Not an expression of sympathy, this kiss expresses mutual intent.

Nadia startles. She quickly slides away, eyes wide with surprise. Murder brought Nadia to me. Murder isn't what brought her tonight.

We realize something we didn't suspect. An attraction exists between us. Did breaking up with Jill reveal hidden potential in Nadia? Scary-beautiful women will always remain out of reach, until they don't.

Nadia smiles shyly, "What a surprise. Different than I expected. You taste of promise. Promise of what? I enjoy being held by you. Didn't expect that reaction did you, Galvan?"

She cleaves to me. We kiss now, saying hello, probing. Are we seeking answers, or answering questions?

Nadia whispers. To me? To herself? "You are in there. You are not what I expected to find. What will you do next? Who were you? You definitely have my attention. Your eyes just flickered. Are you afraid of me or yourself? I'm not afraid of you. You are my mystery, rapped in an enigma, Galvan. Are you afraid I'll hurt you?"

"Why have I started to care about you? Are you going to hurt me? Do you think I should care about you?"

Nadia is setting a trail of breadcrumbs. Leading where? Maybe I am afraid of her. Is she just pursuing me differently for new reasons?

What is she doing? She actually seems interested. Why? The sands are shifting beneath us. I've never desired to kiss an FBI agent. I've enjoyed kissing a secret service agent. I've fraternized extensively with one redheaded Navy SEAL.

Nadia soft, pliable in my arms. Her inviting, tired eyes immerse me. I place my hand to her short hair. I find it thick and soft to my touch. She presses her cheek to my palm. Nadia leans in for a deeper kiss.

Each of us announces our presence, declares our intent. This isn't a getting-to-know-you kiss. This is more, Nadia grinds for an instant against me, pulls back, smiles. Knowing is good. This isn't tease and taste. Meet and greet is over. Doug was right; Nadia and I have something going on. I want Nadia, no doubt about that. The rules have changed. Nadia is starkly beautiful. Is Jill gone? Probably. Almost certainly.

I all but jumped on top of Eva on the dance floor. Eva has always held a fierce draw on me. She offers no more of a future than any sailor on leave. Her life is the Navy. She survived intense battle, lost troops. Exhilarated by survival, she's desperate to be wanted. Been there, done that. Sexual roles have reversed, the plot remains the same. Watching mental contortions cross my face, Nadia recalls who she is. She once again is uncertain of what I may be. She drops her chin, breaks eye contact. She shakes her bang back down to cover one eye. Her motion establishes distance. She has retreated to the middle distance. Out of physical contact, but not gone. I am not in the mood to lose the Nadia I just found. I'm tired of being acted upon. I step into the gulf between us, my hands come to rest on Nadia's hips. She is a strong and athletic woman. She can fight. If she wishes she can break my hold. Doesn't, allowing me to draw her back to me. Nadia wants me to know I desire her. And that she also wishes to be desired. Drawing her tight, I'm done with passive.

Nadia speaks softly, "Understand me, Galvan. I'm not a biker pass-around. I was on a case, in character when we met. Thank you for your help that night. I am not an easy 'A', mister."

She debates mentally before saying, "I was investigating your friend, Doug. Some young girls have gone missing who later turned up in trouble."

She continues, "We theorize the girls were fed Rohypnol and induced to sexual conduct with grown men, eventually being prostituted. There are preliminary indications that the drugs are local because of UPC bar codes on some bottles we found. The drugs are pharmacy grade. Bikers transport drugs interstate as far south as Florida. We need to find the source and shut it down before more are hurt. We were pulled off the Ruffies investigation. An informant identified you as a murderer. Your alibis have checked. We have some work to do, obviously. That's about as far as I can go, it's a federal matter."

Nadia stares into my eyes. "Galvan, I want you to know that I am not a tramp. I'm not trying to slink up on you to get inside your defenses. I don't have any idea what's going on between us, but I'm not opposed to finding out."

"Neither of us expected what happened."

"Galvan, I've been aware of how I can affect men since I became a teenager. You can be a real snot. I got mad. I countered the snide attitude with my own strengths. It got personal for me. I was going to knock the stuffing out of you. Along the way I got a surprise. You might just be worth knowing. You helped me when I needed you. Your little friend from the wedding put those Ruffies in my wine. I was alone. I was fading. I felt I'd pass out."

She says, "Out of the blue you took a side, mine. You were so placid while we tailed you. I didn't understand, I was in such a hurry to bag your ass and throw you in jail, I forgot to be careful. Then I found myself hiding behind you. During the run through the fog, I started to wake up. I got all loose. I'm not comfortable being all loose. I like being in control. I have to be the best. Then for the first time since Quantico, my inhibitions slipped away. I was running down alleys with a suspect. Thank you for not letting me get crazy-wild with you."

Nadia smiles, shyly, "The drugs got to me in a scary way. I was furious when you went downstairs. Then I was out. I think you should know I'm not a prude. I smelled breakfast cooking. I thought you were making it for me. Then I heard you talking to Jill the bartender. Is she really a doctor?"

I nod.

Nadia frowns. "I was furious, so I put on the lingerie show to ruin things with Jill. Sorry."

We are standing close. My palms drop to Nadia's waist coming to rest gently just above her bottom. I lightly tug Nadia. She holds fast, resists my pull. Then ends resistance to smack into me. She smiles broadly, allowing me to settle her against my hips, saying "I told you I'm not a prude."

She's warm in my grasp. She looks up for my response.

I say firmly, "Jill didn't put anything but wine in your glass. I saw Tweedle Dee dump white powder in your glass and swish it around when he handed the glass to you. Jill had nothing to do with that pair. I was watching the whole time."

Nadia pulls my hips tightly inward to her body. "You are partial to women with long legs, Mr. Galvan. As a woman with long legs, I've noticed."

I say, "Doug, Gennaro and I discussed your legs in the street when you left."

She says, "Is Jill special? Am I no longer beyond the pale of decency because of my job?"

Nadia stands in front of me, her feet straddling mine. Her eyes are huge; her lips curl in a faint smile.

"Jill is special. She's been kind to me since I was brought back to town. I wanted to be something special to Jill. I think I mistook kindness for something more. Guys are like that. She's done with me now. Eva Devereaux made sure of that. Little Eva wanted something, Jill was in the way."

Nadia breaks contact, stepping away. Straightens her jacket lapels. She stares at me, her wide sensuous mouth opens, "We'll have to work on it."

"I started the evening surveilling you, as you took what I didn't think was a rival as your date to a wedding. I've ended up at a train station, with you trying to make love to me on a park bench. Progress is progress. I'm not sure what I am doing, but I enjoy what I'm doing."

Nadia wraps her arms around my neck, kisses me lightly. Reaches to her back pocket, withdrawing a large pink cellphone.

She speed-dials. Someone picks up immediately. Nadia says, "He's going to buy me a ticket and we're taking the first train downtown. Get some sleep, George. I'll see you at the desk in the morning. No, we had breakfast. A giant cinnamon roll. He didn't ask about you. That is doubtful, dear. He keeps trying to grab my bottom. OOPs, I wasn't watching, just got me. Stop that, Galvan, I'm talking to my partner. Sorry, George, he likes girls." Pause. "No. Tonight I've run out of ideas. We're fresh out of suspects. I have some questions about the Columbian woman, but he implied the answer. The alibi works, he was with the secret service. We're back to working the evidence. I'll finish checking out the alibi in the morning, by direct interview as the secret service woman."

She concludes, "He'll take me home. I'm fine, George. Thanks for the overwatch."

Turning off her phone, Nadia says, "When the train comes, take me home. We'll pretend we're on a date. When the station opens, get tickets. I assume this train stops at Union Station."

Nadia steps forward to lean her head against me. I'll be damned, she's falling asleep.

I sit on my bench. Nadia sits on my lap, dozing. The station opens. I get tickets. The train pulls into the station. Few commuters this early.

We take over a bank of seats, traveling ever inbound. As the steady rocking motion of train travel ensues, Nadia falls into a deep sleep with head on my chest. I've gone from being a murderer to an FBI agent's pillow during one long night. I contemplate the absurdity of change. I give up, the vagaries of chance. Fatigue enwraps my mind. I doze then wake as Nadia squirms in closer. The air conditioner has kicked in on our mostly empty car. We doze a bit more. I find myself kissing Nadia's hair.

I wake from a dream of a departing dancer. What's done is done. The dream grows immaterial, Jill strolls into the ether. Love those hips, but now gone in the way of dreams.

I lean my battered, overheated forehead against the cool window glass. Nadia slithers up my chest in her sleep. She kisses my cheek in her sleep. Maybe Nadia has her own dancer to dream of, so I hug her gently. She coos softly. A lucky man, he.

In the cooling train car, Nadia curls into a compact ball, snuggles close for warmth. A crazy-beautiful, dangerous, innocent young woman. Doug was right; I don't understand women. I fear potential in Nadia that's worth worrying over. She is drawing me ever deeper into her. Boys and girls are like that. I've been on the outside wishing to be on the inside for too long. Being inside Nadia and her world is incredibly tempting. I gaze down upon her sleeping form. Asleep, she seems more kid than woman.

She shivers, so I drape my suitcoat over her, resting my hand on the small of her back. Well, maybe just a bit lower. She's had a long busy day hunting a dreaded killer. Exhausted, she dozes on his chest. Apparently, I've tired her out. Luckily, I make a nice bed. I wake, my fingers in her waist band as our train slows for Union Station. Barely in her waistband.

On arrival at Union Station, I am rewarded with girl drool on my only clean dress-shirt. As Nadia wakes, she wipes her lips then notices the inelegance of my damp shirt. Embarrassed, she murmurs, "Sorry."

I've been missing the sound and touch of women for two years. Having a pretty girl drool on my chest is oddly intimate. Nadia sees my reaction, blinks, smiles. We share an intimate kiss. Soft cinnamon lips, nice morning.

As we exit the train, Nadia appears disoriented. I take hold of her hand, leading her through the milling crowd onto the platform. She is hesitant at the cab line. I wave one up. Confusion gives way to a warm smile on lovely, thin lips. She paces into step with me, presses the back of my clasped hand to the outside of her thigh as we stroll to my cab. My contact with Nadia's thigh causes me to glance questioningly to her face. A coy, shy smile greets me. She brushes my hand lightly along her thigh.

Nadia gives an address. She settles on the back seat. She remains wrapped in my suitcoat in the cool morning air coming off the lake.

The air carries the promise of rain. Storm coming, Northeaster. The weather and events have been stormy this spring. Being alive is like that. When we arrive, I pay the fare before following her toward her condo doorway. Nadia waits for me to reach her. She grabs my hand, lacing fingers with me. We set off for the door, arms swinging. We set off, arms swinging.

At the door, we're greeted by a guy in a doorman's coat and hat who looks remarkably like the agent who met Nadia at Gaby's that first morning. His name tag says George. Must be a deep cover identity. Looks tired, didn't go home after all. He seems unsure of whether to shoot me.

I say goodnight to Nadia, turn to leave. Her eyes turn sad. Nadia grasps my forearm, "Come on up for coffee. We should talk." Her condo building is nice. From the elevator door I ask, "Will I be recorded?"

Her answer, a smirk and leer. Playful, Nadia asks, "Do you want to be? Galvan, this condo's my home, my unit isn't wired for film or sound."

Nadia pauses, thinking. "Why was Officer Burke killed?"

I ask, "Back to work?"

Nadia says, "Officer Burke was murdered by a pervert. Our behavioral science people say he looks like a serial killer. When I was first assigned to the case, I worked up a VICAP form on the suspect. The critical incident response group likes him, they agree that he's going to go serial, even if he wasn't off the ground yet. To tag him as serial killer, the bureau requires two or more."

I suggest, "I think Secret Agent Calah Morgenthau will give you your two. Call Gennaro and interview them before they leave for the honeymoon." Tell them I suggested the meeting, so you wouldn't bother them while they are away. From what you said, I take it you didn't speak with Gennaro lately."

Suspicious now, Nadia lifts her chin, stares me in the eye. "Why? What am I missing? I spoke with Gennaro the day he interviewed you and collected your DNA buccal swab. He's been busy with the wedding and hasn't responded to my calls. Has something happened?"

Shaking my head, I say, "There are two murders, now. Evidence from both the scenes connect me to the scene by DNA. There is a second, unidentified DNA donor male in both jurisdictions. Each scene shows signs of similar ritual behavior. The second victim was a secret service agent I was dating here in Chicago. She transferred to the service's Baltimore office. The agent's name was Calah Morgenthau; she was a supervising agent in Baltimore. I visited her before I left DC. Both victims were alive when I left town. I was in DC to sign contracts for the secret service Afghan detail. I stayed at Calah's when I was in DC. Left that Sunday from Baltimore. Calah was murdered the next Friday."

Annoyed, Nadia considers developments before asking with a raised eyebrow. "How did a civilian find all this out before I knew? Is that biotch wife of Gennaro's interfering in my case."

A small smile cracks my lips. "Ease up, girl. All of us have a stake in this. Gennaro is assigned to Mary Beth Burke's murder case. Calah was partner of us both in the Marquette. When Calah Morgenthau was in Chicago, she worked on Emma Wainwright Gennaro's team in Chicago. These cases are now an interstate investigation, which gives you UFAP (unlawful flight to avoid prosecution) authority. Thus you have jurisdiction, but the cases remain seated jurisdictionally in Chicago and Baltimore."

I say, "The Gennaros told me at the wedding. Again, if you want to verify, ask the Gennaros before they leave town for their honeymoon. Or his office can fill you in."

Nadia chooses her words, "I need you to answer something for me."

I say, "Are you asking as an FBI agent?"

She bridles, "No, this is between us. Would it matter if I was?"

Girl thing I guess. I respond, "Ask away."

"Were you sowing wild oats? Did you care about any of them? Or was it just hook-ups?"

I answer truthfully, "I had a long-term relationship with Calah which she ended when she transferred to Baltimore. Calah informed me over dinner before she left town by saying the female agents usually start relationships with married guys who are bound for Chicago. When the agent's career requires transfer, they break off the relationship and leave. Cold but it serves them well. Calah wasn't dissatisfied, she was leaving. When I received the notice for my final interview for the Afghan Detail I went to DC. When I got there, I got a text from Calah telling me to stop by her place. I went there after I signed off for Afghanistan. I did so on the theory I was getting a second chance. I wasn't. It was an offer of a place to sleep while in town. I took her up on both offers."

It is a girl thing, after all. Nadia gives me the well-known deer in headlights look. I guess it is learned early in life. She asks, "Just a place to sleep, Galvan?"

"Not just a place to sleep, Nadia."

Nadia says thoughtfully, "OK, I get her. What you described is not unusual. Sad, but not unusual. What about Officer Burke? Relationship seems unlikely as she had lived life as a lesbian woman for years. You left her pregnant. Explain."

Annoyed I ask, "Why, will it help your investigation of the murder in some way?"

Nadia leans in to kiss my cheek, "Maybe it will help the investigation. More likely it will help me to decide."

"Decide what?"

She laughs. "About you, big man."

I say, "I don't really know. We were a couple in high school. We broke up over the time I spent with that crazy redhead Devereaux when we were kids at Annapolis. I ran into Mary Beth in court on returning from Baltimore. Mary Beth knew I took a leave of absence for Afghanistan. There was something between us. Mary Beth decided to take it to a place we hadn't been before. I was willing, since we were in high school."

Nadia says skeptically, "She was a committed lesbian, Galvan. Get real."

I stop to return Nadia's hard look, "I thought so also. Maybe gender and sexuality are more fluid. Maybe, Mary Beth just wanted a baby, and thought mine would do. Maybe she thought I'd get killed in Afghanistan. Hell, she might've wanted to send me to war with a smile on my face. I don't know. I never will. Gennaro says his investigation revealed she wanted the baby regardless of how she felt about me."

I conclude, "It saddens me that she and the baby are gone. I thought she and I might put something together. I expected to experience serendipity. It turned into a whopping big dose of zemblanity. Mary Beth told me she wanted to work on a relationship when I got back. I believed her. In Afghanistan I realized that I wasn't as smart as I thought, and that I definitely had a lot to learn about women. Then I was dead."

We sit on Nadia's couch in silence.

After a long silence, I say, "This guy is choosing to ritually kill women I am emotionally tied to. He isn't seeing a passing woman and killing. He isn't attacking on the spur of the moment. He's killing women with whom I've had relationships. He seems to be afraid of me to some extent. He attacks when he's certain I'm not going to show-up. He lays in wait, plans his attack. He repeats past success. He also demonstrates obsessive, compulsive behavior in the act of killing. He engages in sexual behavior while he views his display. So far he's managed to flee the scene before police arrive."

"I wasn't being callous, Galvan. Thank you for explaining. I wanted to know what to expect from you. I also appreciate your insights about the crime. I have to think about that. You were the link we had. You disappeared mysteriously. Our informant linked you to Officer Burke. I was told you had a troubled history with Officer Burke, that you didn't care for her lifestyle choices. I got lazy. We had you and tons of circumstantial evidence. We ignored the existence of another guy we couldn't identify. I thought that guy might have been a co-conspirator. I figured if we caught you, we'd find him."

I'm getting tired, as I say, "That's water under the bridge, Nadia. Move on, kid. Serial murder cases can have impossible elements. Compartmentalize around blockages. When you eliminate someone, re-cast your net based upon what you've learned."

With interest Nadia asks, "Did you work a lot of serial murders?"

I say, "In the mid-90s my dad told me available computer memory soared. With more space for storage and greater computing power it was suddenly possible to cross-reference incredible numbers of cases and complex DNA returns. He told me the number of what they called linked cases went from a hundred to 12,000 in Chicago in one year. Sex crime linkage was the most common. Some guys were linked to two cases, some as many as twenty."

Nadia says, "I've been looking for you on and off for a year. George and I started out trying to find you dead someplace. The informant insisted you were killed by terrorists in the Middle East because of a drug deal gone wrong. There were a number of rumors circulating around your department that you were dead. Each source we developed told a different story as to where and how you died. Some said it was Turkey. A few Iran. We heard the Taliban killed you. Then someone claimed it was al Qaeda. There is a Columbian rumor involving a Latin beauty and a meeting in Washington, DC, where you pursued white heroin into Asia and was killed there."

She says, "Overnight you went from suspect to sitting on my settee."

Shocked, I ask, "Where on earth are you from? In fly-over country we call this room the living-room. Here, your settee is called a couch. Where you from, beautiful?"

Nadia answers, "I was born in New York. My mother and I lived there with my step-father. My actual father didn't marry my mother; he sent her away. My real father and my mother were Russian. My stepfather, an American, married my mother before I was born. My mother was a prima ballerina in Russia. I trained for the ballet but got too tall. It was difficult for my male dance partners to execute lifts. I gave up dance for college and eventually the FBI Academy.

"Sounds complicated."

Frustrated, she says, "I'm weird. OK. I was conceived in Russia, born here. I'm too fat and too tall for the ballet. My stepfather drank himself to death when my real my parents got back together. My real father moved us here at the end of the Russian/Afghan War. Satisfied?"

"Does the bureau see you as a big, fat bad Russian spy?" I ask facetiously.

In an upset tone she continues disparaging herself, "No, I'm an American girl. And I know I'm a great big mess, mister. Sorry, I'm not a skinny little runner like your doctor-girl. I'm not a petite little girl you can sling over your caveman shoulder. I am so tired, Galvan. I need sleep."

I stand, stepping in front of the seated Nadia as her chin settles to her chest. I gather her into my arms, carrying her to her bedroom, saying, "Good, I liked being kissed on the mouth by a big, fat, bad Russian FBI Agent. With your short boy-cut hair you are as cute as you can be, but you can probably out fight me. I'll never be allowed at any police parties in the future, because you used me and tossed me aside."

I set Nadia on one side of her coverlet as I roll the opposite side back. Looking up she says, "With practice I'll bet you could probably learn to put up with a fat failed FBI ballerina."

I hold out my hand, saying, "Jacket."

Nadia slips out of the jacket, handing it over.

Nadia is squirming around on the bed. Looking around, I find a tall back chair across the room to drape her leather jacket over. I put her black boots under the chair.

While my back is to her, she says, "Here."

I turn back to Nadia. She's handing me her Glock in its shoulder holster. She's still wearing her blouse. How on earth do they take those things off so fast without taking the blouse off? I have a lot to learn about women. Somehow, Nadia's jeans got folded at the foot of her bed. I know because I'm staring at her legs. Very nice legs they are. In one smooth motion Nadia pivots on her bottom, sliding her legs beneath her blankets.

She raises an eyebrow, "Want to have a sleepover?"

Suddenly it is mine to decide. I do. As she begins to pull her blouse over her head, I draw the covers up to her neckline, saying, "No. It's late. You need sleep. If we decide on a sleepover, I want you wide awake. Slinging you over my shoulder will be more fun if you are awake, slim."

I dry rub weariness from my face as I walk to the door. I turn off the bedroom lights.

Nadia says from the darkened room, "I thought you said I was fat?"

I answer a little hoarsely, "From what I've seen, I realize I was wrong. I think I may need sufficient access to study the subject matter more closely."

Nadia whispers as I open the door, "Chasing this guy is like chasing a ghost, Galvan."

"They're all ghosts until you pick up the right thread. Then you start to unreel that thread from its weave. He'll be far less fearsome when you can see him."

She says, "This man is a specter."

"He only seems to be an apparition. He's not a malevolent spirit. He's a sick fuck. We'll find him."

She says, "Homicide is a nasty business, Galvan."

"So, I've heard. You'll get him, kid. I'm at the heart of this killer's fixation. He's killing women close to me to get to me. If I'm around, he won't be far. You need to wait and watch until he comes into view."

"What then?"

"Sweet dreams, beautiful, Things will work out. If I don't get out of this room soon, I'll be in bed with you."

Nadia sweeps back the covers revealing her naked form. Come right in. All warm and cozy in here. I can see that isn't your gun, officer. Come to bed."

Nadia's playful eyes are half-lidding. Time to go

On the bed Nadia's eyes close. She sighs, relaxes onto her back, breasts exposed, her face placid. I walk back covering her with blankets. I lean down to brush her lips with mine. She draws me to her saying, "Got ya. You're a good man, Galvan and a good man is hard to find. You are also a hard man, and a hard man is very good to find."

Nadia releases me from her grasp. I walk to the door, closing it as I leave. She's asleep. Engulfed in the silence of Nadia's home my temples throb. I can say with certainty that Nadia is a girl. No doubt about it.

This Mr. Nice-Guy stuff has got to end soon. Somebody is getting laid. Not tonight but soon. I exit her apartment, locking up as I leave.

Down in the lobby, I pass George the G-Man. He looks worried and tired. Damn, I forgot my suit coat. I'll get it the next time.

George reaches for the house phone. I put my hand on the receiver, saying, "Let her sleep. You all spent day and night tailing me. Sorry, I wander around a lot since coming back from Afghanistan. I don't sleep much. I'm sure it hasn't been easy building the frame to fit me. What you need is more lumber and nails. Give it time, with a little work I'll be framed.

"Funny boy," Agent George says.

"Nadia has my alibi. Don't wake her up, she needs sleep."

Agent George says, "I'm not the police, sir."

"As long as we're revealing sacred truths, George, I'm your long-lost Aunt Betty."

George snatches my bicep, snarling, "Come with me. We'll look in on her."

I say, "Nah, like you said, you're not the police. Let her sleep. If I get back in that condo, I'll put you out in the hallway. I fear she might just let me."

"Is that so, pal?" says George.

I shrug, "If you want to arrest me, you know where I live. I need some sleep."

On the street, the nor'easter has arrived. I walk in heavy cold morning mist sweeping off the lake. In moments, that mist becomes rain.

I stroll the sidewalk in my cold wet shirtsleeves, I think the wedding went well. I got out alive. No coat. No girl. I sacrificed a relaxed morning in Nadia's bed. Jill hates me. Devereaux will eventually shoot me. I'll be dead before I hear the shot.

I can't believe I just turned down a cool rainy morning in a pretty woman's bed. Yes, I do have a certain genius guiding my decision making.

15

MOTHER AND CHILD

Nadia? Haven't seen Agent Dimitrieva since I visited her condo. Called her office a few times, left some messages. Got no response. I suppose striking while the iron was hot was a policy in need of more consideration. Nadia moved on. Evidently, I am a dead end as a murder suspect and have other deficiencies. Life in the big city. I need to be more self-serving.

I don't like Jill being done with me. I was stupid. I let Eva get inside my guard. As a result, Jill and I are through, done, finished. So that's that. Jill and Eva are reduced to shadowy reflections in a dark rear-view mirror. In looking at their reflection I can see lost promise. Would've, could've, should've. If I were a stronger, better man. If pigs were horses, beggars would ride.

I didn't square up to reality. I wasn't ready, afraid of rejection. More likely I was afraid to try. A world with either woman was never real. In each I saw the reflection of a fevered dream existing only in my head.

Jill looked to be the future, but I fooled me. The woman accidently developed the dread personal relationship with a patient. She felt sorry for a goof. How embarrassing for the woman. Her absence makes my heart ache. Stupid fool, she does not see you that way. Grow up, asshole.

Eva is a much different dish. She makes more ache than a man's heart. Eva resides in memory as an overpowering presence. I have often been angry with Eva. I've been saddened by things Eva has done. Eva is always aware she holds the keys to the kingdom, granting admission, or in my case exclusion from the presence. I will never understand that one.

I am tired of being coddled and pitied. I refuse to have my fate decided by the whim of a biotch. I need to put both out of my mind. I can't sit around hoping for the world to improve.

Having decided to mend my ways, I find myself sitting alone in the playlot, north of Gaby's, waiting on developments. I'm halfway between my place and Jill's. My bench is hard and cold. A chill spring breeze sweeps from the lake. Spring holds a bit less promise today.

Nobody is talking with me lately. All I did was create a clusterfuck. So, I sit, I think. I pull at loose mental threads. I hadn't planned to be sitting along the river walk in the playlot. I just ran out of ideas.

I watch the river walk from our launch-deck peering to the northeast. Jill has run by here in the past. Fancy that. Not today or the last several days. The plans of mice, and man of mouse-sized intellect. It has been quite a while since Gennaro's wedding. Haven't heard from him. No word from Nadia and the bureau, which is good I suppose. My freedom may be a thing to cherish while it lasts.

Did I mention Jill hasn't been around? She hasn't. Must've seen me coming. On my last visit to Gaby's I was informed I had been banned. BANNED is the most significant curse in Bridgeport. Excommunication from the Church holds less significance to Bridgeporters. Exclusion and rejection from one's local bar. What's damnation, at least it's warm by the fire. Once, maybe a couple of times, I rang Jill's doorbell. On occasion, curtains above me moved across the window. If I looked, the motion ceased. No Jill, either way. Annoyed, I smirked and waved at the curtained window. I'm quite the jokester.

During my last appearance there, the police rolled up. I left. I can't believe she called the cops. I'm the cops. No, I was the cops. I've become a stalker. Am I now the ex? Do all exs become stalkers?

In my new role, stalker, I waited for Dori yesterday as she came from class. Dori was indifferent to my plight. I requested she carry a message for Jill. Dori enjoyed my squirming. With sufficient whining, Dori accepted a note to Jill, opened it in front of me, read it. On conclusion, Dori shook her head negatively, saying, "She figured you'd pull this stunt. I was told she doesn't intend to speak with you."

Dori concluded, "Give it up, dude, when a woman is done with you, she is done with you. I mean, Galvan, you banged some red-headed ex-wife in front of your date. Really? Give it up, she's done."

Dori had her fun. Enjoyed my begging. Took my note with her. So much for that. It was an invitation to Jill for lunch. I set out for the playlot for sentimental reasons, as in walks in the fog. Probably a bad idea; that didn't go well. I gathered and stocked my parents' picnic hamper from their house.

Jill hasn't shown. Is two hours late in girl time? Maybe Jill came early, left mad because I wasn't here. Maybe she's not coming.

Lunch was meant as an apology for my poor behavior. Do stalkers always say that? I'd mentioned I would leave as soon as she asked. I planned to plead my case. So much for pleading. What a candy-ass I are. On the walk over, I found myself dragging my left leg. I stumbled several times. Damn those big, stubborn sidewalk expansion joints. Fixed parts don't stay fixed. Peace yet remains unrestored in my back, ergo the foot-drop. What a useless sack of shit. My body is punched into a time clock. Time for a shot in the spine. Eventually I'll go. I can't undo what's been done with my body any more than I can undo the developments with Jill and Nadia. Need to accommodate change, adapt and overcome—thereby survive.

I've had a Shakespearean, Hamlet earworm lately,

"To sleep, perchance to dream
Aye, there's the rub." Hamlet (III, i, 65-68)

Sex would be better, but I'm not getting either. I'm out of fuel. In the back of my head one last, deep dive to the bottom of the pool beckons. I hate myself for getting crippled. I was dead. I should be grateful for only being a bit crippled. Crippled beats the daylights out of dead. Who's ever grateful these days? That sounds lame even to me, and I'm so fucking crazy.

I check the time on my phone. Jill told me once that she is off work around noon on Wednesday. Male counterparts play golf. She doesn't. No golf. Not here. Not coming. Oh well. My hamper of wine, cheese, cold chicken with a blanket to sit on has gone to waste. I slide my picnic basket across the bench toward me. Time to go. As I gather my goods, I look up. A slender blond woman is in the sandbox. She's playing with a little girl who has her blond hair. The woman is slender, fine boned. Her back is to me. She's wears a gray hoody over lighter gray leggings. Outfit suits the cool and grey of the afternoon. Feels like rain.

The woman quick-lifts the tiny laughing girl over her head. She's flying. What fun. The woman's long hair streams in her wake. The child giggles in response to mom's whooshing flight noises.

The woman turns side-on to me. Surprise, she displays a hint of the new baby she carries. Her tummy bump something new. Mother and child, fascinating me.

I think of Mary Beth. What causes a woman to be happy carrying some guy's child? The world's such an awful, bloody mess. As I sit on this bench sulking, life goes on. I'll never know why she chose to keep our baby. I walked away from her to play at spy. What a joke, wasn't any better at that than I was at playing father to our baby. Some protector of mother and child.

We are ultimately responsible for choices made and consequences. Confronting reality, one makes choices. Philosophical viewpoint shapes the choices. Western notion suggests saving a man's life indebts the saved to his savior. Confucian thought holds the choice to save a man's life makes the savior liable for the things the saved ultimately does afterward. Fancy that.

I've let myself be lulled into passivity by injury. Didn't act. Lost the right to complain. I abandoned Mary Beth. Murdered, pregnant with our child. She and baby dead and gone. The murders happened while I was off playing. Options? Don't do anything, do something. Do what? To whom?

I sit. I stare blankly at the sand sitting in a sandbox. My mind wanders. Sitting around waiting and whining won't do. Vultures await developments. Not a vulture. I am not passive by nature. My current passivity was nurtured by falling on my face. Time for passive response has passed. I'm gonna do something awful. Action breeds reaction. The son of a bitch needs a good fucking.

I look back to the scene of mother and child. It's not for the likes of me. A starker reality awaits me. It is what it is.

With the family picnic basket in hand, I head for the river. Mother and child head for home. Safe, the child's head rests over Mom's shoulder, watching my departure with tired eyes.

I walk north, lost in thought as I pass a three-story-tall maple tree. From the shadow of its trunk Jill's voice sounds, "Waiting for someone?"

"I was."

"No luck?"

I set the hamper down on the sidewalk, I arch my back to ease the kinks. "Turned out for the best. I got what I deserved."

Jill smirks, "Learn anything?"

I sigh, "Leave before she calls the cops and tells them I'm a stalker."

"I didn't call the police. The Greek called, he thought it was hilarious."

Angry, hands on hips, Jill asks, "Have fun the other night after I left?"

"No. You would have enjoyed how it turned out."

Jill says, "Why did you look like a raccoon all week? Did you and red fall on your faces?"

"Devereaux punched me a few times because I was with you. I'm surprised you didn't see her leave, she was right behind you with the Twins."

Jill smiles a bit wickedly, "I might have seen something, but I didn't really notice. I was busy in the back seat. We gave your buddy Blackmon a ride to their hotel."

We eye each other with bad intent. I say, "See, things turned out for the best. Want some lunch?"

"Had lunch."

"That's nice. Blackmon's a swell guy."

"Really? Are you serious?"

I shrug, "Do what you want to do. He's your business. Just remember, Blackmon would fuck a snake if you held its head."

She smacks me, "Nice mouth, Galvan. When I last saw him, Blackmon was still worried about what you did to his arm."

I say flatly, "Your boy-toy will live. It usually wears off in a couple of hours."

Turning to leave, I pick up my hamper.

"Galvan, where were you coming from? I saw you wandering in the rain on Sunday morning in your shirtsleeves. You walking from the south."

I say, "Late date."

We exchange glares. I relent. "The G had the state police pick me up while I was walking home. They dumped me at the train station with Agent Dimitrieva and her partner."

Jill laughs. "Oh, I'm sorry, I didn't realize it got that bad."

I'm annoyed by her laughter. "Don't be, I took Nadia to her place. When I left, she was sleeping soundly with a smile on her lips. You were right, just wrong about who I was with. Let it go, girl. Tell Blackmon I said hi when you see him."

As I walked to the boatyard, Jill stood glaring under that maple tree as I walked north to my haunted inlet. Home sweet home, I tried not to look back at her. I did in the end, just as she turned and walked away toward Gaby's.

I followed the sidewalk into the barren brightness of our gravel parking lot, where I spot the Pirate of Penzance wearing a large floppy boonie-hat fishing our inlet and watching me.

I come abreast of him across our deep, fast-moving inlet. I stop. We stare. His face is lost in shadow under the hat's broad, floppy brim. He smiles meanly back.

I ask, "Catching much?"

The man shrugs, saying nothing.

I look at his fishing-pole, tip arched downward toward the water's surface. Where his line enters the water, it circles tightly under pressure from below.

Looking at his shadowed face I say, "I think they call that a fish, asshole."

The man's posture stiffens. He reels his line in swiftly. At the shore our watcher yanks a fat two lb. carp with deformed tail from the pond. The man seizes a good-sized chunk of concrete from the ground. Then he drags the flopping fish onto the rocky shoreline, where he smashes it with his concrete chunk.

The fisherman I've rewarded with a splash of fish guts on his pant-leg. The fisherman doesn't notice. Must have stuff on his mind.

His eyes glare at me from beneath his hat brim. He turns to stalk off into the tall weeds clutching his fishing-pole tightly to his breast. Reaching the end of his fishing line the squashed fish tethered to his fishing line dragged by a hook flops into the bushes behind him.

I call after his disappearing back as he disappears, "Nice talking with you. Don't be such a stranger, you're strange enough already."

His car starts in the distance, then roars out of the bushes and across the corner of the playlot before surging southward toward Archer Avenue. He must not fish much. Was I looking for a fight? Probably.

Blackmon and Jill. Lovely, just lovely. Maybe I'll go upstairs and kill that Greek who lives on my roof. Jill and Blackmon. Really?

16

THE LETTER WRITER

I haven't killed the Greek, yet. When I mentioned the call to 911, he played confused. When I mentioned the part where someone called the cops on me for stalking Jill, the Greek was drinking one of my Kirin beers.

It was nice to see him choke. He spit up the Kirin on his shirt. Foam gushed out his nose. One can't laugh and guzzle on the same breath. I timed the choke for mid-guzzle. Got him.

Is it nobler to enjoy one's joke, or enjoy someone else's nose foam. The scene sits lovely on my mind truly sublime.

When the Greek recovers from his choking spell, he says I deserved the police attention for mistreating that poor little innocent. I responded that Jill was a bartender in Bridgeport, a licensed physician and surgeon and had spent last Saturday night tumbling around in the back of his Stinkin' Lincoln.

The Greek smiled brightly, "I figured that would get you. Blackmon did get a little handsy. I had to turn around twice to slap him in the side of his head. I felt warm and fatherly. You know dad and the kids on vacation. In the process, I realized the fear of having a kid like Blackmon could be one reason I chose to forego hearth and home. That kid would make the Pope pro-choice, talk about a poster-child for abortion."

He adds reassuringly, "Anyway, between us, Jill kept frog-boy at bay. Unless you get your shit together, Galvan, that boy might eventually wear Jill down. He is one smooth, insidious lad."

Concluding, the Greek says, "So, what are you cooking us for dinner tonight?"

"Who says I'm cooking dinner?"

"Me, I'm hungry. I'll bring Gaby. She'll bawl you out, but she'll bring Jill. In the meantime, have a good cry, man up and get to it, boy."

The Greek sips another Kirin, "Face it, you've been a little shit. You've been acting like a five-year-old. You got your hand caught in that crazy redhead's cookie jar. Admit it, you little pig. You fat pig. Stop belly aching, and let that sweet young thing know what you want and how much you want it. For Kry's sake, is romance dead? Quit dickin' around; get down there and talk serious."

Not exactly the poetry of Kahlil Gibran, but from the heart.

He says, "Make us all a nice dinner. Atone for your sins."

I ask, "What makes you think I want to atone for my sins?"

Joe says, "You're Irish. You people are always guilty, especially when it comes to sex."

I respond, "Fuck-off."

The Greek smiles broadly, "Look at it thusly, kid, you had your first fight. Make-up sex is grand. Thinking about the sex will even ease the pain from the hot coals you'll have to walk on to get there. "What are you talking about?"

The Greek holds up his palm. He gathers beer and phone, walks onto my deck to make a call. Speed dials, waits, the call is answered, talks. He ends the call, returning to the kitchen. "Gaby said she'll come. She's bringing a friend whose twerp boyfriend thought he was a player. Gaby says the girl wants to enjoy sexual abandon with you because you're such a hot dude."

"You are out of your mind, Greek. That is the furthest thing from Jill's mind. I tried to apologize to her. It didn't work out. We both went away mad."

Innocently, the Greek spreads his open palms, saying, "Who's talking about Jill, I was thinking maybe Dorie."

He reaches for his cell, calls, "Forget bringing Dorie, Gaby. No, not her either. That leaves Jill. Bring her. I know, but he's sitting here in front of me with big tears in his eyes. He wants another chance to apologize."

Silence follows for several moments.

Then Joe says, "Yeah. OK. How about sevenish? I know that's a lot to ask of him. No, he isn't very bright. OK, I'll talk to her. What? He likes black underwear. Oh, you know that? How? What Russian slut on the balcony? Oh. I'll ask him. What do you say for no underwear? You should see his face, girl. Yes, that got his attention."

The Greek says, "OK, I'll come for you two around 6:30. One thing, do I get a preview so I can break the news to this guy. Gaby, he hasn't had sex with anyone since Afghanistan. We don't want him over-wrought. No. He's not young anymore, he might have a heart attack. Is that you, Gaby? Such language. What do you mean the only preview I'm getting is that of my own hanging? The undies were just a thought. I was trying to help young love. OK, 6:30."

He goes for another Kirin. "Now look at the trouble you got me into. Go shopping for dinner. They want dinner by 7:00. Get going; you have a lot to do. Chop, chop, Galvan. Buy more beer, the cupboard is bare."

I got large grilling steaks and large baking potatoes. Found some sharp eleven-month aged cheddar cheese for double-baking, baby green peas. Pressed for time I picked up apple cobbler and vanilla bean ice cream for dessert.

When I returned, the Greek was sitting before my laptop review-ing infra-red video. As I prepare dinner, he speed-edits a trail thumb drive. I let the steaks come to room temperature, mixing a marinade, pouring that over the plated steaks.

The Greek says, "So far, I've seen trees swaying in the wind. A gi-gantic river rat trying to swim across the inlet. Bad idea, he got sucked down into the whirlpool."

Later I look up from slicing broccoli and cauliflower. He found something.

Our game cameras aren't Gen 3 equipment. Having gotten spoiled on Gen 3 systems in Afghanistan, I know the difference. All this type of equipment gathers and intensifies the available light spectrum. Software does the hard part operating on starlight, moonlight, infra-red. In a Gen 3 system the unit receives light images. Then it filters the incoming light as it processes ambient light images. The resulting filtered image presents the viewer with an image. Under starlight, the image runs the gamut from fuzzy to crisp green.

As I watch, he calls me over, "Kid, I got something."

Drying my hands, I join him. A green tinted image sits on the screen. The image is of a man moving through a world of light and dark green tones. He isn't wearing a hat.

I announce, "No wonder he wore a floppy hat earlier. Casper Lewindowski. He wrote many letters to management when I was in Marquette, none extolled my virtues. As a result, I anointed him 'the let-ter-writer'. I worked with Casper one morning before I went on the tacti-cal team."

The Greek asks," What kind of letters?"

"He liked to complain. You know, 'Galvan is the product of a nepotistic culture, he shouldn't be on the takacal team. Dump him, put me up there.' Those kinds of letters."

Perplexed Joe asks, "What is a takacal team?"

I laugh. "He spelled tactical team as T-A-K-C-A-L in his first letter. He sent that one to Internal Affairs. It named Casper and his wine-head partner as admirable candidates for the team.

The Greek says, "The guy is a genius, huh? But the dude does know you Irish are like rats infesting a ship. Once one of you gets on board, everybody has to be Irish."

"That would hurt, if I had feelings."

"You don't have feelings, Galvan."

Casper bumping around on screen in the dark is creepy. A branch from a nearby bush slaps Casper's cheek.

Casper swats at the branch wildly, trying to sweep an unknown assailant aside.

Throughout the slow unsteady process Casper's eyes are opened in a painfully wide manner. His apparent night-blindness is troubling.

We study Casper entering and leaving the area in the dark. Each time he hides among the tumbleweeds as he watches our building. He doesn't do it every night but he's out there regularly.

The Greek asks, "Did your dad make a call to get you on the tactical team?"

"No. he isn't like that. Silky made him work for it, so I had to make it on my own. I don't know of anyone I ever worked for who guessed we were relatives. One captain saw me talking with Silky at the St. Jude's March. He called me into his office to tell me to stay away from Silky because he was a venal man."

In mock shock the Greek inquires, "Your captain thought Silky venal, took bribes? The captain must've known Silky."

I say, "I asked Grandpa about that. "

"What did Silky say?"

I answer, "Silky said he was a good guy. They were partners in the '50s at Chicago Avenue as a detective. Silky said the guy was a mathematician, he divided by two really well."

The Greek says, "My field training officer told me that if you wanted to be a successful crook, Silky was the one to work with."

I begin preparing dinner. "I got on the team by screw-up."

He looks over, as he's reviewing and saving video sections to another thumb drive, "Sounds about right. What did you do?"

"I was still in uniform that day. A stick-up guy was working 'the low-rise' projects. He runs out from between the row-houses with the gun in his hand. Just did an armed robbery in the process of which he tortured an elderly Puerto Rican couple to get their money. The dude was all balls. Seeing me, he turned to sprint back into the buildings. He stopped a second. Laughing, he closed one eye and aimed his pistol at me."

The Greek raises an eyebrow. "What happened?"

"We fired simultaneously, one loud bang. He missed. I shot his hat off."

Joe asks, "Some trick?"

"I had Deuce's .357 snub nose. I figured at the extended distance the bullet would go low. My aimpoint was just over his forehead. I raised it 18 inches at the last second. When I fired, his hat flew like a frisbee. If I'd held my original aimpoint, the bullet would've gone center-mass."

He nods, "That is one small, fat, evil pipe, Galvan. I've fired it."

I finish, "Lucky for him he was wearing a 4-bag, purple, leather Apple-Cap. My lieutenant drove up afterwards. After I'd cuffed the guy. LT wanted to see my gun, to check the cylinder. I gave it to him. LT stripped the spent casing from my cylinder. Then put a live round from his belt pouch in my revolver. The expended one went into his pocket.

The LT then said, "You didn't shoot at the armed robber. Right, Galvan?"

Taking his cue, I said, "Not that I remember. An inspector came up behind me. He demanded my gun. LT gave it to him. The gun was dirty from a morning on the range. The inspector verified all the primers on the bullets in the cylinder were intact. Case closed. Well, the inspector did write me up for having a dirty gun. Old-Timers called my LT, Pug. He used to be a boxer. Pug put me on the tac' team on change day. He didn't tell me he did it until Silky's wake."

The Greek says, "Pug was from the Parks. When they shut the Park District Police down, Pug was gonna quit. Silky found out Pug was leaving. Pug was a good copper. So Silky put Pug on his vice team, which was the tactical team in their era. Pug repaid the favor. That crazy old prizefighter must have thought you were a good copper. Your letter writer was right, you are a nepotistic sonny-boy. Although the old pugilist was a good judge of men."

I continue, "Casper was my recruit on the intervening weekend. Once I went on the tactical team, I rarely saw him. Casper obsesses. He became convinced he should have gone from recruit to tactical. He felt I was a doofus. Because I was a doofus, he should have my job."

Joe says, "You are a doofus."

"If I had feelings they'd be hurt."

"You already said that, go make dinner."

I return to the kitchen counter, he calls, "Go back to the letter writer, you drifted off."

I continue, "I was on the tactical team for about nine months when the first letter arrived. I'd forgotten about him. Summer came. My partners and I were called into the tac' lieutenant's office. Gennaro, Mary Beth and I were working a three-man car."

"A three-person car," Joe corrects me.

I correct, "A three-person car. The tac' lieutenant, our sergeant and Larry from admin were with two 'suits'. The suits were IAD. The suits showed us several letters in sequence starting with the first TACACAL letter. In essence, they were all from Casper or his two partners. They wanted to be on tac'. The trio wanted in and refused to give up until we were out. The accusing letters described me as a corrupting influence, declaring my partners spoiled fruit by association. The trio suggested management compare our output with that of Casper's crew. Eventually, Casper got carried away with his own self-righteousness, describing us in a postscript as an eyesore of a sonny-boy, a dyke and a crazy black dude who thought he was Italian."

"Such language, I hope they were reprimanded."

"Who cares? I know they didn't get their way. Larry compared output from the two groups. Casper's trio had a total of 53 arrests in six months. Mostly misdemeanors. A few were storeowners with guns, closing up on the weekends."

The Greek sneers. "That's cheap shit. I hope you had more than fifty arrests."

I say, "We had around 500 for the same nine-month span. Half of them felonies. We had over 100 guns. We were hustling. Them, not so much. "

"Antecedent to that comparison, we were sent to take a long lunch."

He says, "I assume Casper and company did not get what they wanted. Well, was that the end of it?"

I say, "No. Letters would show up intermittently. Casper's complaints became more insidious. He did learn to spell tactical, which made him much more credible. The last letter was sent to the chief of detectives, informing her that I was promoted to detective on phony merit grounds."

The Greek shuts down my lap-top. "Were you a 'merit' detective?"

"No, I was promoted academically. I scored a 91 on the test, was positioned 250. I was promoted as number 460 out of 250."

He shrugs, "Life in the big city, Galvan. Don't get any tears in my dinner."

Checking his hair in a wall mirror he states, "I scored a 99 on mine. You always have to miss one, it's proper form. I you hit the bullseye every time, internal affairs will want you to shoot the gun out of bad guy's hand."

I say, "That's not what I heard. Anyway, I went to the area. Casper exchanged letters with corrupt practices until they hired him. When I last heard of him, Casper was suing to be made sergeant. I think Casper left the job around the time we went to Afghanistan."

"What was his complaint about the sergeant's promotion list?"

"Casper claimed he was Native American. As an underserved minority he demanded immediate appointment to redress the grievance. His mommy testified she procreated with a man other than her husband which resulted in her carrying identical twins to term. She claims her outside lover was Native American. The man died without other issue. The board agreed, maybe to shut him up."

The Greek says, "This guy does cherish his grudges. Grievance can fester in your head and become a way of life. Finish the dinner, Galvan, I'm going to gather up the ladies. As he leaves, Joe says, "Watch this guy. I do not like being birddogged by a loon."

While the steaks marinaded, I reviewed the history on my computer. Joe has been searching. He gained entry to the IAD computer system from outside by coming from our federal side. Descending from the higher way point he entered the dated portal's security system. IAD has had other visitors in the past. No recent systems update.

While we were talking, the Greek was in Casper's IAD working files. Casper's files remain password protected. Why didn't IAD expire his password as he left the job. The passwords are active.

I wonder where Casper would go upon leaving the job. What would he choose as a password? He can't spell. Probably significant to him, but simple.

Earlier, while I was busy really paying attention, the Greek asked me if Casper went by a nickname in Marquette. Thinking back now, I recall a Casper episode involving two mangy dogs and two young boys in his squad car.

One afternoon, Gennaro and I saw Casper driving around in a marked sergeant's squad car with two dogs and two kids in the back seat. At the time I thought the kids might have been truants, assuming Casper was transporting them home. Several days later Casper's behavior repeated, and that got us suspicious. Casper let the kids out at their home. We made inquiry. We talked with the kids in front of their parents. Neither we nor the parents were comfortable with the kids' response.

Later we found Casper and talked with him. He by this time was a temp-sergeant and he told us off. Several days later on a hot and humid night Casper once again was observed bringing the boys home. Within moments he came up on the air screaming for help. The family took umbrage. We had to rescue him, which was something Casper did not like.

We called for the field lieutenant to mediate. During that investigation, the boys told us that Casper liked the boys to refer to him as Casper da Ghost. Casper Lewandowski was a big fan of the squeaky-clean cartoon character.

We all survived the community uprising. Casper was informed in no uncertain terms to stay off the block and away from the two boys. Before I made detective, I heard Casper answering radio calls, by saying, "I got it, tell 'em the Ghost is inbound.' Such dramatic presence. After they took his temp-sergeant car, maybe they gave Casper a bomber."

Most people began referring to him as that asshole Casper. Only his partners called him, 'da ghost.' I entered 'the ghost', as his IAD password. No luck. The system allows two more tries before issuing an alert. I risked it, entering 'd-a-g-h-o-s-t' (no spaces). That's not it. Time to make or break. Finally, I enter, "casperdaghost." Bingo. I write the password on a post-it and attach it to the Greek's notes. Time to get dinner ready.

The Greek returns, accompanied by Jill and Gaby. Gaby gives me a mildly reproving glance before flicking her gaze to Jill as I was setting the table. I eye Jill, she eyes me. I apologize. She nods slightly.

After small talk, the trio abandons me to my cooking, and they climb the stairs to the Greek's roof garden carrying my Mojitos pitcher, which I had cooling in the refrigerator, made by me with my rum, limes, sugar and seltzer. For the Greek , ,truth is fluid. He mentions making them earlier. Didn't. Orphaned, I cook.

It never ceases to amaze me how many people who knew me before Afghanistan think I'm dead. We left, I died, the Greek came back relating I was a goner.

When he brought me back from the dead, I lived obscurely in this warehouse on the river. My address vastly differs from that where I lived previously, prior to joining the ranks of the undead, I doubt I talked to five people who knew me before.

Beginning right now, I have to quit harping on the past. The past is gone. People have gone on with their lives. Time to make myself a place in this new world. Nobody cares much for the doings of the past. But it is past time to do something. I survived, so what? That makes me smile.

Grandpa Silky was fond of saying, "Life is like a woman, Kid. Grab life by the ass and enjoy." By grabbing someone by the ass do I run the danger that someone will also be attacked?

The killer traveled a substantial distance before I left town. Chicago and Baltimore are worlds apart. In the space of months, he struck twice. Again, substantial distances separate those cities. Why did he start the killing in Baltimore? It appears I'm the focus. I was never in Baltimore before that trip. How did he know where I was? Was I followed to Calah's townhouse?

Did this guy follow me to Baltimore? If he did, why? I was in Baltimore over one weekend. The killer struck five days later on a Friday. I had already returned to Chicago. Before a full week elapsed, I returned to Thurgood Marshall Airport (BWI) for a week, and left almost immediately for training at the farm.

The killing started in Baltimore. It seems to have followed me back to Chicago. I have no evidence there are other murders. I have usually preferred to have relationships with women. For a couple of years I saw myself in a relationship with Calah, until I wasn't.

This dude was in Baltimore, somewhere around Calah Morgenthau. He was around enough to take offense at my presence near her. Our time together had sexual overtones. Even my taxi driver saw Calah in that nightgown.

My visits set things in motion in Baltimore. Serial murder is a very ritualized and personal thing. The guy may have been fixated on Calah before I arrived. It was enough to draw him into action within five days after I departed. An amount of time was spent stalking each woman.

Damn, this nut-case had, or wanted to have, a relationship with Calah. From his ritual he's non-sexual. He does not rape, but is sexual in an inverted fashion. Unrequited love, furious at betrayal of imagined love?

How did he come to focus on Mary Beth? What changed? For one thing, I got Mary Beth pregnant. Because of the time frame I think something interceded to delay his arrival in Chicago. Obviously, I'm the connection which makes this madness of his function. What brought this goof to Chicago, more than seven hundred miles from home. He's a fixated SOB. I'm getting a whopping headache.

Meanwhile, back to reality. I look at the kitchen clock. Time to finish the double baked cheddar potatoes. Out on the deck, heat waves are rising from the grill hood. Developments suggest it's time to broil some steaks.

With this simple dinner, I've cut vegetables for dipping, ranch dip. I cut broccoli, cauliflower, carrots onto a platter positioned around the dip. I garnish the platter with pitted fresh Washington cherries, strawberries and some huge grapes.

Both interludes were bound by chance. I had hotel reservations in Baltimore and Chicago. I canceled both reservations to be with Calah. The killer was birddogging me, otherwise he wouldn't have known who I was with. It started in Baltimore. He popped his cork there. It took him a week to plan and carry out that murder. Could he have already been skulking around Calah when I showed up? Was Calah having problems in Baltimore with somebody? That may be the key. I need to ask Emma to check through the Secret Service. Something changed. The killer took his time stalking Mary Beth. It took months to come for Mary Beth. Why? I was long gone by then. But the baby reflected my presence, ever a reminder. Did she tell someone she was pregnant?

He killed Mary Beth, then he stopped. Why? No more killings connect me to other victims by my DNA which is now in the CODIS registry? My dinner companions return. From the flush on of the ladies' cheeks I'd say the Greek upped the rum in the Mojitos. Gaby's wicked smile speaks volumes. Match-maker, match-maker.

Jill's cheeks are ruddy, her eyes are alight. The sun on the roof? Not at 7:00 PM.

The Greek offers a Mojito, calling it the perfect drink for a warm spring evening. We drink our way quickly through a pitcher before dinner. Dinner goes well. Two bottles of Bordeaux disappear with the steaks. Joking and storytelling ensue. The strawberries americaine I worked up is cool and sweet. The Sauternes afterward is a nice touch. When dinner and dessert are done, we retire to the roof to enjoy the rooftop view of a clear night sky.

By that time, the only chill is in the spring night air. Jill rests her head on my chest as we sit on the glider. We go back to my loft as the mosquitos converge and the lake's off-shore night breeze dies. Later Gaby stands to leave, kissing the top of Jill's head, whispering, "Pleasant dreams, Cherie." Jill smiles serenely

The world has a rosy haze.

Gabby pulls the Greek to his feet, "Come, my brute. I need tucking in. Being ravished in the process would be nice."

They head for his penthouse. Trying out for a brute job of my own, I lift Jill in my arms, carrying her to my loft. Jill is light in my arms. Her eyes are dreamy. I lay her on the bed. She rests her head on pillow studying me closely as I look down on her. I bend forward over Jill, kissing her lips at first gently, then with greater desire. I kick off my boat shoes. Turning back to Jill's body with business on my mind. Not to be. I put lust on hold.

Jill is sound asleep. Too much rum. Maybe I will kill the Greek yet. Chagrined, I climb into bed beside Jill where I draw her to me. As I settle on my back, Jill squirms close getting comfortable. She rests her head on my chest, then languidly wraps a leg over my waist. Before I drift off, I stroke her flank positively contemplating some post-nap sex. Think positive, we'll take a short nap then take up where we left off. I become comfortable with the warmth of her torso over my hips. Sleep is easily won. I fall into a deep sleep with my left hand lightly caressing her thigh. I wake once, Jill is urging me to take off my shirt, murmuring, "Skin is better."

We wrestle me out of my shirt. She tosses her crop top, landing it on my face. In the light coming from the window I am intrigued and aroused by the shape of Jill's breasts. As I move in for a better look, Jill presses me to the bed. I manage to enjoy a moment's touch of her breast's firmness.

Jill presses me against the bed, "Sleep. We'll do that later. Time to sleep. Sleep we did.

17

PAYING ONE'S RESPECTS

Morning has broken. The bad thing is that I may have died last night. Someone has wrapped my face in a white shroud. The good thing is that my shroud smells of girl. I've gone to heaven. I inhale deeply, she smells very nice.

I drank like a fish. I died of alcohol poisoning and I didn't get a hangover. More proof they certainly do not allow hangovers in heaven. I catch the scent of coffee in the air. This might not be a bad place. I snatch the shroud from my face. It's not a shroud. It smells like Jill because it is her mid-riff t-shirt. I remember, now. Suddenly the morning holds promise, I've become sensitive to Jill's scent. When did that happen?

No T-shirt. This is an excellent time to sit up and view the beauty of the day. As I rise, Jill rolls off my chest onto her back. Her long hair sweeps over one breast. Leaning on my elbow I brush her hair from her eyes. Lovely. Her eyes flicker, hazel tones regard me. She smiles seductively, I lean forward to gather Jill to me. At that moment my belt buckle stabs me in the groin. Why am I wearing jeans?

A female voice behind me chuckles. "I hope you didn't hurt it."

Nadia.

Jill sits bolt upright, cupping the sheet over her breasts. She glares at Nadia, "Been there long, dear?"

Nadia says, "A while. Things started getting interesting. I thought I should warn you before we got all involved."

Jill sits next to me. She's wearing the cut offs from last night. Her hair cascades down over her breasts. A nipple works its way through her thick hair.

I reach my free hand out, I don't care if Nadia's watching.

Jill laughs at me, scoots out of reach, asking, "Been up long, Galvan? Did the buckle wound anything? I should take a look. I AM a physician."

Jill's turn to reach out. I do not scoot back. Nadia smiles wickedly. "Maybe he hurt something during the night. I noticed the swelling earlier."

Jill places her hand on my lap, saying, "You should go, Ms. Dimitrieva. As Galvan's physician I've determined he needs a thorough examination."

Smiling Nadia asks, "To reduce the swelling or the smiling? Look at him."

Jill says, "It's been nice seeing you. Too bad you have to leave. You must need to arrest Al Capone. Bye now."

Nadia shakes her head in a theatrical negative. "I'm staying. You go make rounds, Doc, I'll apply direct pressure to relieve the swelling."

Nadia sits on a chair she moved to the bed. Her bare feet rest on my bed spread. Her nails are a vivid red. Jill's nails are as well. I quick check mine. Normal, thank goodness they didn't have a nail polish party, the Greek just wouldn't understand.

I ask, "How'd you get in?"

Nadia says, "The dock door was open on the street side. I waved at the old guy day bartender with the goatee. He was turning table legs on a wood lathe.

Karl.

She says, "I winked at him, as he watched me climb the stairs. He shook his head. I found your bedroom door unlocked."

"How did you get in downstairs?"

Nadia smiles shyly, shrugs, says, "Picked it?"

She says to Jill, "When I came in, I thought Galvan might be expecting me. I was surprised to see you two half-naked in bed. You both looked wasted. I let you sleep and waited."

Jill asks, "What time is it?"

Nadia looks at her watch, "Eleven AM. Do you have somewhere to be?"

Jill frowns, "I have a class."

Nadia smiles brightly at Jill, "You go ahead, dear, I'll make breakfast. Later. I flew in last night. Galvan looks tired and I could use a nap. You get ready, we don't want to halt the progress of modern medicine."

"I think I'll wait for you to go home. You look so worn and frazzled from your travels."

Nadia offers Jill a wicked smile. She, in challenge, suggests "I could join you two. Did you just catch that guy-look? They are such little dears."

Raising her hands behind her neck, Nadia unties the bow of her blue silk halter-top lowering its ends to the tip of her breasts.

Nadia's breasts are delightful when she's dressed for work. Barely draped in a ply of silk, I'm a goner.

Jill is non-plussed as she shoves my support shoulder from beneath me. I fall. Jill laughs reprovingly, "We barely know each other, Nadia. Galvan's right, you are scary beautiful. Nice offer, wrong ball-park."

Jill rises from the bed. Her breasts sway slightly as she steps around Nadia.

Jill steps up behind Nadia. Nadia allows Jill to re-tie the bow at the back of Nadia's neck. As Jill adjusts the bow, Nadia cradles her breasts in her palms, as the pair adjust Nadia's halter top for fit.

I can't take my eyes off these women, totally absorbed by the sight. I watch in rapt attention. Probably drooling.

Nadia says over her shoulder to Jill, "Didn't scare you off, huh? Not me either, but it was worth a try if you ran off in terror.

Jill says to Nadia, "You're lovely. That wasn't my first offer, dear. He did eat it up, though. Guys? Give him just a hint, and their libido boils over. Such simple souls." Jill adjusts the silk at the base of Nadia's neck, sweeping her short hair away from the knot.

Nadia rocks forward in mirth, "We got more mileage with you tying my bow than I got climbing into bed with you two."

Jill says, "My helping you with your top appears to have been fun to watch. It's safe to watch us. When you climbed in bed, you called his bluff. He was in the hospital a long time and has issues relating to people. We threatened his emotional balance this morning. Go easy, Nadia. We might, we might not. He is one lonely soul. He's trying to treat us fairly, but he's a guy."

Nadia says, "He's a nice guy. I've been trying to get to him. He's resisting. Firm resolve and strong will has kept him going in the bad times. He is home now, and doesn't like being alone."

Jill says, "I'm beginning to wonder if I have the time to extract him from his shell. He likes it in there. It's all nice and safe. When I tie your halter it's a safe guy fantasy. Climbing into bed required him to decide. From his expression, he likes both of us. He enjoys his fantasy of being with both of us. Unfortunately for him, I think he's a serial monogamist."

Jill shakes her head and smiles ruefully, "That's all the free medical advice you're getting Nadia, honey. I like him. He has things to work out. We just got him as close as I've seen to rejoining the human race."

Nadia says, "We could fight over him."

Jill glances my way. "He'd enjoy that, too."

Nadia says, "Too nice a day to be fighting over a horny guy. He's made life difficult for both of us. Truce? Can I offer you a ride to school?"

Nadia continues, "I traveled back from DC last night. I spent the last two days verifying Galvan's alibi witnesses." Nadia shrugs, "He told me you two broke up at the wedding over the redhead."

Jill reaches over me for her crop-top. Her left breast brushes my cheek in passing. Erotic innocence? Is it possible to die of lust? She extends a hand to Nadia. "Come on, beautiful, give me a ride to Gaby's, we can pick outfits for class."

They stroll hand-in-hand to the bedroom door. At the doorway they turn toward each other. They smile sweetly back at me. They are enjoying playing me.

Annoyed I say, "We've had such a nice morning analyzing my faults and weaknesses. Don't be strangers, you are welcome anytime. We can have a sleepover. Nadia, Jill and I did break up the night I took you home. You asked me to call. I did. You didn't call back."

I add, "Jill, I enjoyed last night. I enjoy being with you. Thank you. If you wish, I'll stop bothering you two. With both of you knocking billiard balls around inside my skull, I may not make the grade. It could be Jill is right, I am safe and happy hiding from women in my boathouse. Maybe I'm wrapping my head around it.

The ladies come together in the confines of the doorway. Jill looks back between them, saying to Nadia, "He could be right. He's just not ready for us."

Nadia places a delicate kiss on Jill's cheek, saying, "Don't kid yourself, he's ready. Sorry, Galvan honey, you're in the penalty box for telling too many stories. We have to try on outfits."

They exit gaily swinging clasped hands, laughing. I am ready, willing. Able? We'll see. I watch the pair from my balcony, the Greek and Gaby joined them on the stairs. The three women are discussing something funny. What? I'd rather not wonder.

Casper stands on the point. Fishing. I hate that guy. Could I hit him from here with a piece of lead?

He glances at the building, ignoring the people in the lot. Gaby and Jill speak with Nadia for a moment. Gaby gives them both a Gallic shrug, and takes Nadia's offered hand. She hugs Jill and kisses her cheek.

The Greek gives Jill a big hug, speaking directly to her. He shakes his head ruefully, then kisses her hair. Gaby and the Greek, Jill and Nadia depart in separate cars.

Why is Casper's face suddenly so livid? He's incensed. He is shocked and outraged? What is upsetting him? I shrug, not my problem.

The phrase, I have my eye on you carries an emotional and a sensory weight. At some survival level we know when we are being watched. Casper's gaze snaps in my direction. I beat him to the punch. I've already shifted my gaze on over the river to where a fish jumps into the air. I yawn, scratch my head, turn to look at Casper. When I glance to where he was a moment ago, I don't feel the weight of his gaze because he's not there. I shrug theatrically, scratch my stomach, yawn. I go back into the sail-loft where I start coffee. Sipping from my cup, I prepare breakfast. Breakfast this morning is cereal, fresh fruit and wheat germ.

At the kitchen island, I ponder my day. I put off my trip to Brenda's for too long. I've thought about visiting since I heard of Mary Beth's murder. If there are or were two people in the world who loved Mary Beth it was Brenda and I. It is long past time to express condolence. Her parents died long ago. Brenda and I are what Mary Beth left behind. Today is as good a day as any to see Brenda. If I don't do it soon, I won't do it.

I clean up, shave, dress–striving for office casual. I drove to the Leighton Criminal Court Building maze. Then I parked in the county garage. The county jail officer informed me in the lobby that Brenda's new office is on 12. I show my Chicago Police Detective 'Retired' ID and badge. A corrections officer Guzman who knew me in my previous life. He was nice enough to ask, "Why aren't you still dead?"

Not waiting for my answer, Guzman waves me through the metal detector. Last evening's Mojitos make me thankful for small mercies.

I divert to the admin' tower to the south in search of an elevator. I enter the first available elevator, punching 12. There is an even chance that is where we'll go. The state's attorney's offices are on high floors. The public defenders are on lower ones. They call it the state attorney's office for a reason. Proximity to heaven is the province of the select. I am joined by a surging crowd. Stairs access a concrete fire-escape that forces a downward exit.

In the elevator, a public defender nods to me. I vaguely know him. I nod back. The elevator ascends, jerking and banging. On nine the P.D. exits, then spins back to hold the door open. He could lose an arm doing that in these elevators.

The PD stares intently at me, asks. "Galvan? You're dead."

One tries to be witty on overcrowded elevators, so I answer quickly, "I am dead. They sent me back to haunt you. Same place tomorrow, OK?"

The door closes, my elevator ascends to the heavenly gates, or at least the twelfth floor. As I exit the elevator it abruptly rises as I am in mid-stride. That pond at the boatyard isn't the only thing haunted in this town.

I flash an old subpoena, as I inform the receptionist that I'd like to see Assistant State's Attorney Thalburg. The receptionist was a slip of a thing when Grandpa Silky was a young stud. She barely glances at my ancient subpoena. Sheila the receptionist says, "Where have you been, detective. Lost weight? Been sick?"

"No, I was dead, but it didn't take."

Sheila, the receptionist, doesn't blink, "Good, I'll buzz you in. Brenda Thalburg has the supervisor's office, 'D' wing."

She points to the door on my left. Fool that I am, I walk quickly over to grasp the knob. I slip in the door after her lightning buzz. Behind me it relocks.

Silly me, Sheila was annoyed. Information is the price of admission here. I didn't pay for my admission. So, Sheila let me in the door furthest from Brenda's office. I have a half mile circuit around the inside of the building ahead of me.

I should have given Charon the boatman of the River Styx in hell. Sheila's the boss here. If you fail to pay the boatman's fee you are in for a long swim. Gossip is the currency of Sheila's realm. I hike the circuit. A wing, to B wing, to C wing, to D wing. My smart mouth got me a four-block walk accompanied by a substantial hangover. I recall the legend that Sheila has been vexed since the smoking ban was initiated 20 years ago. In time, after a long slow dog-paddle, I circumnavigate my way to Brenda's secretary. She takes my name. I am told to sit. I sit practicing patience.

Ever the keen observer, I study Brenda's secretary. Brenda's secretary is very pretty, has great legs. I notice such things, being a trained observer.

Noting my interest in her legs, she smiles back. She seems so young. Apparently, I've gotten old. Short skirts are back in. Life is good. Does she appreciate my interest or is she just being nice to a father-figure?

Brenda's door opens, ash-blond Amelia O'Malley steps out carrying a huge case file clutched tightly to her bosom in her tiny arms. I've always seen Amelia as petite, verging on tiny.

Amelia was Mary Beth's replacement in Brenda's life. Sensing my gaze, Amelia turns a haughty eye on me. Amelia enjoys admiration from onlookers. Their interest sparks the air around her. I never anticipated Amelia to have a lesbian orientation. Then she pivoted to Brenda, taking her from Mary Beth. She is one tiny, fast mover.

At recognition of my presence, Amelia's jaw drops, as do her files. I stoop to swoop up her spewing file-folder. I extend the file to Amelia. She seems to think the file a deadly snake, stepping away from my hands. She is aghast, eyes huge.

In a cheery tone I say, "Hello, Amelia." Too complicated. Amelia's stumped for an answer. Don't you hate complicated statements.

At the commotion responding to the sound of my voice, Brenda surges from her office. Brenda surges a lot. ASA Brenda Thalburg, like Amelia, is also a tiny woman. With all the surging she seems bigger. Brenda's eyes are huge, almost black set in delicate features. She has shoulder length silky black hair. Her skin is translucent, pale, devoid of freckles. Like vampires she stays out of the sunlight. Bren' considers it the cost inherent to having that pale, perfect complexion.

Bren' doesn't care for males in general, me in particular. We've been 'friends' since law school. She glares at me from the doorway, her eyes sparkle with the quality of onyx. She gestures to her office, "Get in there, you son of a bitch. Why did you kill her, Galvan?"

I answer, "I didn't kill Mary Beth."

Brenda snatches my left arm, trying to hurl me across her office. I weigh too much for Brenda to hurl.

I enter the office dragging Brenda hanging from my arm. Supervisors get the corner windows. I heard somewhere that various things are good enough for government work. The corner windows leak, poor caulking. Nice view, bad on hot or cold days. Otherwise, they're swell. The view gets me anyway. I gaze out. Square miles abandon railyards spread before me.

I await Bren's explosion, thinking of things past. Behind me, Brenda slams her office door. She rushes across the carpet from which comes a sound akin to corduroys brushing. She's quick, up punching the right corner of my forehead from the side. Why do they all punch my forehead?

The impact smarts. Brenda has worn her silver rings as a fashion statement since we met. One gouged my forehead. That stung. Brenda got the worst of the punch. She's jumping around on those heeled office shoes shaking her hand. Amateurs. On TV hitting someone while wearing a ring looks scary cool. Big gouge, blood, villain punished. Rings twist on hitting a hard object, like skulls. Bones break, flesh gets gouged on the striking, as well as the one struck.

Brenda succeeds in gouging my forehead. The gouge stings, Bren's twisted ring finger appears to hurt worse. I'm tall, Bren' unleashed her punch on an upward trajectory. Punching upward dissipates force. Striking up toward a target really dissipates force at an incredible rate, especially if the striking limb's torso joint is lower than the point of impact. Body mechanics is as it is.

I dissipated her force by sliding my rearmost foot back toward the window bank. When Brenda stops hopping and waving her injured hand, she launches a flurry of awkward punches up toward my face. I hand parry each away.

Furious, she is retracting each punch before its predecessor impacts. Arm punches tend to look good in karate class, but don't do much.

I ask, "Damn it, Bren'. Give me a minute to explain. You are a small person. Irish heads are big and hard. They make good targets, but you are punching bone, not a foam pad. Stop it, you are already hurting your hand. Let me see if you broke your finger."

Should I apologize for my head hurting her fist? She's not done, yet. Maybe I should wait.

Brenda's right foot slides forward, snapping up from ground level, targeting my groin as she steps inward.

Bren's throwing a punch-kick sequence. Her hand is sore, so she left out her punch. Maybe I'm not supposed to see her foot.

Her 2-inch heels are bad for her balance. Brenda is mad. If she kicked me in the groin first, my head would now be lower. Her punch then could maximize all 98 pounds of her body weight into my face as she stepped into her punch.

I scoop the heel of her rising foot with my palm, saying, "Bren', you already got your free one. You're not getting another. No, you can't kick me in the balls. Keep this up, I'll flip you on your tush."

As she calms, not trusting Brenda's mood, I still hold her heel, "I'm a guy, Bren'. Keep this up. I'll look at your pink underpants. If I look, you'll get flustered. Stop. Talk to me."

Brenda's face reddens. "Obviously, you already looked. Let go of my foot, Galvan."

I shrug, "I told you I'm a guy. I wasn't in town when Mary Beth was murdered. I've been out of the country for several years. I came back just before the holidays. I didn't discover Mary Beth was murdered until recently.

Brenda settles her weight on her base foot. She stares at me, annoyed. Realizing her awkward position, she glances at her hiked-up skirt, and glares at me.

Very carefully, I lower her kicking foot. Her base thigh flexes as she regains balance. Her base thigh coils.

She's going to bound upward, flip her torso, and backspin her heel into my face.

I counter twist her foot lightly, saying, "Bren', if you spin kick me in the face while I'm holding your foot, I will snap twist your body. You will land painfully on your ass. As a bonus, I will slide your rear end across that 25-year-old nasty carpet for a wonderful rug-burn."

Brenda sneers, relaxes. I lower her kicking foot slowly to avoid tearing her hamstrings.

Brenda grabs my left shoulder with her right hand as she settles to ground. My hand counter-balances her shoulder, allowing her to regain balance.

Furious, she says, "You had to look. You are such a bastard. It's been three years, Galvan. If I hadn't been formally notified by the secret service that you were dead, I'd be holding a murder warrant for your arrest."

I say, "I didn't kill Mary Beth. I was with the secret service when they saw me killed outside Gardez. You were here. You are more likely to have attacked her for jilting you."

Brenda snaps, "You were jilted, not me. After you struck out, I scored."

"Scored Bren', really? I thought you two were in love, until Amelia sashayed up and you weren't. Ever the opportunist, huh, Bren'?"

We eye each other over an unbridgeable void. Eventually, I say, "When I left Chicago that fall, the Greek and I went into training with the secrets. I got banged up, I was in some hospitals.

"I found out I also got Mary Beth pregnant before I left town. You were already with Amelia. Neither of us did well by Mary Beth."

Brenda looks down. "I know. She told me. Why on earth did she do that? She was so happy, intended to keep your baby. I tried to talk her out of it. I offered to go with. But she wanted your baby. What is so special about you?"

I respond, "We'd had sex, I didn't expect her to end up pregnant. We made plans for when I got back."

Brenda smacks the back of my head, "We rarely plan on having sex with a guy. It only takes once, though. Do you know a lot of lesbians who are on the pill, genius?"

That's Brenda, looks sweet and wholesome, but is as hard as a bag of rusty nails. I sit on her couch. She sits down beside me. Her shoulders slump. Brenda shakes her head. She looks at my face strangely. Maybe she's surprised to see me. Bren' immediately produces a lace handkerchief, saying, "Jeez, Galvan, you're bleeding all over my couch."

I answer, "Someone hit me."

Brenda smiles with motherly concern, using her dainty 80 grit sandpaper lace hankie to swab my wounds. Brenda is disconcerting most days.

I found through experience that all women are issued barbed wire handkerchiefs at birth. I didn't realize that lesbian women kept theirs.

Brenda sits back to study me, "You know for some reason she had this bizarre crush on you since you were in high school, right? It was a point of contention with us."

Brenda continues, a bit reluctantly, "Most women get jealous of me, Galvan. Mary Beth's occasional preoccupation with you got me jealous. For me jealousy was something new. Mary Beth would get antsy when you or that bitch Calah you were shagging came around. By the time Amelia and I found each other, I'd had enough. I moved out. I was happy. Melie' and I were in the bloom of love. When I ran into Mary Beth at court, I anticipated a big scene. She wasn't even mad at me. She was happy. She told me you and she were together. Later, Ms. Regularity missed a period. She was even happier about that. The woman was overjoyed at the thought of being pregnant. I asked whose it was. I expected her to say she was out there having sex with every young cop in sight to get even with me. She just laughed at me. She said the baby was yours. I told her to lose it; sooner would be better than later. The crazy girl wanted the baby. We talked about babies before we broke up."

She informs me, "I told her it would be career suicide for both of us, especially me. I was furious, demanded we talk with your dumb ass. I thought you could talk to her, make her sensible. She said you were getting in-service training. Typical guy. Do dirty deeds, hide in the weeds. You assholes. At the time we were busy looking at town-houses. I forgot about it. We were down to messages, mostly texts. After missing her period again, she was convinced. When we did talk, she sounded way too happy. I offered to take her to the clinic. I told her I'd lend her the money if she came back to her senses. She got all huffy, I didn't hear from her for a time."

Brenda exhales loudly. "I read about her murder in the paper, later."

She pauses. "I figured the police would cover for you. I had my investigators look into the murder immediately. Your people found DNA evidence at the scene of an unknown-and-flown male donor at the scene. The semen samples weren't of anyone in the CODIS directory's database. The trail went cold."

Brenda says, "Nobody could find you. You left your job unexpectedly. We were informed the file was held confidentially by federal request. I figured your friends there were protecting you. I was heading up the corrupt practices and official misconduct section of the office, then. My investigators put a non-warrant stop on you. A judge refused them a warrant based on lack of probable cause. I figured they got their friends in the Dirksen building running the interference for you. The bureau couldn't find you. An agent who left the bureau got involved, He started to demand we make a case on you then get a UFAP warrant for your arrest. That went nowhere. I eventually received notice from your department that you died in-line-of-duty. They offered no particulars. You were just dead. It made no sense. Then mister former agent came back demanding we use your demise to clear Mary Beth's murder exceptionally because your demise made prosecution impossible. Your department closed ranks, based on file data in the confidential file."

She finally winds down, "Then one day Gennaro found you, alive. Explain, Galvan."

I slowly explain where I was and gave her the G-rated version of life in Gardez. She sits silently, then retrieves a large, ruled yellow legal pad to make notes. Halfway through my story Brenda asks, "Why didn't the secret service tell the FBI you were with them."

I answer, "Most likely, the bureau asked, but never got a warrant. The bureau doesn't talk much with the service. I've seen secret service agents refuse to shake bureau agents' hands. I've never seen them cooperate unless both sides were forced. The bureau sees itself as white knights."

Brenda says, "Having met that bitch, Calah, the secret service agent, I assume the secret service have a high opinion of themselves as well."

I shrug, "The one bunch *thinks* they are the White Knights. The others *are* White Knights."

Brenda and I sit on the couch for a time. She leans in. I put an arm around her shoulders to give comfort. I don't receive a complaint. Shared troubles bridge gaps.

We sit close in silence. After a time, I rise to open the door. In the doorway, Brenda wraps her arms about my chest. Tears well up, Bren' hugs me, whispers, "I miss her, Galvan."

I kiss the top of Brenda's head. We both miss Mary Beth. A gasp sounds behind me in the hallway. I turn to the sound, finding myself staring into the absolutely crazy eyes of Casper Lewindowski.

Hatred is bubbling out of him. Casper's eyes bulge. His face purple and contorted. Even for Casper, the look is odd. His eyes are usually bulging out about something. This has the look of a pending explosion. It appears the sight of my arm around Brenda has popped Casper's cork.

Casper bellows, "Galvan, you pervert, you sex criminal. Thalburg, you filthy dyke bitch. I'm the FBI. You've been ordered to indict this scum for the murder of Mary Beth Burke. She may be a Dyke whore, but she deserves justice. You've been told to do your duty, immediately. Are you deaf, you debased slut?"

Casper is hyperventilating, "Do what I ordered you to do, tramp. Do it. I don't care if you're letting him fuck you. You strumpet, I'll bring you up on FEDERAL charges."

Brenda explodes, "Casper River Mount Lewindowski, you are a nasty, and smelling, and creepy lesbian phobic, degenerate. You aren't an FBI agent, you got fired years ago."

Stepping between Casper and me, she says, "You got hired on the stupid quota, Casper. You were fired when they discovered you didn't have enough brains to qualify as stupid. Get your unwashed, used-up, pervert ass out of my office." Brenda sweeps in front of me to snatch a giant document stapler from her secretary's desk. Then Bren' hurls the stapler at Casper's head.

I lunge at Casper. Always graceful, I trip over the stapler and flop on my face, missing my grab. Casper's face assumes a rictus of terror. He pivots, bolting from the reception area. The door swings ponderously closed behind him. I see him pass the front desk where he hurls poor fragile Sheila across the doorway. When I get the exit open, I stop to help Sheila to her feet. In the distance Casper escapes as his elevator door closes between us.

As I steady Sheila on her feet, the puzzle solves itself. A fool I am. Casper is Nadia's certified confidential informant because he was FBI. He's certifiable as well because he's insane. Once again, Casper's dogging my ass.

Casper went pointer on me with new FBI Agent Nadia Dimitrieva. Casper's crazed eyes tell me he's much more. Now I need to prove my theory. Missed my chance, could've kill Casper on the elevator. Life in the big city.

Brenda helps Sheila to her chair, saying to me, "He's been writing letters to me about you for two years, Galvan." Brenda chuckles, "Casper insisted it would give Mary Beth peace if I charged you in absentia. The jerk barely knew her. I set him straight."

She continues, "Early on, I tried to explain that in-absentia warrants required an arrest first. The start of proceedings brings the subject into the court's jurisdiction. He refused to get it. Casper was desperate for me to order Gennaro to get a murder warrant. He claimed he wanted Gennaro to get an Unlawful Flight to Avoid Prosecution (UFAP) warrant. Casper insisted he'd do a Rooster Cogburn on you himself.

Brenda shakes her head, "At her wake, Gennaro told me the bureau fired Casper. When no one was watching, Casper sexually harassed a female agent. The complaint came from outside the bureau. While the agencies investigated, some evidence went missing. The evidence was signed out by Casper under his partner's forged signature. He found out in the end that Casper was fired for insubordination. Casper showed up at Mary Beth's wake. The guy was acting heartbroken. His affect was bizarre. He apologized to me repeatedly for not being there for her. I thought they had a relationship so I asked her childhood friends if Casper dated her or grew up with them. They'd never seen him before. I was in charge of the office official misconduct section then and had a lot of contact with your Internal Affairs Unit. Casper worked there before his time at the bureau. The next day I asked around about that wacko. He had visited them before the wake. Casper told them she was an old lover; as a result the bureau gave Casper compassionate leave because they had been so close.

The IAD crew didn't know her and had never seen him with any woman. He also told them she was family. Someone in IAD asked around the bureau about Casper, after my call. Supervisors from the Chicago office later had him brought into the office on Roosevelt Road. It turned out that Casper was under orders not to leave the DC Area because of an in-house investigation there.

When confronted he lied to the Chicago Supervising Agents. Eventually, Casper refused to return to DC. They fired him on discovering a pattern of lies, insubordination and an ongoing unrelated internal HR investigation. Casper later tried to come back on your department as a supervisor on leave of absence to another law enforcement agency. He was refused. He got some connected lawyer to sue for disability because of on-the-job injury. He got the pension."

I think about what Brenda just said. Casper, who else. Simple things are simple. It makes sense. He's compulsive to a fault. He's returned to the scene of the crime to relish the misery he created and to reminisce about what he did. Serial killers feed on suffering and loss.

Facing me, jaw agape stands ASA Amelia O'Malley. An odd expression crosses her face as she studies me. Fear? Recognition? I've given my quarry enough time to settle down. To take a deep breath and rest a moment. Now it's time to begin the hunt. Amelia remains fixed on my face. I extract myself from Brenda. Time to pursue Casper.

Brenda steps in front of me once more, squaring off with Amelia. "It's alright, Melie, I ran Casper off. What a wuss. I scared him half to death with that stapler."

Amelia gives Brenda a sidelong glance, "Casper's not running from your stapler. He's running from Galvan. Casper just saw the devil. Don't ever look at me that way, big man. You already scare me. I don't want a fight, you win."

Time to go. Never be seen is a rule, one hard and fast. Amelia

O'Malley is a conniver. She doesn't like me. The feeling is mutual. She sees through me. Her significant other does not.

I offer a big smile. Must be ghastly. Amelia blanches. Oh well. I offered my goodbyes too late to kill Casper in the elevator, now. I look around, but he's gone.

18

MR. ENCYCLOPEDIA

I lost Casper in the courts building before I started looking. As I surmise, he got gone. On my way out I cross California Boulevard to check the cavernous parking garage. No Casper, no Crossover with tar on the driver's seat. He has disappeared. So much for my bucket clue.

I run a counter-surveillance routine. I don't spot a tail. I double back. I run lights at the last minute. I check mirrors and window reflections. No Casper. I'm happy he isn't following me, but I hope he doesn't go to ground. I definitely prefer to know exactly where Casper is, now. Not knowing locks me into defense. I didn't expect Casper to show up at Brenda's. From his reaction, he didn't expect me to be there, either.

The uncontrolled rage Amelia saw on my face added to a long list of unforced errors. I'm out of practice. Casper the goof is not that goofy. Casper has done what he has done. The trick will be proving what he did. Then doing something about it.

Arriving back at our boatyard, the Greek is studiously ignoring me. He is covered in fine sawdust from smoothing the boat hull with a fairing-board, working the hull lengthwise. A fairing-board is a thin, flexible plywood sheet which has a round handle on each end. The hull smooths with the sweep of the fairing board in long steady swipes from end to end. A simple, straight-forward device suited to create a low friction hydrodynamic surface.

His silence tells me in a simple straightforward way that I need to smooth things out. The Greek won't make it easy. OK. I need his insight, as all my plans and plots need review lately.

I step-up, "In school Sister Eudes told me, 'Don't shillyshally, young man, whatever is worth doing, is worth doing now.' I need your help, Greek. I know who killed Calah and Mary Beth."

Silence. Not silence really—there continues the scratchy-scrape of the fair-board as the Greek thinks. No answer, but he didn't kill me outright, so I say, "Greek, this is bad. I need your help."

He mutters from inside his Plexiglas face shield, "Galvan, you always have a problem, or are about to create one. You were told to tread lightly with that little girl."

I snap back, "Jill isn't a little girl. Nadia isn't a villainess. Nobody planned any of that mess this morning. Well, except you and Gaby. You two poured the Mojitos. Think about your nuclear Mojitos. Jill is not a drinker. We both fell asleep after you left. Nadia and I are a lot closer than anyone, including me, anticipated. She had plans of her own."

The Greek is listening.

I say, "Nadia didn't expect to find Jill half-dressed in bed with me."

The Greek asks, "Half-dressed? I thought you said nothing happened?"

"We were still asleep."

Interest sparks, "What happened? Girl-fight?"

I say, "No. Nadia tried to scare Jill off. Jill didn't scare. The ladies played games with me. They decided to make me pay for my sins."

"How did that go?" he asks.

"I got my brain scrambled."

Setting down the fair-board next to his face mask, the Greek asks, "How'd they look?"

Delaying a second, I answer, "As nice as Gaby half-dressed looks to you, only taller."

"Point taken."

I finish the story. "They are both upset with my duplicity. They left holding hands. So, all is not lost."

The Greek laughs, "Only you, Galvan. Confronted with 'the' fantasy date you blew it. You are hopeless." Resigned he asks, "What do you want me to do?"

I explain, "I went to Brenda's office today."

"I'll bet that went well. No wonder your mug is scratched up."

"It was strange. Brenda clouted me. She threatened to indict me for murder. Then she cleaned up the cuts like she was my mom."

"Come again?"

I explain, "Brenda cleaned me up with mother-spit and her lace hanky. Then I gave my statement to her investigators. When I was leaving, Brenda gave me a hug at the door."

I add, "Casper Lewindowski, the guy from across the spring, was standing in the hallway. He saw Brenda and me hugging. Casper went absolutely nuts. He called Brenda out-her-name and threatened her. Brenda threw a stapler at Casper. He fled. On the way out Casper dumped poor Sheila on the floor, I tripped over her. He escaped on his getaway-elevator before I could catch him."

The Greek says, "Sheila was probably at your father's christening. Any other sterling events during your day, dear?"

Bad news, Amelia caught me giving Casper the stink-eye. She implied if looks could kill, Casper would be dead."

"Why don't you just confess in advance, stupid? We are back in the world. Drive defensively, pay attention. Now, that manipulative, evil little woman is not only after your ass, she's on to your game."

"What game?"

"Bite me, Kid. Do you know how many times in the Kush I saw you give some guy that shit-eye around the time he showed up dead?"

Mildly chagrined I respond, "Sorry."

Joe says, "I'm surprised you like Casper for the murders. After all he's done everything but confess to them."

"You're nuts, Greek."

Joe glances at me skeptically, "The dude has been obsessed with you for years. You came back from the dead three months early for Easter. This fruit-cake has been onto you since it got warm outside. He's sits across your little River Styx out there in the bushes, spending his days peeping at you."

"Maybe he's peeping at you, Greek."

"Even you can't make yourself believe that."

Silence.

In time he asks, "Does Casper have relatives? Didn't you tell me his family was at a Christmas party the year you made detective?"

"Well, he had a twin brother who was a Marine. His mother was alive then. I met the Marine, Gaspar, and Momma at the district Christmas party before I went to detective school. That was the one where I took Mary Beth home after she had a little too much to drink. A police woman who grew up with the Lewindowski boys were identical. She told me they were degenerate child molesters. She claimed they were actually triplets, Casper, Gaspar and Nestor. Nestor was a giant eyeball Momma kept in a fish tank.

The Greek says, "I gather she didn't care for the family."

I shrug, "I think she knew about their degeneracy from personal experience. Sometimes she got wound up in the bar. Usually Casper was around. When she got that way, she'd put her hand on her pistol and stare at Casper. He always left fast. Brenda says Casper legally changed his name to Casper River Mound. That got him promoted to sergeant, claiming Native American blood. Amelia told me Momma Lewindowski in a deposition swore she had carnal knowledge of a Native American chief resulting in Casper and Gaspar. Momma did not mention Nestor."

I add, "Nadia's informant's name is River Mound. I mistook his name as his code name. My letter-writer is Nadia's informant."

The Greek sighs. "I got into his permanent-record at IAD.I have a surprise for you. After Casper completed training with the bureau in Quantico he was assigned to Baltimore. His file indicates the IAD that Casper screwed up some evidence in an outfit hit case. That, lying to supervisors, an AWOL, and a sexual harassment complaint got him fired. The harassment victim was listed as a female agent from another agency. It described her as 'female Agent-A'. That file is held by an outside federal agency's HR office."

He pauses, "IAD wouldn't allow Casper to be rehired, allegedly based on the federal notice. He was getting fired, when we were at the ranch for altitude acclimatization."

I tell Joe, "It just gets better and better. He's my guy. Calah was killed in Baltimore the week after I joined you at the farm. Mary Beth was murdered when we were at the ranch. Brenda verifies talking to Casper at Mary Beth's wake. Joe, the dots are connecting. I haven't found a data point excludes him."

He suggests, "If you are careful, you have time to prove it out first. When we were in Afghanistan, I read an article in a Navy periodical asking for anyone having information on a Marine who was being investigated for rape-murders of young Iraqi girls. The Marine was murdered in Iraq by his unit's interpreter. The girls murdered were from Anbar province. The murders occurred after the Surge. One was the 'terp's little sister. The dead Marine's name rang a bell in my head. I didn't know why. I connected the name to you somehow. I forgot about it when we got busy in the Shahi Kot."

He frowns, "The Marine's surname was Lewindowski. I looked the story up in the old editions on the computer. The Marine suspect was a Gaspar Lewindowski. The 'terp killed Gaspar with an old phosphorous grenade which he tossed in Gaspar's sleeping bag as Gaspar slept."

"Did they swab the remains to identify the Gaspar's body, Joe," I ask.

Joe says, "No, wasn't must left. The dog-tags melted away. The heat from the phosphorous was so great his teeth exploded. The 'terp really killed Gaspar, must've been intense. The 'terp said he woke Gaspar to speak with him before he ignited the grenade."

I ask, "So we can't do an around-end to get comparable DNA on Casper? Is there any DNA on file?"

He suggests, "We may not be at a dead-end. I found a thing called the 'Department of Defense Serum Depository'. The contents are smears dried on hard cards. Samples are stored on them to be processed as needed. Samples stored there are accessible to the FBI on a just-cause basis. They are not entered in Combined DNA Index System (CODIS). Each person attempting to enter the military service is required to submit two blood sample cards during the application process. They've been collecting samples from potential recruit contacts since 1998. Gaspar Lewindowski entered service after 2000, so he's in their card file. I checked, Gasper was dead before Mary Beth was killed. News broke later. Serum records are in the Maryland Central Serum Depository under lock and key. Card content is not entered except by adjudication or demise in action.

He pauses, "You told me his mother told you that Casper and Gaspar were identical twins. We need a comparison of Gaspar's sample to the DNA harvested at those crime scenes. On a roll he continues, "If DNA samples from Gaspar and Casper match, they are identical twins. DNA harvested at the scenes could implicate Casper in the murders."

He concludes, "I assume you know a little about identical twins from detective school. Identical(s) are literally identical in every physical characteristic because they share all DNA characteristics being derived from a single fertilized egg which splits into matching fetuses. Fraternal twins aren't identical. They can look similar. Identical twins can be of different sexes, different eye color, different fingerprints. The babies are not a matched pair."

I nod. "I figured that after I read Twain's "<u>Pudd'nhead Wilson</u>" in school. With Gaspar dead in Anbar before Mary Beth was murdered, that leaves Casper if the DNA connects with the crime scenes."

The Greek says, "It ain't Nestor. He was in the fish tank. Are you out to prove this to yourself, Galvan, before...?"

Confused I ask, "Before what?"

Joe shrugs, "Before you do something awful." Out of the blue, the Greek asks, "What does some obscure Mark Twain book from a hundred years ago have to do with a DNA ID in a serial murder case?"

I say, "I'm surprised at you, from the Medill School of Journalism. You should read more broadly, not cower in the isolation of your ivory tower. Learn, develop a sense of humor, Greek.

He is ordering a copy of '*Pudd'nhead Wilson*', on my computer, bet he charges it to me.

19

SAD EXCUSE FOR A SAILOR'S DREAM

On this beautiful clear blue morning a steady breeze blows stark white floaties out over the lake. Floaties are cottonwood seeds. Pods burst open high up in the giant trees. The pollen rides the heat of morning updrafts. Summer somewhere just over the horizon. The sky is filled with drifting seed clouds.

I come up Archer Avenue traveling northeast to State. I pass the mystery of the beehive projects. The buildings really appear memorials to a de-seeded corncob. Marina Towers on the north bank of the Chicago River are of the same vintage and style. I follow 18th Street to Michigan Avenue, Michigan to Roosevelt Road. There, I cross the long-bridge over the IC Railroad yard into the museum complex. I cross to Northerly Island. It looks more peninsula than island. I pass the Field Museum of Natural History, Aquarium, Planetarium. On to Burnham Harbor.

The south shore of Lake Michigan combines with the modern Northerly Island which sits east of Burnham harbor. Northerly is positioned to protect the Burnham anchorage from the lake's sweeping-current sweeping in out of the northeast. It opens to the southeast.

We have a sailboat at Burnham. I find parking near the harbor. I'll be gone for a while. One must avoid having a vehicle towed.

I haul out my rolling ice-cooler, hauling the boat duffle onto it. It's a good day for sailing with a pretty girl. What could be better? The boat duffle contains a Casper file copy. The cooler has sandwiches, fruit and things to drink on hot days. My cooler contains no file.

I'll need to ask Deveraux for help. Maybe I'll depend on her loyalty. Oh well? I'm after a comparison of Gaspar's serum card from the depository with the crime scene DNA evidence. I think Eva has the pull and cunning to arrange the comparison. Eva will be a hard sell. She is Navy to her core. On the other hand, she's a special forces 'snake-eater'. Snake eaters tend to be more sinuous corner cutters. I've cut a great many corners for Commander Devereaux. I've seen her cut a good many as well. Eva will cut most any corner to accomplish her mission. A lot of us got killed fulfilling her missions. Agents, SEALS and cops died doing for Eva. My own demise comes to mind. Will she cut one for me? Depends on that limited sense of loyalty. Experience says no.

Eva's effect is pervasive, her pull magnetic. The closer she is, the greater my desire to plunge into that pull. I attract Eva, but not for long. My draw dissipates fast in face of distance. For two years she failed to spot me in Afghanistan. When Eva spotted me, we reverted to type. We share a passionate history. Contact ignites a quick burning flame.

I would like to think I'll keep hands-off today. She was good to hold at the wedding. I'll ask my favor late in the day. Eva needs to relax. Like all who overstayed that party in the clouds, being there left her with a dose of PTSD. Only I wasn't there very long. Eva was.

Perhaps sailing on the lake on a day like this will sooth her soul. The day's steady wind and bright sunshine are made for sailing. Eva loves to sail. She'll take the helm. It will hard to get it back. Around Annapolis her desire to command was evident from the first. Eva grew up around the academy's sailing fleet. A day on the lake will do her good. Our boat is of wood, designed to be quick. We dock here just for the windy days.

I stroll to the Rainbow Fleet Dock. That dock is in the northeast pocket of the harbor.

She's moored out at a star-dock in the harbor proper. Docking fees each summer season–the city anchors free floating star-docks in the large harbor. Star docks aren't cheap to lease, but to reserve pier dock space isn't possible.

To get to our mooring at the floating star-dock we have to take a water-taxi from the Rainbow Fleet landing. I told Eva Devereaux I'd meet her at the water-taxi mooring.

There is a prevailing rumor, popular among women, that males think of sex at roughly ten second intervals. The interval seems shorter to me. In the distance I spot Eva studying her watch at the water-taxi mooring. Well, she's not exactly at the mooring. Ever the sniper, Eva remains in the shadow of the tree line.

During the Chicago World's Fair, Helen Gould Beck appeared as Sally Rand performing her 'fan dance'. Sally appeared at the café on the streets of Paris exhibit. Grandpa Silky said there many exhibits at the fair. Sally's was the best. Silky was ten at the time. I was ten when he told me.

Silky said, "Francis, never believe the bullshit. Sally was stark-naked. At your age she answered any important questions I had about female anatomy."

As I reminisce, Eva comes more clearly into view. Before me stands the woman who answered my questions. So much for my iron resolve to keep my hands off Eva.

Eva is preoccupied. As I approach her eyes sweep the harbor seeking. What? Our boat? A distant war? I see the girl I met that summer in Annapolis. A grown woman, now become the amalgam of Naval officer, war tested SEAL leader. In her wispy summer dress, all I see today is the woman. I near her. Eva turns to the crunch of my footfalls on gravel. As her eyes reach mine, my heart pounds. Eva locks on me. Target? Friend or foe? Does Eva see me today as former lover, objective, or opponent. Dropping her beach bag, Eva launches herself into my arms. In mid-flight she wraps her long legs about my waist. Enjoying her leg wrap I hold Eva in place with my hands on her bottom. Eva's enthusiasm is catching. She settles into our embrace. Her hair smells of sunlight. I absorb her warmth. Eventually, I lower Eva's feet to the ground. She is beaming. We walk hand in hand to the water taxi.

The waterman knows me, he stoically ignores our embrace. He just smiles at the sky-line he sees all day long. Must like skylines. I indicate the boat as we approach our star-dock. Eva examines our sailboat with professional interest. Interested in boat speed under sail she asks when the hull was last scraped.

I respond, "Her hull is clean, she just went in the water. Sea-weed and parasites aren't the same problem on the lake as the weed would be in the ocean. On days like this, McCormick Place to the big building to the southwest is a sharp wind-vector as we leave the harbor. The current as we exit into the lake runs onshore, northeast to southwest. The passage can be tricky so I'll take her out."

I say, "When we're clear of the harbor, you can take the helm. She's Yar, responds well. She is quick and nimble."

We loosen our moorings. I maneuver us south through the harbor by jib sail. We do not use the small kicker engine mounted on our stern. The Rainbow Fleet taught me well. Eva, ever the purist, was impressed.

As we exit the harbor, Eva raises the main sail.

I tell Eva, "We have an off-shore breeze out of the north-northwest, but pretty soon we'll see the wind swing around to out of the northeast. There'll be a good-sized northeaster tonight. The lake is like that."

We head for open water. Midweek, pleasure boat traffic is minimal. I relinquish the helm to Eva. Eva has a knowing-hand. I suggest she head further out into the lake. "This boat was the first we acquired late last fall. She was a wreck.

Eva says, "She's Yar? Wow, swift and nimble.

"Who rehulled her?" she asks skeptically.

I answer, "Joe and I own a business in search of a market. We build and repair wooden vessels. Wood boats last longer around here if they're protected from the winters. The lake is a nice body of water to sail on. When it gets stormy the water splashes like a bathtub sometimes."

Studying the setting of my helm I suggest, "You'll enjoy sailing the lake. We have a steady breeze today. When the World Cup was here, the crews loved sailing in this weather."

Eva asks, "How did you learn about Yar, landlubber?"

"Katherine Hepburn, another famous red headed beauty, used the term 'Yar' in dialogue with Cary Grant in 'The Philadelphia Story'. Grant was a naval architect who had designed the vessel on which they honeymooned. The boat was named the True Love. The couple divorces early in the movie. The Hays Code was in effect at the time the movie was made. Hepburn's character was very young and virginal when she and Cary Grant eloped. On their honeymoon Hepburn was frigid. Under the Hays (decency) Code the reason for their divorce needed to be couched in euphemism."

I conclude, "When Hepburn discovered Grant was selling the 'True Love,' she got mad. They had divorced after their honeymoon on the boat. Hepburn commented that while the True Love was Yar, she was not. That was how they got the story across."

Eva frowns, "Is that a snide comment about me? I don't recall we ever had a honeymoon of any kind. You kept running away."

I check distance from the shoreline, then say, "Eva, listen to me. Keep her out at about a mile. The shore runs shallow here." Eva corrects her course.

I say, "You are far more Yar than I'll ever be. You asked me how I knew the meaning of the term 'Yar'. I looked it up after I watched the movie. I was ten at the time. For years I assumed Yar was something dirty."

Eva's mad. She demands, "Are you saying I don't respond well to the helm?"

Watching the shoreline, I say, "On the rare occasions we've been together in the last decade you responded just fine. I have no complaint. The thoughts of having sex with you are some of my fondest memories."

I pause. "Stay out here. Ahead of us a large bay opens. The bay cuts sharply inland. The bottom shallows very quickly. The bottom is a mass of white sugar sand from the ancient dunes."

As we approach the open bay, I take the helm from Eva to inch us further off-shore. My action makes Eva frown. Do I care? She knows Chesapeake Bay which this is not.

I say, "During high water years the lake erodes inland toward the outer drive. The city has a history of back filling erosion along here— construction rubble. In there, huge rectangular sandstone blocks slide across the bottom like skateboards in stormy weather. Sand bars and rubble heaps move around too much to effectively map."

Eva glares at me silently. I respond, "You are wound very tight, Eva. I'm not questioning your skills as either a sailor or navigator. The coast along here has geological reefs interspersed with miles of fill and loose mounds of rubble. Listen up; I know this crazy shoreline a little better. Relax."

I point along the shoreline tree cover, "My family's home is to the west. I live over to the northwest along the south branch of the Chicago River."

Seeking neutral ground, I say, "The water ahead is a darker blue. The depths south of this bay may indicate what was once an exit point which dumped the river into the lake."

A calming Eva changes subject, "Did you cover the entire city when you were in homicide, Trey?"

"When I came to homicide, we had everything from the mouth of the river north of your hotel to roughly three more miles southward.

Our old detective area started here at the lake and ran west of the shoreline to Chicago's western city limits, which are about eight miles west of here. It is roughly eighty square miles geographically. Gennaro says the area is larger now, with fewer detectives."

"Is your family estate in the wooded area way out south there."

"My family estate is a house on a 40 by 60 lot. The forested area of our estate has two trees, a crab apple in front and a boysenberry in back.

"Do you have your own estate?"

Laughing I explain, "My family doesn't have an estate, Eva. My dad was a police detective like me."

Eva has a look of confusion. "You and your father were enlisted men?"

Still smiling I say, "Pretty much. The best comparison I can offer is that in police-work detectives are similar to chief warrant officers in the Navy. The rank of detective is referred to as 'exempt'. They like to call us police officers serving as detectives. Management doesn't like detectives to be exempt because the rank was designed to be able to investigate most anyone, except the superintendent. Command says we are not exempt today. The courts have uniformly disagreed."

Eva asks uncertainly, "You are still a detective? You speak as if you are still active duty."

I explain, "I was retired due to the injuries in Afghanistan. I was seconded to the secrets who loaned me to you. I build boats now. I live in the sail-loft of our business. My living-space was built for sail-cloth storage, between our second floor and the roof of our building. The floors have twenty-foot ceilings."

She looks confused, so I add, "Our boatyard was built on what was once a rock island sitting in a swamp along south bank of the south-branch of the Chicago River. In the boat-yard Joe and I make and repair wooden boats on the first floor. I live in the old sail-loft. Joe lives above me in the third-floor penthouse."

As Eva considers silently. I wonder what is running through her mind. Is she reassessing my value as a mate, based on my confessed limited prospects? I'm very fond of Eva, always have been. I've fought alongside her. I have fought under her orders. I've fought to save her life.

I have on very rare occasions made love with Evangeline Devereaux.

Our physical and emotional attraction to each other has rarely been in question. I just don't know Eva well as a person. Eva in many ways is an enigma. Without doubt, Eva mystifies me.

I retreat into the story of how we got the boat she's sailing. I recount that, "A friend of mine was fishing with his sons a little further downwind of here. They observed this vessel approaching paralleling the shoreline. The vessel was being poorly handled by an inexperienced sailor. The area along here was once sand dunes backed up by swamp until the late 18th Century. Primordially, the area may have been the mouth of the Chicago River where it dumped into the lake. Where my friend and his sons fished is bedrock scoured by the glaciers. The bed rock acts as a reef, running out into the lake. The inexperienced boater was sailing due south onto an east-west submerged rock shelf. To the north of the shelf the water is deep. The submerged rock-reef is blue black in color. Deep water seems to continue but it doesn't. Over the rock shelf, the water is only a couple of feet deep.

I proceed with my story, "When T noticed this boat, it was a broad-reach—out maybe thirty feet from shore, traveling due-south toward the reef at a right angle. The sailor had his sail swung out shoreward, blocking his shore-ward sight line. Like today, a northeaster was brewing up. The boater was oblivious to his danger. The only crew beyond the captain was his young wife who was wearing a gold lame bikini and was perched up here on the cabin roof."

I shrug, "Maybe they were on the way to view the German Submarine."

"What submarine?"

"The WWII Nazi submarine."

Eva says, "There were no Nazi submarines on the Great Lakes."

My turn, "The U-505 was brought here through the St. Lawrence Seaway after WWII. It was forced to surface and captured mid-Atlantic during WWII. Later it was beached and brought ashore at the museum. It's still there. You should have a look at it before you leave town."

Eva frowns, "Why don't you take me to see the submarine?"

"I've seen it. My friend and his sons tried to wave the sailor off. The sailor studiously ignored them. His lovely, blond, amply endowed young wife enthusiastically waved back. My friend wondered if the lovely girl was waving so vigorously to communicate most effectively with the simple natives. Our sailor got upset, because the local tribes-men were cat-calling his lovely, somewhat naked wife. To dramatically speed his departure, the sailor tightened the sheets, and swung his helm toward the sail.

Eva is laughing. "Let me guess, disaster?"

I nod, "He jibed, the boom counter-pivoted. The vessel skidded into a capsize as the keel struck the reef. The impact launched the wife overboard and the captain onto the mast.

I say, "The vessel was hard aground. Momentum luckily pivoted it onto the reef with its mast hanging over the shallows and the captain dangling from it over the water. The blond lady couldn't swim. She splashed wildly in the cool water screaming for rescue. My friend walked out on the rocks trying not to get any wetter than necessary. T was wearing his blued steel service-revolver under an over-shirt. Nobody likes a rusty thousand-dollar gun. "

I laugh, "My friend told the lady to stand up. The water was barely thigh deep where the woman was splashing. The blond goddess rose from the water in all her grandeur. The wife's face wore the most innocent of expressions. My friend, being a trained detective, immediately noted that the lady had lost the top of her bikini. Glancing over his shoulder, he observed his ten-year-old and his eight-year-old boys sharing the view. My friend climbed into the water and removes his over-shirt to cover the lady's exposed torso. "The blond goddess smiled brightly at the boys, they smiled back. I guess we all like to cast our spell. The function of buttons must've eluded the lady. It took her quite a few minutes to figure out how to button the shirt shut. My friend rescued the embarrassed boater who rewarded his savior by trying to get my friend arrested for carrying a concealed weapon when the police boat arrived. The sailor became theatrically terrified. When the Coast Guard boat arrived. Our sailor self-righteously marched over to the Coast Guard Chief Petty Officer to demand my friend be arrested. She told our boater that all cops carry guns as she pointed to my friend's black T-shirt reading, 'Chicago Homicide: My day begins when yours ends.' She told them, they're all show-offs."

Eva notes, "I have one of those. I got it in Afghanistan as a prize for being good."

"You did. I wondered where that went."

"Yep, I took it. Taking your boyfriend's clothes is allowed."

"When did I become a boyfriend?"

Eva says in a more earnest tone, "A long time ago, Galvan. You don't always act like it. You run away a lot."

Eva's view of me is startling blind. I did run for my life to get away from Admiral Grandpa. I frown. The second time Eva sent me up those exploding stairs.

I conclude my story saying, "Our sailor let the boat go to auction. We bought it last winter from the insurance company as salvage."

As it comes into view, I point out the reef by its color change in the clear water.

The day grows warm. We sail out east, then north. I think Michigan was still over there, somewhere. Eva gave me the helm. She went below.

Eva returns wearing a blue, silky bikini. I study her body. She stands facing me in the small cockpit. She raises an eye-brow as I sweep my gaze to the sway of her breasts in motion with the boat. The cool breeze accentuates their shape under taut silk.

Eva has a wicked smile now, "I finally have your attention."

I sweep my free arm behind her hips, pulling her abdomen to me, resting my lips to its soft curves.

Eva breaks free with a giggle, drawing her abdomen away from me. "Galvan, stop that right now. Remember, you are still mad at me, mister."

Eva spins about to hide her abdomen from me. I pull her back toward me, to kiss the base of her spine.

Eva breaks away murmuring, "Ohhh. Stop that. There are people out here." Her eyes flash crystal blue as she glances back over her shoulder at me. Capturing attention is her intent. Now, Eva eyes me from a close distance. Yet, she's just out of my reach. I see the same speculation I first saw in her eighteen-year-old eyes. Eventually, I became this woman's lover at seventeen. Ten years, a long time.

Eva-in-command eyed me with the skepticism reserved for civilian foils about to be used and discarded. During one scant evening in my two-year stay in Afghanistan I became Eva's lover, again. When last I saw Eva Devereaux in the Kush, she eyed me with a disdain one reserves for a failed tool about to be abandoned in the street. Our personal interaction has always run from speculation, to lust, to disdain. Never a boring moment for me with little Eva.

This afternoon Eva's again speculating on my potential. This is different, Eva today considers me with a grown woman's eye. I have a fair idea of her objective. We are that way around each other. Though, Eva's intent in seeking the objective always worries me.

Eva smiles, suddenly sweet and shy. I seem to have passed what-ever test she's posing. I extend my free hand to her. Eva pads bare-foot across the deck to me. Her large toes are cute with dark red nail polish. The fog of time evaporates. Eva sits nestling close to me. She doesn't reach for the helm. I enjoy the study of Eva's body, always have. In the small bikini, she appears in her glory. My eyes sweep up over those long toes, up over thin ankles, strong slender calves, and smooth thighs. I pause at Eva's hips. The breadth of her hips suits her so well. As a teen, I was fascinated by the secrets cradled there.

Lost in thought, I lean in to kiss her abdomen. Who sighed? Eva? Was it me? Will I find home in Eva, or is she just touching bases, check-ing on her holdings? I sit back; Eva and I have come eye to eye. She seems so at peace.

She has always been a woman bound by goals and duty. It has ever been School. Academy. Mission. Most importantly, Duty for her. Eva always charging toward some goal. I've never seen her relax. How is it she can relax in my arms? Maybe she just desperately needs arms in which to relax for a time. Or does she need to rest in my arms? For a day? For our lives? Or just the afternoon. Eva grasps my right hand, placing my palm open over her tummy. She sighs, warm smile on a warm day. Always wants to take the helm.

She's different today. Eva relaxes, sprawled against me, allow-ing my palm to gently caress her abdomen. Not long ago, we argued about who got to lead on the dance floor. Eva from the beginning has been ever aware of her capacity to move me. I think she counts on her ability to do just that when she has the time for me. Can I live like this?

I check the sea lanes around us. The Michigan ocean is currently free of icebergs and oil tankers. I set the sail, lock the helm, slide my arms about Eva's solid slender form. In that moment, I am of a mind to take Eva here in sailboat's cock-pit. Eva appears to agree. Long sepa-rated from her, I've forgotten the soft, warm texture of her lips. I bury my face in her neck. Her skin tastes of salty girl and warm sunshine. I'd forgotten, sunshine has a taste.

Eva moans. Giggles. Do girl SEALS giggle? Mine does.

Eva pushes me off her.

She laughs. "Steer the boat, hot pockets."

Abruptly serious, Eva says, "You get a choice. We go to my hotel or your chateau on the river when we get back. But we're going some-where to do something."

Eva's being good. I like good Eva. When she's good she and I suit each other. What is she doing today? Is she being nice to her vacation friend? Am I her guy in the Port of Chicago? Might she be offering more this time? Do I want more? Should I want more?

Eva squirms into a comfortable position on my chest. I stroke her breast gently saying, "I've always found that your breasts suit you."

Eva startles, "Breasts are just breasts, Galvan. I have no idea what you see in mine. I've never been voluptuous. I don't always understand you, mister. But it makes me happy you still like me and my body."

Eva smiles brightly in triumph, adjusting the top of her two-piece to again conceal her gifts, without hiding very much.

Heavens, I've been talking dirty. Give me a moment's encouragement, I'll talk her out of that suit. To allow catching of breath, I tack far further northeastward into the lake.

My heartbeat settles slowly, as I say, "It's time to head back for harbor. Out on the lake we'll lose the breeze of the heat from the city. There's already a mild offshore breeze developing as we approach dusk. It'll fade away at sunset. It's embarrassing to be caught sculling a sailboat into harbor here."

Eva wraps her arms about my left arm, hugging my arm between her breasts, "Okay, Baby, thank you for taking me sailing. "

Eva settles her head sleepily to my chest and drifts into a sound sleep. Her face smoothed by sleep–furrows gone from her brow.

As Eva rests, I sail us toward safe harbor. The world is good. I suddenly look forward, anticipating our evening at my loft. I want to invite Eva into my home. I was told in Bethesda that time heals all.

When things are going swimmingly, I've learned to watch out for the sharks. But maybe if I give Eva time to clear her head, we can cobble together a life. Eva won't stop being the warrior princess, until they promote her out of the field.

A stray query rises unbidden in my mind. Camouflage must suit the environment. Is red nail polish a proper shade of camouflage for my bed? I once shared Eva's ambition to be a Naval Officer. Boy and girl collided, then paths diverged. I'd be very dodgy as a naval officer's spouse.

The wind shifts, the northeaster is making its presence known. Tonight, I gaze at the darkening sky to the north. I gauge distances. I will need to come-about soon, to re-set my course for the harbor mouth. I study Eva's face, relaxed in sleep. I gauge distance by eye. Only a couple of miles.

I have always been a fool for Eva. One last reach for the brass ring? I bend forward, brush my lips to the top of Eva's head, breathing in the scent of her sun-warmed hair. Eva feels right reclining inside my guard, her head resting on my shoulder. It will be good to have Eva safe and home with me.

The wind vectors. McCormick Place. I jump quickly to correctto set sail into the harbor. Eva's eyes snap open. My move startles her. Eva's eyes are fierce. Not sure where she's at, thoughts are elsewhere. Fear in her darting eyes.

Fool. Peace lulls. Dreaming of peace can get you killed. Eva's violence erupts out of the depths of her soul. Damn, she is quick. I react too late. Eva already snaked her right arm around my neck, back to front.

Eva's left palm cups the back of my head. She glides her right arm under my chin, grabbing her left bicep. Her arm-bar locks over my airway as her palm presses my head into the arm-bar.

The last thought crosses my mind, the Sleeper. Too bad. So sad. Bye, bye. I'm dead.

God, I hate 'the sleeper'. Eva has decided to kill me herself this time. Lights out.

Lights on low, my vision very blurry. I'm back, with a major headache. I feel like I'm going to hurl. Hold that thought. Where I am actually back at?

The wall in front of me is a cool, curved surface. Boat hull? I'm on a long skinny bunk. The wall I lie facing is wooden plank. I'm inside the boat, the stairs to the deck are behind my head. The stern is up those stairs. I'm facing the hull on my right side.

We're rocking gently, hull bumper-pads cushion mild contact. The vessel is bumping the dock on the port side of the hull. Open water to starboard. File that for future use. A light patter of rain on the deck above me. We're moored to a dock. I have a terrible sense of smell, but I smell men's cologne. A light is on behind me near my feet in the galley. Someone large shifts. Heavy, the boat rocks a little.

I inch toward the hidden Rapala knife that is secured to the frame near my head. That I am paranoid seems reasonable at the moment. I withdraw the knife from its secured sheath.

My throat was damaged before Eva strangled me. It isn't any better after being strangled. People have been flipping me around like a pancake for years now. I hate being strangled. I'm done with being acted upon. No more pancake, no more patty cake. Enough.

I think our lovely day ended perfectly. I was thinking about a future with Eva. I got the future; I'm lying on my future. Time to get up and do something. Pacing above on the deck. Eva is giving someone instructions on where to drop me. She thinks I'm dead. She'll need to try harder. I'm not getting tossed into the lake.

Eva sails us to harbor, then contacts a disposal crew. She is straight out of hell. Relying on peripheral vision I look indirectly into the galley. Something's wrong. What? Casper hasn't got Eva. She's the boss. Eva's got me.

In a flash I decide. I'll kill my roommate in the galley. Get up on deck, kill the other guy. With any luck, seeing the dead guy running around will throw her aim off long enough for me to dive into the harbor and go deep. The SEAL princess won't miss. You take the chance you got.

I roll, using my momentum to slide step at my opponent fast and low. I manage to deflect most of a black fist the size of a pizza aimed at my head. The blow clips the right side of my jaw. My jaw snap-pivots to the right.

I miss the slash, keep the knife. My knife arm snakes along the outside of the right arm of my assailant. Pivoting on my left foot, I wheel my right knee into his rib cage, buckling him. I pause my downward plunge at the apogee over his clavicle before I plunge into his heart. I stop just as the razor tip breaks skin. What? Tanner's voice. "Easy, Trouble, it's me."

My voice hoarse. "Thanks for speaking up. You were almost gone, Tanner."

He says, "You scared Eva, she thought you were killing her. She choked you a little. You startled the poor girl. She's up on deck bawling her eyes out. She thought you got yourself killed, again. She's distraught, man. What's wrong with you?"

I snap, "Eva's distraught? I kissed her hair, the crazy woman almost killed me. AGAIN."

I flip the knife in my hand, covering Tanner, then return the blade to its long-tasseled sheath. I keep my eyes on him. I taste blood. He split my lip.

My neck feels like a kinked hose, "Good Lord, we can't have Miss Eva distraught."

Tanner looks embarrassed, "She's a Naval Commander, you perverted turd. You kissed my commander's hair? That's sick dude. I put that French braid in her hair this morning.

"Why are you braiding your commander's hair, chief?" I ask in wonderment.

"I have a twelve-year-old daughter, Galvan; I know how to braid hair. I know all kind of stuff. Eva wanted to impress. You act like a twelve-year-old around her; I knew you'd fall for it."

"Since you know how to do all sorts of stuff, Tan, plug the hole at your collar-bone."

As I exit, I say, "Hair-braiding? What's your rating, SEAL? Hair stylist, E8?"

Heading for the deck, I swipe blood from my jaw, "I hope you go to prison for murdering me, Tan. You'll fit right in with the boyz. You can be chief hair-braider."

Talking to myself, I climb the steps to deck level, "Navy Seals braiding each other's hair? That's disgusting even for SEALS. You guys had a reputation. Rough and ready, my ass."

Tanner swipes his neck. He gazes at blood on his palm, "How'd you do that, prick?"

Long skinny knife. Two seconds, this'd be a text from the Zulu happy-hunting-ground. "

Tanner snarls, "I wash my balls with the hands I braided Eva's hair with, you kissed my balls."

I snap back, "Thanks, Tan, I have a new place to cut in the future."

"That's not even funny. I gotta clean this up. I'm bleeding on my new white silk shirt."

"White silk shirt? If you start singing Day-O, I'll vomit."

I yell back, "First Aid kit's on the bulkhead, better hurry. I used that knife to slice-and-dice a three eyed carp with a rash from the Chicago River. You'll get an infection for sure."

I stumble on deck, holding my pounding head. I hate the Sleeper, always leaves headaches. I stagger past Eva and Black. I open a concealed bulkhead, extracting the Casper File.

To Eva I say, "My head is pounding. Tanner helped by ringing my bell. Thank you for the lovely choke-hold. I had a swell time. I won't ever kiss your hair again. Take this envelope. I need a favor. There's a note inside. We all owe. You owe. This pair owes. Do me a favor, Eva. I'll never darken your door again. Or just shoot me."

She's sits on the cockpit bench, as I toss the envelope in her lap.

"A psycho killed two friends of mine. I was very fond of both women. One was carrying my baby. I need your help to connect him to the murders."

"Between the three of you, one can get the information. This favor cancels all debts. If you can't make yourself do it, give it to Admiral Grandpa. He owes me. Because you're alive to produce his great grand babies because I saved your life. Your bookends owe me a life."

I step onto the star dock. The water taxi slides against the dock. The boatman asks, "You done, Galvan? The boatman has an old police positive in hand along his leg. Retired coppers are everywhere."

I say, "Jack, take me to the Rainbow dock. I'm done with this bunch, come back later.

At the Rainbow Fleet, I hand Jack an extra twenty. Jack, the water-man, smiles as he departs for the far reaches of the yacht basin. As I walk away, Eva looks on, distantly forlorn.

20

DANCIN' IN THE DARK

E va Devereaux is likely disinclined to say yea or nay to my request any time soon. The good commander and her entourage have likely returned to Annapolis and the Navy.

I need to settle this. Soon. Casper will dog me until it ends. If I give him the opportunity to draw this out, he'll connect me to someone and kill them.

This morning I reached Nadia at her office. I've spoken to her partner, George, the guy in the doorman outfit for left messages. She finally called back, but I missed the call because of the racket in the shop. She left a message for me to meet her at a club west of Rush Street.

Can I talk her into helping? Who knows? I park at what used to be the Cabrini-Green Chicago Housing Authority substation. Some low risers remain, most were lost to urban sprawl.

I flip down my detective placard. Inside I ask the desk-sergeant if I can park in his lot. Luckily, we worked together as detectives. He asked, "Still dead?"

Lots of comedians out there lately. I get my free parking.

Heading east from there I walk under dim vintage street lights up-hill seeking the club. Loiterers and lurkers are in the shadows. I know several. We pretend not to see each other. A young denizen of the dark can't resist the temptation. Don't recognize him. Must be new. I was a long gone. A couple of years is a lifetime here. Discreetly, my hand touches my .45.

The callow youth is snatched back by his collar. A Black man saunters up. The Don. He says, "Detective Galvan, I heard you died for God and Country."

"Reports were greatly exaggerated."

The Don says, "Stop by, I have news that might interest you, detective."

Information is the key to survival down here. I say. "I have a meet. Soon..."

The Don says, "Something goin' down?"

"No, a lady."

He says, "My man."

I walk on, working my way up from lower ground into the light. As I get close, I feel the music as vibration in my feet. Vaulted sidewalk? Outhouses and waste troughs carry sound well. The club is in a warehouse, already old when Grandpa Silky left for the Pacific in WWII.

In accordance with rave ethos, the club is outside Rush Street's aura, ostensibly hidden from the cops. Being hidden gives clubs an atmosphere of sin and corruption. Naturally, a thick line extends east from its nondescript, dimly lit red fire door.

The cops will never find it. Anonymity is key to the art of the Rave. Like all clubs, this one draws life breath by being an insider thing. A secret known only to a few hundred people waiting in line out front of the building. The cops will never guess.

As I cut the line at the entrance, an arm thrusts out to push me back, "Get in line, pal."

The cops have already found the club and are working security. I deflect his shove. The arm's owner turns on me exuding menace. The crowd all but claps in anticipation. I recognize security, ask, "Are you working the door at Raves, now?"

Big smile, he answers, "My brother, word was you were d-e-d-d. You don't look dead."

"I'm off the job, and done working in furtherance of truth, justice, and the American way here and in the Hindu Kush, Danny-Boy."

We worked together on tactical in our early days before Danny-Boy left for the bright lights. Danny puts in as much time bouncing as policing. Good in a gunfight, rarely sleeps.

Danny asks, "What brings you to my door? You ravin', now?"

I state, "I'm meeting someone."

"Galvan is meeting a lady? Who would you be meeting in my club? Do I know her. What's does she look like? Maybe I know her. It's dark inside, lots of people. Give."

I say, "You've probably noticed her. She's hard to miss. Very pretty.

Tall, slender, short dark hair, boy-cut. Parts it on the left side, long bang over the right eye. Dances a lot. Nadia."

"The Russian princess? You're meeting Nadia D? Many are called, few are chosen."

"It's business, Danny."

"I forgot how long you been gone. Sorry about what happened to Mary Beth; she was a good kid. Hard to lose a partner. Go inside, Nadia is near the bar. No police work. Capisce?

I agree, "Just passing through, Danny-Boy."

Danny says, "Mind if I watch?"

"No sparks. No smoke. No fire. Nadia and I have issues."

Inside, I allow my eyes to adjust. Good production values, flashing strobes, fog machine, big crowd. Music throbs, postindustrial setting. Patrons seem well-heeled. Dancers everywhere.

I scan the floor. No Nadia.

Danny walks up, points to the bar, "Doesn't drink much. Tonight, she's into Zombies."

I ask, "Zombies? She's into guys who look dead, like on TV?"

Danny laughs. "No. Zombies like, white rum, golden rum, dark rum, apricot brandy, pineapple juice, 151 Proof ever-clear, lime juice."

"That'd gag a maggot."

He says, "I'll get you one you can use as bait to lure her off the floor. Be careful, you'll be chummin' for a great white shark. That girl will eat you alive. Is your poison still Black Barrel?"

I nod and lean against the bar, lost in thought.

Someone steps directly in front of me. I look up. Nadia.

She says, "Hello, you."

She kisses me. She tastes of Zombies. In our embrace her body is damp, overheated. Her feet straddle mine. She's all muscle thrusting her abdomen at me.

Nadia's eyes are intent. Her hips slowly grind against me to the music's beat. She grabs my lapels firmly drawing me tight to her. She's not playing tonight.

I have a six-foot-tall, warm, damp girl swaying with me. In the process I place a hand to each of her hips. Time passes.

Nadia steps back smiling. She's made her point. New rules.

I haul Nadia back. She resists enjoying the moment. Her eyes are bright. Her face flushed—perspiration dots her upper lip. Done with resistance, she relaxes. We collide, lips taste of salt.

I inhale the sweetness of her breath. Her pulse quickens. Promise and fear in her eyes.

A tap on my arm. We break contact. She slips free, regains control. Triumph in her eyes. Danny stands to my right, a Zombie in one hand, Jameson in the other. He sets our drinks on the bar, asks, "Business?" He shrugs, walks away.

Nadia devours her Zombie in quick, long draws on her straw. Sets the empty on the bar. I wonder if Nadia might be more comfortable dancing off some of that rocket fuel.

Her eyes remain wild. Her long stride carries her to the dance floor. She beckons me. When a woman can dance, let her. I accompany her onto the dance floor. We dance. Nadia comes alive in sinuous motion. I'm just here to make her look good.

She is flushed, her body slumped against me. Nadia says something about thirst.

I discover Danny watching, I point at Nadia's glass. He raises three fingers. Fifteen shots of liquor, this woman is gonna die. I look at Danny, shake my head drawing a level plane before me. He nods. Nadia is cut off.

She's nervous around me tonight. The alcohol hasn't stiffened her enough to play seductress. I see it coming. Nadia is pale, sick, her eyes swim. Seductress gone, welcome sick girl.

Time for some fresh air. Taking Nadia by the arm, I brush past security. We get lucky. A city trash basket awaits fortuitously positioned. Danny sees our dilemma. He brings ice-cold water. Danny sees my sudden good luck become a ridiculous mess. Hilarious, in Danny's view.

With cold air and time, Nadia survives. A ride-share pulls to the curb. Danny gestures to Nadia and me. The driver whisks us to Nadia's super-secret FBI lair. She's too sick to care if I know the address of the bat-cave. She gives our driver directions to drop us on Michigan Avenue. She is less sick than I thought. As we exit to North Michigan Avenue, I have the driver drop us a block off, Nadia needs the cool air coming off the lake tonight. We'll walk the block.

Finally, after a pleasurable walk Nadia's gait falters at the door. I gather her into my arms. She is lighter than I figured. I lift, she springs into my lift. Nadia isn't as drunk now. Carrying Nadia along Michigan Avenue, I hear the voice of doom. Jill says, "Galvan, are you taking out the trash?"

I turn, Jill Ryan.

Nadia's head snaps up. She points a long finger at Jill, saying, "Go away, wicked witch. You let him out unattended. I found him. We have stuff to do. Take suit-boy with you."

Jill holds some guy's hand. That annoys me. Jill says of the guy in a suit beside her, "My date, Tom. Nadia dear, do you mind if I ruin your evening? After all, you ruined my morning."

I think I say, "Hello, Jill." Or I could've said, 'Why this stiff?"

I nod to Nadia, saying in a lisp to Tom, "Hello, Tommie, this sweet thing is Nadia."

Jill says, "Hello, Nadia, when we last met you were wearing less and showing more."

Nadia opens one eye, stares at Jill, "You weren't wearing much either, doc."

Jill smiles. "When last we met, I wasn't well. Tonight, you're not at your best."

I set Nadia on her feet. She smiles, leans-in, forming herself to me. She staggers enough for me to place an arm around her to steady her. She rests her head on my shoulder.

Her left arm reaches behind her back to slide my hand into her back pocket. I'm maneuvered and surrounded. Nadia smiles sweetly in triumph.

Unfazed, Jill says sweetly, "Tom is a lawyer practicing with Derwood, Victor & Mann. We met at Gaby's ages ago. Often Tom comes for dinner, but he stays for the scenery."

The saccharine smiles and sweet wholesome gazes pass between the women.

Tom smiles contentedly, slipping his about Jill's waist. That frosts my balls.

Jill clasps her arms around Tom's chest, leaning her head on Tom's shoulder.

Nadia and Jill mirror each other.

Is it OK for Tommy-Boy pa Jill, because he's practicing the law and I'm not? Because Tommy-Boy has prospects, I don't. Is it that I play at making boats and have limited prospects?

Jill's right. A woman has a right to feather her nest with better than the plumage of an old buzzard roosting in an abandoned warehouse along a sewage canal.

Tom's talking. To me? About what?

Tom's saying, "Do I know you? Your face is familiar. Do you work at Gaby's?"

I think to myself, a bit unkindly, 'No, I'm a silent partner in Gaby's restaurant who woke up in bed the other day with a topless Jill. You get a chance, do better than I did,'

It's not his fault I screwed up with Jill. He's gets his chance. I blew mine.

I release Nadia to fawn on Tom-boy and confuse him, "I'm wait-staff, hon'. Jill and I are buddies. From the way you're mauling the poor girl, we travel in very different circles, dear."

I continue, "Gaby lets me bus tables as I study her cuisine. I'm an aspiring interior-designer. Lately I'm trying to break into designer boat interiors. One must sacrifice for one's art. It's a lot like your clerking. You may have seen my work in the paper's Sunday Boating Section.

I say, "Jill and I have been buddies forever."

Tom smirks. "Your lipstick is smeared."

I enjoyed Nadia's amorous embrace on the dance floor. Her red lipstick and mush must be all over my neck. But I ask, "Isn't too dark for my skin tones? I do hate to appear flamboyant."

Jill reaches to slide her finger along my left cheek. Then she pinches my cheek sharply between her right thumb and forefinger. We lock eyes.

Jill says, "Galvan, the lipstick is better suited to, what's her face, here." She turns my face to Nadia, "Have you sobered enough? It's your shade, Nadia. You waste good lipstick kissing him, dear. Knock, he won't answer. Got it shot off, the war you know."

Her grip stings; my eyes are watering.

Sternly Jill stares. For someone I'm helping find the better choice, Jill holds a nasty grudge.

Nadia grasps Jill's wrist, twisting the pinching hand away. Nadia burrows against my neck to plant a solid kiss. This time I lose focus, but my eyes do not water. She admires her work, nods, "The lipstick and guy are mine. Go away, doc."

Nadia smiles wickedly, "That got his attention. He just needs a woman's touch."

Tom is studying Nadia's cleavage. My clumsy carry or our dancing undid two buttons of Nadia's blouse, exhibiting an expanse of red lace and breast. OR, Nadia just undid them.

Jill smiles coldly at us. Frostily, I stare back.

Tom's confused. Am I gay or straight? He knows me from somewhere. To further confuse, I improvise, "Nadia and I are dance partners. Dirty Dancing without all the messy sex."

Now, Nadia pinches my ear lobe tightly.

I stay in character squeezing her hand until she releases my ear, saying, "Nadia had a bit to drink. She's disappointed with me. All show, no go. We'll find her a hetero. You, Tim?"

Jill frowns. I smile sweetly, saying, "No, you're spoken for, of course. Sorry, Jill dear."

Nadia kitten snuggles, saying, "Me too. Nadia's much less sick and sleepy now.

I stand her upright. In doing so, I two-finger pick her back rear pants pocket, extracting her business-card case. I felt it earlier as we danced. The tiny card-wallet has worn its shape into her jeans, like a condom in a teenage boy's wallet. Yes, Nadia's bottom is made for caressing.

Male FBI agents wear starched new blue jeans and wing tip shoes when undercover. Females undercover carry business cards in the right rear pocket of their jeans. Such good spies.

Nadia sighs, squirms slightly, smirking dismissively at Jill.

Jill coldly says, "Don't slouch, it makes your boobs sag so. Sadly, what virtue you have left will be safe tonight. You're drunk. He won't take advantage of a drunk, even a slut."

Jill turns, takes Tom's hand in hers, "We should go. His pavement princess needs a nap."

I grab Tom's arm. "So nice meeting you, dear boy. Happy dreams, you two." In the process, Nadia's business card slides into Tom's pocket. Tom's confused, I wink.

He eyes me in a new light. He was in the bar when I helped Nadia with the Wit Brothers. Tom says, "You're the guy who threw the two bikers on the floor in Gaby's."

Both women point to me, "That's him."

Gave me up for a lawyer. Life is so unfair. I say, "You said it together, you get a wish."

They give me looks weighted with opprobrium. I ask, "Penny for their thoughts, ladies."

Jill sweetly eases her head onto Tom's shoulder. They stroll off hand in hand.

Damn, that pisses me off. Who does Tom think he is? I thought her smarter."

Tommy-Boy looks at Nadia and at her card. All is fair in love and war. Never give up. Never give in. Admit nothing. Deny everything.

Demand a lawyer. Not Tom though. I have to get rid of that one. If all else fails, I can kick him in the nuts.

I walk with my arm around Nadia, my hand on her narrow waist to her building.

Some new G-Guy is on the desk, he wears his black regulation, freshly polished wing-tip oxfords. The guy must be working semi-deep cover. The new guy gives me the fish-eye, Nadia does a wave-off motion. Young J. Edgar Hoover nods. It's hard to believe this crew could sneak up on the Russians.

Then I realize Russian girl has her hand in my pocket. Nadia pulls me into the elevator with her. We fly high into the night sky to Nadia's. En route she goes a little green with motion sickness. At least my Russian FBI agent isn't a paratrooper.

At the entrance to her witches-lair. A question unbidden comes to mind, do I want to be bewitched. Yeah, I think I could use a bewitching. Nadia's pale, paler than usual. I take her jacket before leading her to the shower. I lift her into the shower stall.

Nadia steps in front of me, raises her arms over her head. It appears she wants me to pull her green silk blouse over her head. Instead, I undo the remaining buttons before pulling it over her shoulders to be greeted by her breasts in red lace. It's beginning to look a lot like Christmas.

Nadia comes awake at my touch, she moves clumsily, shoving me out of the shower. "Out, Galvan." The shower door shuts with a bong.

I say to frosted glass, "Clothes."

A shower of green blouse, red lace undies, and blue jeans hurdle the door to plop on the tile floor. Nadia says, "Galvan. I can see you through the frosted glass. Get OUT. "

Reflectively, I say, "It works both ways, you have a lovely silhouette."

Nadia says, "Galvan, please. You're embarrassing me. I'm not lovely tonight. I feel fat, sloppy and sick. Out, right now. Don't be a perve."

I gather Nadia's clothing heap and toss it in the laundry room hamper. In the dryer I spot a dry terry-cloth robe. I tumble it for ten minutes, then fold it tight. I set it on the bathroom counter.

Exasperated, Nadia snarls, "Throw your stuff in the washer. You smell like fruit salad."

She spilled the last zombie on me. I begin to respond defensively. I stop, Nadia's silhouette is leaning forward, head drooping beneath the gushing water. She's exhausted, in search of respite under the torrent.

Beauty stretched beyond capacity. I say, "You are tough. I just put your robe near the sink. I'll be in the laundry room."

Nadia's tired voice says, "There's a small bath off the guest room, wash up there. Thanks for taking care of me. Sorry, I'm such a dreadful mess."

I put my gun and the contents of my pockets on the dresser in the guest room. I toss my jeans and shirt in the washer. I wrap my waist in a large shower towel. As the water warms. I take a quick shower. I'll need to keep an eye on her for a few hours until she's past alcohol poisoning. She got rid of most of the Zombies, but she bears watching. We'll see.

The hot water on my neck feels better than good. My back and neck are definitely aching from lugging Nadia around. A trip to the pain clinic needs to happen sooner rather than later. I dress and wrap my waist in a towel.

In the other bathroom Nadia says loudly, "Towel."

The room is steamy; a long elegant arm reaches from the fog cloud. Nadia says, "Took you long enough."

As the moisture of the cloud thins, her body form appears more clearly. I must be leering. Nadia smacks me in the head with a damp towel, saying, "Robe."

I extend it to her. Nadia emerges, asks, "Are you naked under that towel?"

When I nod, Nadia takes my hand in hers, saying, "Put me to bed. Court in four hours.

Our damp feet slap floor boards to her bedroom. She points the wrong direction to the dresser, "Hand me the pink t-shirt in the second drawer."

I turn to extract the shirt. Turning back, Nadia stands naked. She hands me the robe, takes the shirt, asks, "Never seen a naked woman?"

I toss the robe over the back of the chair. She steps forward as she rips the towel free, "Jill is such a liar."

I re-wrap my towel. Nadia slips into the t-shirt and slides under her covers."

With her blankets to her nose she peers out with large bright eyes. We stare.

Nadia asks, "You got a problem?"

I shrug, "Just so you know, I got my back broken in an IED explosion. A pregnant woman slashed my throat. I killed her. I have nightmares--must have a guilty conscience. Nothing got shot off. Jill's professional judgment is that I'm reluctant to accept being alive. Life is taking chances. In her view I'm hiding in my warehouse because I can't accept life."

"So?" Nadia the interrogator asks.

I add, "I was a paralyzed lump in a hospital bed like many others. Triage works like that. Some of us got lost in the crush."

Nadia's eyes twinkle. "Do things work or not? Or is it just Jill?"

"No, Nadia, it's not Jill. I have no idea where things stand, yet."

"Meaning what?"

Just great, I stand mostly naked before an attractive woman discussing my sexual capacity, or lack thereof. "Let's just say the opportunity hasn't presented itself."

She smirks, "Just did."

I nod, "I've been outside looking in for a long time. Maybe I want to make a connection. The night I met you, something was changing. Joe was closer to you. He had a bat and he was packing heat. First time in a long time I wanted help. Wasn't sure I could help, but...?"

Nadia says, "I could have handled it myself. For your information I was handling both of them when you barged in, Mister Galvan."

I sit beside her, stroking her damp hair gently. "When I stepped into that mess, you were handling it. Before I reached you, I saw Tweedle Dee slip you a white powder. You began to fade after drinking the wine. I figured it was Rohypnol. It's used to do surgery in the Third World. It knocks you out, eliminates inhibition, causes amnesia for at least an hour after consumption."

Nadia is angry, crabby, hung-over and tired. Enough. I ask, "If you don't mind, I'll nap in your chair a bit while my clothes dry. I need to be sure the booze isn't gonna kill you. Get some sleep. You look good so far, but you drank like fifteen shots of liquor."

I check on my clothes. I toss them in her dryer, then return to the bedside to check on her. She's resting peacefully. I sit on the side of her bed. I bend forward to brush her hair from her eyes. She frowns in her sleep. I brush my lips to her forehead. I am so tired.

Damn, someone just tossed a red-hot quarter on my chest. My eyes pop open. Gray-light-of-dawn. I'm firmly pinned to the bed. Nadia sits straddling my hips.

She's wearing the pink t-shirt. She kneels with a leg resting on each side of my hips. I glance up at her. I reach for her. She presses my wrist back down. Her breasts sway seductively.

As my gaze rises to her eyes she smiles sweetly. "You like to be bad in the morning, you little devil. If only I didn't have a hearing this morning."

Nadia glides forward for a kiss. "Thank you for last night. I like waking you up. Will you make me breakfast? Please? I have to get ready for court, or the bad guy will walk. Maybe we can meet back here, or at your place after court? I'd like to talk."

Mildly annoyed, I roll up from the bed. "We aren't being filmed, are we?"

Nadia laughs, "No. Do you think I want guys I work with ogling my naked body?"

Nadia walks away, pulling her night-shirt up over her head, tossing it on my face, entering the master bath. The burn was from the brass of my jeans, now dry and folded.

Later, Nadia sits facing me across her breakfast island. She twiddles toast crumbs off her fingertips. Occasionally she smiles shyly.

Not a word. Hair damp, tousled. Bright blue eyes. She's beautiful, smells of milled soap. Tiny freckles have emerged on smooth cheeks. A touch of peanut butter on her breath.

She says softly, "I'm glad you no longer find me distasteful."

"You taste fine."

Surprised she says, "What? Did something happen?"

"We spent some time kissing at the club."

She lifts a brow. "OH? I have to drink less."

"Why?"

"So I remember things. Did I pull a towel off you last night?"

I say, "Yes, after I put you in the shower."

"Oh, I remember."

Nadia smiles wickedly, "I was checking to see if Jill lied. Sorry. I don't usually do stuff like that."

Her face red she says, "I have to get my stuff, I'm late. Could you pour me a coffee-to-go cup? The mug is in the cabinet."

I brew a cup into her travel mug. Nadia returns. As I face her, Nadia places my holstered pistol, wallet and keys on the island. She picks up my cup, drinking its last swallow, before saying, "Come on, slow-poke."

Things have changed between us. Are we friends? Reading my mind, Nadia leans in for a long kiss. She tastes like coffee. I ask Nadia to drop me at the substation near the old Green.

Downstairs, I wait in the lobby. Nadia goes for her car. Her partner plays doorman. George asks, "Is she OK? You look terrible. You're limp-ing. Did you get fresh with her? Did she kick your ass, boy? You're too young for a little sex to bust you up."

I snap, "No sex, George. She got sick. I brought her home. I looked after her until she felt better. I'm getting a ride to my car."

George smirks, "You are such a nice boy, pal. You in the closet?"

"I'm not gay, George."

George smiles, "I know. She's a nice girl, Galvan. Be nice to her."

Nadia pulls up the side-drive. "George, it gets harder every day."

As we fly toward the Green, I say, "George just told me I'm not gay. He also said that you are a nice girl who needs nice treatment."

"George would know," Nadia says.

"Because he thinks I should be nice to you?"

Nadia glances over quickly as we breeze through an intersection, "Because he's gay. You'll be nice to me because you like me."

We stop for donuts. I have to pay for my parking spot. Donuts, a gallon coffee container and bagels & cream cheese are on the menu. Police tastes vary.

At the Green, I ask Nadia to wait. I walk in to thank the desk ser-geant. The day sergeant is a black guy I used to work with in Marquette. He digs, I return to the lot with a chocolate donut with sprinkles. Nadia leans on her bureau-car smiling brightly at me, as I place the sacred chocolate donut with sprinkles on the files piled on the front seat.

From my car I extract a manila envelope. I walk back to her, say-ing, "I need a favor. Will you look at this file? I wouldn't ask if it wasn't important to me. "

Nadia freezes, her smile slips away. "I've been working on the murders. I stumbled over some leads. There's information here on a suspect. There's context, evidence on motive and a prior modus ope-randi. Please take a moment to look at this stuff."

Nadia is rigidly furious.

Losing her, I throw caution to the wind, "I suspect your informant, River-Mound. It's a personal thing between us. It goes back years. We butted heads when he was Casper Lewindowski. He worked for the bureau in the Baltimore office when Agent Morgenthau was mur-dered there. Casper came back here and killed Officer Burke after I left town."

There, I done did it now.

Nadia is aghast. She physically retreats from me. She shuts down.

Talk fast Galvan, she's almost gone. I quickly add, "Listen, don't cut me out. Casper got involved with a silenced .22 Ruger semi-auto pistol from a bureau case in Baltimore. Bullets and casings are all over the place. Here and in Baltimore."

I say, "Please compare the ballistics reports. Then look at my notes. Give my theory a chance. Casper will connect. He's not the sharpest tool in the shed. None of them are.

I add, "Casper was fixated on me for years. He tried to replicate what I did. He is way beyond where it started. He tried to buffalo you. He likes to hurt, shame and bully women. He's killing women who are near me because of their involvement with me. Casper's always been sociopathic. I think he's degenerated to the point of psychosis. I have foiled his crazy schemes before. I disrupted his psychotic world view. It drives him crazy. Be careful with him. I've shown interest in you. I don't want you hurt."

Silence. Her jaw drops. Not good.

I add, "There's a cover letter inside the packet. If I get the DNA back, I'll let you know the results."

Nadia roars, "Get the DNA back? Who do you think you are? We do that. You're a civilian, MISTER. You can't get anything back. Tamper with my investigation, you'll do time."

I've lost her. She's tired, cranky and hung-over. I've developed a real skill for burning my bridges with women.

I say, "Casper shoved all that serial-killer nonsense about me at you. You know better. If Casper was right, would you have let me give you a bath?"

"A shower." Nadia snarls fiercely, stamping her foot. Nadia's face forms into a grimace of distaste, "You disgust me, Galvan."

"Why? You checked my alibis. Serial crimes are weird. All it takes to break an investigation apart is to prove a suspect was elsewhere when a single incident in the pattern occurred. I'm not giving you one anomaly. You have a bucket full of anomalies. Don't fixate on a theory of the crime this idiot fed you. If it doesn't work, get another. You are stubborn, Nadia. Check what I'm saying. If I'm wrong, tell me."

Nadia glares scornfully. "You violated my trust, you bastard. Last night was bullshit, right? You made me a tramp. The boys at the boat house will get a real laugh."

I drop my packet on her front seat. She roars away, kicking gravel at me.

I walk to my SRX, shaking my head.

The desk sergeant leans on the railing in the dock' s concrete platform watching us. I'm eating a donut, sipping my coffee.

He asks, "No kiss goodnight?"

"First date."

The sergeant laughs. "There won't be a second."

He's probably right. So much for our plans for afternoon delight.

21

GOING IN FOR REPAIRS

Morning had broken, just as any other. I'm sulking. There'll be nothing by mouth this fine day. I hate surgical wards and rides on gurneys.

Lab-coat phobia is my way of life. The sight of one turns my blood pressure to a rocket. Gorkers are patients with such severe brain trauma that injury is irreversible. I was one.

Keep an eye on the kids. They make weird judgments. Residents in hospitals are tired and overworked. They exist to enter patient status changes in the chart. Cut and paste is easier. Its eyes follow you, just reflex. He's a vacant space. Lights on, nobody home, total 'gorker'. IED, traumatic brain injury—vegetative state. Put it in vase by the window, free a bed up.

I wasn't a vegetable. I may have smelled like bad cabbage. Might've looked like bad cabbage. I wasn't a gorker, but my entire soul was devoted to finding a way to bite my resident.

In my brave new world, gorkers received 'MINOR' surgery at the bedside. My resident, Greggie, one day decided it wise to demonstrate an arterial cut to two attractive interns, "Why waste this opportunity. Gorkers are like brain dead. No brain, no pain."

As Greggie initiated the procedure, something changed. Mistreat the dog, he'll bite. I did. I was full of steroids. There is a downside; steroids make days longer and patients crazier. Feeling my own pain, I realized my paralysis had waned I'd begun to get feeling back.

Dr. Greggie stuck my arm, echoing, "He's a total gorker, doesn't feel a thing."

The buts always cause trouble. But I could feel it.

Greggie's scalpel went in. I flinched. Greggie held my face down with one hand, saying, "See? All reflex."

So, I bit him.

Greggie screamed, punched me in the head with his scalpel hand. My cheek got cut.

My attending physician appeared. He snatched the scalpel from Dr. Greggie.

As the interns bandaged my cheek, the attending asked my name, where I was. I said that according to Greggie I was "the gorker. I'm in a hospital in America—one that border's hell."

He asked the year. I was off one. He asked why. I told him I missed that one, I was dead. He told me I was in Bethesda Naval Hospital and asked how I got to the hospital.

I told him I got blown up with an IED outside Gardez, Afghanistan while detailed to the secret service under assignment to a Naval unit.

He asked how long I'd been conscious.

I told him, "Seventy, maybe eighty days. Seventy nights for sure. I count sunrises, I had nothin' else to do."

I told him about a combat flight surgeon on the medivac--Dr. Braxton.

I lost consciousness for a time. Biting residents can be fatiguing. When I awoke Doc Braxton was prodding me. I was sleepy, somebody sedated me. At least they didn't muzzle me. I ignored her prodding as I wondered if this was the best wet-dream I could muster."

Doc Braxton persevered. In this dream she hovered close, listening intently to my heart with a short-tube pink, cardiac stethoscope. Very Freudian, an Irish stethoscope?

I wanted to go back to sleep, until I spotted Doc Braxton's cleavage. Her breasts were framed by white lace. Forget sleep. In the field I never realized she had them.

Dr. Braxton caught my eye movement. She straightened some, improving my view.

I'd died, gone to heaven. Do I see a glimpse of the pearls beyond the lacy gates?

Dr. Braxton frowned, "Galvan, can you see me?"

I answered hoarsely, "Yes Doc'. You smell nice, too. Your hair's better long."

Doc blushed, "Galvan, are you looking down my blouse?"

"Of course," I answered.

Pointing, the female intern from earlier said, "Doctor Braxton, you have his attention."

Laughter.

Doc Braxton said, "He'll live."

So, with nothing better to do, I did.

Things improved. Though I still harbor homicidal thoughts of Greggie and hate lab coats.

I have lab-coat phobia. The morning's pending surgery had me hyperbolic. No guts, has our boy Trey. Downstairs, my SRX started. Sounded throaty. Why did I know my car's voice?

Back to the present. I dress and descend to the parking lot. The Greek loves to rev engines. As I reach the lot, Joe exits my SRX saying, "I can't take you. Gaby and I are sailing from Burnham. I got you a babysitter. You're good unless she strangles you, and you deserve a strangling."

I enter the SUV. Jill gets behind the wheel saying, "Come on 'fraidy-cat, long drive."

This is my first time in my passenger seat. Why do I always feel vulnerable around Jill?

Against my will, I glance at her legs.

Jill's wears a silky off-the-shoulders blue top, draped over her above-the-knee black skirt. Looking at Jill's profile, I am very sorry I screwed the pooch.

She says, "Settle down, Hawkeye, I'm out of bounds. Too much looking, no doing."

The Greek hands me one of my manila envelopes, marked JILL in large block letters. I sit with the envelope on my lap. He says, "Take care of it."

Jill's puzzled, looks at the envelope.

Gaby says, "Jillian, be careful with this one. The doctor's magic potion relaxes him. Duct-tape him to the cart to keep his hands off you. Galvan, you keep your hands-off the girl."

She says to Jill, "I took him for injections. Afterward, I wore my red silk blouse at bedside reading Vogue. Then I felt the lightest touch on my breast. Did I imagine it? Non. Galvan touches my breast. Ohhh, so lightly. Look, Jill, he is red in the face."

The Greek gives me a hard eye, "Show a little respect. I bought that blouse."

Gaby says, "Tchhh. Why do you scold the boy? Is it a surprise that I beguile other men?"

The Greek looks to Gaby, who arches her back, "Baby, you always beguile."

"Oh, you are such a sentimental brute. I think I may keep you."

Jill smiles at Gaby. She smiles back. I don't smile at anyone. I'm in trouble.

Then, Jill flies my SRX out into the street. Jill likes to go fast. Go, Jill, Go. Zoom, Zoom.

I debate pros and cons internally. I flip my JILL file back and forth between my palms. We stop at a light.

Jill decides. "What is it, Galvan? You want something. You're stuck. Nothing to lose."

I say, "The Greek and I have been working on the murders." Always drag others in. It demonstrates clear lack of faith in yourself. Plunging onward, "We're close. The killer is in town. He's probably active. My existence provides his motive. He and I have issues.

"When I met him, he was just a sociopath who had a history of initiating complicated schemes to knock me down a peg. I'd always get wise and ruin his schemes or ignore him. I think he went over the edge, turning psychopathic. They really don't relish it if you attack their world view. I should've thrown a potato sack over Casper's head and broken his legs long ago. If I had, the women might be alive today."

I sit at the stop-light deflated. I have been displaying weakness since I got back. Jill knows me as a milquetoast, afraid to act.

Jill asks, "Who is Casper?"

"You've seen him. He fishes across the point."

"That's the serial killer?"

I shrug. "Look at the letter inside. I'd like your professional opinion on genetics. Casper's an identical twin. The twin, Gaspar, died before the murders. Gaspar sexually assaulted the sister of his Iraqi interpreter. The 'terp burned Gaspar alive with a white phosphorous munition. The DOD keeps DNA sample cards on servicemen. I'm trying to get the red-head I danced with at the wedding to arrange a DNA comparison. Eva was our commander."

Jill snaps, "You were with me. You call that dancing? How many kids do you two have?"

I say, "I'm trying to get Eva to access those DNA serum cards for the comparison."

Jill snarls, "If you intended to plow the red-head's garden, why did you invite me?"

"Until the wedding, I didn't know or care if Eva was still alive. I had no idea she would show at the wedding. I brought you because I've had a crush on you since I met you."

I hurtle onward, "Jill, Eva's nuttier than I am. Her family has been Navy for generations. She's the last of the Deverauxs. Eva's ancestors, if they lived long enough, all became admirals. Since 9-11 Eva has been up to her pretty little neck in the war on terror. She is fried."

I shudder, "War eats everyone. The last time I saw her she actually strangled me. Eva is nuts. I'm to put her on even keel, but her fiancé is inbound. She wants me to take her back to the life she lost as a girl in the pursuit of her Navy ambitions. Sadly, Eva's generation are the first full-time female war fighters. Eva gave a lot to the Navy. She wants her version of happiness but has no idea what that is, so she wants it all."

I explain, "Eva sees you as my bartender girlfriend. In her mind, I was being disloyal to her by dating you. She dumped me as a high school junior. Eva is the center of her universe. Regardless of how she acts, I must be awaiting her return with bated breath."

Jill says impatiently, "Nitwit, your Eva hears her biological clock ticking. As her first lover, your sexuality is wrapped into that concept. You did it to her first. You bastard, why don't you want to make her pregnant anymore? It's transference, her self-induced loss needs a scapegoat. You are responsible for her life choices, you bastard, as well as her PTSD. Why don't you just roll her in the hay? She gets a green-eyed baby boy. You're a guy; you smile and walk it off. The hard part for her just started. Eva wants to be a woman, have a family. Somebody to care for. Somebody to care for her. She may be Wonder Woman, but becoming a wife and mother ain't a downhill ski-slope. Eva wants you to fix it."

She adds a sidenote. "Women are women. We're not men. Our time for child-bearing is limited by biology. Guys can knock-up bimbos forever. Coming to grips with the reality of our biology is a bitch."

I say speculatively, "What if I have a conscience? I want to roll someone else in the hay every time I see her."

She snaps, "Who? Your Russian princess?"

We glare. I say, "Nice woman, but I have someone in mind from the medical field."

Jill eyes me, "Well, aren't you the hopeful one."

Brooding, I stare straight out the windshield. The light changes. We drive in silence.

Jill smacks me hard in the back of my head.

"Don't you ever lie to me again, Mister. I used to like you. I might still like you just a tiny bit. That is shrinking quickly. Are you still sleeping with Nadia?"

Got me, the truth will come out. "I have thought about it. I spent the night watching her sleep the night she got sloshed. In short order she drank three Zombies."

Jill snaps, "So?"

"That's 15 shots of hard liquor. It was a close thing the next morning. I did something that annoyed her. Suddenly, she was not in a loving mood."

Jill asks, "How could you annoy such a lovely girl? You are such a loyal, sweet boy."

"I asked her help on the murders. She blew a gasket."

"That would do it." Jill laughs.

My turn. "How was your evening with Lawyer Tom?"

Traffic slows, Jill says distractedly, "Tom is a nice guy. He's busy litigating some interesting cases. We both like to travel. He's sweet. What went on with you two?"

Bingo. The Marines have not landed. "Nadia likes to dance. I met her with my ulterior motives at a rave club west of Rush Street. For her I'm a sweaty block of Semtex on a hot day. She drank too much, got sick. I took her home. We ran into you."

Jill says, "Knowing you, you tucked Nadia in. Did she give you a quickie, Galvan?"

I ask, "How about you and Lawyer Tom; did you have time to give him one?"

Jill is upset, goes coy, "Too soon. Did you get to rest your fevered brow on her saggy boobs?"

Annoyed, I say, "Nothing sags on her. Trained as a ballerina, got too tall. She has a Russian temper. I was invited to an afternoon rematch, I screwed it up."

Jill is smiley angry. "How is it that you know that nothing sags on Nadia Dimitrieva? Why are you telling me this?"

"I'll answer both your questions. I looked. You asked."

Jill straightens in the driver's seat. "Do I suffer by comparison?"

Catching her eye as we slow, I say, "You are different women. You're both attractive, just different. Having seen you both half-dressed, she's a little ahead at the moment."

Jill says, "What does that mean? Nadia's a little ahead. Says who?"

"I saw more of Nadia. Pull over and park. We'll level the playing field."

We are at a dead stop in traffic. Jill turns to me, "I'd consider your request, but I think you're making the suggestion just to get out of facing down your lab coat phobia."

I say, "I'm hurt. I'm willing to forego a surgery just to answer your questions. For an opportunity to get you out of that skirt, I'd walk on hot coals."

Traffic moves forward. "Galvan, you sound like a stranger. I may not like the new you."

I think before I speak, "There's no diplomatic way to couch this. For better or worse I'm returning to being me. I was harder, once. I may be that again. You met me as a placid man this spring. I'm a composite of him and someone you don't know. You may care for the amalgam."

I rhythmically flip the manila envelope between my palms, "You're right, I found an empty building to hide in. I caused the death of two women I loved, and a bunch of bystanders. In Afghanistan I left a friend to die. In the Kush to stay alive, I killed a pregnant woman. I owe."

Jill drives.

I frown, saying, "I feel like a plague on the land."

Jill opens her purse, rummages inside, extracts a barbwire girl-hanky to wave in my face, "Galvan, you have survivor's guilt. Desperate times are like that. You're not unique. Put the burden down. Do what you need to do. I'll decide if I like you enough to keep you. OR."

I ask, "Or what."

Jill drives into the Surgi-Center's parking-lot. "Or you can borrow my hanky, cry me a river, and never get my skirt off."

22

COMING TO MY SENSES

feel comfortably warm in a cold room.

Someone is trying to wake me.

Why? I feel fine.

Damn this bed is narrow. It feels like a bunkbed. Will I fall off? Who cares? My body feels like I'm submerged in a warm, soft pond. I need to sleep a little more.

No good. I can't stay at depth. Time to follow my bubble trail to the surface.

Someone asks me questions. I reply, can't remember what I said. My answers swim away like little blue fish. Jill's voice, asking the questions. What did she ask? What did I say?

Then I hear some big mouth say, "Yes, I am, I've been fighting it for months." Was that me?

A nurse says, "Wicked, who gets to ask a guy under truth serum if he loves her."

Jill laughs. "It's not truth serum, but as the dose wanes inhibition plummets. All a girl has to do is ask. Patient answers vary for each patient and how open the window remains."

The nurse asks, "Do you think it's ethical, doc?"

Jill's amused. "Ethical? He's not my patient. He's my boyfriend. You can do anything you want with your boyfriend's stuff. Why should the contents of his head be different?"

They laugh. I nap.

I'm awake, foggy, but awake. I lie on my right side, turned to Jill. She sits in profile reading a magazine.

I love her profile, long hair falling to broad shoulders, carriage upright, perfect posture. My eye fixes on the shape of her left breast. She turns a page. The action causes her breast to move. Lovely, so warm in my hand.

The nurse laughs. "I warned you, doc. He's touchy-feely when he wakes up."

Jill stares at me with lack of expression, "Galvan, do you have your hand on my breast?"

Hard question. With a happy-silly expression, I nod.

Jill is stern--lifts my wrist disdainfully between thumb and index finger."

I'm stunned. Jill has outwitted me. How could she? I was so subtle.

Jill releases my hand onto the gurney. She has quick hands, slapping my wrist as it drops. She announces, "Keep your hands in the boat. You got no invitation to touch my breast. You aren't getting one anytime soon. You are on probation, Mister."

Affronted, I decide to leave. I have no pants. I am woozy. The air-conditioned breeze chills my naked bottom. I better stay here.

The nurse catches me mid-rise to keep me from falling on my face. I guess I didn't stay. My gown opens. As I struggle for balance, it billows. Jill looks, blushes. Irish girls blush.

The nurse laughs, "Be careful, doc. It's pointing your way. I think it bites."

My legs wobble. Jill rises to help. My hand grasps Jill's hip. Well, not just her hip.

The nurse and Jill set me on the gurney. I have a firm grip on Jill's bottom. So I almost drag Jill onto my gurney. She grabs my right thumb, bends it back. "Enough, octopus-boy."

An older female voice calls from across the ward, "If you're done with him send him over." Somebody else enjoying their anesthesia.

My head clears. Embarrassed, I clam up. Time to keep my hands off Jill. I dress slowly.

Jill stands at the foot of my gurney, saying, "Nicole is right. You are a brat when your feelings are hurt." Jill leaves, abandoning my ass or gone for the SRX. I settle in my wheelchair, anticipating my ride of shame. Too many nurses witnessed my escapades. Some have a twinkle in their eyes, most a reproving glare. I nod off on the way home. Jill speaks on the phone with the Greek, who says Karl will meet her to drag me upstairs. Karl climbing my stairs is a scary picture, much less assisting me. We'll both break a hip.

At the boatyard, Jill helps me from the car. No Karl. Instead the Twins await us. Black and Tan await me with feral expressions. I who am about to die salute me. Blackmon is charming, "Ms. Ryan, Commander Deveraux asked us to contact this mope to make arrangements for him to meet with the commander at the Fairmont.'

Tanner says, "What's up with that wine-head? He drunk?"

Blackmon smiles ingratiatingly. "We were waiting in your tavern for Galvan. Do you mind my calling you Jill? Karl said you needed a hand dragging this clown up to his flophouse."

The pair sweeps me up in a two-man fireman's carry. They toss me about like a bag of dry sticks. They follow Jill into the building, swinging me to-and-fro. They'll drop me soon.

Black says to Jill's skirt clad bottom., "You look great. The outfit's perfect for today."

We three ogle Jill. She climbs stairs well. Black says, "You've got the legs for the outfit."

Tanner winks at Blackmon, "Let's drop the cripple. He has a mean disposition. We toss him down the stairs. You take the girl to dinner. I'll wait for the ambulance."

Blackmon's head flicks a caution. Tan says, "He stabbed me, Black."

Jill leans back, "What was that last part?"

Tanner complains, "This jamoke is heavy, ought to go on a diet. Get some exercise."

Jill gives them her deer-in-the-headlights look, "What's a 'jamoke'?"

Black smirks, "It's a combination of two Italian words: the words for coffee, 'java', and 'mocha'. A jamoke is a guy who needs something to perk him up."

Tan says, "Galvan, lost the tiger in his tank, honey." Tanner leans in, "It means you're as dumb as my dick."

Jill enters my loft. She turns on the lights and lights stove burners.

The twins do a one-two-three swing, setting up to fling me at the couch. I squirm free, to land between them. I snatch the back of their heads to smack them together with a clonk.

Jill sees me. She frowns. I'm in trouble.

She speaks to the Twins, "I appreciate the help. I need to feed him. He hasn't had anything to eat since last night because of the surgery. I also have to check his injection sites. Time for you guys to go. Let's end the horseplay. I'm his doctor."

I say, "Tell Deveraux I'll make reservations in the Fairmont at Aria for dinner Friday at 8:00PM. I owe her. I'll give you yours later. Don't let the door hit you in the ass as you leave."

Black picks up Jill's phone from the counter, saying, "I'll put my number in here. If you need help with Galvan, call me. I better put your number in my phone. I can check on our patient in the morning. I wasn't aware you were a doctor. This chauvinist is intimidated by a smart woman. I'm the team medic, studied at Johns Hopkins in Baltimore. Are you locally trained?"

Jill smiles watching Blackmon. "University of Chicago."

Black says, "Great. I always enjoy speaking with women who are smarter and better trained in medicine. It might help me to better serve teammates. Even SEALS tested for endurance and proven in the field can fail emotionally, much less a civilian like Galvan."

Blackmon is as slick as wet glass. I'm undermined with a few words. Tanner jumps in to support Blackmon, "Yeah, Galvan fell flat on his face, almost got us all killed. Blackmon's a super-skilled medic. He kept this bum alive until the Medevac got to us."

Jill points the hot frying pan at Blackmon, "The IED broke his neck, then he helped a pair of concussed, barfing SEALS out. Blackmon saved nobody. Your flight surgeon kept him alive."

Tan says, "Ooops. How did you know about that?"

Jill is fearsome, banging the pan on the stove, "You two, OUT. Thanks for the help. Galvan can be a pain in the ass, but he's my patient. Did you forget you owe him your lives? Do you two think I'm deaf?" OUT. Go carry tales to his red-head slut. Tell the General Bitch he'll take her to dinner Friday at her hotel. Tell your fearless bitch leader you thumped the cripple. Maybe she will give you pooches extra kibbles for dinner."

The Twins exit. Jill slams a plate of eggs and two English muffins on the counter. She says loudly, "Eat. I cannot believe you made a date with your red-head bitch in front of me."

Bemused I say, "She's not mine. Eva belongs to the Navy. I need to do a face-to-face with her. Eva can't talk over the phone. NSA listens to everything. All of them are spies."

Jill laughs. "You are really stoned. Spies, really? There's no war out there, it's over."

I answer, "The CIA cannot investigate in the United States. Under the Posse Comitatus Act of 1878. the U.S. Military cannot enforce domestic policy. It prepares future battlefields."

Skeptical, Jill asks, "So?"

"The church committee determined that in the event the military is preparing a future battlefield they can spy, a little. They are watched and are on short leashes."

Jill asks, "And you know because?"

I answer discursively, "I was a spy. Eva is one. I'm seeking secrets. We play by Eva's rules. Dinner is plausible deniability. Set-up through the Twins. Keeps me out of her suite too."

I eat. Be careful talking and eating eggs when stoned, food flies everywhere.

I look up. Jill stands with her arms folded over her breasts studying me, waiting for an answer to whatever she just asked me. Confused I stare back.

Jill says, "Do you and the red-head hook-up whenever she shows up?"

I shrug. "No, I don't see Eva much. We spent an evening together in high school. A night together when we were in Afghanistan. The sailboat ride, that's it."

Jill shrugs, "The Greek told me you went sailing with her. Gaby says she left a bikini in the cabin. Did you two sail, have an orgy or both?"

My vision shrinks. I'm very sleepy. "We sailed, no sex. Eva attempted to strangle me. Scout's honor."

I feel very drowsy, so I lie on the floor to sleep. Jill drags me to my feet. I mutter, "Can I use your phone to make that reservation? I left mine in the car. He put the number in yours."

The black plastic spatula hits me up side of the head. I put Jill's phone down, "Sorry, not thinking straight. I'll go to Gaby's and use the bar phone."

Jill stands across from me, arms folded across her chest once more, tapping her toe on the floor. She's shaking her head, hands me her phone, "Make your call."

I find Eva's number from the directory. Unless she knows another Eva.

Eva answers, "To whom am I speaking?"

"Me," I answer.

Playful. Eva asks, "Me, who?"

"Me, Galvan. I saw the Twins, so-called. Can I take you to dinner downstairs at Aria? They have great pumpkin soup. Oh, no they don't. No pumpkin soup until fall. Will squash do?"

"Are you drunk, Galvan?" asks Eva angrily.

"No, I'm high or maybe low as can be. Nar-co-tics." I laugh.

"What? Who is the JillR listed on this phone?" demands Eva.

"Jill's taking care of me until the drugs wear off."

"That skinny, bartending, bitch girlfriend of yours?"

Jill is listening. Her brow furrows, so I say, "She likes you too."

Jill smiles, snatches her phone, "Hello, Evie, this is Jill the bartender bitch. Galvan is making a reservation to meet you at Aria for dinner on Friday at 8:00 PM. Make sure you're there, you flat chested, freckle-faced, red-headed snot. No pumpkin soup, bitch. Evie, I got him tonight. He has to take his nap. I'll do all I can to soothe his fevered brow. I may even rub his tummy. Yes, bartenders aim to please. Bye fat-ass."

Jill jabs me in my ribs. I moan. On the line, Eva splutters. Jill ends the call.

I'm fading fast. Jill pushes me back onto the couch. My eyes shut.

Someone places pillows from upstairs under my head, a blanket drapes me. I sleep My thoughts ramble. I need to pick ground zero. Casper can't choose the time and place. Should it be out of sight? Plainview needs explaining the why of my capping the prick. If I don't get carried away, I could shape the play for witnesses. That sounds better. I'll still have to arrange another meet with Brenda and Amelia. A warrant would be good. The air beside me feels warm. The scent of Jill's hair. I know her scent, I am a lost cause. As I open my eyes, Jill runs her cool, dry palm over my forehead. Nice. I tell Jill I that I love the shape of her hips. I'm all compliments today. I'm also stoned. I doze.

Later, I wake to see Jill seated at the counter wearing glasses. The contents of my envelope are spread before her. I watch her read. I like to watch her. I'm a goner. I doze, dreaming of Jill's legs, her hair blowing in a breeze. A happy sensual dream. I wake groggy, hot, disoriented. Jill pushes me back to the couch, "Easy, honey, the anesthesia is working its way out of your system. The steroids will make you feel flushed."

I put my hand on her arm to stay her departure. "Are you leaving?"

"No, I'm starved. I called for a pizza. I'm going downstairs to stretch my legs while I wait. Are those tears in the eyes? I thought you were through with me. Don't worry, I'll stick around. I'm not that easy to scare away ."

Jill exits, leaving my door unlocked. Why is that bad? Can't remember. I nod off. In the haze, I hear rain falling hard. Running footsteps on gravel. Someone's outside fumbling for keys against the steel fire-door.

A woman in heels scurries up the concrete stairs approaching the open loft door. JILL.

Heavy male pursues her upstairs. He's trying to catch her.

OH SHIT. CASPER. I roll up, fumbling the stainless .45 clipped in its holster from under the coffee table. I bring it to bear as I stagger to my feet.

Jill, all wet, runs through the doorway glancing behind her. I snatch her wrist, flipping her onto the couch behind me.

On the back swing my .45 covers the open doorway. I'll drop Casper at the threshold.

The Greek straddles the doorway, smiling. He's carrying stacked pizza boxes on his left palm. Under the boxes his right hand points his 5-shot snub-nose centered on me.

He says, "Check. Some chess, sleepy head."

A draw, seven feet separate us. We can walk rounds into the opponent's body.

The Greek shark smiles at me, "Welcome back, Kid. I missed you. You've been off your game. I love to scare you. You're a bitch when you step up your game. I never know what you'll do." He looks toward where I tumbled, "I stopped at Palermo's. Your pizza was waiting. I paid for both. Galvan owes me fifty, plus tip. I'll take sixty from his wallet."

I de-cock with the rolling hammer-lock safety. I slide the old 645 S&W in the hidden holster under the table. I stumble, stretch for balance. Jill's knee? No, too soft. I follow Joe's gaze to Jill. Her hair is wild, wet, mussed. My hand rests on her inner thigh. Her skirt has hiked up to reveal red satin. Jill glances quickly downward, brushes me away, hiking her skirt down.

The Greek puts our pizza on the island, "About time you saw that. Don't let me interrupt, children. Jill, you *are* rather fetching in red satin."

Jill gives the Greek a smile, frowns at me. She's annoyed. "What did I do?"

"Doors banging. Guns everywhere. What is this, Dodge City?"

She points at the coffee table, "Was that thing under the coffee table when I was sitting on it?" To the Greek: "Do all pizza deliveries come with a little gun? Where'd it come from? It wasn't in your hand when you chased me upstairs. Do I get one?"

"You want one?" I ask.

Jill thinks a moment, says, "Not now, show me later. Is it way often? Don't answer that. Galvan, if we have kids, you can't hide guns around under all the furniture."

The Greek chuckles, "On that note, I'm gone. You're on your own, Daddy. Gaby's upstairs waiting for our decadent dinner in a box. I'll tell her you're working on our grand baby."

Jill is anxious in a now small room, "Want us to come up and eat with you two?"

He laughs. "No, Jill. You primed his pump. You two need to practice."

Worried, Jill asks, "Practice what?"

"Making babies? That might get him to clean this dump."

With three twenties from my wallet he sprints upstairs to Gaby. He tips well with my money."

Jill is pale, silent. Standing on the balls of her feet ready to flee my advances.

With large eyes she studies me. Practicing babymaking with me upsets her. I say, "I'll keep my hands off. It's raining, stay for dinner. I have a copy of *The Long Hot Summer* with Paul Newman, Joanne Woodward. You might like it."

"Can I trust you, Galvan?" she asks.

I'm annoyed. "I'm not a bad lover. I want to make love, not fist fight, beautiful."

Righteously, she says, "You fondled my breast in front of the hospital staff."

I feel defeated. "I like them. I'm not just out to hold your hand. I'll try to resist you."

We ate pizza–watched, *The Long Hot Summer.*

Jill says, "I love that line he uses on Clara, in the store, 'Run, lady. And you keep on running. Buy yourself a bus ticket. Disappear. Change your name. Dye your hair. Get lost. And then maybe. Just maybe. You're gonna be safe from me.' Such a good line. Woodward gives it right back to Newman at the end."

She says, "You have sleepy eyes. I put my number in the wall phone directory. I put it in the phone I found in your SRX. If you need me, call. I'm home tonight."

"Thank you for your help. Sorry I screwed up your date night. I apologize for fondling you. Injections relax my inhibitions. I shouldn't have put my hands on you unless invited. I died, was in hospitals for a long time. I'm a silly grown man with a crush on you. To me, you're a walking dream. I'll fight to keep my hands off you, but don't expect miracles."

She says softly, "I plan on an invitation, but not this evening."

Jill shakes her head as she gathers her things and walks to the door. She has the envelope, says, "I'll research this. It looks good so far, I may need to consult a few professors."

She turns to leave, stops, "When this is over, call me. Promise?"

I say, "Thanks for today. For now, stay away. Forget you know me. If I corkscrew into the ground I will be gone or under a cloud. Tell the Greek if I'm right, he'll let me know. I think the killer's convinced you're with the Greek. So, he'll probably leave you alone."

She frowns severely, "We'll see. On the murders, the science is with you. If DNA matches the individual killed in Iraq, and it matches the crime scene, you have a royal flush. I don't know what he can argue in court. The science may be in your favor. Please be careful. I got a little attached to you this spring. Don't grab him and jump off the cliff, Irish.

Jill stops again, thinks, "I'll testify if you need me."

"I'll keep you out of it."

Gaby and Joe meet Jill at the landing. Jill asks them for a ride home.

Joe asks, "Did you practice?"

"He didn't even try. He's sulking. I've been sent home."

I call, "Consider yourself lucky to have escaped."

Jill spins back, "You mean SOB. Thanks for your advice. OK. I'm done with you. I offered my help. You never stop. You can't have it both ways tall, dark and dumb."

The Greek nods in agreement, "That's him. He and Deuce have been the family mean ones. The apple didn't fall far from the tree."

Jill asks, "What happens if this pervert kills him?"

Joe shrugs, "Galvan will be dead."

Rain drums loudly against the windows. Its sound lulls me. The door slams. I drift off. As the rain stops, I wake. I take out Blackmon's McMillan Tac-338 sniper rifle. I climb the stairs to the empty penthouse where I slide out onto the wet roof, where I slither to the tile capped brick perimeter wall. I roll out a neoprene sleeping pad in front of the gutter drain-port with the best angle. I sweep a night camo-grey and black space-blanket over me.

I scan Casper's perch across the spring using the Generation III+

rifle scope we borrowed from Blackmon in Afghanistan. It was with the rifle. After I passed away, the Greek didn't give it back. I hope Blackmon didn't get in too much trouble for losing it. Not my fault, I was dead.

As the scope powers set it to infrared. Heat is pouring off him. He wears what appears a commercial Gen-II starlight system mounted on head gear. It is beacon bright on infra-red. With the rain and clouds there is little starlight. It appears I see him; he doesn't see me.

I lock in the scope, open the silk smooth bolt action to drive a Lapua .338 Magnum round home. I am gonna blow his head to Iowa.

I know murder's wrong and messy. That should inhibit me. It doesn't.

I must still be under the under the effect of anesthetics. I know I'm nuts. But lack inhibition. I'm stoned. Too bad. So sad. Bye, bye. I see something crawling on Casper's face. Sand Fleas? I didn't know they had a signature. Must be itchy.

Take care of your equipment it takes care of you. Blackmon must've been sick losing it.

My aim settles on his chin, not center-mass. We need prints that link him to the murder. All this thinking gives me a headache. I'm getting eye strain from the scope. I look down to clear my head. I look up, he's gone. I wait for him to return. I nod. Dream of Jill in red. Later, I dream of Blackmon. The bastard thinks he is so slick. He denigrated me with Jill while pretending to be the earnest team medic. I pushed it too far. Jill's done with me. Now Blackmon has her to himself. If he can run off Lawyer Tom.

The sky is bright morning blue. I slept the night on-scope. Lucky my finger is off trigger. Somebody is kicking my foot. I'm so stiff under my camouflage shroud in the hot sun.

I turn my neck as far as my Frankenstein bolts allow. The Greek, at least it's not Casper.

Joe says, "You've slept enough, basket-case. I got back about when you positioned. I was watching him. Then I heard the rifle chamber that round. Casper might've heard the sound, too. He left, didn't come back.

"You started snoring, I put on your safety, and shut the scope down. You were out. I was afraid you'd cut loose with that cannon and kill my aunt in Florida."

He hands me a blue Gatorade. "Drink, you look like a drowned rat. Cook me breakfast after you oil my rifle and put it to bed."

23

SOME SHOWERS

When we bought the building last winter, I had spent a long, long time unable to communicate. Home, I couldn't summon any reasons to communicate.

When intubated, I couldn't speak. Extubated, I sat silent, like a lizard on a hot rock.

The Greek has no patience for my sulking. He took me to Gaby's to socialize me. He figured that placed in the company of women and crazy drunks I'd do something, anything.

I developed a crush on Jill. He developed a yen for Gaby. The drunks remain crazy. Gaby's patrons knew something was wrong with me, weren't sure what. The dunk consensus decided I was, at best, deaf and slow witted.

Conversations began, "HOW-ARE-YOU? DO YOU WANT FOOD, OR WATER?

During a snowy endless winter, I went from the Greek's deaf, mentally impaired buddy to being the clumsy guy who falls down regularly. People hoped I wasn't contagious.

Women asked their dates, "Is he drunk? Should I call an ambulance?"

Confined to bed, my muscles atrophied. Muscles need training. We combatted atrophy with exercise and work. When we got the building, we rehabbed it. Hard labor stressed muscles in ways weight training didn't. He kept me on my toes.

We put up the speed bag to quicken my eye. Later we worked Serrada flow-patterns with short sticks for stamina. Progress hastens in the face of fear. Serrada sticks are made of short fibrous rattan rods an inch thick. Rattan vine is scorched and fire hardened. Rattan sticks don't shatter. Opponents work close. Ambient air around Serrada practice carries the scent of smoldering wood caused by stick-on-stick abrasion. Boy scouts rubbing sticks together with murderous intent.

So, we practice this morning on the roof in the hot sun. We work the toxins out of my system. When we warm up, we switch to knives. People pay attention with knives. When we finish, the Greek draws a long, stainless-steel knife from his stick bag. It has the classic Bowie pattern with a weird, slippery-looking knurled tubular handle. The lower blade edge is hollow ground. The upper 'false' edge is not. The handle has an odd cross-guard that sports a single spike on the distal guard. From the upper false-edge to cross-guard there's cross-filed saw-edge.

He says, "It's old-school. Deuce gave it to him for a birthday in the 1980s. It was a prototype in 1985-86 to serve the survivalist niche.

He explains, "It marketed as the SEAL survival knife. It came mounted with two, two-inch-long threaded spikes that screwed into the cross guard. Old-School lost one of his spikes which converted this into a grappling hook by attaching a rope at the handle. I wouldn't dangle from this on a bet."

He notes, "The handle is hollow pipe. The hollow was filled with survival stuff including fish hooks, line, weights, thread, matches, and air-conditioner, whatever. The handle is slippery, like it came from the handle on a universal machine weight-station. The handle plug is not welded to the knife handle, it's sweated. Knife magazine articles reported it separated at the cross-guard, the saw didn't cut. From scene photos, I think Casper used one. I studied the tripled puncture wounds, finding they are consistent with blade and handle spikes. The scales in the photos agree. Don't look away. Look at the photos. We're playing for all the marbles.

He drones on. "There exists an absolute scarcity of the knives today. None are offered for sale on e-bay, no trade among collectors. It's unpatented, experimental, made last in 1986. That .22 pistol is also unique. Printouts of it are in your files."

Grabs my attention with this: "Casper's crazy, needs stopping. Clean up, there's work."

By comparison, it works. The Greek's right--scale measurements against knife are good

I hide the thing inside the sliding panel of a tool storage container in the wall–19th Century utility, repurposed to 21st Century conceal-ment. Storage now protected by a puzzle lock.

Damn, I smell stale and sweaty. I return to my loft, head for the showers. I toss my nasty clothes in the laundry.

Casper's illusive, but has bad habits, like using habitual proxim-ity to harass. One can never can tell when bonehead will turn up. I gather my stainless-steel S&W.38 J-frame. Shower time. Five rounds of crimped, jacketed hollow point 158 grain +p+ do sting. Crimped they're tested to fire after a year in sea water, if you scrape the bar-nacles off.

The shower in-the-wall soap dish conceals a hollow. The revolver slides onto that perch. These days, everyone needs optically concealed storage for the shower-gun.

We bought this building, and refitted factory plumbing for domes-tic use. We built in an open shower, a large free-standing spray-wall, and worked in a jetted tub with a long make-up mirror and vanity on the north wall. Tiles are sealed composite with marble appearance.

As a joke, Joe installed the quartz two sink counter top with a step-down make-up table and an adjustable tri-fold mirror. He positioned a rolling backless beautician's stool underneath. The goofy make-up stool has moved from under the counter twice. The first occasion Nadia visited, the second during Jill's visit. It wasn't me.

My razor, shaving-soap, and toothpaste grace the eight-foot coun-ter with a clothes hamper. The pipes are new, the building big. Water is slow to warm. I let it run. As it warms, I settle under the cascade nozzle. It's warm like summer rain; it feels good, loosens muscles.

I lather up, giving special attention to my hair. I'm convinced bugs nested in the night. Bugs may crawl out of my hair into my ears and eat my brain. Assuming I have a brain. I chuckle.

Exiting from under the spray, I hear clicking. Can't be the new 80-gallon water heater. What? The metronome is close. I retreat into the spray. TDS-time, distance, shielding. I lean back, relax against the wall. I slide my hand into the hollow, grasping my .38. I deploy by a back step. I brace in the Jelly Bryce ready stance, as my weapon comes to bear. Take what you get, use what you got.

Nadia, not Casper. She's languidly posed, eyeing my reflection in the fogged mirror. The metronome comes from the heel of her red-soled shoe marking time. Touching up her make-up?

She wears a crisp bright white blouse open below her neck to her sternum, a hand towel folded over her collar. Turn-about is fair play. Each has time to study the other. A woman making-up fascinates me. Seeking perfection in process. She's preoccupied, intent on the smallest detail. Totally aware, focused elsewhere. My God, I love women.

Some women watch men shave. Studying who knows what? Mimicking the motion. Nadia's blouse rests barely on her shoulders. She whisks a large brush lightly over her cheeks. Nadia's shoulders are pale, board-strong, her breasts full. Naked, I can't escape if I try.

Beneath her tailored blouse, she wears a brilliant white lace bra without shoulder straps. I study Nadia from inside my steam cloud. I've blocked the view of Nadia as a woman to date. Going in to battle soon, I'm not looking back. Jill's gone. Eva's past. Nadia is present.

Nadia's eyes sweep over me. She's safe in my fogged mirror. We assess in silence, regarding each other in reverse. The rest of the world is elsewhere. A few feet apart, lusting with plausible deniability. The past is gone, our future in question. Alive in the present.

Nadia raises an eyebrow, "Shoot or ravage? Life is hard, particularly the decisions."

I return the revolver to its perch, stepping from beneath the cascade. Nadia uncrosses her legs, rising fluidly from her stool. She kicks off her heels, strides into the shower. Decisions.

I reach for the towel at Nadia's collar, tossing it to the vanity.

She asks, "Well?"

I reach for Nadia. Ever the dancer, she lifts easily into my arms. I have limits, just arrived at mine. Time to charge the ivory tower. My lift settles her legs about my waist. Humidity beads her brow and cheeks. A drop falls to my lips. Vulnerable, salty, our bodies centered. It's time. I brush my lips lightly to Nadia's, they part in invitation. I pull her tight to me.

George's voice sounds from just this side of hell, "Nadia dear, we're working."

I turn to pin her against the wall. She exhales audibly, draws me to her. It's time.

George tries to get control, "Aren't you glad to see Nadia? I told her to be careful. You know women, always playing with matches. Did she steal your wits, and discretion?"

I grunt in response, George says sadly, "Now, now. Could we be a bit more discreet?"

Nadia appears through the cascade, eyes wide. She bites the side of my neck. Then focuses breathlessly on Partner George, "You were sup-posed to wait in the car." My lips close on Nadia's neck below her ear. Nadia tastes good, exhales audibly.

George waxes theatric. "So, I lied with good reason. My goodness, Nadia, do you want this brutish municipal thug for your baby daddy. Shall we try a little safe sex, kids?"

I gather Nadia to me. Her tongue tastes of peppermint. Her legs grasp more tightly. Shyly she whispers, softly, "George is right. I'll get rid of him, and we'll take up where we left off."

Nadia orders, "GEORGE, go downstairs. Put me down, we're em-barrassing George."

Her hips flex, legs squeeze, she slithers down my torso, "Things need doing, Mister."

I kiss the side of her corded dancer's neck, nuzzling her ear, "We're past playing games."

Nadia sighs, relaxing against me. She embraces me tightly. Her passion drains away.

The world often changes in a New York heartbeat.

George adjusts his suit-coat as he walks away. From the land-ing George calls back, "You two kids. Really, I mean, I haven't been around this much fun in the shower for years. And, you two are het-ero. Behave."

Nadia ruefully swipes wet bangs from her eyes. Her abdomen presses mine, "It is hard to keep my hands off you. I wish he'd leave, but he will wait downstairs until we go down. He insists on interviewing you about the murders, with me as witness."

Nadia's blue eyes are resigned, "Ballistics came back. I submitted the scene prints against Casper's bureau prints. He wants you to ex-plain some stuff. In the process, I'll tell you what I can. I'm going out east to interviews for a few days. Later we'll have a lot of sex and talk. OK?"

Nadia leans for a kiss. Her eyes lost luster. Her hug goes friendly. Over before we start?'

Choices cost. Warm promise flees. I can recall her taste, missing her already.

I draw back to retrieve a Turkish towel for her. Then fold my robe on the counter, saying, "The laundry is in the hall. It should help with your things. I'll put a t-shirt and basketball shorts on the bedroom dresser. Your stuff will take time to dry."

Nadia sighs. In my home, free to roam. Girls go exploring, but she's reluctant to take up residence, presently. Shyly, Nadia asks, "Can I use the shower and stuff?"

"You're welcome to what I have. I'll make us all lunch. George and I will have coffee downstairs in the kitchen area while you are sorting things out."

Nadia frowns, "Sorry about George. I didn't expect to find you in the shower. I'm glad you were. If I knew, he'd be at the office. We'd be in bed. I'm tired of things coming between us."

I nod. "I was carried away. No excuses, I apologize. I haven't had sex with anyone in years. I got out of control. Lucky George was here. You have worn all my self-restraint."

As I step around Nadia, I run my wet right palm over her taut stomach to her hip. I turn her to me for a parting kiss, saying as contact ends, "You are an incredible temptation."

Nadia says, "Yeah? You aren't so bad yourself."

On the way out, I say, "The soaker tub is a whirlpool, Nadia. Enjoy."

"Save me some lunch. I have an appetite."

"You've frustrated mine."

From the bedroom I grab jeans, a sleeveless sweat-shirt and Tevas as I join George. He made himself a Peet's k-cup. Ruins my day, then makes himself at home. George sits on a tall stool at the breakfast island, watching me with suspicion. He smirks, "Done? Already? Galvan? name must be Irish. I've heard rumors. Got the need for speed?"

"She's not a toy. She isn't here to tickle your fancy, horn-dog."

Serious, he says, "She's a nice girl with proper East Coast ways. I admit that changes when you two get in pheromone range. I'm gay, and even I like Nadia. She's not a tramp."

He rotates his cup, "She wants your attention, but is too little to share you with someone. She's smart, often too smart. She can be domineering. The girl is beautiful and knows it. Her type glides among mortals bumping into someone who doesn't move out of their way. You are the first hetero guy who walked away from her. No fawning. No courting. You just drag her into the shower. She goes, no complaint. You provide her nowhere to hide." George loses flamboyance, "She respects herself. She wants you to respect her. Remember that she's vulnerable, Kid. Only take what you want to keep. Hurt her, I'll get you."

Bemused I ask, "Whether or not I did something? Nadia and I have been on a collision course since we met. You interrupted. Threats won't keep me away. No miracles, James Bond."

"I am looking. Nadia's considering the concept. She's not convinced I'm a good guy. I'm destined for jail or the boudoir. I'll let you know what she decides." George shrugs, "You are both three-times-seven. I assume Mother Nature will take her course. All I ask is that you don't make her feel bad about herself. Do that and like I said I'll get you."

I say, "Never threaten the cook before lunch. I'll make it while we wait for Nadia. She says she's hungry. You can arrange torture implements for my interview on the coffee table."

"Delightful. The straight as cook. Sounds like a TV sit-com." I draw distilled water from the filter into a blown glass pitcher. The pitcher has dark blue striations inside the blown glass. The reflected light from the river surface makes the pattern swirl.

I quick rope Orange-Pekoe bags with cotton string. The bags drop in the glistening pitcher. The pitcher goes in the sunlight on the sunlit deck. Sun-tea brewing for lunch.

From the refrigerator I gather iceberg lettuce which I slice thrice. After rinsing each wedge, they go onto a covered plate. I wash and slice fresh strawberries into large pieces. The berries go in my colander. Rinsed blueberries, raspberries, black berries join my strawberries.

From a cabinet, I pull lightly salted cashews and golden roasted almonds.

I ask George, "Allergies?"

He shakes his head.

I open a bottle of Traverse Bay Riesling.

I often cook with wine. At times I even add it to the food. Today, I uncork it. The cork's inner edge is wet, I don't swell vinegar. I set the cork on the counter next to George, test repeated.

Riesling sits on ice on the island. George docks at the island with stemmed glass in hand. I place two long-stemmed wine glasses on the island just as George empties his. I'll need more Riesling, George is overserved. George, with glass in hand barely gives the contents time to condense on the surface in the humid air.

Humidity? I walk on the balcony, scan inland. Thunderheads are building north/northwest of the city. Been there all morning. Stationary front? Rain tonight, late. My Frankenstein neck bolts are spiking like a barometer.

George sips wine. I cook. I carefully lower three eggs into a rolling boil salted water, 12 minutes will do. Grandma was French, she did that. Must be a reason? The timer pings. I remove it from the heat, allowing cold water to drizzle away hot. It loosens egg from shell. It also stops the cooking. I want flaky yokes, not golf balls.

George opens the second bottle. The man can drink.

I gather up sweet green-pickle relish, ketchup, mayonnaise, Worcestershire, red pepper and white vinegar. From the cabinet I grab ground cloves, white sugar and a jar of black olives.

The jar pops, fresh.

I dice olives. Core and dice the red pepper finely. The pepper and olives go into a bowl with mayo and ketchup. I add a teaspoon of sugar. Whisk in Worcestershire and white vinegar. Time to carefully fold in the relish, until the color contrast is vivid.

I crack and peel eggs, chop them finely; I whisk them with the other ingredients a bit at a time. Whisk, not smoosh with the spoon.

I glance to the counter. George has the wine bottle in protective custody in the shade over the deck. George's watching the river flow backwards to the Gulf of Mexico. We'll need at least a third Riesling. George has woked up a thirst somewhere.

The dressing goes in the refrigerator to cool. I add an open Riesling to breathe in the cold air. That way, Nadia may get some.

I'm tired, need to pay attention. I study George as he sits on my balcony. He has a plan. These two are hunting me. I'm to be hunted over lunch.

George asks, "I saw you on the roof. You guys renaissance re-enactors?"

I say, "He taught me to use it to help my equilibrium. It took me a long time to recover."

George laughs. "Amazing, dude, a whole year malingering. Bethesda, Landstuhl, Asia.

I nod. A good interrogator knows the answers before he asks. Omnipotence.

George couldn't be bull-dogging me, blocking my avenues of escape. OK, pretend to scare me, George. Ruin my sex, drink my wine, eat my food. Do it all in one day in my own home.

George has downed the better part of that first Riesling. It is not dulling his wits. He asks about life in Bethesda, must've been there. Time to act Irish, answer questions with questions. It throws off the guest's pace, sets back his plan.

He fires at me, "Was your stay in Bethesda nice?"

I ask in a distracted tone, "Were you there long?"

Retaining his smile, he says, "I was there about three months after Desert Storm. Banged my leg up. I hear during the period you were there, Galvan, the patient census increased. I heard it was a little tight."

Is he seeking information to broaden his attack platform, or am I just paranoid? I answer, knowing the bureau is prone to hiring officers, "Am I right to say yours was a fixed tank battle war? What kind of injuries did your men suffer?"

His eyes are haunted, "I deployed my Recon Marines in an effort to obtain intel as the Qatari tanks were fighting their way into Khafji. We tangled with Iraqi Commandos near the coast. They called in artillery on us. Our medic lost his supplies during the barrage. The medic had to use safety pins to put my leg together after blast force shredded my lower leg. My boys got me out on a Saudi National Guard LAV-25 amphibious vehicle. They swam it parallel to the beach to get past the commandos."

Silence, he's lost in thought about the bad times. Been there, done that.

George says, "The mess you were in was an overinflated insurgency. Desert Storm; that was a real war."

He's picking a fight. Is he doing it to set the stage for his role as bad guy to Nadia's good girl? I hope she didn't stage that scene in the shower. If she did, it got away from her. I'll kick his ass if George makes the girl testify about what I did to her in the shower. That would be shaming. I hope George has more class.

I shrug, letting the argument go, "War is relevant to someone who was there. A vet at the VA Hospital told my grandfather the Viet Nam 't-weren't nothing but a squirmish. Like you, I got caught in the switches. Was I warehoused too long? Was I lost because of the numbers? Or is it just that life's a bitch, and then you die? Who knows?"

He shrugs, "I got out of Bethesda with a bronze star with a combat V and a partial disability. I still get a disability check. Marines retired me. I joined the bureau."

He must be recording now. I've been informed he is a federal agent. We're on the record.

Oh my, don't lie to me! I've been told! If I don't lie, he'll say I did. The G does that.

Nah, shucks, George is a good guy. A goof like me. Two old timers telling war stories. George mistook me for a stupid goof. That's folksy, George.

"By the way, pal, these are some digs. Fancy. How do you manage it?"

Here we go–out to prove I'm living beyond my means. I thought we were pals. I got it, anything I say can and will be used against me. I guess George forgot reading me my rights?

I answer carefully, "Wasn't I on leave of absence to the secret service? They said my concussive injuries would leave me with blank spots. They said I'd never remember things. Was the concussive effect the same for you, George? Do you know what they did in your case, buddy? I look confused, mind wandering, "I think I receive disability payments, like you?"

George demands, "Who told you that?"

I respond, "I don't know. I was in and out of comas. Some doc or docs or maybe a VA lady told me. They said I had hearing problems from the explosion. Tinnitus, ringing ears, or something, I forget. What does it say in the hospital records?"

George is beginning to flush, "I don't know. I haven't seen them."

Dully I say, "Do you think they don't want you to see my hospital records?"

George snaps, "What are you talking about? Who doesn't want me to see your records?"

I shake my head sadly, "Who knows, buddy, the Navy, the secret service. president or one of the other ones? I have no idea. You mean you don't have them?"

George snarls, "No, I don't have the records."

I say, "Oh, they must not want you to have them."

George frowns angrily. We exchange stares.

He resets, "Well, let's go on."

"My lawyer suggests I cooperate," I say. "She said to give you her card. I'm glad to help. But she said to notify her immediately if you get adversarial."

George goes on reading the card, "What's this bullshit? Judge Standish is on the northern district of Illinois bench. She's your lawyer?"

I say, "I think I was her law clerk. Her firm agreed to represent me. After today, I'm instructed, as her client, to relay all requests and inquiries to her."

George asks, "Why did she allow it today?"

"She's at that Over-Reach conference with your director. Something about new FISA court rules. I'm limiting my response on her counsel. Can I record our interview?"

Nadia pads up on bare feet behind me. She folds warm arms around my neck, laughing. I turn to her. Her skin is pink, fresh from the bath. Her short hair is loose and wild. It has reddish highlights. My Russian princess must have scandal in the family. Why do I rate Nadia as my Russian princess? She wears my threadbare Ryukyu Kempo T-shirt, once black, now washed grey. My clothes are loose on Nadia's frame. I like this Nadia.

It will ruin my faith in humanity if I fall for her, only for her to slam the jail-door on me. I feel old. Nadia is young, earnest. Sophisticated agent reverts to young woman. No wonder her effort at seductress felt so tenuous. George is right. Nadia is just a kid.

Was I ever that young? I always felt old? So, it's true, you're as young as you feel. Looking at Nadia in shorts and t-shirt, I feel like a cradle robber.

My expression startles Nadia. I let her inside my guard, first and last time, that.

Nadia happily beams like a girl. She hugs, buries her head on my chest, and asks, "Can we eat? I'm starving. I went to the gym this morning, no breakfast."

I walk to the balcony for sun tea I put there as I started on breakfast. Nadia joins George settled at the island. To the tea I add sliced lemon, crushed ice, white granular sugar.

I set tall narrow glasses of crushed ice on the island. I place a white Corian plate with more lemon slices between them.

I set the bowl of sugar on the island. They sip tea, while I place my lettuce wedges on larger Corian plates drizzling my Thousand Island over each wedge.

He says, "More dressing, dear. I watched him make it. You'll love it."

Nadia glances at me shyly from beneath her damp bang. "I enjoyed everything else he cooked for me. I wonder if he can make peanut-butter-and-grape-jelly sandwiches in the dead of night with cold milk and chocolate chip cookies?"

The tenor between Nadia and me changes, I say, "You have plans?"

No answer, beyond a sweet smile. I arrange strawberries, raspberries, blueberries and blackberries over each wedge, add peanuts and cashews last. Salt, sweet, tart. That will do it.

I produce the last Riesling, pouring each of us a glass. A lot of dead soldiers lying about this afternoon.

I retrieve a loaf of pretzel bread from a warmed oven. I place cold, fresh butter on the island to partner with the bread. As we lunch, Nadia says, "Did George tell you we have the preliminary ballistics. The report supports the theory that the bullets recovered at the scenes are from the same gun. Detective Gennaro was right, it's a .22 Ruger semi-automatic. Probably had a suppressor with metal baffles. Extractor marks on casings from both scenes match."

George places a restraining hand over Nadia's forearm. Nadia brushes the hand away, "Ballistics indicate the bureau inventoried the weapon well in advance of the murders. Our agents inventoried it in Baltimore."

"Was the inventorying agent the guy I mentioned?"

"No, it was inventoried by an agent who was training River Mound. The man you mentioned was present when the Ruger was recovered. River Mound signed out the gun for court in his partner's name. He claimed it was stolen in court by the cops who worked the case."

I say, "Gotta watch those crooked cops."

Nadia smiles, "I try to."

George frowns again, he does that a lot.

I ask, "Was a large stainless-steel Buck Knife, Model 184, inventoried in that case?"

Nadia shakes her head, goes coy.

I plow in, "But you found one."

Nadia shakes her head negatively, "No, but Casper inventoried one which local police had recovered antecedent to an unlawful-flight-to-avoid-prosecution. A wife castrated her spouse with that knife in Virginia, then fled to Maryland, where she was arrested."

I answer, "Beware the woman scorned."

Nadia raises an eyebrow. "You should."

I ask, "Was she Russian?"

Nadia says, "They're the worst."

I note, "That knife is a rarity on the collector's market. It is listed with open offers to purchase; none are available in any marketplace I could find. For the sake of argument, it was a prototype, going out of production in 1986."

George furiously flips pages in a file, "How did you prove that? Why do you know?"

Reaching into the file, I lay the printout of the SEAL survival knife. Beside it I place the autopsy photos with the ruler scales in the picture. Beside them I place a photo of Old School's knife with its single spike attached in down-blade position. The puncture wounds were photographed exhibiting millimeter-ruler scale adjacent to the wounds.

I say, "The scales match."

The pair argue. Their photos freeze me. I fixate on their faces. I lean on the island. I loved the women, now dead, naked, cold on stainless tables. I don't hear anything for a time. When I was someone else, we were very close. Confident in my own invulnerability I went off to play war. Along the way we all got dead. Mine didn't take. I need to fix what I can.

I wish I could see our baby. I'm so empty. Baby would be child jabbering at me through lunch, not my guests. In my mind I see Mary Beth smiling on her brood, as her child rambles. I loved her, but Calah was done with me. I'd been dismissed. Mary Beth was creating life with me. Throughout all of it I was oblivious.

Something is missing in my head. I'm older, more callous. Wiser? I doubt it.

Nadia is speaking as she extracts the now crumpled photos from my clenched fist, "Give me the pictures. George needs to see them."

As I sit on a stool. I can feel her touch and hear her voice. She's indistinct, a blurry shape. I must have sweat in my eyes. As they clear I see round spatters that mark the photos.

Nadia rises from her stool, steps between my knees. She hugs me. She's murmuring something foreign very softly. She has a lovely voice, soothing. I wrap my arms about her.

George has become silent. I bury my face in her breast, tears wet her breast. My vision clears. Embarrassed, I step away to walk to the balcony. Beneath me our inlet empties clear water into the murky brown of the river. Across the icy barrier of our spring, a figure stands among the tumbleweeds. Casper gazes back smiling. I am gonna kill this prick. He waves, smirks. Turning, he disappears into the six-foot tumbleweeds. Gone now, time for him later. Not soup yet. When it's soup, Casper will be in the pot.

I feel George's eyes boring into my back. The FBI is watching. Be cool fool. He can't see what I saw. They refuse to look for fear of seeing, even as I tell them. Resolve descends, cloaking me. I return to

Nadia and George. My face assumes an inquisitive expression, "Sorry, I got distracted by the autopsy photos. You were saying?"

Nadia points to the SEAL knife photo, then directs me to the medical examiners' photos, saying, "You need to explain what this all means."

Resisting the evidence, out of phase with events, George seeks to regain control, "Similarity doesn't prove they are identical. He could've flipped the knife around, making a second stab into the wound to confuse us. "

I say, "The wound channels don't indicate the possibility."

Enraged, George snaps, "And how do you know that, Barney Fife?"

Nadia says, "Who's Barney Fife?"

I respond, "He was a TV cop on a comedy show about a town called Mayberry. Clyde Tolson here is making a funny. He's alluding to me as inept."

I say, "In answer, Georgie Porgie, I can read ME reports, can you?"

Nadia says, "Boys, boys be good. I get the Clouseau reference. Steve Martin, right?"

George sighs. "No. He's referring to my moustache. Peter Sellers is the only Clouseau."

Nadia asks, "Why won't you let him explain, George?"

George says, "In the proven timeline, this fool had love affairs with both women. The Morgenthau woman was murdered in Baltimore after he visited. I have TSA footage of him entering the gate to board in Baltimore. He went back to Chicago to kill the police broad."

My right hand pinches his Adam's apple, as my left passes along his right side popping his thumb break safety and drawing his snub-nose upside-down. The gun goes to his temple with my little finger taking up trigger slack. I say, "I bet I can hit ya."

With him on tiptoes, I continue, "I was going to war. I'd been in love with Agent Morgenthau. She ended it. I came back to Chicago in a dark mood. I found a very old friend and rekindled a ten-year relationship. We made a baby. I left to play war. It got me killed. That didn't take. I was paralyzed for a year. You play at crazy, George, I am screaming bat-shit crazy. Learn to be courteous to crazy people."

Nadia says, "Put my partner down, Galvan. I signed him out today. You're making his face purple. Stop it."

I set the gagging George on his feet. I turn away snapping the cylinder open. As the crane swings open, I palm his live rounds as I toss the revolver on the couch.

George lunges past me to the couch, snatching the revolver to point it at me. He pulls the trigger. I drop his bullets in my pocket. George cross reaches for his speed-loader. He yells, "Where is it?"

I say, "Downstairs on the loading dock somewhere. It fell off your belt when you were sprawled on my lounger drinking two bottles of my wine. George, you couldn't pass a breathalyzer on a bet."

He demands, "Did you kick it off the deck?"

I say, "Maybe. I was mad."

As he registers, I say, "I was here when Calah Morgenthau was murdered in Baltimore. I was in training at the 'ranch' when Mary Beth was murdered. It's like the 'farm', but colder. "

Nadia sit sits on her stool shaking her head, "Boys, be nice."

She says, "George, you have a filthy chauvinistic mouth. The woman was a police officer carrying this man's child. She was murdered in her home by an armed psycho-sexual serial killer who killed her and their baby. You're lucky he didn't snap your pencil-neck. Obviously, you drank your lunch again."

George gets huffy, "So?"

Nadia is annoyed. "Galvan has half the secret service for an alibi. He was signed into a court here testifying at the time Agent Morgenthau was murdered in Maryland. I talked to the judge and state's attorney on that case. They alibi Galvan."

She's exasperated, "He left Chicago after the murder of Agent Morgenthau. He flew to Williamsburg, Virginia, where he was transported by the secrets to the 'Camp Peary Farm'."

She finishes, "Enough, George. There is work I need to do. Galvan didn't do either murder. He was always somewhere else. Impossibility is the ultimate defense. I know you hate Chicago cops. You have a history with them from another time. Give it up.

Silence. After a time, she says, "He didn't know of Officer Burke's murder until Detective Gennaro told him in front of me. Galvan almost fell on his face."

"I have an audiovisual recording of Detective Gennaro telling Galvan about the Morgenthau murder at area central. On screen he passed out, split his head and had to be resuscitated. It's all on tape in the file, WTF George. Illinois records all murder interrogations,

"Prints recovered at both scenes match the same unknown third party.

Distractedly I ask, "Do they match Casper?"

Nadia says, "They don't match a known suspect in our AFIS Criminal Database. I have to get permission to compare against an agent, or former agent. I haven't sold the idea yet."

I say, "Try against his Chicago Police Department former personnel prints."

"I submitted the request. Chicago likes us as much as George likes you."

"I'll call. God help us if we ever have to cooperate fast. What could happen?"

Nadia leans in for a kiss. She tastes of mint. Must be a Russian thing, "Pre-conceived notions are a bitch. I just showered with a guy who isn't sure he can trust me yet. The city and the bureau have had troubles longer than he's been toying with my affections."

Nadia says, "That's a first, my kissing a guy makes him sad. Why?"

I say, "Girl."

Nadia watches me tightly, saying, "Girl? So what? So, I'm a girl."

Surprised, I say, "It's a first."

George snaps, "A first what, nutsy?"

I say, "My grandmother always wanted a girl. She had all boys. I just allowed myself to look. Our baby was a girl. She's the first girl in generations. A girl would have made Mary happy."

Caressing her shoulders, I say, "I may have an outside DNA comparison with Casper cooking. I'll let you know if it pans out."

He snaps, "You nobody. Who do you think you are? Did you submit it to '23 and me'?"

I say, "They've caught more serial killers than you have. Read the file, J. Edgar."

George explodes, "I thought I was Clyde Tolson. We handle the big DNA cases. You're a nobody. We're the experts. You are a never-was."

Disappointed, Nadia says, "Boys, why can't we all just get along?"

"Sorry, beautiful," I say, "but you're no Rodney King." Resigned, I ask George, "How many murders have you investigated?"

George smirks. "Six."

I say, "I've investigated several hundred."

"How many serial killers have you arrested?" I ask.

"I interviewed two serial-killers in post-conviction settings in prison."

"George, I caught six, I did the follow-up on eleven others, who were also charged."

"What's that supposed to mean, Buddy?" says George.

Nadia studies George with tired eyes, "Your buddy is telling you that he's the expert on murders in general, and serial murder in particular."

Anger cools, I walk Nadia and George to the door. She's wearing my Teva's carrying equipment in my gym bag with her dry clothes and shoes on top. She looks cute struggling with her bundle.

I open the door to the stairs, watching her shuffle along with her burden. She looks better in my clothes than I ever have. She smiles shyly. As she exits, Nadia catches a Teva sole on the kick-plate, stumbling forward. I catch her to prevent a fall. She kisses my cheek as my hand steadies her hip.

At that moment we collide with Jill coming up the stairs. Nadia stumbles, retaining her hold on the equipment bag containing her gun. Her clothes spill.

Reflexively Jill catches part of Nadia's clothing with a free hand. Unfortunately, she catches a handful of Nadia's lingerie, the rest cascades.

They end up jointly clutching the loose bundle.

Jill utters an exasperated, "Ick. Really, Galvan? Couldn't you hang a note on the door?"

They are frozen almost nose to nose.

Jill swings wide with her other hand as she smashes a hot bag of Ricobene's on my head.

Nadia's embarrassed, says, "Sorry, Jill."

Jill snarls, "Don't explain. I tried, you succeeded. Your alley cat now, sweetheart."

Jill bounds down the stairs, wiping her hands on a napkin. The street door slams.

Chortling George, drunk as a lord, thoroughly enjoys the wreckage of my love-life. I try to help Nadia gather her bundle. Nadia shoves me back, "You are just too complicated. I'm tired of getting sent home to bed. I've work to do. I'll try to help. But stay away from me. Something is wrong with you."

George smirks. "You fried your own self. Enjoy. You are a real idiot."

I have a dull headache. Did I just get a Ricobene's sandwich concussion?

24

LOVE LONG GONE

I woke this morning to the sound of my mailbox slamming downstairs. Mailmen come awful early these days. Joe gave me power of attorney to collect his mail. He's too lazy.

Resigned, I walk to the boxes in the hallway. I slip on some orange slop, yesterday's Ricobene's. Scrambling, I get my feet under me. The post-box contains a single item, a shiny new house key on an FBI key-fob. Outside, Nadia peels away. No FBI romance for me, doesn't want the key she cut. Something very complicated in that. Looking upstairs, a line of mushy marinara sauce footprints. Good food, had it for dinner. Waste not. want not. Won't happen today, nobody loves me.

Oh, that was me. I walked in that blob, before I fell down the stairs. Tired I reclimb as the sauce odor peaks. Another county heard from. I spot a key lodged in the Marinara blob. Jill dropped hers when she bashed me with the Ricobene's.

Proof positive I have time for a late morning nap. No sense in planning on visitors. I spruce up late, set out early for the Fairmont Hotel. Early is an unfamiliar Galvan trait. Tonight's dinner with Eva is business. For business I'll leave early.

I rightly acquired the antipathy of Nadia and Jill. To keep them safe, I'll take the antipathy. If I wanted alienation, I succeeded. Serendipity, could do it again if I tried. The average guy would have been satisfied with group sex. I had to be a perfectionist.

Beauty is in the eye of the beholder. For the pair, I am a manipulative pig. Each clearly sees a bum illicitly cavorting with a loose woman when he as easily might cavort with a good woman. Good, bad? That depends on perspective. Complicated to think on, but effective. I got rid of them, they're gone. Man cannot rejoin what has been put asunder. I have little to do. If I see him, should I loosen his neck with a hedge trimmer. Gas or electric? Decisions, decisions. Should I buy a hedge as an alibi?

He destroys good women in service of pleasure. Serial killers remained an all-male club until Aileen Carol Wuornos showed up. What the heck, exception destroyed that rule. Now, every demographic has its own. Sociologists everywhere need to know. WHY? Who cares? They're all screaming bat-shit crazy.

Casper isn't stupid. He's nuts. But he's a sociopathic nut. He enjoys the safety of rules. He cleaves naturally to using the rules that bind others to behavior. Then Casper da' Ghost does as he pleases. You accept the rules, so he can plan what you'll do and where you'll do it.

Tonight, Casper keeps his distance. I distally started my vehicle. No kaboom. He wasn't doing his fishing thing across our inlet as I walked to the SRX. But he was there, calling me from the tumbleweeds.

Casper asked in his high-pitched odd voice, "Big night? Got a date?"

Making my own luck, I swing the car door between us as I ask, "How's the fishing?"

He is doing something with his hands. My pistol is in my hand below the door frame. Casper flings a live, bloody carp from his fish stringer onto the shore line. A river rat emerges from debris to drag off the struggling carp. As I watch, Casper does it again. More rats. He's drawing rats to him. Pure genius this boy. I'll just shoot him so the rats can eat him. I'm gonna actually shoot this prick.

Casper looks out of the shrubbery at me, "You should have warned me. Nods to the cross street where the woman and child are coming from the park at the foot of our inlet. Casper says, "Wouldn't want to scare that little breeder and her brood mare mother."

Casper tosses the flopping, strung fish to his rats en masse, "Garbage. They have to go. So many breeders, so little time." His laughter recedes into the brush.

I swing from my view of mother and child to acquire my sight picture. Casper's gone into the weeds. Got me. Talk or shoot, don't try for both.

I drive south to pick up Archer. Ahead of me ragged red cross-over races under the viaduct, heading my way. Everyone is going to the Fairmont. Casper has me tailing him.

Theory holds that intervals between attacks shrink as the killer approach's personality dis-integration. Not a ray-gun obliteration of the personality, but the disassembly of the killer's reasoning process.

Deuce and I experienced three and one-half bureau training regimens on serial killers. Aloof reserve on the part of the killer becomes a growing thirst for the kill. They become overconfident. Getting closer to the suffering of the prey is no longer sufficient. As in heroin use, the high is gradually ebbing. Killing becomes life, but its thrill becomes ever more fleeting.

That is the theory. Theories change. We'll see.

Will Casper appear behind me? Such disrespect for prey. Pay attention. Maybe he wishes to join us for dinner. Casper is following me in his nasty cross-over. Try as I might, I can't get close enough to put the grab on him. He ain't soup yet anyway. I proceed for my date at the Fairmont. What could go wrong? I think I have an evening with Eva. How could that go awry?

Casper maintains perfect distance. Obviously, he has excellent bureau training in the art of the obtrusive tail. He does obvious things well, though the raggedy tail-car stands out. The cross looks like a junker. Crap is heaped back on the cargo deck. That is probably Casper's important papers. Over it is crazy man junk heaped in boxes in his car. Casper is falling apart. Looks like his personality dis-integration is setting in. He will become ever more unstable. Frantic need surmounts careful planning.

I need to become the picador dashing in to prick the angry bull. It is important to focus Casper's attention on me. I need him confused and madly rushing in at me. My effort is not to understand. Understanding will not fix what he has done, nor will it deter the next guy. Casper lives, women died. He needs stopping. Drawing him in is what it is.

Jill and Nadia are gone. Tonight, I'll send Eva away. With no one else to play, Casper and I can then chase each other around in the dark to our heart's content.

Casper's behavior tonight is prophetic. He repeatedly rushes in, only to back off with a confused expression. Whatever is going on in his head, confuses him. As we close in on the Fairmont, I consider Eva. Eva needs special handling. But I suppose everyone does. Eva has the killer instinct. She got it at the cost of her girlhood. Our generation of women was raised to equal males of the species. Now, girls like Eva are as badly soiled as we are.

Hemingway wrote, "There is no hunting like the hunting of man, and those who have hunted armed men long enough and liked it, never care for anything else thereafter."

In service of Deveraux Clan ambitions, Eva became scout-sniper, a killer of men. Now the clan wishes her to step away from who she has become in order to be the next Admiral Devereaux. What would the Navy be without an Admiral Devereaux? Who the fuck knows? I don't give a shit. But I am dumb enough to care what happens to Eva. What a dumb SOB I am. If Eva realizes what I'm doing, she'll want to join me. By nature, Eva is the over watch. I need to keep her out. How to do that? Reasoned argument? Impassioned pleas on love? Make her mad?

The last shall be first then. I'll make her mad.

There are no women in the special forces, unless there are. Operating overseas the woman is seen as a girlfriend. Ignore the girl, she's nobody. Until she shivs you. A woman in special forces is as likely as a gay man in the FBI, except for J. Edgar, Clyde Tolson and, well, George. The Delta Force doesn't exist. Government bureaucrats are like little kids who hold their fingers in front of their eyes and say, "You can't see me." Really?

Eva has danced on the edge of the knife. Skillful war-fighter can't afford being seen as a psycho killer bitch. No. That won't do. The old-boys have plenty of crazy SOBs. If Eva goes wild, a crazy bitch she'll be. Crazy would soothe fragile male egos, thus obviously proving Eva unsuitable for a spot on the admiral's list. The boys can say, "Daddy, Daddy look at me."

Most institutions are chauvinistic, it's tradition. Like wine, organizations sour with age. Rivals in Eva's service lack my murderous love's intestinal fortitude. They labeled Commander Evangeline Deveraux a snake-eating bitch. I never saw her eat one, who knows?

I make wooden boats in a style nobody remembers. I do it because I like it. Mine is not a niche with a broad future. Darwin's surely coming for my ass. I can see me chatting with my fellow Navy wives, "Would you bitches care for more marzipan? I whipped the shit up myself." Does one whip up marzipan?

If there's something awful that needs doing, do it yourself. Truisms are like that, filled with bountiful advice, I suppose. Unless you can trick somebody into doing it for you. I'm done kidding myself. When I look at the mature Eva, I am overwhelmed with the desire to place a bun in her oven. I know Eva knows. She's walking down the aisle with someone else's.

As Eva's spouse, I would be proof positive that Eva not only eats snakes, but likes her men down and dirty. I won't support an admiral's course. I gotta go and she knows it. As always, Eva wants what Eva wants. The Navy doesn't care what Eva wants.

Eva's bored. Eva's looking for a fight. If Eva Deveraux gets a whiff of Casper's intent she and the Twins will go hunting. Eva is juggling too many balls. Her Marine--her post SEAL career. An admiral needs to have had a ship and a crew. Annapolis has midshipmen to teach.

I'm not stupid. Eva's eyes see forever these days; she wants kids and wants them soon. If she ain't ovulating, the Pope ain't Catholic. Eva needs to relax. That trio would find killing Casper and skinning him out just that, relaxing. But the G is all over this thing. That bunch is audacious; audacity won't do.

Edmond Locard mentioned that when entering crime scenes, one leaves things behind, and on leaving a scene, one takes things away. Facts of life which have nothing to do with duty, honor, or country. The Navy is 100% behind Eva and the Twins when right. But Eva and the Twins don't need them if they're right.

If they are wrong? Well, the trio is on their own. If I live, I'll tell 'em what is what. Right or wrong, who knows? Casper gets to fill his hand. Hang? So what?

Eva and the Twins are the good guys. Me? Doubtful. I'm a dead guy with little to do. Casper rolled the dice. We shall see what we shall see.

My mind wanders, I lose sight of Casper's car. Dumb thing to do. Daydreaming will get me killed. I wish I gave a shit. No, he's back there. The most dangerous game plays on.

I weave the SRX into valet parking under the east portico of the Fairmont. I signal the chief attendant. I show him my favorite picture of U.S. Grant folded to display a nice view of the bill's lovely engraving. Ah, I have his attention.

I say, "I'm meeting a client for dinner. Can you keep my SRX handy? President Grant wants to meet you. I'll introduce you to his twin on my way out."

The attendant nods, "It will be here at the curb."

I add, "I am being followed by a very odd competitor. He plays detective. Male white with weird blue hair not found in nature. He has issues with the lady I'm meeting."

"Would you like me to call the police when I see him, sir?"

"No, he's unlikely to be a problem here. I do think he'll approach you with some story. He's looking for info, and will be the soul of generosity. He may offer a couple of engravings of George Washington for your help. Tell him I had a meeting about a job and the woman I met didn't care for my act."

"Very good, sir. I'll keep your Caddy near the door. I'm the soul of discretion."

We shake like old friends. The fifty travels from palm to palm.

I enter the lobby glimpsing Casper's reflection in the glass door at the curb. He exits to speak with the chief attendant.

I'm wearing a blue shirt with red tie under my one remaining gray suit. Casper wears a red shirt with an askew grey tie under a blue suit. Are we schizophrenic twins?

Eva exits the elevator. Naval punctuality. I forestall a hug by extending my hand to shake. Eva appears puzzled, before shaking limply. Casper lurks in the background. I ignore him, speaking very loudly. I thank Eva for seeing me about my application. She plays along, remaining perplexed. We enter Aria from the lobby.

Eva's hair is in a soft curl, hangs loose. Warrior-girl, come home a woman. Lovely. As Eva walks ahead of me, I admire her form. She's in a royal-blue lace summer dress with a haltered neck and a thinly belted waist. The hem is steeply slashed from her upper left thigh seeping behind her right knee before returning to that naked left thigh. This ain't gonna be easy. Eva has lovely thighs. Her dress draws my eye.

A shiny blue silk sheath embraces her slender form beneath the lace of her dress. My mind desires to chase her away. I'd rather keep Eva. Sadly, wild can't be tamed. I read somewhere that a man can be aroused by his woman's scent from far away. I have no sense of smell, something to do with the St. Thomas Wrestling team in cowboy boots punting my head. That was then, this is now. Tonight, Eva's scent is driving me nuts. A miracle, I can smell. Steady Galvan.

Eva catches me studying her bottom in the glass of Aria's door. Warm blue eyes study me. She nods, smile curving thin lips. Eva likes to win. I doubt this will be the last I see of her.

Does Eva care? Who knows? We all see the world in hues of our own making. Eva enjoys my daft expression, "Aren't you still mad, baby? You are nuts, but I'll always love you. I just want to disappear in your arms. Dinner first, I need you strong like a bull."

We glance at the menus. We share Naan sesame bread. I recommend the Squash Bisque.

Eva's playful, "No pumpkin soup?"

Without thinking, I say "Not in season."

I recall what Jill said; Eva won't be here for pumpkin soup. Jill is gone. Eva soon will be. No, Eva won't be here for pumpkin soup. Time passes, it doesn't disappear. You get the life you get. With small room in Eva's for me, it is time for me to slip from her orbit.

Eva catches the signs of my abstraction. She knows me. Her pale cheeks redden. Under fire, Eva's first response is to attack. She always goes for the throat. Stopping to consider foibles in others is a weakness Eva does not have. "You called me on that woman's phone. Who is this JillR? Besides being a skinny tramp of a waitress that you dragged to Emma's wedding to the Black Man, who is she?"

Eva's not asking, she's demanding. Why wait for an answer, when you can provide the bulk of the explanation yourself? Eva is suppressing fire with rhetorical questions. Don't lie, I know. This will be easier than anticipated.

Eva brooks no idols before her. Eva was my first love. She was my last lover. Fitting. Time to live and let live. Eva is upset, the war is done for her. Was it worth what she gave up? Is it good to be happy to be alive when others are not? Then up pops Galvan, the jack-in-the-box. As a vignette in the fresco of her girlhood sways the boing-boing boy. All is not lost, party time. For a time, we can cohabit our own passion bubble. In due time, Eva will become bored.

Sooner or later, she'll exit her love bubble to pursue that which defines her. The Navy will beckon. Eva always answers duty's call, which is often much easier than a relationship. Thus, I will not be offered the position of consort to the admiral.

No recriminations, I give Eva the door without summoning regret. Eva may leave mad, but she's leaving. I say, "JillR is Jill Ryan. She tends bar, evenings, at Gabrielle's Restaurant in Bridgeport. Your bookends have been there."

"Gabrielle, Joe's friend, is French and a Le Cordon Bleu Chef. She serves Bourgeois cuisine. Her menu reflects what my grandmother served me as a child. Grandma was French-Canadian."

"You have never talked to me about your family. My family's French from Louisiana."

We've spent the little time we've had together, fighting, having sex and talking of Eva, but I never knew she was Cajun. I say, "My grandfather, Silky, was a policeman, a detective, and finally a sergeant. Grandmother went to French Dominican Convent School."

"My mother is Spanish/Irish specializing in emergency medicine. My father, was a policeman and detective,"Eva snaps, "as I hear, were you. Your daddy was the old fart who wanted me as the older woman arrested for molesting you at Annapolis. I was listening. Such a poor little boy."

I say, "The old fart out for an arrest was Admiral Grandpa. You, I remember fondly."

Eva bristles. "You'd better. You stole my youth and forced me into the Navy."

Hard to like Eva. I forced Navy life on her. Really? Eva was very well on her way when we met."

Eva demands, "Why is the Ryan woman always with you?"

I answer, "She was the first woman to see me as a man, instead of a crippled mess."

Eva roars, "Was she? Well, she told me she got you high on dope and was bedding you. You should have called. I'd have gotten you help. And I wouldn't have done it with a bag of dope."

I ask, "Eva, how could I have called you? I was paralyzed. My throat was cut. My neck had a ventilator stuffed in it. Where would I call? Maybe, 1-800-GIRLS-WHO-R-NOT-SEALS.

Changing course before the storm, I ask, "Did you have time to decide on the favor I requested?"

Eva's face is a scorching scarlet. "Of course I did. I read your letter. Inquiries were made. A comparison was requested. Ick. Seminal material? They found a one hundred percent match to a deceased Marine enlisted man named Gaspar Lewindowski. He was dead before your crimes occurred."

She demands, "Who were those women? Your DNA on bedsheets in Baltimore at one girl's house. How did you get the policewoman pregnant?"

I raise an eyebrow, "If you stick around, Eva, I'll show you. If you get confused, ask Emma; she's very familiar with the process."

I add, "Gaspar Lewindowski's identical twin killed both women. The killer calls himself Casper River Mound/Lewindowski. Identical twins are identical. They come from a single egg which splits into two halves, identical DNA, fingerprints, blood type. The dead Marine was a serial killer in Iraq. Whether the flaw is nature, nurture, or it runs in families, Gaspar raped and murdered young Iraqi girls. One girl's brother was Gaspar's unit interpreter. The 'Terp tossed a white phosphorous grenade in Gaspar's sleeping bag. "

Eva nods, "Mostly he was fried crisp. In the remains there was serialized titanium hardware. PFC Lewindowski broke a leg in basic. The hardware's serial numbers matched."

I owe, I owe her. "Thank you, Eva. I'll keep you out of this. Emma's husband can acquire a court order for further comparison. Warn Blackmon's guy–the cops aren't after him."

Eva smiles. "Girl."

I rise, saying, "Silly me."

Eva is suddenly angry, "What am I, a fair-weather friend? You got what you wanted and you're off. Wham-bam-thank-you-ma'am? SIT. Explain your bizarre behavior with your dope-pusher girl. You need to shape up and fly right, mister, or I'm done with you."

I say loudly, "Eva, you were done with me years ago. You chose new companionship on your first 'summer-cruise'. I didn't hear from you again until you recognized me in Afghanistan."

I add for effect, "You are Eva Deveraux, Commander, United States Navy. I'm a bum. I live in a boat house. Sometimes I have a hard time walking across the room. You are United States Navy down to your blue four-inch heels. Nipping my insubordination got me killed."

Tears swell in Eva's eyes, she croaks, "Damn, Galvan, you aren't dead. I didn't get you killed. I need you. I want you here for me. Baby, I love you."

I'm a lot of things, but not a baby. "Eva, you are a highly regarded naval officer with proven skills, and great courage. I would disgrace you, or at the least try very hard. Navy house-cats fear your record as a war fighter. You've got clout, backstabbing is the order of the day.

"I'd ruin you, Eva. Especially, when you go back to your wandering ways. I tend toward monogamy, sailor. Can you see me hanging out in Annapolis raising your babies, while you're pursuing new interests and friends at your next posting? Tanner told me you were awarded a Navy Cross after I went belly up. You're a good fighter and a superb leader. So good, you talked me into getting myself killed. Go be an executive officer, command vessels. Finish the job. Be the next Admiral Deveraux. You'll be the one with beautiful legs all the way up to your lovely neck."

I smile sadly, "I'd ride you hard and put you away wet. I might even get you pregnant when I got the chance. When boys and girls have fun, someone gets a baby bump. It won't be me."

Greeted by silence, our squash soup arrives. Show-time. Center stage in the role of bumbling buffoon I become the drugged stupefied dolt. Taking a mouth full of hot soup, I dribble some down my chin, saying, "Commander Baby, you look SOOO hot in that dress. What do ya say we scurry upstairs and I snatch your fine ass out of that blue handkerchief. We'll make the beast with two backs. After a quickie, we'll order room service." Was that indelicate enough?

I quickly slide the case folder from in front of Eva and into my pocket as I rise, grabbing her arm. On the four-inch heels, Eva collides with the table as I drag her toward me. I drool more soup onto my shirt as the table flips. We both get splashed with soup. I mutter obscenities. I blot soup around on my shirt. Mumbling, I theatrically dip my soup-saturated napkin in a neighboring table's water glass. Disgusting is as disgusting does.

I take the now cloudy glass, dumping it on my chest to wash away the remaining soup. The cloudy mess is ghastly cold as it seeps down my pants. I holler, cursing the world in general and Eva in particular for the mess.

Summarily, we are asked to leave. Staggering out, I snatch napkins from occupied tables. I curse Eva as an untrustworthy tramp. As we enter the lobby, Eva stops short. I stagger into her trying to smear my goo on her dress.

Eva spins on her heel, smacking me across the face with her handbag. Owww, must have a pistol in that bag. Taking a new tack, I loudly beg her to forgive me, to listen to my pleas. Her eyes are flaming. Nothing. So, I stumble into her again. I then deliberately smear the soup goo around her breast. Noting her countdown to launch, I say in a weak voice, "Boss, I got to get my job back. I can't get off these oxy'. I'm high all the time. Help me ,would ya? Gimme my job back, I need the money. I'm broke for Chri-sake I'm begging, Boss."

Eva is volcanically beautiful. Eva roars over my clamorous storm of apology as only a naval commander can, "Mr. Galvan, you just ruined my dress. You are a waste of my time. In fact, you are a sick waste of space on an already crowded planet."

As I go limp, Eva grabs my shoulders, fiercely shaking me. "Snap out of it, Galvan. Act like a man, straighten up, fly right. We do not exist as a reason for your existence. You have few friends and don't deserve those you have. They definitely don't deserve you."

As icing on the cake, I slide my right hand to her left hip, then fiercely grab Eva's ass. She drives a ridge-hand against the right radial nerve between my wrist and hand. Even anticipating the move, it hurts. I step back shaking feeling into my hand. Distracted, I'm resoundingly slapped across the face.

I sit forcibly, ass to concrete, with a thud. Chagrined, Eva says, "I was crazy to have dinner with a jerk like you. You are a mean, spiteful, and manipulative bastard. I hope you got what you wanted. Debts owed. Debts paid. Now get this loud and clear, mister. You won't be joining us. We hired you to do work you're suited for. What work you could do, you can't now. For us you rated just above mule."

Eva sends me on my way with a kind word, "You are a drug addlepated ass. Get gone." She surges into the elevator, zooms to safety. I stand dangling my dripping napkin

I rate at mule level or below. That's a cruel thing to say about a mule. At the door to Aria I hand my sopping napkin to the horrified Maître'd.

As I exit, I approach the nervous chief attendant to recover my vehicle. As I request my keys, the man says, "Can we get you a cab, sir?" I wink at him, whispering, "I'm not drunk."

I display the second folded, engraved portrait of Ulysses S. Grant nested in my palm. I pat his jacket shoulder with my clean hand saying, "I think that went well. She'll never talk to me again. Did 'Oddgar the Cheap' see the show?"

The man relaxes, "Yes, I made sure he had a clear view. He is to the east near the fireplug. You were almost right. He presented me with a lovely portrait of Abe Lincoln, telling me to, 'keep the change'. A true gentleman that one, I did appear very grateful as you suggested."

I say, "Sorry for the disturbance. I want him away from her. Pretend to give me a hand to the car. Ask me loudly about the cab, again. That's a nice touch."

He assists me to my SRX, again offering taxi service, "Are you sure about the taxi, sir? We'll park your car overnight, no charge."

I straighten my coat's soup-stained lapels. I need to be careful, I'm out of suit coats. Women must be collecting suitcoats this season. I growl loudly, "She refused to re-hire me. After all I did for her. Women bosses?"

The hiker says, "A pleasure doing business, sir. Anything else?"

On reflection I say, "Tell security to keep 'Oddgar' out of the hotel. Please let her security team know that Galvan said he's the pigeon and the pigeon is pure trouble. From his reaction, he's not likely to come back. Better safe than sorry. though."

"Yes sir, I had security record and copy the interaction. Security will provide printouts to the Navy gentlemen accompanying her. Do come again, sir."

For show, I burn rubber, losing Casper and fast. Good tail, horse-shit pursuit. Figures.

I last saw Casper chugalugging. I wonder if the Greek put cigarette filters in Casper's tank. It seemed starved for fuel. I'm just out to kill the guy, the Greek is really mean."

Returning to the boatyard, I review Eva's note. Not a note, rather a laser printed document in Times New Roman-12, the most common print type. The DNA is a match, Gaspar was Casper's identical twin. An addendum notes Gaspar's leg hardware serial numbers match the ones the Navy installed. There are no source identifiers on the printouts.

I scan the pages, sending copies where they need to go with a cover note explaining the Who, What, Where, When and Why. Then I shred Eva's printouts to eliminate any chance of recoverable prints or DNA from the paper. Theoretically, Eva is out.

I check for voice mails and texts. There's a cryptic text from Nadia, timed 5:00 PM Friday:

"Two prints of R-index found at MBB scene in 'C'. One print matches a print in 'B' at CAM scene. Several little-finger prints and others from 'B' match those of CRM-L. Agt. G says suspect CRM-L tore gloves on zipper playing with plums. Quaint. 'G' wants to visit again for lunch after the Holiday, your treat.

All prints not yours or of the deceased ladies in 'C' and 'B' match CRM-L on print card from Home Office file. Evidence request(s) forwarded DC. Traveling there today. SORRY. Talk? Please. Yours, N."

In short, George thinks Casper tore his gloves while fondling himself at the Baltimore murder scene, and in Chicago as well. Casper left two R-Index fingerprints at the Chicago scene. Apparently, other prints at both crime scenes connect Casper to the crimes.

Tears swell. Why? Sad, I realize I knew Calah on intimate terms for a period of years. I guess we were just visiting, we were close but not as close as I thought. I slept once with Mary Beth, but knew her and worked closely with her. It bothers me they are reduced to shorthand. It saddens me to discover I've been held at arm's length. I missed things simple and things enormous. Calah had a middle-name. Anne? Alana? Don't know, never will.

For years Mary Beth was by nature indisposed to me having a place in her life. In the end, I had sufficient presence to get her killed. We made a baby. The contact got her killed. Maybe if I had asked, they would've answered questions small and large. When I could I didn't ask. I won't get another chance in this life. Life passes and is gone, not to return.

I'm gonna reduce Casper to a cipher. In binary terms, light on, light off. One goes zero. The doing will be the trick. Going out, I call Gennaro's cell. He says he's off through the weekend, home with his beloved rubbing her sore feet. He tells me to come over, they're watching the end of *"The Thin Man"* with William Powell and Myrna Loy.

I forward the file as it is to his work email as an attachment. He won't get it until Tuesday. Fancy that, Gennaro on honeymoon. The bureaucracy halts.

After the wedding, they moved into a home owned by a Wainwright Family Trust near the University of Chicago. Emma's father said the newlyweds need to save on rent.

Rumor has it the Wainwrights own several small states out on the East Coast. Maybe the Wainwrights bought the property from the Native People before there was a university.

Emma meets me at the front door; I inform her she is looking lovely. In Chicago, allowing one to enter by the front door without a pat-down is a sign of high regard. Emma snarls a little; I guess crabbiness is permissible. Mrs. Gennaro slouches back to the couch. Ever-elegant Emma is wearing baggy basketball shorts and Gennaro's old Bears jersey. She informs me she feels fat. Em is every inch the summer-pregnant, hungry, mother-to-be. She then insists she is not lovely in any way. Throwing her slippers at me, she hollers, "Stop it, Galvan. You are a phony, lying weasel."

I offer vodka, amaretto, clementine (s), orange and cranberry juice to the happy groom. To Grumpy, the bride, I offer a bouquet of flowers camouflaging my large white confectionary store bag which conceals a large strawberry milk-shake, concocted with fresh strawberries. Into the thick shake are speared large vanilla wafers.

One would think an erstwhile Chicago Bear turned homicide detective would be too embarrassed to drink Cranberry Kisses as his drink of choice.

Emma says, "You can stay."

I take the wins I can get.

In Afghanistan the lot of us talked of favorite things, especially food. Emma told me she had a secret boyfriend back home. On their first date, he took Em', to his friend's pastry shop. That date was her favorite memory when we were in the mountains.

At the wedding it all clicked. The pastry shop made their wedding cake. I stopped last at the pastry shop on my way over.

Emma tells me to put the flowers in a vase. As I fill the vase with water, Gennaro mixes his vulgar Cranberry Kiss.

Emma fixes me with a suspicious azure glare, sullenly slurping the strawberry shake. She remains perched on the couch. Her feet resting on the coffee table ensconced in fuzzy socks. Pregnant women allegedly suffer permanently cold feet.

Emma is annoyed with the outsider in her nest. Wants to know why, says, "Well?"

I bide my time.

Emma harshly whispers, "Galvan, you treated Eva like shit tonight. So, why do you think you're welcome in my house after mistreating my best friend?"

I shrug, "I brought a strawberry milk-shake?"

I receive a baleful glare, followed by a quick straw slurp. Gennaro sits on the edge of the couch to rub his wife's swollen feet, saying, "If you kick him out, dearest, he's gonna take his strawberry shake and his cookies with him."

Emma frowns, glancing sidelong at Gennaro, "Like hell he is. Explain, Trouble."

I shrug, "Eva and I ran our course. There isn't an us in it anymore. When you told her I was alive, you told me she was already meeting her Marine colonel to receive his proposal. Eva's just visiting, Emma. Do you think I would help her by putting her in the mommy way? Just think--you'd have someone equally as miserable to slurp shakes with."

Emma announces, "Maybe chocolate malts, Eva doesn't like straw-berries. Why don't you just be nice while she's in town. Be careful, be nice. Bang her brains out. Both of you would benefit. Just maintain, Trouble. Yank off that blue bikini and bounce her around your sailboat. When she's tired and happy send her home to that stuffed shirt fiancé. You are a guy, Galvan. Eva likes your company. Enjoy the side benefits of friendship."

Displeased I say, "Em', I'm in the middle of a shit-storm. I am not suited to hanging around naval bases attending teas as a Navy wife. She booted me long ago. Ask Eva about the events leading up to that."

"She told me when you showed up in Afghanistan."

"Showed up? I was in the back of your land rover. Eva recognized me two years later."

Gennaro comments, "I can't see my former partner hanging about with all those young Navy wives. With Eva gone, in spring there'll be the plague of Galvans looking sternly around Annapolis."

Gennaro gets kicked. Better him than me.

I say, "I'm here for help, Gennaro. I have a problem."

Emma snarls, "What a surprise. You are a problem, Trouble."

I say, "Casper Lewindowski killed Mary Beth. Casper Lewindowski River-Mud killed my girl Mary Beth and that pretty little secret service agent with the tiny ass and long black hair. Why?"

Emma says, "Mr. Gennaro, if you start talking about pretty tiny white women's bottoms you'll be sleeping on this couch." Emma con-tinues, "Give, Trouble. What did you find out?"

I extract the documents, fanning them across the coffee table. They both read the documents. Silence.

When done, Gennaro looks up, "You got him, Galvan. You have preliminary evidence, ballistics, DNA comparisons and manner, mo-tive, and opportunity on my coffee table. Obsession mutating to psychosis."

He argues, "As a devoted sociopath he put his faith in the rules of the police department. When he didn't succeed in misusing those rules to get his desired outcome, he moved to the FBI. While there, full-on Psychosis got him. He stole evidence to further that obsession. He attacked Calah with the items he took out of the evidence locker. He pursued you back to Chicago. He eventually murdered Mary Beth here. Then you disappeared. Having lost access to the object of his obsession, he brooded, fearing he'd be caught."

Gennaro frowns. "Casper's fear of getting caught kept him close to the case. psychotic obsession led him to attempt to force Brenda to indict you 'in absentia' for Mary Beth's Murder When he couldn't Get Bren' to play by his crazy rules, He went to your girl at the FBI for a UFAP. Absolutely fuckin' nuts."

Emma looks over half-glasses at me, "That and he's in love."

Gennaro asks, "With who?"

Emma smiles, "It's with whom, dear. This Casper person is in love with at least the idea of Galvan the cop if not with Trouble himself. He attacks Trouble because he wants his attention. This man most of all wants Galvan to fear him. He is a sick, sick puppy."

Emma studies my reaction, "What I said didn't even make you blink, Trouble. Did it?"

Gennaro swings his gaze intently at me. "It'll take me the weekend to organize the paper for warrants. Monday I can request subpoenas for records. Is Monday enough time?"

I answer, "Sounds good. I'm planning to visit Brenda's with this packet tonight. Yours is attached to an email I sent to you at area central."

Gennaro shakes his head negatively, "Do it tomorrow night. They brought in a murder jury. She and Amelia are celebrating. They'll be pub-crawling in places you aren't welcome."

Emma says reflectively, "Dear, you said that wrong. You would have been better off saying, 'The soonest we can indict Casper will be Monday.' Don't you recall the conversation that way?"

Gennaro frowns at Emma, looks back at me. "Yes, dear, I do believe I remember the conversation that way."

Holding Gennaro's gaze I say, "I'll make arrangements in the morning. Maybe I'll take them a Palermo's Pizza; it's excellent hangover food. I'll let them know we spoke tonight. I'll say they'll hear from you early in the new week."

Gennaro putters with the file. I get up, rinse my glass in the sink, set it to dry.

Emma smiles slyly, because she knows, "Do be careful, Trouble. This Casper person is after you. If Eva were around, he'd be after her. But he won't be after Eva if she's not around, you vile, duplicitous bastard."

I say, "Goodnight, Emma. Eva is a big girl. I warned the Twins. Hotel security made a film of Casper. He saw my job application. Eva rejected me. I begged, alas I was rejected."

Emma snaps out of her slouch to yell after me, her strawberry shake aimed at my head, "Life isn't a Victorian novel, Galvan. Eva loves you, you bastard."

I say, "I know."

Gennaro says, "Let it go, baby."

Emma growls. Gennaro tries again, "Galvan's jumping into a puddle. Mud will splash. Friends shouldn't be so close as to be covered with muck. Your friend Eva's life is Navy. For her there is first duty then country, then Navy. Love and family follow behind. That's how she stays sane."

Emma's face softens.

Gennaro concludes, "Eva's on furlough. She and Galvan have had a thing forever. In the end the Navy will call and she'll fly. That's how she is. Galvan's a man, not a vacation plaything. Reality is happening, let her go home mad. He ain't got time to play."

Gennaro asks, "Coming for the grand jury on Monday, Galvan?"

Looking Gennaro in the eye, I say, "Tuesday. No grand jury on the holiday. If they need me, they'll call."

Gennaro nods. "My mistake. Take care, man. Enjoy your weekend. Tuesday the wheels of Justice roll, be available. Need anything, we're here. With Mary Beth gone, I'm out of partners."

Emma snaps, "BULLSHIT, Galvan."

Gennaro placates, "Honey."

Emma says sharply, "Don't honey me. He and I killed people together. Let the law run its course, Trouble. I'm a pregnant, my constitution is very delicate. You been dead. Don't do it again this weekend. I'm running out of my supply of vengeful, crazy bastards."

I quickly close the door. Emma's empty shake smacks the door. Who would think she cared? Nobody gets out clean. If your luck holds, you get out as you are.

25

SATURDAY NIGHT PIZZA

"**Jeremiah Johnson**"
(Director: Sydney Pollack, Warner Brothers, 1972.)

(Scene: Hunting elk in the Rocky Mountains)
"Jeremiah: Wind's right, but he'll just run soon as we step out of these trees.
Bear Claw: Trick to it. Walk out on this side of your horse.
Jeremiah: What if he sees our feet?
Bear Claw: Elk don't know how many feet a horse has!"

Elk see that which is before them. Human beings see what is before as well. The sight is then subjected to rationalization. Does the viewer suffer from paranoia? Is that paranoia valid? Does that paranoia distort the view? Or is that view studied for important insight. This horse has too many legs. Run. Given the option human beings view things they see in the light which best supports strongly held conviction. In worst cases, the viewer will see what he most needs to see. That is a lake glistening out on the desert not a mirage. Wish upon a star. Ignore the god damned extra feet.

I got up Friday to work the speed bag in high humidity during the grey light of dawn. Bad guys like to attack in the grey light of dawn; it's a tradition. I like to attack in the grey light of damn. Does that make me a bad guy or wise beyond my years? Or, just a wise ass?

Forms are indistinct in that light. The world is shifting grey. It lacks color and depth. Low light requires you to trick your brain. Your eyes' receptors contain both rods and cones. Rods are sensitive in poor light.

Rods make the brain allow indirect sweeping input, which forces the brain to sort in black and white. Brains like cones. Easy-peasy, Cones require less brain effort, seeing the world in the depth of living color. Brains like easy.

Training with the speed bag in semi-darkness wakes speed and hidden capability. As in lock-picking it requires the gentle touch. Don't stare, just see.

Fog is a cloud on the ground. Once we stopped on the side of a mountain in the Kush. We positioned among sun warmed rocks in a wide spot on the trail as darkness settled in. As dawn broke, the fog slowly evaporated as the sun rose in the sky. At a slightly lower elevation, a sizeable group of men wearing the Pakol Pakul hats popular with the Taliban and al Qaeda emerged from the night's fog. Maybe they were from the Afghan branch of the Audubon Society. Few bird watchers gone a-birding arm with machineguns and rocket launchers, unless they're in Chicago. Some of them weren't Taliban clothed in earth tones. The latter bunch were amateurs on a jihad sabbatical.

They stood out like sore thumbs in brightly colored track suits. Poor little rich boys. I acted quickly because the world isn't fair. I popped the last downhill bird in the line, before their eyes adjusted. I worked from back to front. My gunshots echoed strangely off rock and fog walls. The would-be ambushers got ambushed. Turning as a man to fire downhill.

Joe woke to a spray of hot brass sliding down his collar. Black and Tan appeared to lay down aimed fire. SEALs are good like that. The cacophony was deafening. Silence followed. The tour group tumbled from the trail, leaving a few hats and tidbits of equipment.

I yelled, "Cease-fire. Reload." Obviously, I had been there too long by that time. Eva swept in from the trailhead. Her rifle was positioned along the trail to our support. She focused on my voice to guide her in. That day I received my first strange looks.

Since that ambush, Joe hasn't faulted me for early morning speed bag drills in the grey light of dawn. In passing he merely suggests I need more focus. My drill runs an hour. In the end I need to lift my arms above my head onto the rebound platform plate to stretch tight muscle. In stretching, I see a woman dart past in dying fog along the river walk. She doesn't look up, her dark wet pony tail sways in her wake. Gone.

Jill? Or just a tall slender brunette with a pony tail? That was it--here then gone. I have set the table. Now, I'm afraid to attend my own party? I may not succeed in settling this mess, Win or lose, it is getting done. From the balcony, I look down at water surging from the spring. An icy thermocline is visible. The water crinkles. For the first time I see a rocky port on the bottom. An eye looking back at me in malice?

A white gull lands at shoreline distracting my thoughts. It clutches a clam in its beak. The bird looks about, then smacks the clam shell against a rocky pile. The clam rebounds, audibly cracking. The shellfish splashes into the shallows. The gull lunges to snatch it back. The gull smacks the shell against the rubble again. The shell shatters. The meat half rebounds into deeper water. Shell and meat plunge, spiraling to the bottom. The bird manages to spear the whitish meat against the sandy bottom. The exertion makes lunch even more savory.

In that second, the under-tow snatches the gull into the depths of the spring.

The gull is sucked beak-first into the deep. The carcass is battered along the rocky bottom, only to surge limply to the surface of the icy torrent. A moment later it is sucked to the bottom, skimming the rough bottom outward to the murky brown vail of the Chicago River. Such is life.The gull is gone. The clam meat is gone. The shell alone remains, pink half-shell open.

Time to go. After I clean up, I drive to my parent's home. If one leaves a trail of crumbs, one hopes someone follows. I visit with Deuce, waiting for my mother's return from rounds. I explain my trip to Palermo's. Deuce goes to get his thermal pizza carrier. He has a lot of weird stuff. I sip coffee.

While Deuce searches, Mom arrives and asks how Jill is doing. My evasion shows. Doctors are detectives in their own way, Mom retorts, "That's a lot of pizza for you two."

So, I confess, "We broke up."

She asks rhetorically, "You bring one girl home in ten years, and then dump her?"

I attempt to explain, "Jill has reason to be unhappy with me. The wedding was a disaster. Eva Deveraux was there. Jill left mad. Then she found me with a drunk FBI agent."

She asks, "Jill's mad because she saw you with some drunk FBI guy?"

To close the inquiry, I say, "The agent isn't a guy. Jill's dating some lawyer now."

Deuce says from behind me, "C'mon. There's more. What happened?"

Changing the subject, I say, "I met Eva Deveraux for dinner, she blew her stack."

Deuce says, "The Devereauxs are always blowing their stacks about something."

Women pay attention to details. She asks, "Why?"

"I needed her help on Mary Beth Burke's murder case."

Mom says, "Go on, there's more."

"Jill took me in for a back procedure. Afterward I was stoned. I called Eva on Jill's cell. She got in a fight with Jill. Jill and I had a fight. She came over with lunch; Nadia and her partner were at my place. There were issues, I got smacked in the head with a breaded steak sandwich."

My mother laughs. "I assume Nadia is the FBI Agent."

I say, "Yes."

Deuce asks, "There's more?"

"Nadia was all wet and wearing my T-shirt and shorts.

Deuce says, "Go on."

"No. too complicated to explain. I have everyone working on the murders."

"What murders?" they ask jointly.

"I discovered who killed Mary Beth Burke. The man also killed a secret service agent named Calah Morgenthau that I dated. I had relationships with both women. I'm linked to both."

Deuce asks, "DNA?"

I nod, "A second male is also linked by DNA to both the crime scenes as well.

I needed a difficult-to-get DNA cross-comparison to a Marine who died in Iraq. Eva helped. She proved the killer had an identical twin who had been a Marine in Iraq.

Deuce asks, "Any weakness in your theory?"

My mother asks, "Who killed Mary Beth? Why?"

I ask Deuce, "Do you remember the Letter Writer?"

"Casper Lewindowski,"

"He killed both women because they were close to me."

Mom asks, "How close?"

I say, "Ma."

She gives a stern look, "How close?"

Deuce says, "Tell her. She's not going to give up, son."

"I broke up with Calah. We had sex when I stayed with her in Baltimore. She was killed the week after I left."

Mom smells blood. "Mary Beth?"

I shrug, "The night before I left for Afghanistan, she invited me to stay with her. When she was murdered, Mary Beth was pregnant with my child."

Deuce smiles, "Finally."

Mom asks Deuce, "How on earth? Her mother told me about her change in orientation. At the wake her mother was heartbroken. The medical examiner told them about the pregnancy. She didn't know the father. The baby was their first grandchild."

Deuce shrugs, raises an eyebrow, speaking volumes without words. I continue, "We were together the one night before I left."

SMACK.

My mother cracks me to the side of my head with a full, open hand slap. She hasn't hit me since I peed in her flower pots at six. Our Labrador and I were bored.

Some men haven't hit me that hard. Mom is mad, "It only takes once, my bone-headed son. I liked Mary Beth. I've always liked Mary Beth. She followed you around like a puppy, until you blew her off over that red-headed tramp from Annapolis. Mary Beth suited you then. Jill does now. Deuce, our bone-headed obtuse son is saying this character killed our grandchild. Talk."

Deuce says, "I know him, Nicole."

I rise, pick-up the thermal pizza-bag and move for the door.

My father calls me back, "Get back here, Curtis Lemay; you just dropped a stack of bombs."

I say, "Deuce, I'm going to get you a file copy from my car."

Mom asks, "Will you be back directly, or can we expect you in four or five years?"

Families have issues, but I deserve the jibe.

On return, I set my file in front of Deuce. I explain the contents of my folder.

They skim the file in silence.

I pick up the pizza carrier to leave. They spoke while I was gone. They hold hands, the air around them electric. This might not have been a good idea. They need to know in the event I screw-up.

I say, "I have to go. I ordered the pizza. I'm taking it to Brenda's."

Shocked, Mom says, "Mary Beth's roommate?"

"Yeah. I'm asking her to handle the case locally."

I shrug at the door, "Based on the file, I'm going to ask Brenda to approve a murder warrant for Casper. Gennaro has the case. He says he'll take the case to the grand jury early next week. The FBI agent, Nadia Dimitrieva, has connected ballistics and prints to Casper. Jill guided me on the DNA of identical twins."

I ask, "Mom, I'd like to keep Jill out of this. Would you be willing to act as a prover on the identical twin issue? It's in the notes. The autopsy photos of Mary Beth and Calah are in a sealed envelope in case Dad needs them. You may not hear from any of them. You know everyone else. Nadia is a tall, very pretty brunette with short boy-cut hair."

Deuce shakes his head. "Her too?"

I shrug, "No. Almost. Maybe. I don't know. Issues."

I point to the file on the table. "There's a lot of stuff you may not want to see in there. I just wanted to make sure you had a copy. A copy needs to be around in case you need it."

My father asks, "How long you got?"

"Tuesday."

Deuce asks, "Stalking Horse?"

I nod.

"Be careful."

"Always."

My mother's eyes well-up as I close the door. I've hurt everyone near me, genius at work.

I'm guessing Casper's mind is decompensating swiftly. If theory holds, Casper will only get worse. It is time to get it done. This fool is coming, might as well meet him halfway. Act or be acted on. KISS, keep it simple stupid. Find the source, end it. My plan looks as strong as steel. Then, my trip to Afghanistan seemed a swell idea--at the time.

I drive to Palermo's on Cicero, arriving early to beg. We chat about my travels in the Kush. We discuss my uncles and their pizza driving days. I tell the crew I'm making a proposal. We conclude I need an inside-pizza for such a special evening. The evening crew gives me an 'inside' extra-large deep-dish cheese pizza. The 'inside' pizza is a trade secret. Sweeter, cheesier and thicker, as closely guarded as the Grail. I am told in parting, "Be sure you tell your little lady where you got it and how easy it was to get." That makes me feel guilty.

I smile on my way to the car. Bren' might consider being my lady revolting. I weave through traffic heading toward Brenda's. Casper is tailing me. Spotting a tail can be as simple as a series of right turns around a ball field. His decompensation is greater tonight. He sits posted behind me at a fixed interval, running rough. He doesn't see or doesn't care I circled that park. I turn into the parking area behind their home where I park near the rear of Brenda's. Her townhouse is two stories. It has a balcony facing the creek. As I approach, I see a so-lar powered light and hear a fountain gurgling. The light and fountain sit on a small grotto patio with railing. The solar battery is fading. In dim reflection Casper parks along the creek.

I stroll the walkway with my file on top of the thermal bag. The glass door has no brace. I knock at Brenda's front door. In the back-ground the creek makes an audible burbling tug-boat sound. A car re-flects off the trees as Casper shuts down the cross-over. Good getaway car. The creek isn't truly a creek; maybe it once was. Today it is a shal-low flood reduction canal. Kids once had an AMC bike track back there under the trees.

Brenda opens the door, at present I'm in good graces. Thus, I re-ceive a one-armed hug. Brenda is a girl under the cut-off sweat-shirt and old sweat-pants. Amelia appears behind Bren', wearing extremely short, frayed cut offs and a Northwestern University t-shirt. I follow the couple to the second-floor kitchen. I glimpse lime-green lace and deep tan through Amelia's frayed shorts. Strange, Amelia looks over her shoulder at me as we climb to see if I'm looking. Why is she teas-ing? Probably tempting the straight with a glimpse of forbidden fruit, ever out of reach. Amelia likes to play.

I feel awkward. I don't know Amelia. What I know, I don't like. Above us Brenda laughs enjoying my discomfort, asking, "Scared of girls, tough guy?"

I smile as my hosts share an inside joke. Amelia's eyes glitter. I fol-low them up to the well-lit kitchen. The kitchen is pristine. Nobody cooks anymore.

Brenda catches a whiff, "Is that an inside-pizza?"

"I groveled."

Brenda says jauntily, "Do you have inferior motives regarding our virtue? Two beautiful, but unattainable women are dining with you. Alas we aren't susceptible to male charms."

As guest, I play along with a sad shrug. Amelia winks my way. Dust in her eye?

I add quickly, "Manly charm? Not much. Inside pizza I got."

Bren' is happy. "Let's eat while it's hot."

I set the thermal bag on the breakfast island and am directed to the dining room table. While we eat, I'll explain my presence, suggesting they throw me out when I get boring.

I begin, "I'm now more sure who killed Mary Beth and Calah Morgenthau."

I then retell my much-told story, explaining the murder cases from the perspective of my findings about Casper. It's in overview, we're eating. The receipt sits on the island, deductible. Amelia has set place-mats before each of us. Brenda's plates bear a French Bistro motif. Or they could be tattoo parlor ads; my French is poor.

Palermo's deep-dish pizza has thick crust, sweet sauce. The thick sauce and cheese topping are hot. The warmer bag worked. We eat quickly to sate appetites. And kill hangovers.

I tell them, "We had a character hiding in the bushes outside our place near the park swings. He hides in some tumbleweeds along the river. Earlier, I couldn't get a good look at him. For the kids' sake, Joe took a picture of him with an infra-red camera. I recognized him."

Brenda asks, "Who him?"

I say between bites, "Casper, him."

"Over time we put things together. When he came on the job I worked for about a minute with Casper. Later, I met his family when working with Mary Beth and Gennaro. Casper's Mom was alive then. She told me Casper and her son Gaspar were identical twins. A policewoman told me the Lewindowski twins molested a young girl who became a police-woman. The officer told me the pair were sadistic little perverts."

Brenda snaps, "That makes Casper a serial killer?"

Amelia smiles with delight, bouncing her gaze between us. Tennis match?

Amelia asks, "Gennaro—is that the gorgeous Black guy who thinks he's Italian. Great big shoulders, wasn't he a White Sox, Bren'? He just married the pretty blond secret service girl. Do you think she knows he's not Italian?"

Annoyed, I respond carefully, "Gennaro was adopted as an orphan by the Gennaro family. They couldn't have kids. Mr. Gennaro liked his spunk. They adopted him as their own. Vito spoke Italian before he spoke English. He sees himself as Italian. The Gennaros were the only family he knew. For Gennaro, it's not melatonin level, it's family."

Bren' interjects, "Nature over nurture, Galvan. That is immutable."

Not out for a fight, I shrug, "You may be right, Bren'. Although, it might be argued Gennaro chose his identity without a no for societal stereotyping. Thus, sees himself an Italian."

Amelia claps her hands, laughing, "Galvan turned your argument back. I like him."

I say, "When Mary Beth, Gennaro, and I were on tac' Casper wrote nasty letters about us to anyone who'd listen. He wanted us off tactical and replaced by him and his buddies. I made detective. He kept writing. Only by that time his letters obsessively focused on me. When the secrets offered the Greek and me a contract in Afghanistan it heated up Casper's pressure cooker. Gennaro's wife told me Calah Morgenthau had a sexual harassment complaint in Baltimore that included allegations of him stalking her."

Casper had changed his name to Casper River Mound, become a sergeant and left the job for a bureau spot out in Baltimore. As a newly minted FBI Field Agent in the Baltimore Field Office, Casper got fired for cause by abandoning his duties and returning here not long after I did.

I explain, "Casper may have been transporting the knife and gun which eventually became the murder weapons to court when I was seen by him with Calah. Neither he nor the evidence including the gun made it to court. I'm betting Casper seeing me with Calah drove him over the edge."

I look at Brenda. "I came here for court on the dope torture murders from the westside. Mary Beth was in court. By now both of you are aware I got her pregnant that evening before I left town. Casper got back here later. He stalked Mary Beth, maybe discovering she was pregnant and by whom. He was already a murderer and I was gone. There's no knowing the mind of a madman. Eventually he killed her. The ballistic evidence from the murder scenes is being compared to the prior FBI Lab ballistics tests by Agent Dimitrieva. Nadia told me there were two active investigations of Casper under investigation including the missing inventories when he got fired for insubordination. The other two cases were terminated. I think Nadia's investigating the loose ends in DC this weekend."

I conclude, "It's all in the file. In short, Casper's prints were found at both scenes with a myriad of other lab links."

Bright eyed, Amelia asks, "Did you investigate the Dread Pirate Roberts when you were on the Silk Road website?"

"'Melie, Different Silk Road," says Brenda, "Galvan wasn't on a website case; he was on the actual Silk Road in the Himalayas."

I explain, "The Silk Road I was on is a caravan route through Hindu Kush. It runs west to Italy, north to Scandinavia, northwest to Russia. Along the road, opium processes into heroin."

To keep their interest I add, "Anyway, I think something snapped in Casper's head. Who knows what did it exactly? Maybe my visit to Calah. Maybe the rubber band on his squirrel cage broke. Knowing why will not change the situation or prevent the next. They pop, they kill. When I saw Casper at your office, I realized he'd tipped his apple cart. Seeing me hugging you knocked an already odd bird completely off his perch. He's extremely dangerous."

I become annoyed. "Don't laugh, Brenda. I'm warning you. He attacks women who he thinks have a sexual relationship. My proximity to women inflames Casper. "

Both are laughing, Amelia shoves Brenda to me, "Give her the big bamboo, Galvan."

Brenda theatrically flinches away as she falls toward me. I manage to stop her forward plunge.

I give up, what happens, happens, "Be careful, Bren', we're dealing with a madman. Gennaro says he'll come to your office Tuesday to indict him. He'll have the paper done then."

"You may hear from Agent Dimitrieva when she gets back."

Brenda smirks, "Would that be Nadia? I thought we have a thing?"

Amelia frowns.

Brenda's turn to be annoyed, "How did you get this information? You're not the police. You're a nobody. You are an itinerant chauvinist boat bum. You did it in a few weeks. WTF."

I say, "Everyone else couldn't see the forest for the trees. You were all too close for too long. I came back with the answers locked in the cobwebs of my head. I'm just coming back to the world, Bren'. I have been gone a long time. He found me. I didn't find him. Casper hates the ground you walk on because you two are lesbian. You gave him a verbal dressing down in front of me. He'll want to get even. Watch yourself. Look after Amelia. This boy is losing it."

I say, "His dogs don't bark at the same time, ladies. He's unpredictable, quick as a snake. He needs to act before he disintegrates. His family is all dead. He hides in the bushes watching the world go by. He can't focus well. Fixating on hurting me keeps what's left together."

Brenda snaps in annoyance, "Oh, Galvan, this is the real world. I get what you're saying, but please. I can handle mister smelly pants."

She states firmly, "Galvan, understand this: Casper will be tough to prosecute. He has the cleanest of resumes. He's spent his life in the highest of callings, hunting corrupt cops. He's been in the corrupt practices unit, a sergeant in IAD, and investigated official misconduct in Baltimore."

Her tone shifts, "Mr. River Mount insists he was fired in a dispute with bureau administrators over his fervor to see justice done in a political case. He can't be specific because of the sensitivity of the case. The bureau says nothing. Do they ever?"

I try, "Casper is a pooch. He never could cut it in law-enforcement. He's afraid of the bad guys. He preys on good guys. Good guys won't hurt him. He's all poseur, not a crimefighter."

"Stop right there, Mister. You are a washed-up, self-satisfied, overbearing, heterosexual, egotist, 'know-it-all' prick," Brenda growls.

Amelia posts herself behind Brenda, smiling and nodding. This is getting scary.

"Bren', you are defending a guy who ordered you to indict me for the murder of Mary Beth while calling you a dyke. But I'm a chauvinist."

I nod to the file, "Casper murdered Mary Beth, Calah, and others. You've been calling me a prick since you realized I'm not dead. Are your words symbolic of your own antipathy?"

We stare intently at each other. "Bren' darlin', Casper eats shit, barks at the moon and hates the baby Jesus."

Brenda sags, tired, relents, "How did you find all this stuff? Why is the knife unique?"

I extract a printout to show Brenda, "They were only made in the mid-1980s and it was designed to spur sales. It had design and durability issues. They are almost nonexistent, today."

Brenda says, "I know this knife. My boyfriend's uncle had one in a glass case on the wall. He claimed he was a SEAL. He claimed he wasn't a pervert. He claimed a lot of things."

Amelia's eyes grow the size of golf balls, "You had a boyfriend?"

"Yes, 'Melie, I've had boyfriends."

Amelia breaks in, "Bren', this isn't what or who Galvan may be. It's about what happened to Mary Beth. We're looking at a strong prosecution case. It is perfect to our long-term plans. Read the file, I'll put Galvan on the deck to cool his jets."

Amelia says, "If the file supports the charge, we'll get a warrant. Solving the murders of a pregnant policewoman and a secret service agent is exactly what we need. Cop murders draw publicity like flies. We'll sweep the local news market just before the elections, sky's the limit. If not, we got a free pizza, and a good story."

Amelia grabs my bicep, "C'mon, James Bond, Bren' will decide your fate."

On the small balcony, I lean out, looking at nothing in particular. Peripherally I spot Casper in the bushes. His shiny glasses wiggle intensely; he's having loads of fun.

Amelia pushes me onto a chaise lounge, saying, "Sit."

I sit. Maybe I can get a job pretending to be a golden retriever.

Amelia leaves, returning momentarily with a Guinness draught, "Drink. You're beet red."

I drink. Amelia leans her back on the railing. I rest my Guinness on my belt buckle.

With a quick hip-snap Amelia launches from the railing to straddle my waist. Somehow, Amelia snatched my beer from my hand inflight setting it onto a side table. Amelia gently lowers her warm, tiny bottom as she settles about my hips. The things one endures solving crimes. Amelia braces her hands on my shoulders as she does a quick pelvic grind. Her face descends over mine to deliver a wicked kiss, parting my lips with a flick of her tongue.

I fear Amelia isn't as committed to a monogamy as Brenda might think. Amelia brushes her lips to my ear, "I'm the 'B' in LGBT."

Surprised at myself, I find myself cradling one of Amelia's small breasts in my palm.

There is the sound of flip-flops being donned in the kitchen.

Amelia bounds up and away. I really like that hip flick. She lands with perfect balance to lean, gazing vacantly outward.

Amelia has garnered my attention. I see lime green lace visible through her frayed cut-offs. I've been seduced by a pixie. I didn't expect that from her, nor my reaction to her.

This may not be Amelia's first foray into the deep pool of infidelity. I lean back into my chaise, closing my eyes. Brenda halts beside me. I await doom.

Brenda says, "This doesn't look good."

Expecting to be struck with a blunt object I say, "Why doesn't it?"

Bren' is gesturing at my face with the file, as opposed to my pants.

I was about to consider singing, 'Gimme one step, lady. Just one step toward the door.'

Oblivious, Brenda proceeds, "Actually you really may something here, Galvan."

Amelia bobs her head affirmatively in the background.

Brenda continues, "We may be able to work with you. There's a lot yet to be done. You're infamous for rough product, Galvan. We'll try to work something up."

Amelia again nods affirmatively, delicately brushing a fingertip across her breast.

Brenda continues her analysis, "Assuming Gennaro is up to it. They can't do paperwork. "

Brenda must suspect Italian literacy. Have I missed something? One would think Caesar's commentaries, and the Aeneid sufficient to argue against her argument. Quick, call Joe Colombo and the League. It ain't right.

"Melie, get Galvan up to speed while I reread this."

Amelia watches from her railing. Brenda returns to the kitchen table, donning bifocal half-glasses to review the file. Bren' sits with an audible thump in her chair with her back to us.

Amelia trails Brenda, handing me my mug. It sloshes on my lap. Amelia returns with a dish towel to grab the front of my pants tightly, whispering, "You're not a saint. Got to be dead to be a saint. You aren't even close." Her tone has a husky timbre, "Your monastery on the river is done. We're gonna play."

More beer on my lap and splashed on the floor than remains in my glass.

Amelia studies me, cradling her left breast now in the palm of her right hand. She rolls her thumb and index finger over her nipple. She nods, "Yeah, you're ready."

Amelia returns to the kitchen with her towel.

I lean back into the chaise lounge. My face is the picture of delight, as I study the bushes along the creek. Nature is at peace, except for that one bush which apparently contains a wombat vigorously thrashing in ecstasy. Then it could be Casper, doing whatever moves him.

Amelia returns without her towel. Enough silliness. I stand, as melia walks past. Surprised, she turns back to me. I pivot Amelia by her shoulders to initiate my own theatrics. I lift her hair from the nape of her neck to provide my own kiss, as I guide her back against me.

How graphic. If Casper was having fun a moment ago, he's having a picnic now.

Amelia is surprised by the heat of the fire she sparked, up here on the balcony but also down in the bushes. Casper will be coming. She primed his pump.

26

THIS AIN'T A GAME

Quite a while later, Brenda is still addressing the difficulty of this murder case for her. Amelia is for getting up to speed fast enough to time it as part of their election moves.

Brenda remains fidgety, scandalized by the elbow grease she'll have to apply to save the case from my slip-shod work in order to salvage it. Brenda argues neither the right nor wrong but the hard.

I rummage through cooling pizza for something to do. There's more talk of which local TV anchor might want an exclusive most. Choices narrow on which print reports will best serve her needs. Brenda wants me to guarantee it will be like shooting fish in a barrel. Lawyers trouble me who are at work in service of ambition, with justice as a far second in their considerations.

Before I depart, it's time to thank them and go. They've made this easy. As I rise, Amelia is suggesting, "It's simple, we can play up her and the baby. We don't request the infanticide charge, that's primordial. Let the grand jury do itself. That might make enemies; the girl in Baltimore will add another life sentence. Who cares he has only one life? Forget your relationship with Burke. Play up the connection to Lothario, here, mother and child abandoned, father off playing war. Pure sugar, man's inhumanity to woman."

Brenda perks up, "Man oblivious, self-centered and off doing bad government's bidding. Faithful woman abandoned. Our boy plays war. Woman bravely carries a bum's child." Brenda, glances my way, "Sorry, Galvan, buck-up; it's a tough world. 'Melie I think I like the sound of abandoned to her fate–plays on the heart strings better."

Amelia beams, "The role's made for you to play, Brenner. Noble crusader hunts down fiend to bring a bad-cop to justice for the sake of women scorned."

Who'll play this pair in the movie version? In the fall an election, slots opening, no limits in sight. I better leave before I throw my legal team off the balcony. I collect my thermal pizza sleeve. Time to sat bye-bye.

As I leave, the ladies scheme and plot. I feel better, things ride easy on my mind. One does what one can. On the scale of justice how would it be possible for the weight of a child unborn to outweigh ambition? Justice's statue is that of the goddess Lustitia. A blindfolded woman armed with a sword and scales in balance. We'll see?

I glance out the window at Bren's creek where one major player plays with his plums. Then I descend to the first floor, calling back, "Could one of you let me out the back? "

Brenda hurries after me. I watch her shuffle along in flip flops and half-glasses. The last few years haven't been kind to either of us. Time and tide;--would Mary Beth recognize either of us?

I fear for Bren' with Melie more than Casper. She lacks remorse, him I'll deal with. Amelia is in her ruthless youth, raven haired, cat-eyed. Bren's been at the books too long.

Bren's lunge for one last brass ring is unbecoming. Tonight, I discovered that Amelia is drafting on Bren's tailwind, ready to bail. Amelia's an apex predator with a taste for red meat, her future beckons to an Amelia waiting with sharp elbows to meet it.

The grotto light is assisted by a light switch on the wall. Bren' slides the glass door open. In the new light I feel naked. Casper is out there in the bushes. The weight of cross-hairs rest on my forehead. Time to distract him with performance art.

Brenda has a happy smile. She hugs me, gives me a peck on the cheek. I pull her to me for a tight hug. Brenda pushes me back with a loud, "Down tiger." She tells me to cool my jets. Now, satisfied that she still has what it takes, Brenda whirls just out of reach of my well-lit grasp, saying, "'Melie, lock up after the nice man leaves."

I'm not a nice man. If I were, I wouldn't be here. Brenda heads upstairs, Amelia slides before me. She peers intently into my eyes, searching. Ooops, I have my male war-face on again.

Amelia says, "You scare me, Mr. Ice green eyes. I had you on the balcony. I've lost you."

I drop my hands, grasping Amelia's bottom, drawing her to me.

She springs up, wrapping her legs around my waist. With her arms wrapped round my neck she forces a tight kiss. We remain enwrapped a long moment in profile in the patio lights. Eventually, I release her to slide down me to her feet. My hands rise to caress her breasts.

Amelia steps back a half step. My hands caress her torso gently. Her expression shifts from surprise, to arousal.

I am an awful person. It is time to say in warning, "Be careful tonight. Keep a sharp eye out. Casper is a dangerous man."

"You're the dangerous man, Galvan. I can handle either one of you."

I say, "Don't get cocky. He's out there. Don't ever underestimate him. He has already killed two tough women."

Amelia smirks. "If you can make yourself unhand my breasts, I'll lock up."

I release her, giving our watcher a last glimpse of me squeezing her bottom as she steps away to close the door. Amelia snatches my arm, "I have this bad-girl thing. Stealing Brenda from Mary Beth was a lark. I wanted to work in the office. When this is done, we should start over. I liked you when we met, still do. OK?"

I answer, "Sure, we'll do just that."

I walk to my car annoyed at my duplicity. I see Brenda and Amelia inside arguing. Amelia waves Bren' off, saying. "OK, mom. Whatever you want, dear."

Bren' glares at me in the doorway, before slamming the sliding door shut and flicking down the tiny lever. No cross bar is added. I shrug, hitting my remote start. No explosion. Good

I like the SRX until I get a parakeet, she's my only pet. Casper's crouching in bushes. He appears abstracted. Does he even know I see him? I leave the lot, cornering out of sight to the east behind a little league park. I park with the Little League wall between us. I then sprint back west on foot along commuter tracks that parallel the creek bed. I run the BMX track to come up behind Casper.

He's gone, not good. In the moonlight I sprint for Brenda's. The door is ajar. As I fly toward the townhouse, I snatch an empty Corona bottle from the ground. Fine dust puffs as I tread. The path is rough, uneven underfoot. I stumble in the back lot.

From inside, I hear Casper's nasal tirade, an incoherent rant. Should have run faster. I recover my balance, but I'm off stride. No time left. I step up onto the steel patio railing to vault for the porch railing. As I spring, I fling the Corona bottle through the open lower door glass. Glass shatters, I vault.

Unfortunately, neither railing is steel. Their aluminum folds like cookie dough. Not an Errol Flynn day.

I'm just able to grasp the upper railing long enough to mount and sprawl across the beer wet balcony sliding on my ass. What momentum I retain carries me in a tumble toward their kitchen.

Thank goodness her whole house is earth friendly. It may have gotten all of us killed, but the environment thanks her. I need to avoid stupid in the future. I bleed off the last of my momentum to rise in a full forward roll as I come up on my feet. Everyone turns to the sound of shattered glass on the first floor.

Casper spins back at me. Damn, he's quick. He smells awful, looks worse. Neither clumsy nor slow, he's tightly focused on me. His Bowie knife sweeps down at me in a right overhand slash at the left side of my neck.

I side-step. Casper misses. It's a close thing. His tip scrapes across my chest. My clock is ticking. No time. If I bleed out, Brenda and Amelia are dead.

Casper over-compensated as he turned and he overswings, stumbling forward. He quickly rebounds into a figure-8 back-slash reaching for my neck beneath my right ear which I parry away. Casper recovers instantly, sweeping wide into another right crossing down-slash once more. He's puffing, out of breath with a chest rattle. I step into an overhead cross wrist block of the down-slash. My move catches his knife hand continuing his swing backwards at Casper's right thigh to slash thigh and groin as I step through behind him.

At this point his torqued wrist drags his blade across his ribs, scoring the intercostal space. I pivot smoothly, stripping Casper of his and slashing his back hip to shoulder.

I slide the knife between his right ring and little finger, catching the blade above his ring and driving the blade into the finger. My cut severs the ring-finger and ring which is flung skidding across the mantelpiece of the fake fireplace.

Screaming, Casper stagger-steps forward trying to get away. He breaks free, lunging his injured hand into his waist-band to draw a pistol which is attached to a long silencer which makes him look like he has an erection. The silencer catches somewhere in his pants.

Casper shrieks, "Galvan, you have to die. You bastard. You are a slippery prick. You stole her. You ruined my life, you son-of-a-bitch. You stole my career. You became me. Always you. Never me. Always you."

He sucker punches me so hard I gasp but we struggle round and round fighting for the gun. He gets a finger through the trigger guard.

I torque his wrist. The gun fires down his pants. Two, three, maybe a fourth time in his pants. Casper tanks the gun from his pants. I knock it from his hand. The pistol slides across the floor.

Damn, he's fast. Got to be on something. He crashes bodily into me. He lifts me bodily to hurl my body into the dry-wall. I cannot believe I'm stuck sitting inside a twenty-four inch center piece of dry-wall.

Casper starts for me only to slide and stagger on the wet floor. He collides with Brenda who is duct-taped to a kitchen chair. Wide-eyed, Brenda and chair flop over backward.

I thrust upward from my thighs, breaking and dislodging an avalanche of drywall on my head. My feet now touch the floor. I repeatedly hammer-fist the drywall on my right side. It slumps into the void behind me.

Casper kicks Bren' in the side. Apparently, she didn't handle Mr. Stinky pants after all.

As Casper tries to stand, he slips again on the blood- and beer-splattered floor. He over-reaches for the gun. Stumbles, fighting for balance.

Damn it, I have a knife in my hand, but I too am trying to regain my footing. I jerk myself out of the drywall hole as Casper extends his right hand to grab his automatic. The hand snaps back as he howls at the sight of his missing finger.

I grab the .45 on my hip. Not quite steady, but well-armed.

Casper whirls at me frantically. "You were supposed to groom me to replace you, you old bastard. You stole my tactical spot. You kept me from making detective. You ruined the job for me with your filthy gossip..."

I refrain from firing. I just have to hear his deranged railings.

"You stole my women. Well, now you have no job. The tactical team is over. Detective is done. You live in a stupid abandoned warehouse on a sewage canal. Now I'll smash your Frankenstein face and knock your knobby neck off its hinges before I kill your lesbo tart lawyers. Your world is gone. I took all your women. Now even your whores are mine. As I kill them, I absorb their lives into me. The whores will be mine soon." I have to chuckle.

"You abandoned me to scorn when I was a recruit. Now you whine about love lost, but they are mine. I'm taking the gun I killed the bitches with to kill you. You and the sluts will be me.

Casper again reaches for his pistol, as my barrel levels at his forehead. Shocked, he looks down the bore, before returning his eyes to me. I take up trigger slack.

Fast as ever he spins shrieking and runs for the door. I bring my weapon to bear at the back of his disappearing head. The Springfield isn't elegant. It is brutally efficient.

I make a slight tick to my right, firing a round. Casper bobs his head, weaves through the doorway. Something floats in a bloody spray to his right.

Casper screams, "I give up." Then he scrambles down the stairs.

Amelia's eyes are as big as golf balls watching, as she is also taped to a kitchen chair. Golly, the state's attorney just saw me shoot an unarmed man in the back. That just ain't done. I must not be one of the good guys.

Suddenly utter exhaustion. I drag myself over to pick up Casper's automatic. Amelia's face is horrified. Carrying two automatics I walk toward Amelia, planning to set her free first. She cringes, shutting her eyes. Reaching out my left hand to free her, I realize at the last moment I'm holding the gigantic suppressed Ruger. I tuck the Ruger in my right armpit, and rip the Bowie knife from the drywall.

The front door slams, as I return with the SEAL survival knife to free Amelia. She screams under her tape. I snarl, "Would you please shut up, I'm cutting you free."

I hand Amelia the knife as I step over Brenda, lifting her and her chair to a sitting position. "I have to call the police, I'll be downstairs covering the doors. Cut Bren' free."

I lock the front and barricade the back. Using a landline, I call the interested parties. Then I establish my watch with a view of both doors. I don't think he'll be back, the blood trail led out front and down the block. Spacing of cast-off blood spatter indicates be broke into a fast scurry if not a full out run.

I climb the stairs to help Bren' and Amelia. The skirmish brought an adrenalin surge, which has now burned off. There are muffled grunts in the kitchen. Silence returns as I enter. That's a shredded ear on the second tread. I glance at both frantic women. Each woman has two ears. I can't hear very well after shooting up the kitchen, but seem to have both my ears. My scalp has a gouge which is bleeding.

The ear on the stairs must be Casper's. I need practice; I was aiming at a pumpkin. The muffled howling continues as a cross the kitchen. I spot the ring and related finger lying on the mantel. The Bowie knife buried in on the floor.

A Saran-wrapped pistol is on the counter. Brenda is preserving evidence.

In the silence, I feel eyes on my back. I turn. Amelia is staring wide-eyed at me. Brenda is flat on her back, still tied in sitting position to the kitchen chair.

Returning my .45 to its holster, I ask, "How you two doing? Let's calm down and free Brenda."

I've stopped shaking and my head is clearing. I reach into my back pocket for my Bali-Song. Click-clack-click. I flourish my blade. Brenda scoots away from me as if I'm attacking her. I cut her loose anyway.

Removing the tape, I have to peel it from her sweater, exposing her bosom a bit. I relent, allowing Amelia to peel it off her mouth and thighs.

As I wait for the police, I leave a message for Nadia with her night crew at the bureau office on Roosevelt Road. I walk to the liquor cabinet, where I pour a couple of stiff shots of Absolut for the ladies, giving each woman one.

Nothing for me. Things yet to do. Oak Lawn was already on the way. A neighbor called in the shots.

Amelia shouts, "Galvan, go outside and shoot Casper."

I say, "He's gone, your doors are locked. His gun is on the counter. His knife is on the floor. Both of you stay out of the blood. You'll get the ick and blame me."

Brenda says, "When he slashed Galvan's forehead, he got blood on the handle. You can see the prints on the grip, 'Melie."

Amelia is wide-eyed. She tries to flee down the stairs. I grab her bicep saying, "Stay here. Casper's ear is on the stairs. There's blood all down the stairs."

I gesture to the vase on the mantle, "His ring finger and ring are up there on the mantel near the flower thing. Drink your vodka."

Brenda laughs. "That's not a flower thing, it's a vase, Galvan."

"OK. Casper left his ring-finger on the mantel by the god-damned vase."

Brenda says sharply, "Melie, don't play with Casper's finger."

Amelia snaps, "You two are such assholes."

I await developments, covering entry points. Hearing the police arrive I pin my star on my chest. Hopefully it will prevent them from shooting. I only have one star; the ladies are on their own. They huddle off to the side, quiet. I suppose it's not that funny for them.

I hea a racket at the front door. I set my gun on the table saying loudly, *"Poleece officer. I will open the front door."*

When it's unlocked, I raise my hands over my head stepping back, *"Police officer. The door is open! "*

I still end up on my face on the floor, hands cuffed behind me.

I call out loudly, *"Chicago Police, the offender fled. The floor and stairs are covered with evidence. The women are upstairs. They are safe. The scene is secure. Give a slow down."*

Eventually they'll discover I'm not the cops. Maybe they'll lock me up with Casper. Won't he just shit. I'll be yelled at, but at the least I'm not dead. Yet.

As I lie cuffed in the front hallway, blood from the wound on my forehead puddles on the red oak flooring. My head is beginning to sting.

Oak Lawn asserts local jurisdiction. Julie asserts federal jurisdiction. Gennaro doesn't assert any jurisdiction, just smiles at me lying on my face bleeding out.

Gennaro shakes his head at me. When asked whom he might be, Gennaro states, "I'm the Lead in Chicago on the murder that is at the bottom of events in Illinois which led to this mess."

Eventually, everybody consults with Gennaro out of my earshot. Afterward, my cuffs are removed and a paramedic gives me first-aid. I don't bleed out after all, but it's a good puddle. I have no jurisdiction. I don't want any. I've done enough on my own.

Oak Lawn takes my gun. 'Evidence'.

Too bad, so sad, bye-bye.

I answer similar questions for the succeeding jurisdiction. None of the jurisdictions talk to each other unless they need to. Nobody talks to me beyond what happened. My story? I returned to my car. I remembered the open rear door in home, went back to tell them to lock up. Casper tried to kill us.

My answers are monotonously similar. "No, I couldn't call her, I only had Brenda's work number; we don't socialize or travel in the same circles."

"Why'd I go in the way I did? I heard the suspect threatening the victims. I distracted him to rescue them. Stuff happened."

"Like what?"

"We fought over the knife. We both got cut. We fought over his gun. In the process we shot several times down his pants. I think he shot himself, trying to shoot me. Why'd I shoot him? He threw me through the wall. I got stuck. I was terrified he'd shoot me. As he came at me, I fired one shot. Thought I missed until I found his ear."

"Why didn't you chase him?"

"I was slipping around like I was punchdrunk. Then I was afraid he'd come back for the ladies."

"Why didn't you shoot again?"

"Gun jammed."

"It is not jammed now. How?"

"Cleared it. Might have needed it if he came back."

Peat and Repeat.

The jurisdictions don't like each other, so they talk in small groups. I have no idea what was said. I'm not in the need-to-know. That's spy talk. I used to be a spy.

Gennaro spends more time watching me than talking. Amelia and Brenda fight with the Oak Lawn Detectives over their file.

An officer squeaks then gags. He found the ring finger, or maybe it was Casper's ear. Casper must be bleeding like a pig. I know my forehead and scalp are. Head wounds leak ungodly amounts of blood.

A new-guy G-Agent decides to bad cop me. He asks me if I think I'm a tough guy. I shake my head no. Which gets him a splash of cast-off blood-spatter on his face, shirt, suit-coat. New-guy agent leaps back with a screech.

Gennaro coughs to cover his laugh. Bren' goes all mom on me, demanding medical treatment for me.

I'm instructed to go down to the ambulance at the curb. I do, my cut is cleaned and bandages applied. The paramedics tell me I need x-rays. They suggest the local ER. I ask if it's OK to see my own doctor, too. The paramedics tell me it would be a good idea. I thank them and walk away into the street.

Seed planted.

The townhouse is ringed in spotlights and flashing blue Mars light bars. As I reach the outer darkness, I walk to my car behind the baseball park.

In the distance I see Casper's SUV disappear, traveling north on Central Avenue at the speed limit.

He must have stopped for an inventory of wounds. Darn, Casper has escaped. I wonder where he's headed. Would he try and self-treat? Maybe we can meet for coffee and compare notes later. Simple things remain simple. Perhaps someone might take some initiative and follow the goddamned blood trail? Then that might be too much to ask. Crime scene analysis requires devotees to stay close to their screens.

I remote start my SRX. No boom. If nutsy found it, he didn't do anything I can see. Inside, I retrieve my 9mm Springfield from a clip-holster concealed beneath the dashboard. One must be properly accessorized. I press check for a live round in battery. Fifteen rounds. I got this, unless the Mongol horde jumps me on the way home.

I go home, not to the hospital. If I go to the hospital not much more will happen. Time to nudge. On the way, I pull over on a residential side street of mostly abandoned homes where I slip a fresh battery and sim-card into a burner-phone I keep in the glove box. I call Mom, everybody calls Mom when they have an owie. She and Deuce agree to meet me at my place at 4:00AM. Two hours. Enough? It will have to do, things need doing. I remove the sim-card and battery from the burner. As I drive, I deposit various phone parts into Deep Tunnel vent ports. Fans spin, water roars down deep. Must be raining along the lakefront. I crumble the chip into various mid-street sewage drains when I stop for traffic lights. I drop the battery which kerplunks in a storm sewer near McKinley Park. Almost home. At the boatyard, I slip the outer lock on my staircase. Everyone else is doing it. I carefully pad up the concrete stairs in silence. I walk around to the hidden rear loft entrance, slipping that lock as well. I heel toe through my loft from the rear. Concrete rarely creaks when walked on.

A blackout drapery below the stairs creates a shadow cloak beneath the inner staircase. I stand in a balanced, open stance, unmoving in the dark mouth opening. It's a ninja trick that improves hearing. Listen before acting. Wait out a nervous opponent, he'll move first. Casper is crouched in plain view, my side of the couch, facing the staircase door. As I watch, he fidgets constantly. In the moonlight from the open balcony, he's a mess. The moon glow reflected from the river surface shines off blood pooling at Casper's feet. He's hurt, mind slow. Didn't bandage his wounds, foolish.

I sneak up behind Casper whispering, "What we doing, ghost?"

Casper surges up from tight crouch, gasps, tries to spin at me, staggers. As he comes in, I side-step, smacking his injured ear with my palm. He squeals. With the speed of a madman, Casper produces what appears to be a kid's silver baseball bat. He tries for a quick overhand right strike for my head. I step aside to bob-and-weave. He misses, breathing heavily.

His backhand swing flicks my right shoulder with a glancing blow that staggers me.

Threatening again, bat aloft, Casper snarls, pointing his uninjured hand at me, "Your ass is mine, you bastard."

Sorry, I beg to differ. I'm not a nice man. I sharply slap his bad hand. Casper howls.

He swings his bat at my head. I step outside to his right, deflecting the bat's orbit and snap punching to break his nose. He gets in the quick groin punch that makes me want to puke.

He's come with too little, too late. Time to end this. I let my shoulders slump as if I have faded. Taking the bait, he rushes in, eyes gleaming with insane ferocity. He swings a fierce left under my guard.

I turn, grabbing his incoming fist above his wrist, torqueing it inward, jerking it under and down.

Casper pivots mid-stride to end up standing with his back to me. His bat cloinks on the concrete as it bounces away.

Cloinks? Casper just tried to kill me with an aluminum Little League bat? Really?

Finish it. I mid-knuckle his kidneys. It's called 'the silence'. A victim loses the ability to speak. Having experienced the silence, I know it's ghastly, painful and indeed evokes silence. Old School believed 'see one, do one, teach one'. He taught that way, we learned that way.

Time is forfeit for Casper. There won't be any last words. I took them. No judge. No jury. No human-interest. No last interview.

I grab his greasy, dirty hair with one hand and snatch the back of his belt, frog marching him through the open sliding door onto the balcony.

I snap-kick the railing-latch free. The gate swings outward. I whisper, "This ain't a game; you ain't a hero."

Releasing Casper, I boot him in the ass.

Casper flies, tumbling face forward to flip through the air. His body slaps flat-back as he strikes the spring water up-well. He then plunges downward. The man is sucked deep. He surface-pops, struggling weakly for a moment. Casper's terrified. I consider the murders. Mary Beth, our baby, Calah. I snatch up his fallen bat. When he bobs-up again I fling the bat at his head. It bounces off his skull.

Casper is sucked into the vortex. The hollow, buoyant bat bobs away downstream. He appears in the moon glow far down in the shimmering depths. Casper's riding the vortex to oblivion. His body riffles the sandy bottom outward.

Casper rides the current into Bubbly Creek. Then glides into brown murk. Gone.

With the weather this warm, Casper may turn up on the mud flats in Maywood. If he gets below the locks, then the Asian carp will get him. Too bad, so sad, bye-bye. Time to clean up.

When my parents arrive around 4:00 AM, my concrete loft is as clean as I can get it. The floor has the scent of lemon bleach and damp concrete. Fans and air-conditioner are blasting.

I cleared the floors yesterday. Living in an old warehouse with no wall-to-wall carpets has its benefits. Bleach and the firehose have obliterated Casper's essence, spilling it into Bubbly Creek. A hard bristle brush and a squeegee serves well on concrete.

Mom cleans my wounds, applies stitches where needed. Deuce stands guard facing outward into the night, armed with my/his old five-inch, stainless .45 S&W from under the coffee table. Around the time he met my mother, Deuce got shot, they say he's been on watch since.

I don't mention Casper. They don't ask. Ben Franklin's right, three may keep a secret if two are dead. Some secrets you carry to your grave. A patch is shaved on my scalp, before I get an incredible number of plastic surgeon's stiches. Well, it seemed that many. Shot of antibiotics, pill for pain, nap-time.

Mom finishes, Deuce hands me a sixteen-ounce Pilsner Urquell to wash pills down. Then I sleep long and hard.

I dream of Jill, where I swept her onto the couch as Joe entered. Her skirt hikes up. I stare at her red satin covered bottom. I must like that memory, that scene, because it keeps repeating.

I dream my dream. You dream what you want. I sense my parents watching over me for a time. Parents do that for their children.

I wake at 7:00 to overcast skies. On the coffee table sits a bakery bag with two chocolate-frosted, cake donuts, a thermos and a silver bullet. The thermos holds cold chocolate milk, nectar of the gods. I study the single silver bullet. Deuce sees the Silver Bullets funny. I think of the Lone Ranger on late night TV. I scarf milk and donuts before heading out.

27

DAY INTO NIGHT

I gather my Sea Baidarka and double paddle from the kayak rack. Donning my wet suit, buoyancy compensator, and brain bucket only to discover that it chafes my sore head. I glide upriver on still water past talkers, walkers, and gawkers.

My dull headache occupies my thoughts, I barely see anything along the river walk. A tall brunette with a pony tail stops with the rising sun's glare to stare back at me. She runs southwest away from me. The sun's glare makes my head pound. Sorry, Lady, nothing to see here this morning.

Humidity loosens my sore muscles. In due time, I portage my Baidarka.

A group of young Black Men stop playing round-ball to watch a strange white dude in a wet suit walking down the street with a boat on his head. White guys are strange. I walk east on (Teddy) Roosevelt Road through the museum campus with my boat hat. White people ignore me. Hispanics laugh. There were no Asian people present.

In time, I launch from 12th Street Beach.

The lifeguard hurries down the shore at me, too late. The kayak glides out into rising surf. I decide I need to get out in this heavy chop, betting it won't kill me. When paddling a kayak in rough water one needs to pay attention. I focus closely on my bow's cut-water to part incoming surf. The proximity of danger takes all my attention. Reaching slack-water beyond the surf line I execute a quick pivot to discover I have an audience. At first, I take the onlookers to be a strange crowd. Some have long grey hair and tie-dyed clothes. Others are in business casual and have styled hair in shades of brown, copper-red, and blond not found in nature. Ladies seem better dressed and in better shape than the guys. Most are sharing cigarettes, which pass from hand to hand. Weird smoke, cold around them, damn the whole group is passing spliffs around. They're all stoned. Ahhh. There are Grateful Dead concerts over the Fourth of July weekend. The Fourth already? June's gone already, what have I been doing with my summer?

The senior-ravers urge me on to: I don't know. Maybe, they want to see the waves kill me. OK. We'll see; I return back out into the roiling surf.

Thought evaporates in desperate effort. I glide between three wave sets—big, medium, small. Sometimes big, bigger, biggest. The Baidarka's bow tooth slices white water to keep me running straight and mostly stable. Steering by the seat of one's pants wears out one's ass.

I paddle south with the sweeping current. As I fatigue, I make fewer runs in-shore. Exhaustion wears me down. Getting old, donuts and chocolate milk only carry a man so far. The dead-heads have gone to wherever they were bound. I wrestle with heavier wave-action. Rough water is breaking south of 47th Street. That puts me on notice. I begin seeking out protected shallows, a protected rock wall with a safe leeward bend suffices.

I guide across the stiffening northeast wind. In time I work carefully into that leeward hollow. I lug my Baidarka onto grass away from the surf spray.

I extract my life-cased cell phone, calling Gennaro.

I sit a safe distance from the Outer-Drive, thinking of Alioto, Haynes and Jeremiah *Lake Shore Drive*, which rapidly morphs to an ear-worm.

Gennaro arrives before winter sets in, driving a black plain-clothes car. We tie the kayak on its roof. Gawkers gawk. Life goes on. Gennaro drives to their place with me in tow. A little later, Em' shuffles around her kitchen making us breakfast. Mine could've fed the Marine Corps. Must have used up my donut protein.

Em' sips tea from a large mug, studying me over her table.

She pokes at my interesting stitches with a wooden spoon, then brushes a hand gently over my cheek. She eventually says, "Trouble, you look like Frankenstein. Fun evening?"

"So, so. Didn't right wrongs or make anything right. But, done stays done."

I tell the Gennaros what I can. Each knows more, neither ask for more.

I suggest Casper hopefully ended his life by jumping in the river from the Damen Avenue Bridge not far from where he was born.

Then maybe he didn't. Who am I to ruin a happy ending? Either way, Casper's on his way downriver toward the Maywood river flats.

History continues to be writ to suit survivors' fancy. Gennaro informs his wife that Casper's crossover was found stalled on Damen Avenue near the river bridge.

He says Nadia found all Casper's worldly goods in the crossover. Nine boxes of moldy paper, evidence envelopes of blood-stained clothes, Casper's scene notes on his crimes. Maybe he planned to arrest himself.

No Manifesto?

Gennaro nods, noting that Casper wasn't an ardent fan. Wow, what a surprise.

After breakfast Em' says something about done being done. Gennaro takes me home. We carry my baidarka to the dock. He surges in past me to clear the premises. I make coffee during his search.

Gennaro holsters his automatic, then says, "Upstairs is nice. Did your swimming pool break? Smells wet and bleachy, let it air out, genius. Get some sleep. Do I have to arrange a watch-over? No? Don't you think he'll be back? Then nothin' left to do, huh? Done all that needs doing?"

I shrug, no answer seems necessary.

He inquires, "Why didn't you drop him at Brenda's? You had him dead to rights, pardon the pun. Why did you come back when you did?"

"I told Amelia to lock-up. When I was the other side of the baseball diamond, I realized she didn't lock up. I was distracted. I came back when I remembered the open door. I heard Casper ranting inside. The shit hit the fan." I shrug, "It got intense fast. He was quick as a snake. He scared the daylights out of me. I barely got Bren' and Amelia out alive. I was stuck in the wall and panicked under fire. I missed. He dropped the gun and knife in his flight. I'm not the cops, no more. Non-cops can't pursue, or shoot an unarmed offender in flight. Done is done."

Gennaro gives his 100,000-watt smile, "What a nice answer, been thinking on it a lot?"

I say, "Seems like months, but it all happened in a flash."

"Seems like months?" After a moment he asks, "You consider Brenda who took Mary Beth from you a friend?"

I answer, "I went back."

Gennaro inquires, "Did you set them out as bait while you played stalking horse?"

I answer, "I told you last night I was going to give Brenda the case. I warned them Casper was dangerous. I went back because I realized neither woman took their danger seriously. I guess Casper didn't know how many legs a horse has. End of story."

Gennaro smiles, "Much remains unanswered. Why did you take you so long to return?"

I say, "Heavy traffic? Or, maybe I was thinking about what could have been with Mary Beth. Gennaro, if you came in search of the secrets of the universe, I can't help you. Try Tibet."

Gennaro smiles, "Well, when you die, you'll get total consciousness on your death bed for this one jagoff. At least you have that going for you."

I say, "Swell."

Gennaro walks to the coffee table and picks up Deuce's silver bullet. He flips it in the air, catches and sticks it in his pocket, saying as he leaves "See you later, Kimosabe." As Gennaro exits, I wonder if he intended Kimosabe to mean, 'friend who has been faithful', or as in the intent in Apache, 'idiot white guy'. Secrets of the universe are like that. Later I slept soundly, dreaming of slashing knives and gunfire in the nick of time. A disembodied, bloody finger dances across my mantel singing *Happy Days Are Here Again*. I awake at 6:00. It is dusky light outside. But do it be morning or night? The alarm clock swears it is the Fourth of July. But what year? Time passing is important only in light of having a place to go or something to do. Before I roll back over to sleep, I check my texts. The White House didn't call. The entire law enforcement community of America wants to see me immediately. That will be after the holiday. It's the Fourth, after all. Hopefully, they have lives. Dr. Mom told me that I can't play until I'm in my right mind. That may be nevermore.

I find a message from Gaby. She's distressed, crying. She needs me to close for her. I have a place to go, and something important to do, after all. I'll bring a gun. She may need someone killed. Quickly, I shave and shower. I note a large, swollen bruise across my left hip and abdomen. Casper's bat? He got a good one in after all. I was in the zone, didn't feel it.

Or maybe I got it crashing through drywall. It was a busy night.

My clothes hide my bruises. There is no one around to see them, anyway. I stroll into Gaby's through the bar. Karl is bartending, talking to some other old guy.

I request a leaded Pepsi.

Karl looks me up and down, "You look like shit, Kid."

Karl is wearing a navy polo with gold breast emblem reading, 'Team 2-Little Creek'.

I ask, "You a SEAL, Karl?"

"Yeah, Vietnam. Meet my LT. Steve, meet the kid I was telling you about."

The old SEAL LT shakes my hand, "Your face is a mess."

I say, "Lost a fight over somebody's granddaughter." They laugh. It's funny when it isn't your granddaughter. Admiral Grandpa's first name is Steve. I didn't know admirals had first names. I look into Steve's eyes for the first time in a decade. In his SEAL polo, he doesn't recognize me.

I say, "Thanks for your service, guys. Welcome home. You guys on the way to a team reunion?"

Carl says, "LT is in Chicago to celebrate his granddaughter's engagement. We're seeing The Dead later tonight. I lined up some ladies."

Breaking contact, I say, "Congratulations, sir. Hope you guys have a nice evening. Karl, Gaby wants my help tonight." Karl points to the restaurant. When I reach the restaurant, Gaby looks at me with haunted eyes. Her anxiety strikes me a physical blow. Gaby's put on weight. Is everyone pregnant?

I give Gaby a hug whispering, "Does he know?"

Gaby leans into me, "No, I'm on my way to tell him I'm keeping this baby." Gaby has a faraway look, placing my hand to her abdomen. I don't feel the kick but smile anyway. I kiss the top of her head.

I say, "Good. Tell him, I'll close up." After Gaby leaves, I study the room. Antipathy, smiles, disdain, chagrin, hatred. What a nice mix. Is this the annual meeting of my fan club?

I study the crowd. Two distinct groups. One is the prosecution. The other the Navy balancing the room. Ashes to ashes, dust to dust, if the Lord don't get ya', the devil must. What, I only get two choices?

At the head of the prosecution table Brenda sits primly with Amelia to her right. Gennaro sits nearby, his chair reversed. What expressive body language.

Gennaro's glazing eyes strive but fail to be attentive to Brenda's monologue.

Nadia, George, and the Oak Lawn detective from last night and his boss at Bren's table.

At the head of the Navy table sits my new friend Steve, alias Admiral Grandpa. He's talking to a handsome blond man with a 'high-and-tight' haircut. The guy was born to be on a Marine recruiting poster.

The Marine and I stare at each other, exchange a knowing glance. I have met the groom. Eva sits next to her guy glaring sourly at me. They all take in my Frankenstein costume.

Emma meets my eye next. She sits flanked by an empty chair. Gennaro? Em' glances my way frowning, then she shrugs it off to smile back. Blackmon and Tanner sit at the officer's mess, how egalitarian. The help eating in the presence of royalty.

Eva says something to Emma who becomes pensive. She glances between Eva and me. Eva is speaking heatedly to Admiral Grandpa. Admiral Grandpa follows Eva's eye to me. Something clicks. Admiral Grandpa just made me. Admiral Grandpa snarls, I wink at him.

First things first, I head for the prosecution table. 'Trouble' like wine, has his own time. Amelia studies my Frankenstein face. Her irises widen as I approach. Oh no, 'Melie likes my Frankenstein look.

Gennaro takes in Amelia's focus, then gives me his shit-eating grin. As I approach, Gennaro rises to give me a biker hug and chest bump, whispering, "I hope you got your strength back. You are gonna need it, my brother."

Gennaro turns to prosecution, "Thank you kindly for the drink, Brenda. I have to get back to the little woman." His glass sits untouched before his reversed straight-back chair. He adds in passing, "Come say hello to my bride. Brenda was just chatting about you, Zorro."

I whisper, "He was my mother's cousin. I'll be over shortly."

Stepping up I say, "Brenda, so good to see you. I hope you've gotten some rest. What an awful experience. We're all lucky to be alive. Any news on our attacker?"

Amelia asks, "Where'd you disappear? We checked all the hospitals."

I say, "I got dizzy from my head wound. The paramedics suggested I see my doctor as soon as possible. I made arrangements, got a house-call."

Amelia says sarcastically, "A house call?"

Brenda says laconically, "He had his mother stitch him up. She's a physician."

I point to the river behind me, "Mom made a house call to fix up her little boy. I not well—may have a concussion. "

Amelia snaps. "Your ass hit the wall. Where'd you get a concussion, Galvan?"

I say, "When I hit the wall the force punched the back of my head through the drywall. Mom called it a coup-contrecoup injury. Very serious, especially with the broken neck. You know, head hits wall, brain collides with skull. Jell-O bouncing in a box."

I shake my head, looking worried, "Mom cleaned me up, gave me shots. I fell out, slept a long time. Just woke up."

"Sleeping? Weren't you afraid Casper would get you? "Amelia asks.

"Last saw him, Casper looked worse than I did, 'Melie." Amelia does not like her new name.

Nadia visibly dislikes my interaction with Amelia, she asks, "Why would he? Brenda told us she saw you slash Casper with a big knife before shooting a gun a hundred times down his pants. Then you shot off Casper's ear with a 9mm."

"Nadia, I shot Casper's ear off with a .45. Oak Lawn has it."

I ask, "When can I get it back, Bren'?"

Brenda states, "You aren't the cops. You shouldn't have a gun. If you fulfill your responsibilities, I'll release it after the trial on a court order, unless an appeal is pending. You're lucky we didn't lock you up for carrying a concealed weapon."

"My goodness, I was in your house saving your life, Madame state's attorney. If I didn't have it, you'd be very dead. I have a concealed carry permit. I gave Oak Lawn a photocopy."

George says, "Galvan did this routine with us earlier, Madame state's attorney. You owe him your lives. Give him back his gun. He'll just get another. "

Amelia sneers, "You almost didn't make it back, Galvan. Can I visit the bat-cave?"

"Did you lock the door, Amelia? You are both welcome to visit. You'll enjoy the motif. I'm thinking about turning my loft into an amusement park."

Amelia shrugs with a leer, "I was distracted."

Nadia smiles. George laughs. Bren' frowns, looking perplexed.

In the ensuing silence, I ask, "May I get anyone a dessert? Perhaps an after-dinner drink? Coffee?" I take orders. George wants a double Dom on 'a' rock. George likes a good drink. I drop the orders at the bar.

Time to face the music. I walk to the Navy table. Admiral Grandpa glowers. What's new?

He snaps, "You fooled me, Galvan. You grew up, never thought you'd make it. Figured some little girl's grandpa would have killed you. Now there is more of you to be useless. I'm thrilled to see an arrogant rich boy reduced in station to a lowly waiter."

Rich Boy? Where'd I put the money? A lowly waiter? Elitist. I get your food.

But I say, "Nice to see you, sir. May I get anyone a dinner drink, coffee, dessert?"

Grandpa laughs, "Typical, waiter suits you. I would mention your poor character to your employer, but she fled in tears when you entered. My family was defending our country while you made latte's."

I respond, "As you say, admiral."

Emma looks pregnant, uncomfortable, and upset. Then I note Em's building steam. I fear she has something to say.

Emma blasts Eva, "Don't you sit there and let this self-important old fart lambaste one of OUR team members. You egotistical bitch, Big Bob got killed in the Kush. You got Trouble dead, too, you righteous bitch. He just wouldn't die. We are alive 'cause he came runnin' and gunnin' to save your narrow ass. You damn well know why he did it. We'd be up there raped and baked in the sun now."

She shouts, "Galvan ain't a sorry pooch sniffin' at your back door. How you sit silent, while this pompous old prick makes fun of a man who got killed for you. I saw him beat armed men to death with a goddamn hammer to save you. I saw who slinked up to whose back door. I gotta go, the bunch of you make me sick." Emma struggles from her chair.

Gennaro is out of his chair, to assist Emma to her feet, saying, "My dear wife hasn't been resting well. She's with child, she is in a delicate condition. Please excuse us."

Gennaro passes close to me, saying, "Call me, Dude. There's a lot Emma hasn't told me. Em' is all bottled up. Come talk when this is done. I ask it as a personal favor, Compare'."

"I'll try to get over your way. If I get sidetracked, see the Greek. She talks with him."

I turn to the table, "Anyone care for dessert?" Silence "No? I'll see to your check."

I turn to the Marine as I take my leave, "Congratulations on your engagement, sir, you are a very lucky man. Commander Devereaux will make a lovely bride."

I pay both checks and give the staff substantial tips. Then cut the staff loose as I tend bar.

Eventually the dinner parties exit the restaurant into the bar, talking among themselves. I lock the restaurant's double doors, telling Karl, "Head out to the 'Dead' early, I have this. You guys have fun."

Karl shakes his head as he walks over to Admiral Grandpa, "Galvan, you were the dude with his granddaughter? He was gimping around with a bad knee for a month after that fight."

Tanner walks to the bar. I ask, "What can I do for you, chief?"

He says, "What's the status of the guy on the security tape?"

I say, "Gone."

He replies, "Detective Gennaro said you fucked the dude up and shot him in his dick, but he's still out there."

I nod. "If Detective Gennaro says that, must be true. I doubt you'll see Casper again."

Tanner looks tired. I've never seen Tanner tired. He nods, "Good. Done is done." Tanner extends his right hand to me, "I won't be seeing you again, Galvan. Got my time in, come fall. Until then I'll train new operators. Then I'll get gone. You ain't a frogman, but you'll do." Tanner turns back, "Thanks for the staircase. We were fucked. I puked 24/7 for days before I heard you were KIA. Eva is all about the mission, dude. You make the girl crazy." He focuses behind me, grimaces with distaste, "Sorry, man. Hasta Lumbago. I'll go."

Karl approaches me with Admiral Grandpa in tow, saying, "Come on LT. It's gonna be a picnic, we'll be walking barefoot in a field of bubbles."

Admiral Grandpa stares at me over the bar, "Didn't know you were over there. Eva doesn't say much. War's like that. Karl and her guys told me. I have one grandchild. I was afraid I lost her at the Annapolis. Thank you for saving her life in Afghanistan."

I break the ensuing silence, "She barely knew I was there. Didn't recognize me until the end. We were kids at Annapolis. We did what kids do. It didn't work out. She's happy with her Marine. I wish them the best. She'll make a good mother and a good admiral."

Karl says, "Come on LT, we're late for the party, I got sweet weed for our glaucoma. "

Nadia saunters up to the bar, "Thanks for dinner. Why'd you give my card to the lawyer? He's a sweet guy, but I didn't say you could give me away. Any plans for the evening?"

"Twenty hours of sleep."

"Need company?"

"Neither of us would get any sleep." I touch the softness of her cheek. "Some other time?"

Remaining Nadia-the-G to the very end she says, "We found Casper's car west of here on a bridge. Think he killed himself?"

I say, "You got me."

Nadia smiles sadly. "No, I fear I screwed that up. I want you, but I ain't got you."

I say, "My rusty, professional opinion is that he's faking us out. Or maybe he did get hurt, and had nowhere left to go. His family are dead. Maybe he came home to die."

Nadia chuckles. "What? Did something happen to his mother?"

"Somebody threw a bucket of water on the witch and she melted."

I explain, "Dorothy killed the Wicked Witch with a bucket of water in the Wizard of Oz. I hope you don't have a taste for bad boys, Agent Dimitrieva."

She says, "No, I'm a Russian girl who likes cowboys. I found mine and let him get away."

Nadia lunges over the bar to wrap her arms about my neck, hauling me in for a long kiss. We draw back, sharing a breath. Nadia brushes lips across my ear, "I'll keep you if she doesn't."

I wonder, she who?

Nadia saunters to the door, checks to see if I'm watching. Yes, I am. George follows Nadia out.

A feel something touching my right arm from behind. I spin expecting Casper the ghost.

Jill. It is good to see Jill. She has a nice black wool man's suitcoat draped over her shoulders.

I start to worry. The shoulders of the coat are broad. Under the coat Jill is sheathed in a little black dress with a medium-low neckline.

She stares back without expression, "That looked like fun. How do Nadia's tonsils taste?"

I shrug, choosing silence because of Jill's tone. With a frown she asks, "Did you slay your dragon? "

Jill palm-snaps my forehead with her palm," Earth to Galvan, you've been gone for days. Did you save Nadia's maidenhood? You know, the bitch who just choked you with her tongue." She plows on, "I have news that bitch hasn't been a maiden since primary school. Maidens are in such short supply these days."

Jill glances toward Brenda and Amelia, "Those two? I may not be very bright but they're a couple, Galvan."

I'm shrugging a lot tonight.

Under the black suit coat, Jill crosses her arms over her breast, "Poor Galahad. he had too many candidates and forgot to choose. Should've picked one. Go home alone. After all your nonsense, I discovered you'd rather cut bait than fish."

She turns away, stepping back into Gaby's office, calling, "Come on, handsome. I need you to give me a ride in your fancy car. I'll show you the real fireworks."

I'm forgiven after all. I say, "Sure."

Jill then draws Blackmon into the bar, as she coldly brushes me away, "Too late, Galvan."

Holding hands, Jill and Blackmon push past me. I made choices. Time to reap what I've sown.

Blackmon smirks, slipping an arm about Jill's hips. Jill leans into his grip, smiling. Then slipping free, Jill disengages his grasp to slide her arm through Blackmon's.

Blackmon chuckles, "All's fair in love and war, buddy."

Time to go with the flow, never let them see you sweat. I suggest, "Have a good time, the fireworks are best at Soldiers Field as the concert ends. If you can get out by the Planetarium, you'll have both music and fireworks."

Turning to face me, Blackmon appears amused by my equanimity, saying, "Thanks, guy. Good to see you can accept that you're beaten. You know, may the best man win and I did."

Silly boy, he let me position a forearm away, directly in front of him. My hands close on his torso. I drive my fingertips under each of Blackmon's pectoral muscles. My thumbs lock down, pinching into the nerve plexus on each side. Bracing my elbows on my hips I lift Blackmon on his tiptoes. Black is immobilized with white-out pain.

I lean in to whisper, "You know me. She gets to choose. She helped me retain an iota of sanity. At present that's gone. I got time on my hands. My promise to you--hurt her I'll find you. "

I smile at Jill like nothing happened, saying," My friend Gawall has the Planetarium detail tonight. Tell him you're a friend, Black. He'll let you watch the submarine races."

I take a detective division parking placard, "Put this in your window as you enter the museum campus. Tell the guys working you're there to see Sgt. Gawall."

Jill hazel eyes blaze with fury, as she says, "Mr. Galvan, I'm a Chicago girl. I know all about submarine races."

Blackmon is perplexed. Perhaps wondering how one might watch a submarine race. I'm ready for my suite at the nut-house. Crazy is so liberating. Jill is upset. Did I do something? Do I care?

I think positive, if I develop multiple personalities, at least I'll have someone to talk to. Beneath my angry surface I think of Jill. I've spent a lot of hours thinking about Jill.

Jill and Blackmon stroll out the door. Transfixed, I enjoy the sway of her little black dress as Jill walks out of my life. I'll miss her. How about that, parting is such sweet sorrow. I realize now that I fell for Jill when she left with someone else. Jill spots me hawking her, but her eyes go opaque gazing back. Here we go, more fun. Amelia saunters over, leaving Bren' near the door.

Amelia vaults onto the barstool before lunging across the bar toward me. Resting her elbows on the bar. Amelia adjusts the long collars of her blouse. The motion pops open the one securing it at her delicate cleavage. Amelia theatrically drops her chin, glancing at her mostly exposed breasts. She has perfect small alabaster breasts. The woman can bring out the lusty Victorian in a man. Makes me want to tip a bodice. Amelia taps my sore forehead with an index finger, saying, "Gotcha. You're human. We should lose my chaperone."

Has everyone lost their minds? Amelia leans in, I offer my cheek, leaning in. She's been through a lot.

She snatches my ears, pulls me to her lips, whispering, "You savage. You almost didn't make it. Why all the sword fighting? With that hand-cannon on your belt, you should have blown his head off. It wasn't a goddamned movie, that nutcase almost murdered us."

She's upset. "Why go all Marquis of Queensbury? You should've just shot him."

I gaze into Amelia's cold sparkly blue eyes, to say, "You should have locked the door 'Melie. You didn't. He needed to know. When he knew, he ran away."

Startled, Amelia pushes me back from her, she slides from stool to floor. Hands set on slender hips She stares up, saying, "You are a scary bastard. Now, Brenner won't be getting her big trial, will she? Damn, I like you. You bastard, do you always have to even the score?"

I add, "I already suggested that you ask the locals to keep an eye on you two until they catch Casper. He came at you because he thought you were with me."

Amelia arches an eyebrow. "I'll sleep over; you guard my body."

My expression says no, she shrugs, "Your mistake. Poor baby, you just let that gorgeous Italian take her from you. Too bad. You lost. He won. If you don't reach for it, you won't get it."

Amelia strides toward the door. Brenda shakes her head, impulsively walking to the bar. She stops, arms akimbo before me. I hope she isn't out to break my already sore nose.

With distaste, Brenda lunges at me. I flinch. She wraps her arms around my neck, kisses me on the lips. She tastes of Crème Brule. She feels like a woman. Our kiss lasts a moment. Brenda pushes me back, steps away to say, "Thanks for coming back. Don't worry, I wanted to find out what the kissing was about. Nice, but not for me. You kiss like a guy."

"We're just not made for love, Bren'. Sorry I got carried away. I had to try."

Brenda laughs at me, "It's OK, I thought you needed to know. You're an impetuous boy."

I respond, "Gee thanks, Bren'. Couldn't keep my hands off you."

Bren walks out the door. That leaves dear Eva and her beloved. They'll team up and kick my ass.

Said beloved steps to the bar. He sizes me up, reluctantly extends his right hand to shake. I look stupid. I may be stupid, but I see his forearm muscle set. Marines are tougher than the day is long. SEALS lift weights, swim the bottom of the ocean, and fight sea serpents. I'm a wreck.

But I've been doing finger-tip push-ups with old school since I was twelve. Well, I cheat too. I make him reach over the bar. I glide back a sconce. He resets his footing. He can't focus his full attention on two muscle groups at once. If he tries a bone-crusher, he's coming over my bar.

The colonel still has an extremely strong grip. My elbow centered grip ruins his torque.

Surprised, he relents, with a sneer, "Thank you for saving my fiancé. You surprise me. From Eva's description, I expected more. I thought you'd be taller, better conditioned."

"Sorry to disappoint."

"Been ill?"

"Captured by pygmies, they ate me and shrunk my head."

The colonel smirks, "I seem to always come between. I won't see you again, will I?"

"Not if I see you first."

Eva's listening, her eyes glistening. His princess likes to be fought over. Her colonel has won his prize—beat me. He's got Eva, lucky him.

Should I mention Eva keeps coming back? Perhaps he doesn't understand the cuckhold thing? Eva is prone to stray. She's a SEAL. Maybe she'll be chaste in the future. What're the chances?

Eva and her problems belong to her champion. What's done is done.

Thinking before I speak, I say, "Colonel, congratulations. You're a lucky man. You two are well suited to each other. May you have a long and happy marriage and a house full of red-headed children. Be careful going back to your hotel."

The colonel flexes his shoulders. Darwinian triumph of the most fit. He tells Eva it's raining, so he'll drive up the car to the door.

Eva folds arms over her breasts. Time was, I got crazy watching Eva pout. Not tonight. Have I grown up or just gotten old? Eva is looking down, scribing an arc on the floor with the tip of her shoe. Her toe returns, centering on me. She's ready to launch. Her first volley is a wide-eyed innocent gaze.

Jill does it better. I polish the bar, waiting.

Eva rushes in thrusting her index finger in my face, "Is that all you gonna do? Just stand behind that stupid bar looking at me with icy green eyes? I'm worth fighting for, baby."

Fantastic. Eva lost with the choice of one word.

I say, "Congratulations on your engagement. When he gets back, I suggest that your beloved take his prize and go. We all got our just desserts. Enjoy yours. I'll savor mine."

Eva's eyes sparkle. "I almost got you, huh?"

I say, "Almost. Come on, Eva, can you see me as a Navy spouse?"

Eva shrugs. "In a word. No. What happened to your face?"

I say, "Long story, Pirate Queen. There was some swashbuckling. He gone. Thanks for the information, it helped."

"Who is the short haired Glamazon?"

I chuckle, "Nadia, an FBI agent. She thinks Casper killed himself in the river."

Eva studies my eyes, "What do you think?"

I answer, "Casper was coming apart at the seams, just needed a little push."

Eva laughs. "I take it he's gone on. Too bad, I haven't killed anyone in weeks."

"Except me."

Eva nods, "I didn't kill you. I almost killed you. Don't I get a second chance?"

"No. I wish you well in your new life, Mrs."

"I helped you solve your murders."

"Yes, you did. I owe you. I assume you'll collect when you want something."

She smiles, "That was a big one. I'll let you know."

"Why did you bring your fiancé for your engagement dinner to my house. You told everyone, including me you are marrying."

Eva says sharply, "I wasn't thinking. *I was mad at you, you son-of-a-bitch.* You had years. You should have looked for me. I had to find you banging Blackmon's new squeeze. Serves you right, you bastard."

She roars, "I can't believe you. What are you, some punk bitch? You let your bitch run off with my forecastle-Lothario. Black eats snakes when he's not fucking them. You're letting me go. What is wrong with you? You don't want me. OK. Fight for her. Fight for that Glamazon. No? You fool."

I say, "Eva, let it go."

Eva's face is crimson, "You let us all go. Did that pregnant Afghan bitch chop your balls off? Stupid, Blackmon is banging your bitch over the hood of his rental car."

I nod at her explosion, "Who is sleeping with whom isn't my business. You decided long ago where and with whom you laid down your head. Jill gets the same choice."

The outer door opens. The colonel forcefully strides in as I say, "Your ride is here, commander. Time to go."

Eva demands, "Is my chief safe? I don't want him arrested with a dope-dealing whore."

"When I got out of Bethesda, Jill babysat me. Jill was my doctor, not my lover."

Eva goes sly, "What did you say to Blackmon when they left?"

"I wished him well."

She snarls "BULL-SHIT. You vengeful fuck. Do not kill my chief over that woman."

I say, "I told your snake-eater I'd find him. If we come to that, I have nothing else to do, I'll be waiting for you."

She says, "You never did anything like that for me."

I laugh. "Eva, I've killed men to save you."

The colonel marches toward me. I polish my bar. The colonel dislikes my proximity to Eva. The feeling is mutual.

He announces in his parade-ground voice, "Problem, buddy?"

I say softly, "Thank you for your service. Take your fiancé. Go, closing time."

They remain stationary. I say, "I refuse to waste anymore time listening to you two. Go tell somebody else how clever you are. Cherish your bride. Go away, take Eva with you."

Sullen, Eva takes the colonel's arm, walking out. Gone for good? Doubt it.

I check the locks, close the bar. As I leave, I carry a bottle of Dom Perignon, which I paid for when I anticipated I had someplace to go. The register is closed. I'll leave it in my loft for the Greek.

It is not being left on the bar for Admiral Grandpa and Karl when they get back with cotton mouth in the morning. Assuming they can survive Karl's field of boobies.

I stroll toward the boatyard thinking. Black has my girl. I got the Dom. Poor trade, that. My girl? How possessively medieval. Jill's right. I chased them off. She, I, we all chose.

Jill will have to be satisfied with Mad Dog 20/20 Blue Raspberry. Looks like wiper fluid, tastes like it, too.

I saunter home, champagne under my left arm, I carry my black 9mm Springfield in my right hand. Closing time has its dangers. I left change for tomorrow in the cash register. Karl will need it in the morning. Big money is a temptation for local thugs. Ergo, the 9mm. Bad things always wait around the corner. I have nowhere to go and am in no hurry to get there. The boatyard is destination, not goal.

Just up ahead the pregnant woman from the park paces back and forth on the sidewalk carrying and soothing her over-tired daughter. I discreetly holster my pistol as she paces away. I stop a distance from them. I cough to let her know I'm there. I ask if things are alright.

Startled she says, "Oh, it's you. Daddy's inbound. Must be holiday traffic."

"Does he work on the Northside?"

"No, silly. Jack's coming from Afghanistan. He was a Recon Marine. He finally mustered out. Well, I suppose he's a 'former' Marine. One last tour. He's done." In the distance a cab rounds the corner coming off Archer toward us.

Mother murmurs reassurance. Her daughter peers blearily at me from Mom's shoulder. Mom bounces her, resettling her weight, "It's OK, pumpkin. He's the sad-pirate from our park. Remember? He waited for the food palace princess when we were flying in our playground. "

The girl shifts in her mother's arms to take a better look. The child points from me to Gaby's, "*Mommmmmy*, he was a cry-baby pirate. He had too many lunches. He didn't go to the food palace with the princess. He's not a very good pirate, he ran away."

From the mouths of babes. I'll be remembered locally as a cry-baby with too much lunch. Mom shifts her child again. The child has gotten bigger. Mom asks knowingly, "How's that going. You two haven't been around. We saw her earlier with that other guy."

I watch the airport cab bear down on us. I say, "Wore out my welcome."

Stop signs slow the cab. The lady spots the cab, hands her daughter to me, saying, "Hold her, stand right there."

The lady fluffs her hair, dons a welcoming smile. She laughs at me. "Had much experience with kids?"

The child squirms in my arms to face me. asking, "Why do you eat so much?"

I say, "I get hungry."

"The big ogre and you are pretty bad as river pirates. You cry too much. You eat too much. You'll get fat. Your princess ran off with the black prince. She doesn't like fatty pirates."

I say seriously, "Wouldn't want her to do that."

The little girl says, "Done it, dum-dum. Too late for you. The black prince has her. Those guys never give them back. We waved at them. Princesses and princes wave a lot."

I look to Mom for explanation.

The ladies have a secret, Mother is non-committal. "You and your partner are the river pirates. The brunette you used to be with is the princess from the food palace, we had brunch there once. My daughter saw a pair of the two big guys carry you into the warehouse. The big guys are the saracen and the black prince. While we were waiting, the princess, wearing a little black dress got into a car with the black prince. My daughter thinks the black prince is pretty."

I say, "He's a SEAL. Most princesses seem to agree with her."

Mom shakes her head, "My daughter thinks the black prince kidnaped your princess and took her to Ogre's Island. Ogre's Island is the point of land across from your building."

The island has lost its short one, its ogres.

The cab zooms to the curb. A large familiar-looking man wearing much-worn Marine Pattern Camo Fatigues exits. The Marine snatches the woman into his arms, spinning her about him in a circle.

Things calm, I hand them their frantic squirmy daughter. I set my Dom at their feet, lifting his bags from trunk to porch. After paying the cab with my last cash, I'm jumping free.

With limited plans, the sky is the limit. Before I leave, I extend my hand, "Welcome home, Marine, Thanks for your service." I get the official Marine fish-eye.

He tilts his head, to say, "I know you. You were the spook who worked for the Greek. You were with the Hindu Kush Swim Team."

He nods, "I was recon out of Gardez."

I know him, "A truly lovely place. Loved the guys sitting behind the half-wall of the Afghan public bathroom by the road."

I change the subject, "The Greek and I build boats now in the warehouse at the end of the block down by the river. We work with recycled woods. My name is Galvan. The Greek is my partner."

Pointing to the Dom I tell the Marine, "It's a little warm, store it nose up. You two can enjoy it after the baby comes. Stop by the boatyard when things settle down. As I remember, you know engines top to bottom. Joe needs a small engines and power plant guy. I say on impulse, "Stop by and take a look. Maybe you'll like the set-up. Think about it, if you're looking for something to do until you figure out life back in the world.

I say, "Tell Joe I offered you a spot." I nod my goodbyes. Turning away, I take a stroll toward the river. Seems a good misty night for a spooky walk. I'm in no hurry. I meander across our gravel lot. I feel individual stones shifting beneath my feet. Glancing back, I find no tracks. Gravel rarely notices one's passing.

I vault up onto our dock to unlock the steel access door. I enter the shop gingerly. The shop is shrouded by long shadows in an industrial array. Ambient moonlight breaks through fleeting rain clouds to illuminate machines from a somewhat distant industrial past. Some of these machines weren't new in 1900, much less 2000.

I wonder what the Greek will do with this stuff. Sell it? Knowing him, whatever he does he'll make a hefty profit. Probably sell it to the idle rich as loft space.

Walking south in my hall of machines, I feel insignificant. Does the blue marble we ride through space consider the specks riding its back? Such melodrama. I was given the gift of life twice. What did I do with those lives?

In the Bible, maybe the New Testament, I remember the parable of the slaves and the Talents of silver. A silver talent weighed about 30 kg. or 66 lbs. Today that would be? I guess maybe $17,000, give or take. Each of three slaves got silver talents. The boss went on vacation. Nobody ran off with the cash. Different times. When the master got back, he asked the slaves what they did with his gift. One buried his to protect it. One made a big profit, one a little profit.

I don't recall what the master thought about the use of his gifts.

I took mine and killed a murdering bastard. I'll pay my bill back at the tent in the dunes. Did I do good or bad? It wasn't bad. I didn't serve the mores of modern justice. What I did has a biblical overtone. Was it worth it? Yeah.

I'm a rotten bastard. I was told by most everyone at Gaby's tonight. Having been sent back, I was informed of what happened to Calah, Mary Beth and our baby, I did what I did. I abandoned a woman pregnant with my child. I went off to play soldier. A young lad fancy free. Sorry I got you killed, ladies. No harm meant.

I like to think Casper da Ghost was not of my ilk. Perhaps he was of my ilk. I am an arch hypocrite, a flawed doppelganger of Casper who finds no joy in his work. I do know I am tired to the bone. I feel incredibly heavy, as if when I stand still, the weight of that fatigue will sink me into the concrete shop floor. To keep from sinking, I continue walking the length of the floor, like a penitent seeking forgiveness in a silent industrial cathedral.

I slowly climb the south stairwell. I don't have the strength to ascend to my inner loft. There'll be no rest for the wicked this night. This night my business hinges upon the sail-loft proper.

I walk through, must keep going, don't want to fall through the concrete. I exit the sail-loft bound for the balcony. The rain and fog have cleared. I look back to my recent living space. Must have left the lights on upstairs. Forget it. The Greek will unload the building before he has to pay the bill.

I'm tired and I'm done and I'm out of tricky ideas. I get it. No dunes for me this time, boyo. My misdeeds bind me over to a warmer clime. Decision made. It's time. Let's get it done.

I kick off my shoes, face west to glance into the moonlight playing over our surging pool. Our spring surges up between me and Ogre Island. Ding-dong the witch is dead. I know because I killed the bitch.

On the bottom of the spring, incandescent light emerges from a small cornucopia spiral on the bottom. A cave opening? Bright, inviting I have not seen the like previously, nor will I see it again. The icy current shimmers along the creek's bottom. It glistens in the moonlight rushing into the river's murk.

Spring is ebbing into summer. If I don't go tonight, I'll miss the rollercoaster to oblivion. So, I step up on the railing, aim my swan dive at the up-well. Here's lookin' at you. I spring into damp, warm air, gliding down, I gulp a last breath. Why would I do that?

A woman screams. Who? Where?

My head and shoulders pierce the surface. Brain freeze. Damn this water is cold.

28

FEW PLANS SURVIVE CONTACT WITH ICE WATER

I plummet into the depths head down through a frozen thermocline. I am a genius, that's me. This is really dumb. Damn, it is cold. The depths are far deeper than I expect. I arch my back, slicing through the central rising inner column to discover the outer shaft plunging me precipitously downward.

The current doesn't relent. By plunging my hands, head and shoulders into the inner vortex I come about to leap toward the surface. The cold burns fiercely across torso. The icy cold in the rising vortex is blinding. The force twists me into a rising spiral. This damn thing is a rip-current. Don't fight, flex. Let it spin me. Save air and energy, steer for the outer edge. I have to let it spin me outward. As I am flung upward away from the bottom fissure by water pressure, my ears pop violently. Swallow, swallow or you blow the ear drums.

I'm spewed violently into the air. Inhale, inhale. Do it quick, this won't last. I belly flop, exiting its vicious spiral. I edge-slice this bastard. Inhale deep, deep. Do it now. Oh shit, the undertow has me. Relax. Take it easy. Don't fight, move with the flow. Work the edge. Oxygen is life, don't waste the life you have in you. As I am dragged along the bottom, I note the irony of my stupidity.

Like Casper, I'm gonna die on the bottom of bubbly creek. There is crap everywhere down here. Wire spools, drifting wire clouds, rusty bicycles. A Harley Shovelhead nose down in the mud.

Stroke, kick, glide outward. Repeat. Angle for the edge of the flow. Keep fighting or you die. Steady breaststroke, frog kick those long legs. I once could hold my breath forever. Tonight, I discover the sorry span of forever.

In this mess, forever won't be long enough. Time to die trying. Life hangs in the balance. Find something to fight for. Give in, Blackmon gets Jill. There. That prick has to die. Hate is a strong motivator. Truth, justice, apple pie ain't cutting it. No, I'm gonna kill Blackmon.

Don't panic, it burns oxygen faster. I am the only one who can save me. Adapt and overcome. A shard of metal hook slices my shirt. The shard hooks around my chest. I'm dragged back into toward the column. Crinkling ice water numbs my mind. I lose.

My ears pop, again. Can't any get more, Once the oxygen in my lungs goes, I'm dead. The wire in my shirt drags me back. Involuntary exhalation. That all, folks. My vision tunnels; life shrinks to straw width. Becomes a speck. Is gone. Dead again.

I flop onto my back on a hard surface. I up-chuck my stomach contents. My head is forced left, my airway cleared. I get slammed back on the deck, cracking my head. Pushed flat, I receive the breath of life. I gag violently. My chin is forced over left. My mouth is forcibly pinched open. Someone goes finger fishing in my throat clearing my airway.

Mouth to mouth starts. 1-2-3-4-5. My chest is crushed. Got to stop that. Whoever is doing chest compressions is built like a bull elephant. My face is turned again as I vomit more water, coughing and rolling on my side.

I take painful, burning inhalations. The Greek and the Recon-Marine kneel on either side looking down at me.

Where did they come from? My gaze wanders. Our long aluminum boat lies beside me. Ahh, the wire that curved around me.

They watch me breathe. The Greek asks, "Done, stupid?" He gives me a callused slap to the cheek. "Listen to me. Let it go. They're all dead. It ain't about you. You didn't kill them. Calah's dead. Mary Beth and the baby are dead. They are not coming back. That pregnant Iranian bitch is dead. If you kill yourself, you'll be dead, too. All you did was use up another second chance."

The Greek says, "I assume Casper's gone?"

I croak, "One would think."

"You did what you could. Learn anything?"

I answer, "It is really cold down there. I won't do that again."

The Greek says, "Move on. Try as hard as you might, you can't fix dead. You are such an idiot. I should have tied you up this afternoon."

Jack the Marine offers a comment, "Deep, Greek. That's really deep."

Why are Marines always so coolly taciturn?

The Greek stands. "Jack, as I was saying. He gets wound up, he does something awful, then crashes. He's as loose as ashes, but he means well most days."

Wonderful, they know each other. I'll never hear the end of this.

Jack says, "Joe, he looked like he lost his best friend when he walked off. Pale as a sheet. You know the look. I decided I had to get you. I seen that too often. Lost too many Marines to PTSD."

Jack is apologetic, "He gave me a bottle of champagne. I thought he had Evie Devereaux or someone here. Then I realized he was on his own looking for a building to jump off. Seen that look before. I double timed it down here.

The marine says, "Some woman screamed, I looked up to see Galvan dive off the railing. Galvan went straight down as you got here with that boat-hook, When I was young my buddy rode a stolen Harley off the parking lot into the creek only to be sucked down by that undertow. We saw him swept out into the river. He disappeared. Never saw him again."

The Greek shakes his head. "No more Eva Devereaux. My fiancé told me the Devereaux clan threw an engagement party for Eva in our family restaurant. Galvan wasn't on the guest list."

Nobody's talking to me. Am I here? My sex life is being spoken of discursively as I sit at their feet on the concrete in my puke puddle.

The Greek laughs, "Galvan, you're a little tramp Eva visits when she needs a quickie."

He grabs my wrist, turning my hand over, "What are you hiding in your hand?"

I open my hand. The pink clamshell from the bottom.

Joe snaps his fingers in my face, "Earth to Trey, you back? Good. Go to your cave and take a shower. You stink. No more bottom feeding tonight. Go, sin no more. I have a fiancé to tuck in."

I ask, "She told you?"

He nods, "Gaby told you, Galvan. I already guessed. I'm a sensitive guy. I had the ring upstairs. Got a good price, two carats. Besides, can you imagine a woman who wouldn't be honored to carry my child?"

I think before saying, "Brenda?"

He nods, "The exception makes the rule."

The Greek says, "Come, Jack. Walk with me. I'll give you a quick run-through of my operation. It's like that other thing, but different.

You know what I mean?" Joe has an arm wrapped around Jack the Marine's shoulders as they stroll to the door.

I sit on my messy concrete. Obviously, I missed a bit in Afghanistan. They laugh over the Johnnie Walker Blue label scam and the quality of Mr. Boston products. The Greek laughs. Joe is saying, "It's not what you serve, it's what they think they're being served that sells."

Jack the Marine strolls home smiling. I call after Joe, "Your operation?"

Joe responds, "I inherited the operation after you jumped off the balcony to your death."

I pat-down my torso, "I'm not dead."

The Greek walks back, lifts the boat hook like an ax. "A technicality, easily corrected."

I duck away, rising carefully. He leans the boat hook on the wall, saying, "Put that away when you're done playing in the water. Please take a shower, you smell ghastly."

If somebody steals it, I'll get a new one. I walk up the stairs. In the staircase, I smell badly of fire and brimstone. It has the scent of sulphur from decomposition on the river bottom.

My door is unlocked, I must have left it open when I came in or maybe when I left for Gaby's. Inside I strip to the buff and walk to the balcony to drop my reeking clothes into our dumpster. Bombs away, Curtis LeMay.

I wander bare-assed up to my loft. Good to be alive. I'm plumb out of visitors. I can walk around naked if I want. There'll be no unexpected maidens leaping out of the ether. Damn, that was a close thing in the ice water. My soul feels clean and empty. I'm so tired I could sleep a month. I stub my toe in the dark. Ouch. My proud naked saunter becomes a stumbling limp.

On to the showers. Game over for today. I'm exhausted but light on my feet. I glance at my shell. Snatched it from the depths of despair, leaving my burdens in the bottom clutter. I set the shell trophy on a shelf. Fight as hard as you want, life goes on. I need to get a puppy to keep me company. I'll devote all my time to training him on the river walk. I'll call him Fang, maybe Sam. There'd be purpose in my life. Women like purpose. Who can I impress? Not Nadia, she wandered off. Brenda likes girls. Amelia apparently likes everybody. 'Melie really scares me.

Eva's gone. Unless she wants a favor. Wouldn't that would piss the colonel off.

Jill left by choice. Have to respect that. She's right, Blackmon can be Jill's summer boy-toy fling. Fun and games between med school and residency. She's blowing off steam.

Serious possibilities scare us both. I'll start again in the morning.

The first time I saw Jill she was shuffling through calf-deep snow between mid-street and curb. The world was wet and quiet with large, heavy snowflakes dampening all sound.

Jill wore a brushed-out shearling jacket—suede out, fur in—for warmth. The jackets large loose hood shaded her long dark hair. The suede was bloused at her waist. She was stunning. That day I wanted to feel the texture of her long brown hair. Her hair had a cute hippy frizz in the cold damp air. That white shearling inside the hood framed her face perfectly.

Some good-looking cliché had just dropped Jill off in the middle of the snowy street. Pretty boy didn't walk her to the door. Must've been afraid to muss his manly hairdo.

I was jealous of the cliché man, feeling angry he possessed what I was desperate for. I looked idiotic, snow-plowing the sidewalk on my walker. Even human detritus on the sidewalk can have feelings. It must be primal. Stumbling along dreaming of crab lorraine one minute, horn-dog hawking somebody's lady in a heartbeat.

Reconciled with reality, I went back to my snow plowing. The sidewalk was slippery, my feet unsure. I picked my way carefully in the snow afraid to become comedy relief on her walk. Lift walker, shuffle forward. I wasn't a foot race, but it was progress. The Greek saw my walk as a character builder.

I shuffle, lift and collide with Jill, who faces me dead on, holding the walker's cross bar in her hands. I stumble into her road block, floundering. In the end I hugged her to me to keep from falling on my face. It was a long time since I'd hugged a woman. Under her hood she had a wicked look for me.

We held each other a moment, loosely. Sharing a foggy breath, smiling. Lightning struck. Embarrassed I released her, mumbling apology. Jill slid an arm through mine. Unaccustomed lately to speaking, I remained mute unable to come up with anything to say. Jill wasn't having it, "Did you just get back? What branch?"

Terrified, I had nothing to say. I'd been back a year. Never had a branch. Wasn't in the service. There, but not there. Loyalty to people who listed me as dead triumphed. I tried to honor promises that no longer mattered. I said unsurely, not believing myself, "I was an imbedded newsman in Afghanistan, an IED. Wrong place, wrong time. Not heroics, just bad luck."

Jill's saucy eyes challenged, "Bull-shitting pretty girls already. You're on your way to recovery, good-lookin'. Come on, you can tell me pretty lies about how nice I look in this coat which cost me my first paycheck."

I nod, "Worth it."

She says, "I bet, I look like an angel."

"You do," I answer.

"Guys always say that.'

I suppose they do.

I retired my walker that night. Stagger I might, fall down I did, but to Gaby's I walked. I hauled myself along brick walls. Stumbled through intersections. I was out to speak to Jill. Never saw the guy in the BMW again. Didn't miss him.

In the end the Mr. Cliché and I both screwed the pooch. Male stupidity is contagious. I follow my hallway to the shower. Dark, quiet, cocooned in shadow. Reality at bay. Other than my river bottom dour scent the place smells of home. I catch the faint scent of a woman. It's faint. Pew, what I really smell is grossly arranged on me. I run the taps to warm them. This building is a monster; warm water comes slowly.

As steam spreads in the humid spring air it becomes fog. No, it isn't spring, its mid-summer, the Fourth of July. I was busy this spring, had only enough time for that idiot. Oh well, he's gone. Jill and the others are safe. They're gone, but they're safe. Jill's not ever going to be safe with Blackmon. Too bad, so sad.

I soak my head which needs it greatly. In time the sulphur smell in my sinus passages fade. I note my hair is a little shaggy, my beard in need of some work. I climbed the mountain, time for the mountain man look to go. Mostly dry, I walk, light of foot, but fatigued toward the bedroom's glow.

Must've left that light on earlier. When I went to Gaby's? That was a million years ago. Grateful for the light as I navigate the darkness. Good, I'll be able to find my way to bed without falling from my loft.

Lost in abstract thought, I decide I'm a little better alive than dead. My senses are hyper intense.

The scent, again. I can taste the Miss Dior on Jill's abdomen from that morning in bed. I haven't noticed her scent so intensely before.

The sheets? After all this time, that is *some* perfume. The taste lingers on my tongue. Let it go. Someone else may be taste testing that tummy tonight. What an awful thought. I'm not going to torment myself tonight. Time to roll with the changes. Life is what it is. I can't help it. I smell her skin. I won't need a dog. I've become one. Woof.

My bedroom is air-conditioned cool. The quilt stirs. A woman's slender arm elegantly flips it back.

Naked, Jill is stretched out, lounging beneath my covers. Hazel eyes regard me as I study her body.

She smiles in triumph, "Fooled you. You were soooo mad. But you so deserved it."

Jill says after a moment, "Surprised? Not mad anymore? Obviously, you're happy to see me."

I frown, thinking.

Jill laughs brightly at my discomfort, saying in mirth, "Oh my goodness, I did not allow Blackmon to get to the fireworks. We came straight here. You are a jealous troglodyte."

She then says soberly, "I'm involved with someone. You get to guess who. I sent Blackmon on his way after he drove me here. He tried, but that's what guys do. You've been trying since we met in the snow. He left a bit upset, but he left laughing at how mad you'd be."

If she said anything more, I missed it. I was busy

Jill laughs. "My, I seem to have your undivided attention. I thought you didn't like me. It appears I was wrong."

My palm glides gently along, tracing the shape of Jill's hip. I roll her onto her back to kiss the softness of her abdomen.

She giggles, pushing me away, "What was that, a taste test. How do I taste?"

I say, "About right."

Jill asks, "I taste about right. What does about right mean?"

I join her, answering, "You taste as nice as I remember. Which is just about right for me."

During the evening we explore such things extensively from different perspectives. Much later I wake to dull sunlight and occasional distant fireworks. There is the smell of good coffee in the air. Jill appears to be elsewhere. I yawn, stretch. I'm good with life. I must've slept a long time. I hear female voices in the sail loft. I don basketball shorts and a T-shirt.

The metal door to the stairwell closes softly, locks. Someone left.

Panicked, fearing Jill has departed, I rush to the loft stairs. I stub my toe on the stairs.

Jill is seated in one of my Sea Island Cotton dress shirts at the breakfast island, smiling wickedly at me.

She asks, "You sure stub your toes a lot."

I say, "I have big feet."

She's amused. "I noticed. You woke me up making demands on my person. I was sound asleep up in that Olympic playground you call a bed."

"Sorry, you infatuated me when I saw you undressed."

She smirks, "Don't apologize, we need to do more sleepovers, mister." She adds, "I heard you howl in the shop as you came in. Who do you think ran upstairs, half-naked to get the Greek when you dove off the railing?"

Her face serious, Jill says, "Don't ever do something stupid like that again. You scared the daylights out of me. Talk to me if you get down."

"Were you down there, too?"

Jill grimaces. "I went back down and got dressed but the Greek and his buddy had you out and laying on the driveway. You were sitting up talking to them. I went back to bed as you found me. There wasn't time to dress again. Besides you seemed happy finding me as I was. I succeeded in encouraging you to finish what we have been working toward for the last six months. You just needed to see me naked."

She shrugs. "The Greek saw me mostly naked, but it couldn't be avoided. It was that or let you drown yourself."

Jill wags her finger at me, shaking her head negatively. "They saved you. I'm not letting some cute stranger in Marine fatigues see me naked."

I respond, "That Marine is Jack. We knew him in Afghanistan. He's also the husband of the pregnant lady with the little girl in the park the day I had the lunch basket on the bench."

Watching Jill's eyes, I ask, "Who was at the door?"

She asks, "Why?"

I shrug.

Annoyed, Jill answers, "It was Nadia carrying a bag of pastry. She wanted to have you for breakfast. I told her we hadn't had breakfast, but I had you. She started laughing and offered to trade the pastry to get you. I turned her down."

I ask, "Was she offering good pastry?"

Jill frowns, "She wasn't offering hot buttered New Orleans beignets with praline ice cream. For those beignets, I might've let her have you. I'm starving, we had a lot of exercise last night."

I smile. "I was that bad?"

She smiles, "Don't smirk. Beignets would have been nice. I'd just steal you back, later."

"Pretty sure of yourself?"

Jill's turn to smirk, "Oh yeah. We definitely have something here."

"Might I ask what the lovely FBI agent wanted?"

Jill eyes are bright, "Nadia said they found what you were looking for below the First Avenue bridge over the river. What's there?"

"The river bumps north there. Bodies, usually suicides turn up on the mud-flats below the bridge. Nadia's saying Casper's dead."

Jill raises both eyebrows, appearing shocked, "I wondered where you put him."

"Funny girl."

Brow furrowed, Jill says seriously, "Do you have to meet with her?"

"I seriously doubt it."

Jill puts her hand in mine. "Promise you won't meet with her at her place."

I raise my right hand. "I promise."

"Just you and me, Galvan. I've barred the door, thrown away the key. We are each setting up new lives. Whether there is a long-term, we know that will take time. Okay?"

"Yes," I answer.

Jill walks to the balcony to point at the chaise lounge chair saying, "Sit."

"Why? You making breakfast, Jill?"

Jill shakes her head no, snatching a folded throw from the couch. She walks to the chaise, settling catlike on my lap, drawing the throw over us, she says, "We're taking a nap. You ravished me, I'm tired. You can cook us eggs Benedict for brunch, later. A lot later."

Playing with her hair I whisper in her ear, "I know a spot for your beignets and ice cream."

Jill mumbles as she drifts off, "Figured you might."

The End. Every beginning starts at the end of something else.

CPSIA information can be obtained
at www.ICGtesting.com
Printed in the USA
FSHW011842060621
82020FS

9 781977 239754